P9-BYF-638
39042014659251
WITHDRAWN

A CRY OF WHITENESS

By the same author

Fiction

ALL GOOD MEN

THE GOD OF LOVE

KING OF THE HILL

Non-fiction

NOW WE ARE ENEMIES

BEAT THE LAST DRUM

ONE SMALL CANDLE

AFFECTIONATELY YOURS, GEORGE WASHINGTON
A Self-Portrait in Letters of Friendship (Editor)

A CRY OF WHITENESS

by Thomas J. Fleming

WILLIAM MORROW & COMPANY, INC.
New York 1967

Published simultaneously in Canada by George J. McLeod Limited, Toronto.

Printed in the United States of America.

"... Who is this Mr. Kurtz?"
"The chief of the Inner Station."

JOSEPH CONRAD
Heart of Darkness

Chapter One

"Let's go."

Harry Kurz watched Bill Moser sling his worn brown holster over one big shoulder and strap it swiftly into place. Under the harsh lights of the 13th precinct's squad room, sweat glistened on Moser's black forehead and great patches of it stained his cheap white shirt. It was July 5th and on the sunbaked streets outside the temperature hovered around a hundred. It was at least a hundred and ten in the squad room.

Idly Kurz let his eyes drift from Moser to the window. On the stoops opposite the old station house sat a half dozen teenagers staring blankly into space, numbed by the heat. There was nothing strange about it. On hot days teenagers sat listlessly on stoops all around the city waiting for the sun to go down so they could start raising a little hell. But these teenagers made Harry Kurz blink, while inwardly he felt another tremor of disbelief. It was the dream sensation again. He had been in the 13th Detective Squad for two months and he was still getting it. Like Bill Moser, the staring teenagers were black.

The 13th Precinct was in the center of the city's Negro slum. Most of the local whites called it Niggertown. The cops called it the Congo and with magnificent disregard for history and geography, nicknamed the precinct house The Alamo. The grimy barred windows and battered stucco walls, streaked and smeared with cracks and halfhearted repair jobs, did have a certain resemblance to the ancient fort, and Kurz's ex-partner Eddie Reardon, who had put in two years as a cop in the 13th, solemnly predicted, "Someday it's gonna *be* another Alamo. The whole goddamn precinct's gonna make a last stand against them boogies down there and I don't want to be one of the heroes. No names on plaques for Reardon. He likes his just where it is—on a doorbell."

Kurz's first reaction when he got the transfer was a straight line to Chief Inspector Harold Clark's office for a workout with the crying towel. Harold Clark had been his father's best friend—a fact which had once puzzled Kurz enormously. What did Big Jim Kurz, with his booming voice and take-over personality, get from palling around town with a wispy little tongue-tied character like Harold Clark? Kurz had finally decided it was a case of pursuit and capture. Big Jim put up with the creep, took him for a partner when they both made detective, even named his kid after him, because he couldn't get rid of him. It was like trying to lose your shadow. That was how Kurz had got the name Harold, which he detested and never used, even when signing checks. And why Harold Clark became his unofficial father, when Big Jim Kurz died in an alley gunfight.

It was all very fine and touching. But Harold Clark was a bore. At least once a year, all through high school and college, Harry Kurz had to listen to a sermon from Uncle Harold about his father's "great legacy." Meanwhile, Clark was plodding his steady, unimaginative way toward the top of the police department. It was logical for young Harry to become one of the city's first career cops. A college graduate, no less, devoting his life to the profession of law enforcement. SON OF HERO COP JOINS POLICE. FIRST IN CITY'S NEW PROGRAM.

Yeah, yeah, yeah. It was a good move no matter how you sliced it as long as Uncle Harold was in there saying the right words at the right time. There was only one thing wrong.

Uncle Harold thought the ball game was for real. Kurz sometimes forgot this and it caught him badly off balance. His scream about the move to the 13th precinct had been one of these awkward moments. "Now, Harry," Clark had said, stubbing out his 120th cigarette of the morning and letting his wizened puppet face smile for the first time in a month. "A cop can't go nowhere in this department unless he's got some of the 13th precinct under his belt. Ya gotta know how to handle them boogies on home base. It'll only be a year and then you'll be ready for 1st Grade Detective—and Homicide."

"Oh."

Murmuring like an idiot, Kurz had only let himself in for another long discussion of his career, a club-sandwich monologue in which promises were piled on top of veiled warnings that he ought to settle down and get married and take said career a little more seriously. Yeah, sure, like sister Susan, thirty-eight years old and six kids in a five room flat. No thanks, Uncle Harold. I know that as long as I keep my nose reasonably clean you'll stick with me because you've got no place else to go.

So Kurz had trekked obediently down to the 13th and reported for duty. Getting Moser as a partner had been shock number one. Aside from the color of his skin, it was quite a switch from Eddie Reardon's continuous chatter to Moser's almost continuous silence. But for some crazy reason he could not entirely understand, Kurz found himself liking it. Maybe he was bored with the uptown duty. He knew godamn well he was bored with Marion Kelsey and her alcoholic spasms of guilt.

Oh, Harry, we really shouldn't. You know we really shouldn't. It had seemed too good to be true from the start—a Catholic divorcée, nicely stacked, no worries about getting married because it couldn't get her off the hook in the first place. But in the last few months it had turned very sour with sobbing midnight phone calls and even a performance on the precinct house steps. Uncle Harold, president of his local Holy Name Society, hadn't liked that one at all when he heard about it. Maybe putting a good dozen miles between him and Marion was one reason why Kurz liked the 13th. Maybe another was the work. There was so much of it, boredom was out of the question.

Bill Moser was good, as good as any detective Kurz had ever seen. Inside his head he had the 13th precinct knocked-up, cross-filed and prefabricated. He could tell you to the minute when every card game broke up, to the penny how much each numbers wheel paid. He knew the straight ones, the scared ones, the big shots, the crumbs. He knew who to trust and who to kick in the groin and he was capable of doing both without even a change of expression on that wide, slightly rounded impassive face. Maybe it was Uncle Harold, or maybe it was dumb luck, but Kurz was glad he had drawn the best detective in the precinct. Talking about it to his mother, who was all upset about him working in such a dangerous area, he would sternly denounce her fears that Moser would desert him in a tight spot.

"Listen, he's a hell of a partner. We get along great."

Which was a slight exaggeration. They were friendly enough. Riding in the car they would talk about the weather, the Major League races, even sometimes about how Moser's kids (he had three) were doing in school. But the deal somehow fell short of being friendly. They never kidded around and except for the remarks about his kids, Moser was pretty much all business. There was never the slightest hint of inviting Kurz to his house for dinner or any of the other let's-get-together jazz a married partner might pull on a bachelor. Maybe that was why every so often Kurz had his what-am-I-doing-here reaction.

The hell with it, he thought. You're here and today we may land a big one, that lovely stuff from which promotions are fashioned. About two weeks ago, the city's warehouses had discovered they were being taken by one of the cleverest dodges yet. Up would roll a freshly painted, absolutely authoritative truck. Out would step two characters wearing uniforms from one of the city's biggest department stores. They would shovel in a handful of orders stamped, signed and as official looking as a U.S. Marshal's badge and proceed to load the truck with television sets, radios, washing machines, cases of booze, whatever. Away would go these hard-working characters, never to be seen again. For three months now, using a half dozen different trucks and order blanks from a dozen different stores, they had been racking it up. When the accountants finally got around to shuffling their papers and found out it was all going out there and not coming in here, the police commissioner managed to silence their screams long enough to convince them that the smart move was to say nothing. Only by catching these characters in the middle of a performance would there be any hope of finding out where the loot had gone. Half the detectives in the 13th were working on it because the one thing everyone remembered was the color of the truck drivers: black.

Three days ago Moser had gotten a call. He didn't say anything except hello and goodbye but he slammed the receiver down and said, "Let's go" to Kurz. In ten minutes they were groping up the foul front stairs of a river-side tenement. On the fourth floor, Moser peered at a nameplate on the door, then kicked it open. A Negro with a face like a black harvest moon and a belly to match was sitting in a beat-up easy chair drinking beer and watching television. He jumped up, shaking all over as Moser walked toward him.

"Hey, Pork," Moser said. "Seen Dancer lately?"

"Dancer?" the fat man said in a high husky voice. "Hell, I ain't seen him in six months maybe a year—"

Moser drove his knee into the fat man's belly. He screamed, his beer splattered against the ceiling and he went back over the chair into a corner and lay there wailing.

"The next one will be in the nuts," Moser said.

"He's runnin' a wheel. You know that," the fat man whimpered.

"Sure, I know that, And I know he gave you that TV set. Where'd he get it?"

"How do I know?" the fat man sobbed.

"Twenty-five sets got stolen from a warehouse last week, Pork."

"I hear. But that don't prove—"

Moser's foot lashed out. Kurz could not look. He had worked over a few uncooperative types in his time, but never anything like this mayhem.

"What else do you hear, Pork?" Moser said when the fat man stopped screaming.

"Medicine," the fat man whispered. "There's a real hot market in medicine."

They left the fat man slobbering on the floor and charged back to the precinct house for a fast check of the warehouses that stored medicine. There was only one. So for the last three days Kurz and Moser had spent between eight and ten hours down there watching the trucks move in and out. The accountants had printed up a whole new set of order blanks, indentical with the old ones except for a small star in the righthand corner. If the warehouse foreman got any orders without that star he was supposed to stall until Kurz and Moser got there.

Outside, they debated for a moment whose car to take. Not that it made much difference. Both were worn-out Chevvys, with 100,000 miles on their weary motors. Moser usually let Kurz do the driving, no doubt hoping to stave off a visit to GMAC by letting his heap get some rest. Kurz couldn't have cared less. Among the joys of bachelorhood, he counted a fire-engine red Volvo 1800S home in his driveway, panting for some weekend roadwork.

"It's a bitcheroo, isn't it?" Kurz said, throwing his hat onto the back seat.

"Yeah," Moser said. "I'm glad I got my kids out of it."

"Where do you go?" Kurz asked.

"Up in the mountains. My wife's family comes from up there."

Kurz tried to picture exactly what a Negro family did on vacation in the mountains—or anywhere else. He had vacationed often in the state's northwest corner; it was lovely territory for a bachelor. All the secretaries up there for their two weeks of sun and sex. But he had never seen a Negro at any hotel or lake he had visited. Maybe they had segregated lakes, slightly more scummy, with fewer trees, more dilapidated boarding houses.

The warehouse was at the bottom of a dead-end side street. The grey tenements lining the sidewalks were among the worst in the city. There were black holes where steps had rotted away, at least a dozen windows where cardboard had replaced glass. Some buildings seemed about to fall forward into the street, others leaned wearily against next-door neighbors. But as usual, the street was lined with cars, some flashy. They could be living in one of these ratholes, down to their last can of soup, and still want that creamy Cadillac out front. Screwy. Someday you ought to sit down and really talk it out with Moser. Find our what the hell he feels about that sort of idiocy. Kurz had been thinking this way off and on ever since Moser had given him his lecture on Dancer, two days ago.

They had been alone in the squad room after their trip to see the fat man. Moser looked at Kurz in that halfway open, almost friendly way, and said, "I kinda smelled Dancer in this deal. If I'm right it's real bad news. Dancer is always bad news."

He got up and walked over to the window as if he wanted to take a long look at the tenements outside before he said the next sentence. "He's a hater, Dancer. Which isn't exactly news. You spend most of your life fighting hate when you're born colored. I mean fighting inside yourself."

He looked back at Kurz. The dark face remained an impenetrable mask. "But not Dancer, he doesn't fight it. And he's smart. I wouldn't be surprised if he's the only colored man in this city smart enough to work out an operation like this one."

Moser suddenly looked out the window again and his voice was edged with bitterness. "I couldn't do it myself in a hundred years."

Kurz was amazed by how uneasy that little speech made him feel. He found himself suddenly wanting to ask: *Do you hate me, Moser?* But that was hardly the right reaction for Harry Kurz, professional policeman. So instead he asked: "Has he got a record?"

"Juvenile mostly. They finally grabbed him when he was seventeen or so stickin' up a liquor store, and he got one to three. I remember him tellin' me that was the last time. It was, too. He hasn't made an honest dollar in his life but no judge's seen him since."

So Kurz drove slowly down the side street toward the black blank face of the warehouse, thinking about Dancer. There was a stick ball game in progress at the head of the street and Kurz expected the players to move as he approached. Everyone stepped back until he got to the pitcher, a long slim-hipped kid with a bullet head. He kept right on pitching until Kurz's bumper was an inch from his shins. Kurz tapped the horn and he turned around, put his hands on his hips and said, "Blow it out yo' ass, Whitey."

Kurz sat there somewhat stunned by his inability to answer him. Instinctively he let Moser do it, hoping he would see another knee in the groin. But Moser just looked straight at the kid and said: "Will you get out of the way, sonny? We really don't want to run you over."

The kid stepped back without another word and they drove to the warehouse parking lot. Inside the warehouse it was beautifully cool. They kept it that way for the drugs, not the people. But it was nice. The foreman was waiting for them. He was a small, grey-headed Italian, built so square he looked like he had been carved out of marble. He never used less than two obscenities per sentence.

"I got some——coffee up there in your——roost waitin' for ya. I hope these——bastards show up——soon."

"So do we," Kurz said.

On the second floor there were two containers of coffee on the packing cases by their window. They sipped the coffee, which tasted like it had been brewed three days ago, and watched the trucks begin to arrive.

The first hour was strictly routine. Trucks lumbered and

rattled down the street blowing angry horns at the stick ball players who retaliated with obscene gestures and shouts of defiance. Kurz could see why the bullet-headed kid got excited about the horn.

"Those kids ought to play stick ball on some other street," Kurz said.

"Can't," Moser said. "That's probably the only turf they got."

They finished their coffee. Outside the sun beat down with steady ferocity, dissolving the stick ball game, seeming at times even to slow the oncoming trucks to a weary crawl. Otherwise the scene remained routine and Kurz began thinking about what he wanted for lunch. The foreman sent a guy out to a good delicatessen about ten blocks away. Corned beef or roast beef? You had corned beef yesterday. . . .

A small blue panel truck turned into the street and drove briskly toward the warehouse. Maybe it was the air of confidence implied by its speed; maybe it was the obviously new paint job glistening in the sunlight; maybe it was just cop intuition. Moser and Kurz both stood up.

"It could be," Moser said. "It could be."

Squinting through the glare, Kurz made out two Negroes in the front seat. The truck pulled around and backed up to the loading platform directly below their window. The two Negroes got out and walked slowly across the black asphalt toward the warehouse steps. They wore blue zippered jackets, snug at the waist, and visor caps. The pants were a slightly darker blue. Their shoes gleamed in the sunlight. In white lettering on the blue truck was LADLAW LABORATORIES.

Kurz picked up the phone they'd installed by the window. "Two guys coming in from Ladlaw Laboratories. They come here often?"

"Maybe twice a month," the foreman said. "Usually just a small truck."

Moser was still standing by the window staring down at them. "I know one of those guys," he said suddenly. "Yeah, I know 'm."

The phone rang. "I can't find nuthin' wrong with their papers," the foreman said.

"Stall them anyway," Kurz said.

Moser was already in the freight elevator. They rumbled down to the first floor and strolled casually over to the foreman's office. It was in the center of the building—a small blockhouse-like structure with its own connecting elevator to the upper floors. The foreman kept the two truckers talking until Kurz and Moser were right behind them. They were both very tall, bullet-headed types like the stick ball pitcher. Kurz suddenly remembered the way his mother used to complain about Negroes: *they all look alike to me*. Mother, you are so right.

But Moser had no trouble. He grabbed the guy on the right by the arm and said: "Hey, aren't you Dukey Anderson?"

The two of them turned and the fingered one said, "My name's Allison. James Allison."

The James was a mistake. They were hot all right. Kurz could feel a small twist of excitement in his chest as Moser said, "I never forget a face. I arrested you in the summer of 1960 for mugging a woman in Greystone Park."

"Then why ain't I in jail?" Allison said.

"Because the lawyer talked the judge into puttin' you on probation."

Kurz beckoned to the foreman. "Call up the Ladlaw Laboratories and find out if James Allison drives a truck for them."

"And William Toland," the other guy said. "Check us both out."

The four of them stood there eye to eye in the silence while the foreman dialed, asked the question and waited for the answer. It was lunchtime and they were betting there was no one around who could confirm or deny. Not a bad bluff. They were well trained.

The foreman came stomping back to the window. "Never heard of 'm," he said.

His words seemed to hit both Negroes in the back like a

small gust of wind. "Where's Dancer?" Moser said. "You two guys help us bring him in and we guarantee you a good deal."

The two said nothing. Their wide pink lips just drooped a little.

Moser sighed. "Okay," he said, "I guess we got to go upstairs and talk this over."

"Keep the second floor clear," Kurz told the foreman.

The loading boss, a square hairy Italian who looked like the foreman's son and probably was, came squawking up to the office window at this point wanting to know what the —— they were going to do with the ——Ladlaw truck. There were six——trucks waiting to get their——before lunch.

"Pull it out and park it," Kurz said. "We'll pick it up in a few minutes."

They marched their captives over to the freight elevator and went rumbling up to the second floor. Kurz suddenly found himself wincing at the prospect of Moser working these two kids over. Somehow, bad as it was, it did not seem so brutal with the fat man. With these kids he could see bones breaking, blood spurting. It could make for some very bad copy in the newspapers—especially since they had to get what was left of them out of the building.

But Moser surprised him again. "Now look," he said, "I don't wanna hurt you. I don't wanna even touch you. But I will, Buddy. I'll make you wish you were dead, then I'll make sure you're dead." He pulled his gun out and held it under Allison's nose. "You get the message?"

"Okay," Allison said. "The stuff's at 26 Boona Vista Avenue. But I don't know nuthin' about Dancer. I mean I heard about 'm, but he ain't in on this deal."

"Okay," Kurz said, "let's go. We can straighten that out later."

He started pushing them toward the freight elevator. Moser hesitated. "Maybe we ought to call in," he said.

Kurz shook his head. "Let's find out if this bastard is lying first. We could look pretty silly."

And if he isn't lying, we win the whole ball of wax. Can't you read that citation in your record, Bill? I can practically hear those promotion bugles blowing.

"Okay," Moser said.

They went down in the elevator and out past the foreman. "Good luck," the old man croaked.

"Thanks," Kurz said.

Out on the loading platform the heat was like a wave of fire. The loaders were all stripped to the waist, even the guys running the mechanical lifters that ran into the big trailers with five and six packing cases in their bright orange claws. About half the loaders were Negro and Kurz thought he noticed a brief pause in the nearest team as they walked past them. They went down the steps and across the broad plaza where the trucks did their backing and turning. The panel truck was parked at the very end of the street, half of it sticking into the plaza.

"How the hell are we all going to fit in this truck?" Kurz asked.

"You ride in the back with one of them," Moser said. "I'll ride up front."

"Why don't I take Roger here in my car?" Kurz said. "I'm afraid if I leave it in that parking lot after five o'clock it'll get stripped to the axles."

"Yeah, maybe you'd better," Moser said.

Kurz took alias William Toland's arm and turned right, leaving Moser on a straight path toward the panel truck. He had gone exactly two steps when the noon factory whistles began to blow. Some shrill, some deep and harsh, they permeated the hot air with sound. In the same instant William Toland's arm came up in a vicious arc and caught Kurz in the throat. It was karate stuff but poorly done—just bad enough to hurt like hell. Half blinded by pain and rage, Kurz spun, his hand on his gun as Toland sprinted toward the panel truck.

The whistles still drowned the air. Ahead of him in the blazing light Kurz saw unbelievable things happening. Allison-Anderson was running toward the panel truck too. One of the truck's back doors was open and there was a shadowy figure kneeling inside with a rifle in the traditional sharpshooter's position. Bill Moser was stumbling toward him, one hand raised to his throat, the other clutching for his gun. The rifle jerked slightly as the sharpshooter pulled the trigger again and again and bullets tore into Moser, stopping his stumbling run as if he had been hit at the waist by an invisible 220-pound tackler. Moser fell forward on his face, his gun skittering across the black stone.

The roaring, screaming whistles, the fierce sunlight, the heat, all conspired to make it a slow motion nightmare. Kurz stood there unbelieving, frozen for a fatal second. Then he dropped to a crouch and started firing. Allison-Anderson and alias William Toland were almost to the front doors of the truck. Kurz would have liked to take one of them, but he had to get that rifleman first. His first shot shattered the window in the closed door of the truck. Kurz was squeezing off a second shot, he could still see the rifleman, a faceless shadow, the black snout of his gun sticking into the sunlight when something smashed him in the chest and knocked him flat on his back.

The whistles stopped and in the tremendous silence Kurz heard a motor starting, then the rifle crack. A bullet whanged into the asphalt an inch from his head. He wasn't hit. There was no pain. Someone had thrown a rock. He pushed himself up on one elbow as another bullet shrilled against the stone. The blue truck was moving now with the back door still open and the rifleman still firing. Moser was not moving. He lay there on his face, a tan puddle in the blackness. Kurz tried to push himself to a sitting position but it was impossible. There was no strength in his arm. He rolled over on his side and squeezed off one, two, three, four shots at the truck as it zoomed between the parked cars. He hit nothing as far as he could see.

Feet pounding now as he flopped over on his back and the sun scorched his eyes. There was a dull pain in his chest where the rock had hit him. He put his hand under his coat and it came away red. That was no rock. He looked up at faces. The foreman, the loading boss, square-jawed scared Italians. Other faces, black, no expression. The stick ball pitcher was there with the whole team. "Man, they give it to Whitey good. Did you hear that pow pow pow? That's some gun."

"And the other guy. Must be a member cop."

"I think he dead."

"Just what he deserves, son of a bitch. Ain't no member cop in the world any good."

"I think whitefuzz here gonna be dead pretty soon too."

"Yeah, looka dat blood."

"Shut up! Get out of here, you sons of bitches, give him some air."

The foreman was taking charge. He pushed them back a good ten feet. He knelt beside Kurz. "Hang on, pal, we got an ambulance comin'."

"Thanks. How's my partner?" Kurz said. His voice didn't sound too weak. Maybe you're not too bad. But the chest is always bad. Where the hell can you get hit in the chest and not get hit bad?

"I think he's had it," the foreman said. "I was in World War I. I never seen a guy hit that bad and live."

A dull ache spread slowly through Kurz's chest. He tried to take a deep breath and the ache became a hot coal of pain radiating down into his belly and up into his throat. *Jesus, are you dying? Then why aren't you scared, you dumb son of a bitch? You haven't been inside a church since you went to midnight mass with your mother last Christmas and then there's Marion Kelsey. At least say an Act of Contrition. O my God*—The hot coal began burning in his chest even without taking a deep breath. Little electric spurts of panic ran down his gut into his legs. Okay, now you got what you wanted. You're scared. Are you happy, you stupid son of a bitch? He tried to take one more deep breath just for luck and the pain was like an ax blade crunching through his chest. The blue sky suddenly turned dark. Jesus, where was that ambulance?

"You wanna cigarette, pal?" the foreman's son asked. He didn't say yes or no but someone stuck a butt in his mouth and lit it. Menthol. Nice and cool. Douse that goddamn fire downstairs. He took one drag and could not breathe at all. Coughing, gulping at pure sweet air in the blue sky. Jesus, something in his throat was hot and wet like vomit. He choked and spit and saw the pool of bright red blood beside him. A murmur swept through the watchers.

"Hey, man. You see that? Old whitefuzz really got it."

"Yeah, he got it. You start spittin' blood you got it."

"I tol' you once I tol' you a hunnert times, stand back," the foreman screamed.

A siren. Thank Christ, a siren. It had to be the ambulance. Jesus, God, make it the ambulance, not some motherless police car. If you get me out of this one, God, I swear to Christ I'll play it straight. No more Marion Kelsey, no more dames, period. I'll find some nice girl and settle down and have nine kids.

A bull voice roaring: "Out of the way. Out of the way."

The crowd opened up fast and through it loomed the wide red face and wider shoulders of Deputy Chief Inspector Patrick O'Bannon, the top cop in the South End. Behind him, gold braid gleaming, was Captain Timothy Crotty of the 13th, his his long-jawed deacon's face looking almost intelligent.

O'Bannon knelt on one knee beside him. They had met often at Harold Clark's house. "Where ya hit, Harry?" he said.

It was an effort to talk now. "Chest," he said.

"How'd it happen?"

"Guy in the back of the truck—rifle. Creamed us at fifty yards."

"Did you get the license?"

Christ, you're going to die here talking shop with these two sons of bitches. He let his head roll back and forth. Nothing. Harry got nothing. No citation, no promotion, just a big hole in the chest. Suddenly he wanted to scream. *Jesus, where is that goddamn ambulance?* It would be a hell of a thing to lose control that way in front of O'Bannon. But didn't they realize he might be dying? Thirty-six years old and dying. That was too goddamn young to die. There was too much on his agenda. Like a Mexican vacation, that hunting trip to Canada, a few more weekends at the shore with Marion in that glass dream house her stupid husband left her. Getting married. Maybe even to Marion, if that's what you want, God. But that's asking an awful lot. *Jesus, where was the ambulance?*

A figure in white seemed to grow out of O'Bannon's shoulder. He had an oblong, lumpy face with a long, sad Jewish nose and large black rimmed glasses. He walked around Kurz's feet and knelt on one knee beside him. For some reason, just seeing him made the hot coal in Kurz's chest get bigger. The doctor picked up his wrist as if it were a stick of wood and held it for a few seconds. "Let's get him in the ambulance." His voice was nasal and vaguely unpleasant. He sounded bored. *You Jew son of a bitch. I'd like to see how you'd act with a hole in your chest.*

Two men in white, one a Negro with shoulders as big as Moser's, came through the crowd and lifted Kurz onto a stretcher. Instinctively he tried to push himself up as they grabbed him. It was laughable. He didn't have the strength to lift a piece of balasa wood. The sky went dark again and it came through very hard this time: *You dumb bastard, you really are dying.*

As they got close to the ambulance, a strange sound hit him. It was like heavy rain on a roof at first. Then he could hear hands clapping, voices. As they lifted him into the ambulance he got a glimpse of the street. There were two and three black faces hanging out of every window of every tenement. They were all cheering. He caught a few of the flying shouts.

"How's it feel, Whitey?"

"Next time we give it to you up yo' ass, Whitey."

Closer he heard O'Bannon snarl, "Black sons of bitches."

Why the hell aren't you mad, Kurz? You don't know, you just aren't. Too tired. You've got other things to worry about. Like breathing.

It was shadowy inside the ambulance. To the right he could make out Moser's black face. He was not moving. The Jewish intern climbed in between them and slipped Kurz's right arm out of his coat sleeve.

"How's my partner?" Kurz mumbled.

"Bad."

The intern rolled up his sleeve and hung a bottle of plasma from the ceiling above them. A needle gouged Kurz's wrist. Another needle nicked his forearm.

"Listen, work on him first. He's got three kids."

"Don't worry, we'll do everything we can for him."

It was the kind of promise fathers made to children, nice words that meant nothing.

Through the glaring summer streets they hummed and up the long hill toward the city's medical center, the politicians' pride. Are you feeling better or worse? It was hard to tell. In the dimness everything was slightly fuzzy. That was probably morphine he slipped you. What was he doing for Moser?

The intern was rigging a plasma bottle above him. Watching, Kurz saw the black head move. Once to the right. Once to the left. "Harry," Moser said. His voice sounded very far away. "It was Dancer, Harry. Dancer."

Suddenly his black arm leaped up like a live thing, knocking the plasma bottle into a crazy arc. "Can you hear me, Harry? Can you hear me?"

The intern tried to grab the arm but Kurz caught it first. "I hear you, Bill. I hear you," he said.

"Dancer!"

Suddenly the arm was no longer a rigid, reaching, living thing. It was heavy, inert. It fell out of Kurz's feeble fingers down into the shadow between the two stretchers.

Fuzzy. Fuzzier and fuzzier. Too goddamn fuzzy wuzzy to worry, much to less pray. It was all the Jew's fault, the son of a bitch with his morphine. No, stupid, he's only doing his job. "They're ready for him in the OR," a crisp voice said. It was hard to tell whether it was a man or a woman.

"The Negro's dead."

Marble walls drifted past. Bronze plaques with politicians' faces staring through the antiseptic smell. Hospital smell that takes you all the way back to tonsils, the age of five, your arms around your father's neck screaming *Please, don't leave me, Daddy, please don't leave me* and the square face giving you that Humphrey Bogart smile: "I gotta go to work. I gotta catch some crooks, kiddo. If I stay here with you the whole city might get stolen." Big laugh. Three years later it did get stolen as far as daredevil Jim Kurz was concerned.

Jesus, you are going to die. They are going to stuff you in a box and drop you in a hole. Two weeks ago up to there in Marion Kelsey. Down at the beach last weekend, your hand on that splendid snatch. Oh, Harry, that feels so nice. Impossible. You are not going to let some boogie with a rifle knock you out of the picture. Impossible.

Suddenly bobbing along above him like something on a balloon was an old man's face. "I'm Father Hartke," he said in a weird singsong voice. "I'm going to give you the last rites of the church."

The fuzzy wuzzy stopped. He could see the Jewish intern clumping along beside him, the bottle of plasma in his hand. He looked down as the priest spoke and Kurz could swear he saw a look of contempt on his face.

"Get the hell out of here," Kurz said to the priest.

"My dear boy, there's no need to be frightened. It doesn't mean you're going to die. We call it the sacrament of healing now."

"I don't want it," Kurz said. "I'm not going to die."

The fuzzy wuzzy came on again, buckling the walls, dissolving the ceilings, making the worried old face dance. The priest had very bushy eyebrows and under the eyes, deep dark circles. He was spooky looking, the son of a bitch.

"I'll give you absolution," he said. "Are you sorry for all the sins of your past life?"

"Yes," Kurz said.

No point in fighting that one.

The hand wavered up and down, the thin, rather womanish

lips murmured the Latin and suddenly everything stopped. The rolling stretcher no longer moved ahead. Instead it was dropping down down down through a hole in the floor, while the priest's tired balloon face drifted up toward the ceiling. There was a great spasm of brightness, then darkness, then brightness again, as if someone was blinking a searchlight in his face. This was drastic. He tried to say something, but he could not make a sound. He could only stare straight up at the Jewish intern who stared back with dismay on his mournful Semitic face. Then even he disappeared and there was only darkness and a voice: "Cardiac arrest! Help me!"

He smelled soap, soft lips on his mouth, soft skin against his beard, smelled sweetness, lipstick, perfume, no tasted it on his breath, not his breath but sweet Jesus air down his throat into his tortured chest, suddenly painful *Jesus* every breath a blast of fire. The lights came back. He stared into a mass of black air, *black* forehead, *black* cheeks. A Negro nurse or wardmaid was giving him mouth to mouth respiration. *Kissing niggers Jesus.* And every breath a blast of fire. Kurz wanted to curse her, fling her aside but he could not even raise his hand. And pain. The intern's fingers now, clutching and unclutching the good side of his chest. Up and down, up and down went hand and breath as if he was some ridiculous rubber toy that they were trying to keep from collapsing and all he could do was stare into the pores of the smooth black skin. What a crazy way to die.

"I think he'll make it now," the intern said. "I'm getting a pulse."

Lips, eyes vanished. "You bettah run all the way," a soft Negro voice said.

The operating room had to be on television. Everyone standing around with their masks dangling, one nurse really stacked. He could see them coming right through the floppy uniform. But there was no small talk. Weren't they supposed to joke with him? Who the hell wrote this script anyway?

Gently, efficiently, they lifted him from the stretcher and two nurses began cutting away his shirt. There goes fifteen bucks. Save the tie, girl, that's worth five. Moser couldn't afford those kinds of prices. Three kids, the poor bastard.

Overhead chatter: "Pulse . . . respiration . . . cardiac arrest . . ."

Someone put a mask over his face. There was darkness.

There was light. His mother sat about six inches from his right eyeball, weeping. Her double chins were bouncing up and down, her button nose was red. "What the hell are you crying about?" Kurz said.

"Oh," she said, leaping up. "Nurse. Nurse."

"Yes?"

His eyes revolved to the rear of the bed.

A nurse stood there, crisp and white, unsmiling. The lips had a small bow in them. The hair was very dark, the face rather narrow with a very fine nose. One of those willowy types.

"He's—awake," his mother said, as if it was a catastrophe.

"It's about time," the nurse said. She walked around the bed and picked up the patient's wrist. She smiled more to herself than at Mrs. Kurz and said, "He's doing fine."

She looked down at Kurz: "Is there anything I can get you?"

"A bulletproof vest."

"You won't need one of those for a while," she said, smiling in a small careful way.

"Guess what I was doing the last time I was awake."

"I give up."

"Kissing a dame. Right in the doorway of the operating room. Kissing a dame. As black as the ace of spades."

Her smile was slightly warmer. "I heard about it," she said. "She's a friend of mine."

"Give her a message, will you? Her lips are sweeter than wine."

"Harry!" his mother said.

She gave him a cool look, very professional. "He's been a little delirious," she said to his mother.

"Go to sleep now." She stepped back from the bed and he

had a chance to see all of her. Long legged, with a high slim waist and well rounded bottom. He could hear his mother sniffling on the other side of the bed.

"Tell her to stop crying and go home. I'm not going to die now, am I?"

"No. He's going to be all right, Mrs. Kurz. You really ought to go home."

"Can I kiss him?"

She must have gotten an okay. A moment later her lips brushed his forehead.

"Okay, Mom, I'll see you later."

"Thanks f'everything, Miss Macy," his mother said.

Miss Macy's smile was very professional but sincere. "We'll take good care of him, don't worry," she said.

His mother bumbled past the white curtain around his bed and disappeared.

"I could use a drink of something," Kurz said.

"Water is all you can have," Miss Macy said. She held a glass with a straw in it under his chin and lifted his head so he could sip it.

"Thanks," he said. "How long have I been out?"

"Almost twenty-four hours."

She stopped back from the bed again, a long slim hand spread out on her thigh. There was a skittish, coltish quality about her, something animal and natural and proud in the way she held her head.

He tried taking a deep breath to check on the pain and found it was impossible. He could only breathe in small, shallow gulps. It scared him a little.

"On the level," he said, "am I going to make it?"

She nodded, a small smile on her lips. "They took you off the critical list about two hours ago. Now you're just serious."

And tired. I think I will take your advice, Miss Macy, and go to sleep. I am seriously tired. But maybe some one of these days you and I can get serious, Miss Macy. You have a torso that is worth serious attention.

He slid slowly down a long, black hill and at the bottom

Miss Macy was waiting for him, pure white against the black and she knelt beside him and put her lips on his lips and his hands began exploring that long, lithe body. From somewhere a voice began calling. He did not listen at first, but it soon became impossible to ignore. It was Moser saying, "Dancer. Dancer, Harry." Go to hell, Kurz thought, I've got what I want. He went on kissing Miss Macy. But the voice kept calling and gradually the dream faded and there was only sleep.

Chapter Two

Up from sleep Kurz came like a diver surfacing into sunlight. Yes, it was sunlight, speckling the walls and ceiling of the ward. You really are alive, Harry.

But you wish you were dead.

Marion Kelsey stood beside the bed wearing a wide, round flowerbed of a hat and a pink suit. She looked like a leftover from the Easter parade. She was wearing too much lipstick, as usual, and you could see where the makeup ended on her neck. "Oh, Harry," she blubbered, "you're gonna be all right. I talked to the doctuh, thuh surgeon. He says you're gonna be fine. You're strong as a horse. When I heard it on the radio, Harry, I thought I'd die. I said to myself, God's punished us. I got right down on my knees and prayed. Oh I prayed for Him to forgive us both, Harry. I said take me, what good am I. I'm so glad He listened, Harry—"

Kurz closed his eyes. "I'm afraid I'm not out of the woods yet, Marion," he said in his feeblest whisper. "My heart, you know. The doctor said absolute quiet, no excitement. And you know how you excite me, Marion."

"Oh. Oh, dear, I shouldn't even be here. Why didn't the nurse tell me?"

"She probably doesn't know it yet. The doctor just left."

"Oh. Well, I won't stay anothuh second but" (blubbering again) "I'm so glad—I don't know why they sent you down to that awful precinct in the first place. My fathuh always said the police department was like the army, the right man in the wrong place. I just hope it didn't have anythin' to do with me comin' over to see you at the station house that night. I just felt so blue and you know how I get tiddly when I get blue and you laugh me out of it—"

"I'll see you later, Marion. Thanks for coming," he whispered, eyes still closed.

Marion gave him a farewell peck on the cheek and the odor of My Sin was like a gas attack. It made Kurz sneeze and the pain in his chest was excruciating. A few minutes later, Miss Macy came striding past with some medicine on a tray. Under her crisp white uniform she rippled in all the places where Marion Kelsey sagged. She stopped when she saw Kurz was awake.

"Well, Rip van Winkle," she said. "How do you feel?"

"I don't know. I'm too busy coping with my visitors," he said.

"Oh," she said.

"If she comes back, tell her I've been transferred to the Mayo Clinic."

Miss Macy's face remained a mask. "Would you like to sit up?"

"I'd like to stand up."

"That'll come soon enough."

Miss Macy put down her tray, seized him under one shoulder and told him to push with his other arm. No perfume for Miss Macy, just a nice clean soapy smell. "Ready. One, two, three." Jesus, he was like a slab of tapioca pudding. Miss Macy stuffed another pillow under his neck and took his pulse.

"What's your first name?" he said.

"Ann," she said, giving him a very professional stare.

"Mine's Harry."

She didn't say anything but he got the message. It was not going to be Ann and Harry. She must be used to fending off bedridden wolves.

"Miss Macy," an old man's voice croaked on the other side of the ward. "Miss Macy."

"I'll be right there, Mr. Palmer."

Kurz watched her swish away to Mr. Palmer's rescue. Miss Macy liked a tight uniform around the hips. It was a very stimulating view.

Kurz lay there just looking at the sunlight. It was white, lovely. He thought about sunlight on the beach, on the blue sea, on tan skin, all waiting for you again, Harry. Jesus, it really was good to be alive.

He discovered he was hungry. It came on very slowly, just a small whisper of discomfort at first and then a big hollow ache. Miss Macy came swishing past, tray under her arm.

"Hey," he said. "When's chow?"

On the other side of the righthand curtain a voice yelped, "You won't want it when you get it, brother."

"You just missed lunch," Miss Macy said. "It's about three hours until dinner."

"Not even a sandwich?" Kurz said.

"Miss Macy. Miss Macy." The old man's voice was shrill now.

"I'm coming, Mr. Palmer," she said sharply.

"If I bring you a sandwich, Mr. Kurz, just because you are hungry, that means I would have to bring a sandwich to anyone else on the floor when he was hungry. There are thirty-six beds on this floor, Mr. Kurz, all full of hungry men."

"But you feel so sorry for me and I'm such a nice guy, you're going to get me that sandwich anyway, right?"

"Wrong," Miss Macy said.

Miss Macy, I am getting a new picture of you. That sweet girlish glow is strictly for the television scouts. I thought going beddy-bye with you would be like a large sweet slice of mother's apple pie. But you are looking more and more like steak tartare with lots of pepper on top.

"Pull my curtains, will you please," Kurz said, "so I can see my companions in misery."

She pulled his curtains without a word. He was in a semi-private ward, six beds. Two of the three beds along the opposite wall had their curtains drawn. The third was empty. On his left was a white-haired Negro who looked like Ronald Colman with a deep tan. On his right was a young hawk-nosed white man with unruly black hair and excitable, if friendly, eyes. "How ya feelin', Detective?" he said.

"Pretty good," Kurz said.

"The name is Finnegan," he said. He swung his feet over the side of his bed. "I read about it in the paper. You got half the front page."

"No kidding," Kurz said.

"Yeah. Too bad you didn't nail one of them black bastards."

"We tried."

"I bet you can't wait to get the hell out of here and start lookin' for 'm."

"Yeah," Kurz said.

He had seen this type before. He thinks every cop is a tiger who eats, drinks, sleeps his job. But this was by no means Finnegan's only problem. His thin lips twitched, his hands raced wildly through his black hair which stood up in all directions like grass on top of a coconut. "There's only one thing them boogies understand, the gun and the club. Right, Detective?"

Kurz remembered the Negro in the next bed and gave him a glance. He was staring straight ahead like a carving on a sarcophagus. Finnegan did not bother to wait for Kurz to agree with him. "In another twenty years, the way things are goin', we'll be the slaves. Goddamn black bastards. I tell you the more I see of this civil rights shit, the more I think the only good Nigger is a dead Nigger, like they used to say about the Indians. Right, Detective?"

A bellow of laughter came out of Finnegan, a crazy sound that didn't seem to belong to him.

Ten seconds later who should come walking into the room but Miss Macy and a plump smiling Negro nurse who looked like Aunt Jemina's granddaughter. Did they hear Finnegan? It was hard to tell. Ann Macy gave him a cold stare and then smiled gravely at Kurz. "I thought you'd like to meet the girl who saved your life," she said. "Helen Johnson."

Helen giggled and said: "It's the first time I ever had to do that."

"He said your lips were sweeter than wine."

Helen giggled some more. "I think that's sort of beside the point."

"Helen and I graduated together," Miss Macy said.

"I sure appreciate what you did," Kurz said. It sounded lame. But what the hell was he supposed to say? If Helen was white, he could add: *And it was a lot more fun than kissing that intern.* But it didn't go. Even the crack he had made when he was delirious didn't go. "Yeah," he fumbled. "I wouldn't be around without you."

Helen stopped giggling. "Just my job," she said, shook his hand and departed.

Finnegan stared in disbelief. He didn't know what the hell to say or think. Fortunately Kurz was rescued from further conversation with the idiot by the grandiose appearance of Deputy Chief Inspector Patrick O'Bannon and Chief Inspector Harold Clark. O'Bannon's wide, thick-lipped mouth seemed sneery even when he smiled, as now. "Look at the son of a bitch," he chortled. "Sitting up already. I always said you can't kill an Irishman with one bullet, especially when he's half Kraut."

"How does it feel, Harry?" said Uncle Harold in his usual solemn style.

"They guarantee me I'll live," Kurz said. "I told them if they're wrong I'll sue hell out of them."

O'Bannon chuckled. "You're a godamn *nut,*" he said. "Listen, you feel good enough to talk about this thing?"

"Sure."

He told them about the driver Moser called Dukey Anderson and described alias William Toland.

"What about the guy with the gun?"

"It was too dark inside the truck to really see him."

Uncle Harold shook his head regretfully. "Anything else?"

"A guy named Dancer. Moser kept saying he smelled Dancer in the whole thing. He might have been the guy with the gun. In the ambulance just before he died he said, 'It was Dancer, Harry.' But I'm not sure what he meant."

O'Bannon nodded, all business now. "We'll have a little talk with Mr. Dancer."

"We'll have a sketch artist come in and see if you can reconstruct those two drivers," Uncle Harold said.

"Any time."

"I'm sure you can't wait to get out of here and go after those guys."

"You bet."

Uncle Harold looked slightly disappointed by his small enthusiasm. Screw you, Uncle Harold. I would not have this hole in my chest if you were not such a square. Your Little Boy Blue has to have a well-rounded career before he gets the big promotion. Maybe I will surprise you by rounding off the whole thing with a two sentence letter of resignation.

Kurz lay there for the next two hours thinking about it. The sunlight faded from the room and someone clicked on a cluster of shielded lights in the ceiling. The maids came with the food and Miss Macy paraded up and down supervising with the aplomb of an admiral directing maneuvers. The food was two dried-out pork chops, a few teaspoonfuls of apple sauce and a baked potato. Kurz forced it down to fill the growling void in his belly.

"I see what you mean about the chow," he said to Finnegan.

"It's shit," Finnegan said, pushing his tray aside. "Think you'll get this guy Dancer, Detective? I heard you guys talkin' the case over . . ."

"Who knows," Kurz said.

"Is he a boogie too?"

"Who knows?" Kurz said with a silent curse for Finnegan's stupidity. Miss Macy had heard them and delivered a very disapproving stare.

The next morning Kurz was confronted by the largest

woman he had ever seen. Miss Donaldson was at least six feet tall with arms and shoulders that qualified her for the Green Bay Packers and a line coach's mate voice and manner to match. She flipped Kurz around the bed as if he were a ninety-six pound weakling, meanwhile telling him all about her brother who was a Marine Corps specialist in guerrilla warfare.

"He's given me the whole course in judo," Miss Donaldson roared.

Kurz shuddered, picturing the carnage Miss Donaldson might wreak on anyone insane enough to make a pass at her. After seven hours of her booming we're-all-buddies manner, it was a distinct pleasure to have Miss Macy back, even if the femininity she exuded was only one degree above freezing. Kurz immediately turned his back on Finnegan and tried to start a conversation with the tan Ronald Colman on his right. It was impossible. The guy was deaf, for one thing, and he had a drawl that made it sound like he was mumbling Swahili. But as long as Miss Macy was in the room, Kurz kept trying.

Later in the afternoon, when she took his temperature, Finnegan was downstairs getting more X-rays to decide the fate of his gallbladder. "You like nursing?" Kurz asked.

"That's why I'm doing it," Miss Macy said.

"It must be a drag, putting up with characters like laughing boy here."

Her eyes brightened. It was hard to tell whether it was just surprise, or pleasure. "He is rather loathesome, isn't he," she said.

And that was that.

About an hour later, down the aisle came the slightly wild-eyed old priest who had tried to give Kurz Extreme Unction on the way to the operating room. He peered at a slip in his hand and then smiled faintly.

"Harry Kurz," he said. "I'm Father Hartke."

"Hello, Father."

"How are you feeling?"

"Better every day, Father."

"You're a very lucky young man. An inch the other way,

the doctors tell me, and that bullet would have been fatal."

"So I hear."

"I must say I was surprised that someone like you—a college graduate—would refuse Extreme Unction."

There was a lost sheep dog quality to Father Hartke's face. Deep lines ran from the corners of his mouth, framing a rather weak chin. His cassock was stained and scruffy and the few graying hairs left on his head were disorganized and droopy. He made you feel sorry for him.

"I wasn't thinking too clearly, Father. I was concentrating on staying alive and you sounded like an invitation from an undertaker."

Hartke smiled faintly. "Yes, of course, of course. You don't have any—problems about your faith then?"

"Of course not, Father."

"You'd be surprised how many do." He looked nervously around him as if his revelation might offend someone. "You'd be surprised how many terminal cases here refuse to see me. Refuse to see a priest when they know they must face God's judgment."

"Is that a fact, Father," Kurz said, making an effort to sound interested.

"Of course, there are some like my friend Finnegan here—daily communicants."

Finnegan had returned and was eavesdropping as usual. "It makes sense, Father," he said. "Ya gotta have spiritual strength if you're gonna uphold spiritual values."

"Of course, of course," Father Hartke said. "How often do you receive the sacraments, Mr. Kurz?"

"Oh, every week, Father," he lied.

"That's good. Better than most. Are you a member of you Holy Name Society?"

"Oh, yes, Father."

Anything to keep you happy, Father.

"Fine. Fine. I'm sure those things had a lot to do with your narrow escape. God does watch over us, you know."

"I'm sure he does, Father."

About six o'clock, four detectives from his old uptown outfit, the 23rd squad, dropped in. Eddie Reardon led the way and his death's head grin was a welcome sight. "Here he is," he said, waving his spidery arm. "The only dick in the history of the force that shot himself tryin' to get his gun out of his holster."

"Up yours, holster and all," Kurz said.

Finnegan was so excited to see four detectives he almost wet his bed. He sat there, his ferret ears taking in every word. The conversation was probably one hell of a disappointment for him. The boys spent the first half hour on the latest laughs in the uptown scene. Reardon gave his usual superb imitation of Captain Clarence Mahoney lecturing a mounted patrolman who had had his horse stolen. Then Bill Prince, Reardon's new partner, pulled out a flask and they had Scotch all around. They were on their second drink when Miss Macy went rustling past.

"Hey," said Reardon, "look what loverboy has got on his dinner menu."

"Yeah, in bed twenty-four hours a day, what else can he do?"

"But what will Marion say?"

Miss Macy poured some medicine down a throat on the other side of the room and once more crossed their line of fire. "Oh, Nurse," Reardon said, "could we see you for a moment?"

"Yes?" she said coolly.

The four aging wolves stood there devouring every curve. "We're from the police department good conduct squad," Reardon said. "We want to know whether this young man has been behaving himself. He's been recommended for a good conduct medal, you see."

"Miss Macy—" Kurz began.

"Quiet," Reardon snapped. "The good conduct medal, you see, depends on whether the recipient has been strictly obeying the Ten Commandments. Now this young man has had trouble with certain of these commandments. The sixth, for instance."

Miss Macy gave him an icy stare. "Is that all you have to think about in the police department?" she said. "No wonder the city's a mess." Then she saw the bottle and really blazed. "Don't you know better than to give a patient liquor without asking permission? You ought to have more sense, Mr. Kurz, if your friends don't."

She stood there until they sheepishly put away the bottle. Reardon watched her go, then reeled back and put up his coat collar. "Wow! You haven't made any time on that front, loverboy."

"For Christ's sake, I've only been off the critical list two days," Kurz said.

"Listen, I think we got this guy all wrong," Bill Prince said solemnly, "I think Marion's got him hooked. Why, just the other day she was telling me how she was working like a little Trojan to pay off a couple of cardinals and get her marriage annulled in Rome so she and darling Harry here could start a new life together."

This broke everybody up. "You want a second mortgage on that property, you got it," Kurz said.

"I'm a happily married man," Prince said.

"There's no such animal," Kurz said.

"Jesus, he hasn't changed one of his crummy opinions," Reardon said. "I thought maybe going down into the shadow of death might have caused a spiritual revolution in your soul, old buddy."

"It did—for twenty-four hours."

Reardon shook his head cheerfully. "It's enough to make a lad stop believing in sanctifying grace."

"As if you ever believed in it, you bastard."

They continued in this vein for several more laughs, finishing off the rest of the Scotch. The married boys then pulled themselves together, announced there were irate wives at home with burned or cooling dinners on stoves and said good-bye.

Fellow bachelor Reardon lingered. "Oh, by the way," he said, "they're giving Moser an Inspector's funeral."

"Why the hell shouldn't they?" Kurz snapped.

Reardon shrugged, grinning. "It's just going to look a little odd, all that brass marching into the First African Baptist Church."

"He was a damn good cop, Eddie."

"Take it slow, kid."

What the hell is wrong with you? In seven words you had shot down half the old-buddy feelings of the visit. But it was true. Moser was a hell of a cop and Eddie Reardon was wrong including him in the digs he was always taking at the Negroes on the force.

"Hey, Detective," Finnegan said, "I guess that was code you was speakin'."

"What?"

"All that stuff about Marion and the cop that lost his horse. I didn't know you guys used code."

"When we've got to talk like this—in public—it's necessary."

A feverish delight danced in Finnegan's eyes. Kurz could practically hear him telling the story in bars for the next twenty years.

About an hour later, Miss Macy suddenly appeared beside his bed. "Mr. Kurz," she said, "I—I'm afraid I should apologize for losing my temper that way."

"Forget it," he said, "we all deserved it."

"No," she said. "I realize you weren't responsible for—the way they acted."

She stood very stiffly, her head slightly raised, reminding him of the way girls used to recite in the fourth and fifth grade when they were afraid of the nun.

"Forget it," he said again.

She stuck the thermometer in his mouth. "Are you married, Mr. Kurz?"

He shook his head.

A small smile. "But that wasn't true—about your reputation in the department."

He shook his head again.

She gave him a very dubious smile, and read his temperature.

"Actually," Kurz said, "I'm shy."

She just looked at him, not believing a word of it, but not really disliking it either. "Time for temperatures," she said to Finnegan.

That night Kurz had the cage dream starring Ann Macy. He had had the dream for a long time. It had begun about a year after his father's death. In those days he was alone in the cage, a monkey-like creature. Sometimes the cage was in the middle of a jungle. All kinds of grotesque animals, lions with rhino horns in their heads, wolves with giraffe necks, came and peered at him. Other times the cage was on a dock and a huge crane picked it up and lifted it hundreds of feet straight up in the air and then swung it far out over the water to drop it on the deck of a ship where it was instantly surrounded by grinning apes in sailor hats.

In later years the cage grew bigger. Sometimes there were animals inside it wearing human faces. Uncle Harold, for instance, often appeared as a lion, the most ridiculous possible costume for a man never known to raise his voice. Sometimes these animal people attacked him, sometimes they performed obediently when he barked orders or cracked his whip at them. As he grew older, the dream (which had once terrified him) lost most of its nightmare power. Lately he had grown to regard it as almost comic. But there was one vestige of the old terror left. It always ended with him trying to get out of the cage and finding the door locked. Usually at this point he woke up.

The dream starring Ann Macy was human. She wore her white uniform and stood on one of the little platforms, mocking, serene, refusing to obey a single one of his shouted commands. He walked slowly over to her and let his hand move teasingly up her thigh beneath her skirt until his fingers found the softest, warmest parts. She tried to hold herself erect, but it was impossible. She trembled from head to foot and suddenly crumpled forward into his arms.

Instantly he was enveloped by the long gleaming green coils of a boa constrictor. He staggered back fantastically frightened, struggling to get his right arm free. He had to get his gun. He had to get his gun. Backward he reeled to crash against the bars of the cage. Mindlessly the great coils continued to entwine him, reaching below his waist now. *This can't be a dream, I'm not afraid anymore. I'm cured—I——*

"Did you say cured, Mr. Kurz?" Miss Donaldson's square-jawed smile refracted the morning sunlight. "We like our patients to be optimists, but you're in too much of a hurry."

Later in the morning, after limbering up by throwing him around during bath time, Miss Donaldson dragged him out of bed and stood him on his feet. His legs felt as if they were made of bamboo but he managed to get up and down the corridor once and sit in a chair for another fifteen minutes. The following day he got up by himself and made it out to the solarium. After each trip he would sleep for an hour. But on the third day he made it back to the bed without that sensation of imminent collapse. He sat there feeling very satisfied with himself, looking forward to an afternoon of idle strolling, notably in the corridor where Miss Macy had a desk. But at three o'clock, when Miss Donaldson departed with a cheery longshoreman's wave, in her place came a squat little Irish nurse with gray hair pulled to a bun in the back.

"Miss Macy sick?" Kurz asked as she strode briskly past his bed.

"No, gone back to her own ward. I'm Mrs. Murphy, the regular three to seven nurse here." She peered at Kurz's chart. "Hmm," she said. "You're the one with the bullet. I hope they got it out."

"So do I."

"Let me have a look." She pushed him back on the bed and peered under the bandages swathing his chest. "Oh, what an incision you've got. It's healin' very nice, though."

Thank you, Kurz thought. Please keep your infected fingers off it. "Where's Miss Macy's ward?"

"Oh, in the other wing. Kids and old men. All incurables. I don't know how she stands them."

Mrs. Murphy waddled away. Kurz lay there cursing. It

would take another week for him to get strong enough to penetrate the other wing, wherever the hell it was, and even then, how was he going to explain his casual visit? I just happened to be talking my daily three and a half mile constitutional that the doctor ordered for my punctured lung. Or gee, it's great to see you again. All those laughs we had together back in the old ward. Oh, well. Maybe you'd better consign Miss Macy to that large closet full of unrealized hopes like Grace Tarentino, who led you to believe she adored cute young detectives and then you found out she adored fast-rising politicians like Jake O'Conner even more. In fact, night after night. Or Helen, the blonde at the beach last summer, who turned out to have a seminarian brother who lifted weights and topped out at about six feet four inches.

Who should come wandering along but the Jewish ambulance intern. "Mr. Kurz," he said, "we're going to change your bandages."

"No more ambulances, doctor?"

"Weinberg's the name," he said, snipping away. "No. That was my last day, thank God."

"We made it pretty lively for you."

"Yes. I'm sorry about your partner. There was nothing we could do for him."

He lifted away the bandages. Kurtz peered down at his chest and winced. A raw ugly incision ran from his nipple down below his rib cage. In the middle, even uglier, was the brownish red bullet hole. "That son of a bitch," he said.

"Who?" Weinberg said, swathing him down with freezing disinfectant.

"That boogie with the rifle. For the first time I really want to get him."

"What's the point?" Weinberg said, his voice still carefully impersonal. He hesitated. "I don't believe in shooting people, white or black."

"Neither do I, but sometimes there's no other solution."

"I think there's always another solution if we look for it."

"When you're in an alley, Doc, and the guy at the other end is pointing a gun at you, there's not much time to look."

"Oh, well," Weinberg said, relapsing into impersonality again, "each profession has its ethical problems, doesn't it?"

Silence while Dr. Weinberg put new dressings on the incision.

"I was sorry to see Miss Macy go. Watching her walk around was about the only thing that made life interesting in here."

"She's a very pretty girl," Weinberg said. There was a mournful note in his voice. Have you swung and missed, Doctor? Hardly surprising with a face like yours.

"This other nurse was telling me she works in an incurable ward."

"Yes. A waste of nursing talent, in my opinion."

But you are not going to tell me where, are you, Doctor? "Give her my regards, will you, the next time you see her."

Dr. Weinberg gave Kurz a very small and somewhat knowing smile. He packed up his scissors and gauze and said, "I will," and lumbered on his way.

After him came Bill O'Boyle, the police department artist, and a Negro detective named Jackson, a stocky, peppery guy with a flashy, nervous smile. He had a mug shot of Dukey Anderson which Kurz identified with no trouble. They worked their way through a hundred other mug shots but found no one who rang a bell as alias William Toland. O'Boyle then went to work asking a hundred questions about the size of his chin and the width of his mouth and the depth of his forehead and finally showed him a rough drawing. Kurz had never had much faith in this idea. They had picked it up from the New York Police Department.

"It looks like him," he said. "But I wouldn't want to take it into court."

"That's not the idea," O'Boyle said testily. He liked his job. It was a lot easier than gumshoeing around town.

"Okay, it's a perfect likeness," Kurz said.

"What about this guy?" Jackson said. "He ring a bell?"

He handed Kurz a shot of a face which was obviously different from the run-of-the-mill mugs they had just been studying. It was a Negro face, long and angular, with a flat nose and an unusually high forehead. But it was the expression that made the real difference. Defiance blazed from the eyes; a kind of bitter pride dominated the mouth.

"No dice," Kurz said.

"That's Dancer," Jackson said. "Dancer Washington."

"You picked him up?"

"It was easy. He wasn't running anywhere."

"No score then."

Jackson shrugged. "He's like them little monkeys, hear no evil, see no evil, speak no evil."

"What do you think?"

Jackson looked wary. "I don't know. When it comes to Dancer, I just don't know."

"Bill Moser knew."

"Moser. Yeah. He was always kinda hooked on Dancer. I just think he's too smart to go around shooting cops."

"Maybe he wants to teach some cops a lesson. One cop in particular, Moser."

Jackson shook his head, his eyes blank. Kurz decided he did not like him very much. But now was hardly the time or place to start an argument. They left, with Jackson suddenly urging him to get back to work soon, even throwing in a line about all the guys in the squad room missing him. "Everybody's just waitin' to see you back in action." He grinned.

Kurz decided he did not like him at all. "Tell them not to hold their breath."

The afternoon paper arrived and he read the story of Moser's funeral. It wasn't at the First African Baptist Church, it was at the city's Episcopal Cathedral. It was an Inspector's all right, with the brass, the commissioners, even the mayor there. As if Bill Moser gave a damn inside that coffin. There was also a bulletin from the police department informing the public that Detective Kurz was recovering nicely and another story about the strenuous search for Moser's killer. But in between the lines, it was easy to see that so far the results were zero.

They had found the panel truck, abandoned near the city dump. It was recently stolen, of course. Inside it, likewise abandoned and no doubt stolen, was the rifle, a pump action Remington model 760 Gamemaster. Mr. Sharpshooter had fired .280 high velocity slugs, the kind hunters used to stop a charging grizzly. It grabbed him again, an odd clawing anger at the brutal simplicity with which he and Moser had been sandbagged. Underneath the bandages his chest alternately itched and ached.

The next ten days drifted by. The city's heat wave continued. From the solarium windows he watched the sun beat down on the broiling roofs and gridiron streets. Thank God this new wing of the hospital was air conditioned. Finnegan was finally sent home complaining about his unremoved gall-bladder and assuring Kurz in a conspiratorial stage whisper that he would undertake an immediate check of the local bars to see what he could pick up on the escaped killers. He was replaced by a Jewish shopkeeper with hemorrhoids whose family brought him half a delicatessen for an after-dinner snack.

Every night Kurz's mother arrived looking worried and refused to believe his assurances that he felt better every day. "When are you coming home?" she'd demand. He was unable to tell her, and this confirmed her fears that he was still secretly on the danger list. Marion Kelsey stayed away—that was his only consolation. That s.o.b. Reardon probably was making time with her. It did not take much charm to knock Marion over when you got down to it.

Boredom became his chief enemy. He bought a couple of James Bond thrillers from a perambulating book wagon and spent a few hours imagining himself wrestling superbly stacked broads around the Caribbean and other exotic locales. He was halfway through his third volume—right in the middle of one of the juiciest episodes, in fact—when Father Hartke's nasal singsong interrupted him.

"Ah, Mr. Kurz, the doctor tells me you're doing extremely well."

"I'm glad to hear it," Kurz said. "He never tells me anything."

"Oh, yes, yes, very well. It occurred to me that a man like yourself—a member of the Holy Name Society, that sort of thing—it occurred to me that you might help me out in a little crisis I've got on my hands."

"Oh," Kurz said warily.

"We have a group of children in the other wing. Rather tragic cases, most of them incurable. It's my responsibility to see that they get religious instruction. We usually have volunteers from the local Catholic colleges, but during the summer their attendance is very irregular for reasons I'm sure you can understand. I myself will be away for the weekend—"

And you want me to teach them catechism. Father, that is almost good for a laugh and ordinarily I would institute an immediate sinking spell to dodge it. But little bells are ringing in my cerebral cortex as the incurable children's ward connects with Ann Macy.

"I was wondering," Father Hartke rambled on, "if you'd mind teaching them their catechism. It wouldn't take more than a half hour and I think they'd be very favorably impressed to see a man like yourself."

"I'd be glad to, Father."

He lay in bed the next morning telling himself he was insane. He did not even know Miss Macy's hours. The chances were no better than fifty-fifty that she would even be there. But he was so bored he decided even teaching catechism was better than staring at the walls of the ward. After breakfast he put on his bathrobe and told Miss Donaldson where he was going. She roared her hearty approval and gave him directions to Ward 12-H.

Down a dozen floors in the elevator and across a glass-walled bridge between the new wing and the old section of the hospital he trudged. The air grew thick and faintly nauseating. There was no air conditioning in the old wing. The place seemed almost eerily deserted. It was built on a blockhouse pattern with a long, many-windowed corridor running around all four sides and the wards sunk in the center. He saw no one except a few hurrying nurses, their rubber-soled shoes thumping hollowly on the marble floor. He was sweating and it made his bandages itch furiously. He cursed himself for an idiot but he had gone too far to turn back now. There was Ward 12-G.The next one would be H.

Straightening his robe, clearing his throat, Kurz strolled casually down the corridor toward the bright rectangle of fluorescent lighting. He was in the middle of working on a good opening line for Miss Macy when he heard a cool, familiar voice.

"Oh, Mr. Kurz. Mr. Kurz?"

She was standing out in the corridor, crisp, white, self-possessed. He walked toward her, confused and a little annoyed. "The children are down in the chapel," she said.

"Oh."

"How are you feeling?"

Be encouraged, you goofball, it's almost a friendly smile. "Great. Until I got into this non-air conditioned nightmare."

"Now you know how lucky you are."

They walked side by side. He could see little beads of perspiration on her forehead, just beneath her black hair. It is nice to think of you sweating all over, Miss Macy. It makes you almost human.

"It's good of you to volunteer," she said. "For the children's sake, I mean. It will be interesting for them to meet someone like you."

"You mean they'd rather talk cops and robbers than catechism?"

"Can you blame them? Well—you haven't met them yet." She gave him an uneasy glance. "If I had my way I'd eliminate catechism for good."

"Why?"

"Because it's an insult to them. Making them sit in there week after week, month after month, studying about this God that supposedly loves them."

"You don't think He does?"

"Oh, it doesn't matter what I think. This is really part of your job, isn't it? That's why you run things like the PAL, right?"

There was something more than a little bitchy, even sarcastic, in the way she said this, but Kurz had to let it pass. They were almost to the chapel. "In there," Miss Macy said, pointing toward the door. "I'll be back in three-quarters of an hour to help you wheel them down to the ward."

"Thanks," he said. He turned on his best smile. "Relax. I guarantee I'll give them a good time."

Her smile was brief. "They could use one."

She left him standing in the doorway confronting and confronted by his pupils. His first reaction was: good Christ, what have you gotten yourself into now, Kurz, in the name of nooky?

There were six of them in the chapel, which was not much bigger than a semi-private room; no pews, just a few folding chairs, and an altar at one end. A bright-eyed grinning little Negro lay on a rolling cot. He was about ten years old. Besides him was a husky, stupid-looking kid in a wheelchair, his wasted legs in braces and another brace on his neck. Then came two somewhat older boys with spastic paralysis. They were both inhumanly thin and twitched and jerked in their wheelchairs like grotesque puppets. Beside them sat a younger boy with the vacant smile and swollen head of the mongoloid. Last, sitting very straight on a folding chair, was a remarkably handsome little boy. His skin was a very light tan; he might have been Negro or Puerto Rican or even East Indian. There was a vaguely foreign quality to the expression on his face. His bright black hair was carefully combed and parted. While the others smiled or twitched uneasily, he gave Kurz an indifferent stare.

Kurz took a deep breath. It was too late—much too late—to

back out now. "Hello, fellows," he said, "my name's Harry Kurz. The chaplain—you know, Father Hartke—asked me to come down this morning and teach you guys a little religion. I haven't been near a catechism in twenty years. You'll probably wind up teaching me."

Feeble smiles. None at all from little bright-eyes at the end of the line. He could feel sweat oozing under the bandages. Hot needles of itching would not be far behind.

"Well, let's get to know each other."

Quickly he collected the names. The Negro on the rolling cot was Bert. The kid in braces was Bill. The two spastics were named Frank and Eddie. The mongoloid was Pete and bright-eyes was Harry.

"What do you know, another Harry," Kurz said. "Does it stand for Harold?"

He shook his head. "Just Harry."

Kurz sat down, stealing a glance at his watch. So far, so good, we have killed five minutes. "Well, like I said, I don't remember much about catechism any more. Maybe we just ought to go over what you know. Have you got books?"

Everyone nodded and held up the thin tattered books. They looked exactly like the ones he and his classmates had sweated over at good old St. Patrick's parochial school.

"I lost mine," Harry said, looking Kurz straight in the eye. "You're the cop who got shot, right?"

"That's right," Kurz said, finding the admission a little painful. "Who told you about it?"

"I heard it on Eddie's radio."

Eddie confirmed this with a series of twitches and nods and goofy smiles which made it seem like it was the best news he had heard in years.

"Yeah, I forgot to duck," Kurz said. "But I'm okay now."

"But the other one is dead, isn't he?"

"Yes," Kurz said.

"Was it a Negro who shot him?"

"Yes."

"That's good."

"Why is it good?" Kurz snapped. "He had three kids, one about your age. How would you like it if your father—"

"I don't have a father," Harry said.

"Oh," Kurz floundered for a moment. "I still don't see why you like to see cops shot."

"He was a Negro. Any Negro cop deserves to get shot."

"Why?"

"Negro cops are traitors. They play the white man's game."

"Who told you that?" Kurz said.

"It doesn't matter who told me. It's true."

Kurz found it difficult to conceal his amazement. The kid was not more than ten or eleven years old. "Well, whoever it was, they're nuts, and so are you if you believe it."

Everyone laughed uproariously. Kurz had no idea he was being funny. Before he could stop them Bert was flipping around on his cot, shrilling hysterically, "That what I always saying. He crazy. He always talking crazy. You crazy, Harry, see."

Harry just glowered.

"Wait a minute," Kurz said. "I don't think it's funny. I'm serious. There's only two kinds of games, Harry, and they don't have anything to do with being white or black. There's the honesty game. And the dishonesty game."

Harry's mouth compressed into a stubborn line. "White men aren't honest with Negroes. They never have been and they never will be."

Steady. Remember he's only a kid. "Some white men aren't honest, Harry. Some Negroes aren't either. Nobody specializes in honesty."

"You ever catch any crooks?" Bill asked, looking almost alive.

"Sure. But most of the time it doesn't go the way you read it in the detective stories. You usually nail them buying a paper at the corner or having a beer in some bar or fast asleep in bed. They hardly ever put up a fight. They save that for the courtroom."

With vast effort, Eddie, one of the spastics, jerked out his question. "You—ever—shot—one?"

"Oh, a couple."

"Negroes or whites?" Harry asked.

Kurz grinned. The kid was so bugged on the subject he was almost funny. "Whites," he said. "Does that make you feel better?"

"How long have you been on the cops?" Harry asked.

"Ten years."

"And you've never shot a Negro?"

"Nope."

Harry obviously did not believe him.

Kurz glanced at his watch. They were killing time nicely. He picked up Bert's catechism and flipped the pages. "What are you guys up to in this thing?"

There was an uncomfortable silence. Their eyes wandered along the walls and out the windows. "We . . . don't have regular teachers," Bill said.

"They come once or twice, then they stop. Then we got to start over," Bert explained.

"That's too bad," Kurz said. "Well, maybe we ought to start around the beginning and just sort of go over in general what you already know."

No one objected. "What do you know about God, Harry?"

"Nothing."

This kid was too much. Kurz turned to the urine smell. "What about you, Bert?"

Bert's eyes rolled comically. But he was deadly serious. "God make us. He watch over us. Here—and in heaven."

"That's pretty good," Kurz said. "Why don't you know that, Harry?"

"I know it." The childish face blazed with a surprisingly adult contempt. "But I don't believe it. He won't believe it either when he's dying."

"I ain't gonna die," Bert said. "God's gonna cure me. I've been prayin' and prayin' and my momma's been prayin'."

"You're going to die. I heard the doctor say so."

"I ain't," Bert screamed hysterically.

"Wait a minute, wait a minute," Kurz snapped. A pain throbbed in his chest. He was pouring sweat. Of all the stupid goddamn idiotic situations you have talked yourself into, Harry, this takes it.

"You never heard any doctor say that about Bert. Admit it."

The kid stared at him for a full minute. Then he broke, stubbornly. "I just wanted to see what he'd do."

"You saw. And it's not a very nice thing to see. Right?"

Bert was sobbing quietly now. Kurz patted him on the shoulder. "Come on, Bert, he was just kidding."

The thing was turning into a shambles. "Look," he said, "why don't we just sort of refresh our memories. We'll have Harry here read the first ten questions and answers."

It was a dirty trick and he knew it. He handed Bert's catechism to Harry. The kid glowered at it. "What's the point?" he said. "You're like all the other teachers. You're not coming back."

He caught the sadness of it in all their eyes. "Who says I'm not coming back? I don't mean as a catechism teacher. But when we go back to the ward I'm going to find out something you guys need—maybe some kind of game or a TV set—and I'll get it for you."

"You could really get us a TV set?" Harry said, impressed for the first time.

"Sure. Don't you have one?"

"There's one in the ward but the old men won't let us go near it."

"You've got one. I guarantee it. Now will you read that catechism?"

Harry nodded almost eagerly.

"I'll read the questions. Who made us?"

"God made us."

"Who is God?"

"God—is—the—Supreme—Be—ing—who made all things."

Harry did not read very well. He had to concentrate fiercely and follow the words with his finger.

"Why did God make us?"

"God made us—to show forth—his goodness—and to share with us—his ever—lasting happiness in heaven."

"What must we do to gain happiness in heaven?"

"To gain—happiness—of heaven—we must know—love—and serve God—in this—world."

"From whom do we learn to know love and to serve God?"

"We learn to know love—and serve God—from Jesus—Christ, the son of God—who teaches us through the Catholic Church."

The same old questions and the same old answers. Suddenly he was back twenty-five years, a skinny little kid in St. Patrick's second grade, with Sister Sophia, a hundred and ten if she was a day, standing over him with a yardstick, whaling him on the rear end every time he missed a word. What a crazy way to teach kids to know love and serve God. Take the Kurz method for contrast. All you have to do is promise a television set with every right answer and you get superb results.

"Smile, everybody."

In the doorway ballooned Herman Cass, rotund photographer for the city's morning paper. They all looked up and the camera flashed, blinding them.

"What's this?" Kurz growled.

"Human interest," Herman barked merrily. He always talked like he was cabling a world-shaking story from Bangkok. "Hero cop teaches religion to cripples while recuperating."

Kurz did not like the smirk on Herman's face. He liked even less the look on Ann Macy's face when she slipped through the door behind Herman and announced the lesson was over.

"Whose idea was this?" Kurz demanded.

"Who knows." Herman shrugged. "Maybe the chaplain. I've got to get the names of these kids. Can you give them to me, Nurse?"

Miss Macy gave him the names while Kurz brooded. He

was inclined to take the film out of Herman's camera and flush it. He could hear the guffaws from guys like Eddie Reardon. On the other hand, it wouldn't hurt if Uncle Harold saw the picture in the paper. So Kurz said nothing. He even sat down and let Herman take another picture for good measure.

Herman left and Miss Macy assembled her troops for the trip back to the ward. She was very natural and friendly with the kids, none of her brisk professional bitch act. They went down the corridor in a disorganized procession, Harry and Miss Macy leading the way, the other walkers pushing the wheelchair cases. Kurz waited for Miss Macy to ask how the lesson went. But she didn't say a word.

Finally, in what he hoped was an offhand way, he asked, "What's wrong with Harry? He doesn't act very sick."

"He has a kidney condition," Miss Macy said. "He's been very good the last few weeks." She gave the back of Harry's head a maternal pat as she spoke.

"Mr. Kurz says he's going to get us a television set." Harry managed to make it sound like he didn't believe a word of it.

At least it made Macy look at him. "Really," she said. "That's awfully nice of you."

"No trouble. It will just take a little arm twisting, that's all."

"Oh. Well—it's still awfully nice. They could use it."

In another minute they were in the ward. Huge fluorescent lights glared down from the ceiling. There were no windows. The walls were white and totally blank. The boys occupied six beds along the back wall. The first twelve beds held old men with bored, shrunken faces and button eyes.

White curtains encircled the last bed on the right. The curtain in front was drawn slightly aside and an old man could be seen clawing the sheets, gurgling and whining, saliva shiny on his upturned bony chin. As Macy passed the end of the bed, the chin moved. "Nurse, nurse," a voice squeaked as if a mouse were talking inside the head.

Macy hurried to his side. Harry stopped and stared unflinchingly, his small child's mouth twisted in contempt. "He was always telling me to study my catechism," he said.

Kurz helped Macy slide Bert into his bed. The others stayed in their wheelchairs. Harry stood by his bed, a small frown creasing his forehead. It deepened when he caught Kurz looking at him and he began fiddling with the knobs of Eddie's transistor radio. Eddie promptly grabbed it away from him. Kurz felt a twinge of pity. There was something about the kid, his pride, his stubbornness, that reached him.

Lunch arrived in a huge rolling steam table. A Negro maid slung the trays unceremoniously on the bed tables and wandered off. Macy worked her way around the ward cutting meat for one old man, pouring coffee for another, moving a tray into position for a third. The children were far less trouble. Even the spastics cut up their own food and ate it rapidly.

There was nothing for Kurz to do. He wandered aimlessly down the ward and into a small room just off the exit corridor. On the wall bedpans and urinals gleamed like silver trophies in the dim light. A big icebox throbbed quietly in the far corner. Macy's desk was by the door with charts racked on either side. A chart lay on the desk and Kurz studied the neat firm handwriting. The figures and comments meant nothing to him.

"Are you still here?"

She stood in the doorway. Kurz studied her casually. She was really a great looking girl. There must be a way to improve her disposition.

"Somehow that doesn't strike me as a very friendly question."

She got the message and the message got her, a little at least. "Can I help you in some way?" she said, lifting her chin just a trifle to let him know she was a girl who could take care of herself.

"Doesn't it puzzle you a little that I dragged my shot-up carcass down about eight miles of corridor to spend an hour in that oven of a chapel?"

She didn't get it. Or she refused to get it. "It did."

His bandages itched crazily. He felt like he was wearing a hair shirt. "It's all your fault."

"Mine?"

"You left without saying goodbye."

In the fluorescent glare he could see her face change color slightly. An old fashioned blusher. "I really think——"

"That we ought to get to know each other a little better. After all, why fight it?"

"Fight what?" There was a delicious edge of scorn in the *what,* which meant she was not quite as naïve as she was playing it.

"Fate, or whatever you want to call it. I didn't go out and get myself shot on purpose, you know. And you didn't volunteer for duty on 14 Surgical. Humility, that's what we both need. Who are we to decide we weren't meant for each other just because you hated me on sight."

She blushed again. "I didn't hate you on sight."

He stopped her with a look. "I'm kidding, for God's sake."

"Oh, really——"

"Look, I'm getting out of here in a couple of days. They tell me it will be two or three weeks before I can go back to work. That means I've got nothing to do but crawl in my car and head for the beach each day. You must have a day off now and then. How about coming along for the ride?"

She sighed. "You take an awfully long time to get to the point."

"That's half the fun in life. Can I call you as soon as the doctor gives me permission?"

"All right," she said, with a little nod as if she were really making up her mind about something else. "I haven't been to the beach all summer."

"Why not?"

"I go to school on my days off. I'm working towards a college degree."

She slipped again into that slightly self-conscious little girl manner, as if reciting for Sister. Wait until I touch you on the right places, Miss Macy. We'll see how long that act lasts.

"Well, I'd better get back and see what's left of lunch."

She glanced at her watch. "Yes, you'd better."

"But first—the vital statistics—address and telephone number."

She gave them to him. "Did you—really mean that about the television set?"

"Sure."

"Oh, that's—awfully nice."

Awfully nice. He padded wearily back through the heat feeling very tired. Awfully nice is what you are, Miss Macy. Awfully nice between the sheets. Awfully nice between your legs. Awfully nice before breakfast and after lunch. Awfully nice is a girl with a figure like yours, Miss Macy. Awfully nice is a touch of the tongue on those ripe breasts. Awfully nice is my hand on that rounded rump. It will be awfully nice knowing you, Miss Macy. Awfully nice all the way.

Chapter Three

Back in his room he found Miss Donaldson had kept his lunch warm for him, probably by breathing on it. She was ecstatic over his catechism work. "I could tell the moment I looked at you, Mr. Kurz, that you were one of those policemen who refute all those vicious rumors we're always hearing about graft and corruption. I'll bet you do a lot of youth work in your spare time."

"Well—whenever I can fit it in. Detectives have—kind of irregular hours."

"Of course, of course. Well, I just wanted to tell you how wonderful I thought it was for you to hike all the way down there."

"They're nice little kids," Kurz murmured. "I hope I get a chance to do it again."

He forced down the lukewarm food and pondered the television set he had promised to deliver. He could get on the phone and have Uncle Harold pick one up from a sheriff's sale tomorrow, but he decided against it. Better to wait a week or two and make it seem like a really big deal. Then he remembered the flash of eagerness on little Harry's face. A week would be long enough. He would have it down there within the week.

The next day the surgeon who had operated on him finally

showed up. His name was Keller and he was a double for Eric von Stroheim. He even had a faint German accent. "Goddamn, that's a beautiful incision," he said, after he had ripped half the skin off Kurz's chest along with the bandages. "You are one lucky son of a bitch, young man. You know that? A little to the left and that bullet would have smashed your shoulder, maybe made you a cripple for life. A fraction to the right and it would have been in the lung. It creased the lung as is and it may give you trouble. I hope not. Anyway, you go home tomorrow."

"Can I go to the beach? Go swimming?"

"In pools only. No vigorous exercise of the upper torso until I give you permission."

"What about the lower torso?"

"Aha, bachelor. That's your business, sonny boy."

He went home the next day. Uncle Harold drove the car himself. His mother sat in the back seat saying over and over again, "It was Saint Jude. I got right down on my knees and prayed to Saint Jude the second I heard the news."

Who, Kurz found himself wondering, did you pray to the night the old man got it? Whoever it was, that saint got scratched from your list of favorites.

Home looked good. It wasn't their home, of course. The squat little two-storied house was owned by Luke Tully, a lean, crabby, retired railroad engineer who lived on the first floor. Old Luke was alone now, his wife had expired quietly after forty years of trying to get a smile on his pickle puss. His two daughters had long since taken to the road. They were named Martha and Mary and were as different as the two in the Bible. Mary was sweet, plump, serene. For a while the nuns were sure they had her. But she had married a cop and now was on her eighth kid. Martha was a hellraiser who had given sixteen-year-old Harry Kurz some of his first lessons in sex. During World War II he used to sit on the porch on hot summer nights watching Martha neck with sailors in borrowed cars. She knew he was watching. One night she came up the steps and walked over to him in the darkness. He breathed enough perfume to make him wonder if she had taken a shower in the stuff. Then he realized she was crying.

"The son of a bitch," she muttered through her tears. "You want it, Harry, it's all warmed up for you."

He was standing up in more ways than one. His hand touched her wet cheek. "What the hell's wrong?"

"Never mind. Come on."

Down the alley they went into the backyard, past the long rows of lettuce and cabbage and tomatoes and beets which Luke Tully worried over a lot more than he ever did over his daughters, to the sweet-smelling grass in the back of the yard, separated from the garden by a hedge. Pitch black. He had to work by radar, touch. Remembering Martha's hot whiskey breath, whispering, "Jesus, Harry, you're a man. A real man. Thank Christ—"

A night to remember. Where was poor old Martha now? Doing it for five dollars a drop on New York's West Side, he wouldn't be surprised. They had met a dozen more times out there behind Luke Tully's garden during that hot wartime summer, the last she spent in her father's house. In erratic spurts, Martha had given him her philosophy of life. "Jesus, you're a man, Harry. You're really hung. Don't let anyone take it away from you, no goddamn nuns or priests or son of a bitch of a father."

Good old Martha. She was the first person to make him wonder if there was something to be said for having your father gunned down when you were eight.

Mother led the way through the double glass doors into the cool hum of the air conditioner Kurz had bought over her violent objections. "I didn't have that thing on all the time you were—away," she said. "The chills it gives me. We need a cup of tea. And you can stay for a minute, Harold."

The Irish ritual. Uncle Harold was well trained. His lined spaniel face fell in a mournful nod and they trudged behind Mother Kurz to the old-fashioned kitchen with its long deep sinks and ancient spindly stove that still required matches.

They sat at the battered white table which Kurz had been promising to paint for three years and hot tea was soon steaming under their noses. Next came the Uneeda biscuits for Harold and some pound cake for Kurz. It was uncanny the way women remembered a man's minor preferences. It was the major ones that they specialized in frustrating.

"And how is Kitty?" his mother said, sitting down before her cup. The same old gas. Yet it was good to be here, good to see the sunlight filling the faded polka dot curtains with a vanilla glow. Good to know that old Luke was toiling away in the garden below them, his gnarled fingers deep in the gritty earth. Good to know you could still see and feel all these things. Home made you realize how close you had come to seeing, feeling nothing.

Harold was explaining why the heat bothered Kitty's sciatica. His voice was the same weary monotone he used when discussing the latest burglary reports. Not too surprising when you considered old Harold's wife, a faded little woman whose battle-ax of a mother had lived with them for the first thirty-five years of their marriage. But you could tolerate Uncle Harold and Mother today. You could tolerate just about anything.

By the end of the day he was ready to change his mind. His mother insisted on treating him like a cripple. When he refused to take an afternoon nap, her eyes filled with tears. When he considered going down to the neighborhood bar for a drink, she became almost hysterical. He sat watching television and she sat watching him as if at any moment he might stop breathing.

About nine o'clock his sister Alice and her husband, Ed Brant, dropped by to welcome the martyr home. Alice was two years older than Kurz, tall and plain with lanky brown hair and a schoolteacherish manner. Physically, according to the family mythology, she resembled her father, while Kurz had inherited his mother's heavy-boned, stumpy build. But Alice had not inherited her father's easygoing personality. She was a fusser, an order-giver, like her mother. In her teens she had tried to play second parent to Kurz but he had soon made it clear that one was more than enough for him. She had been a brilliant student at the local Catholic schools but there was no money to send her to college. The son had first call on what little cash there was in the bank. Alice had accepted the decision without complaint but Kurz sometimes wondered if she occasionally looked on him with a discontented eye. Would she be married to a nice guy with a second-rate job in the post office if little Harry had conveniently neglected to get himself born?

But tonight she was all sympathy, too damn much sympathy. She and his mother sat around looking at him as if he were a corpse in a funeral parlor. His mother even talked about him in the past tense. "I never liked the idea of him going on the force. I remember saying at the time 'Is that why you went to college?' "

"I said that," from Alice.

"What do you think of those Yankees, Ed?" Kurz said.

Ed was a fanatic Yankee hater and you could always get him excited by asking his opinion of the American League pennant race. But with the Yanks in a state of collapse, his vitriol was a little pointless. The conversation drifted around to politics. The new mayor, Jake O'Connor, was a friend of a friend and Kurz had done some drinking with him in prepolitical days. His relatives liked to think this made him practically a member of Jake's official family. They agreed he was doing a pretty good job trying to reconcile the old pros to a cleaner political style.

"But I'm telling you one thing," Ed declared. "If I hear one more announcement of a new housing project or a new school for those boogies downtown, he's losing my vote."

"Why?" Kurz said.

"Because they don't deserve it, that's why," his sister Alice snapped. "Why should we live in a twenty-five-year-old rundown flat that costs us twice what it's worth and some nigger who never did a day's work in his life gets a clean new apartment with a modern kitchen that he'll ruin inside of six months?"

"Maybe you got something there," Kurz said. His agreement was lukewarm because he did not see the shufling no-account Negro that was in his sister's mind. He saw Bill Moser and there was no rational reason why Bill Moser would ruin an apartment any faster than a half dozen white men he could name.

"O'Connor's paying them off, that's all," Ed said grimly. "They voted down the line for him."

"Well, I don't know," Kurz said. "Maybe he figures it's about time they got a couple of housing projects. The rest of the city's got a good ten to their one."

"And look what they've done to their one."

Greenwood Gardens was the oldest housing project in the city. It had originally been all white but when the Congo expanded, the whites had pulled out and now Greenwood was one hundred percent black. It was also a wreck. Kurz had gone down there once with Moser to check on a burglary suspect's alibi. His nose wrinkled, remembering the urine smell in the elevators, the scraggly brown lawns covered with tin cans and blowing paper. Moser had said nothing, of course. He just stared and smelled and asked the questions and Kurz took down the answers and they scrammed.

Alice was beating her gums about desegregating the schools now. "That'll be next, you watch. They'll be dragging our kids around in buses like they're doing in New York. Two hours on a bus each day, little first grade kids. Dragged up to Harlem. Why? Because the white politicians don't have the guts to tell them where to go."

Kurz was about to ask her why she was so worried. Her kids were all in parochial schools where a black face was about as common as a yellow one. In his sixteen years in Catholic schools, Kurz had sat in class with exactly one Negro, a girl named Nina who had enlivened his eighth grade classroom with a figure that was pure jailbait. Kurz and everyone else, as far as he could remember, had been a lot more interested in her shape than in her color. Words like *black meat* took on new meaning in the cloakrooms. But he realized finally that his sister was just echoing what was in the air around town and her brother getting plugged by a Negro gunman constituted a weird sort of proof that everything her friends were saying was true.

Kurz sighed. The subject just didn't interest him. He was a professional, and as long as integration didn't make waves that rocked his little boat, they could all beat their gums about it until doomsday. Getting shot by a Negro did not change his mind. White or black, a hood was a hood and it was his job to catch them, not worry about their color. He wasn't for the Negroes, he wasn't against them. Sure he called them boogies now and then and laughed at Reardon's savage jokes about them—the first Negro airline pilot who told his passengers, *Now just sit tight till I get this mother fucker off the ground.* But he never made the kind of speeches he was hearing tonight or went out of his way to be snotty to Negro cops, as Reardon sometimes did. Let the philosophers and social scientists figure it all out. Kurz was neutral.

"You just wait," Ed was saying. "In ten years we're going to have a black face in City Hall. Unless we get together and stop them now."

"There's really not that many of them, Ed," Kurz said. "Only about twenty percent of the city. They give you a rundown on them before you go into the 13th precinct. You know, numbers, crime rate, family problems, the whole social work bit."

"Yeah, but there's more coming in every day from the South."

Ed was not going to surrender his doomstering on Kurz's say so. But why argue? You always thought the guy was a jerk anyway.

His sister gave him a very irritated look. She sensed, as only a family member can, his disagreement. "Well," she said abruptly, "how did it feel getting almost killed?"

"Not good."

"I should think it would have given you some second thoughts about the life you lead."

"What's wrong with the life I lead?"

"You know," she said darkly.

"I thought this was a friendly visit. Here I am just back from practically knocking on the Pearly Gates."

"You sure they were pearly?"

Suddenly he wanted to tear into her. Just because you were afraid to play around and grabbed the first wedding ring somebody stuck through your nose, don't start—but he caught a glimpse of his mother, her eyes wide with alarm. No, Harry, no. You have to keep on being a fine fellow until death do us part.

"They were pure pearl," he said, "and I could hear those angels strumming on their harps."

"On the level, Harry," his brother-in-law said, edging out on his chair. "We called the hospital that first night. They said you'd had—a cardiac arrest."

It really was like a wake now, with a talking corpse. For a second he was almost angry again. But instead he smiled. "Sorry, Ed, I hate to disappoint you, but it isn't a big deal at all. You don't even have time to get scared because you don't really believe you're dying. You don't really think it can happen to you. And before you have time to get convinced, it's all over."

"Oh." Ed laughed uneasily. "None of that stuff about seeing your whole life?"

"Not for me, anyway."

"Crazy." Ed ogled his watch. "We've got to get back. There are some of us who have to work."

His sister kissed him on the forehead. "Stay out of the line of fire from now on, will you."

"I'm going to bulletproof everything, right down to my underwear."

They left. Watching his mother waddle to the door with them, Kurz suddenly felt bored enough to punch down the walls. It was the college feeling. The four years he had spent inside St. Ignatius of Loyola's hallowed halls had been the dullest time in his whole life. He had had it again in the army for a while, but at least the army went somewhere like Korea where it suddenly made sense, all of it, the orders, the drill, the ass-breaking marches, the obstacle courses. Maybe waiting is harder to take when you get older. Maybe you are just frustrated, Harry.

Ah. While his mother was still saying goodbye at the head of the stairs, he charged into the bedroom, dug through his suitcase and came up with Ann Macy's telephone number. "Greetings," he said, "this is your ex-patient. Also ex-catechism teacher, ex-corpse."

"Mr. Kurz."

"You remember my name. That's a good sign. When is your next day off?"

"Tomorrow."

"There is a God after all. One more day with my mother and they'd have to throw a net over me. Shall we head for the beach?"

"Can you drive?"

"The doctor said I could do anything but battle the surf."

"Then why go to the beach?"

"There's a swimming pool I know. And I want to see you in a bathing suit."

"Oh. In that case, I'll bring one along."

"Nine too early?"

"I always get up early. I'm a working girl."

His mother insisted on some milk and cookies before bed. "You've lost weight, you know. I bet you've lost ten pounds."

"Mahatma Gandhi would lose weight on that hospital food."

"You were looking so good just before it happened. I was thinking to myself how good you looked."

"Yeah."

"What do you think you'll do tomorrow? I thought maybe we could take a ride out to see Uncle Bob. He was awful worried about you. I bet he called five times the first few days."

Bob was their rich uncle, a plumbing contractor in one of the city's booming suburbs. In one horrifying glimpse Kurz saw what she had in mind. She wanted to visit every relative on the list exhibiting her wonder boy, just back from the dead.

"Sorry. I'm going down to the shore tomorrow. Date."

"Oh."

Her eyes filled with tears, but she said nothing. He felt guilty but he dismissed it, as usual. "A nurse I met in the hospital. Nice girl."

"Oh. I wish you'd bring some of your girls home sometime. I'd like to meet them. You always used to bring them home. But lately—"

Oh, that is a dandy idea. I can just see me bringing home Marion Kelsey and listening to your lectures on hell and damnation for the next six months. Well, maybe he would bring Ann Macy home, just to shut her up. She had a nice sweet clean look. Pure. Pure bitch. But your time is coming, Miss Macy. Your time is coming.

He slept poorly. He kept dreaming about Greenwood Gardens, of all places. Once he found himself walking across it in the moonlight. A Negro in a cheap white shirt with a frayed collar was raking all the garbage on the lawn into one gigantic pile. He turned as Kurz walked toward him and it was Bill Moser. He had a terrible look on his face, half rage, half suffering. For some crazy reason, Ann Macy was there too with a big rake in her hand. "Mr. Kurz," she said sternly, "you'll have to do something about the mess you're making. We just can't go on cleaning things up indefinitely, you know." He looked down at his chest and was aghast to find his shirt soaked with blood.

He woke up sweating in the air conditioner's artificial chill and listened to its mindless hum. Like shrapnel from the dream, some very unpleasant thoughts kept hitting him. Thum, thum, thum, the song of the air conditioner. Thum thum thum thum. Is that all you are, Kurz, another variety of air conditioner humming away day and night, slowly wearing out? He could feel his heart beating against the bed. A week ago it had suddenly stopped beating. A boogie with a pump action rifle had turned you off, Kurz, just as quickly and as neatly as you turn off the air conditioner when the first cool wind of autumn hits town. Thum thum thum. Jesus, it didn't seem right. It didn't take into account all the things you had going on in your head. All those lovely plans and belly-haunting desires, that month in Europe at the department's expense Uncle Harold had practically guaranteed you last Christmas. A week in the Bahamas with someone like Ann Macy. One whole crazy week alone in a hotel room with a balcony that went out over clear blue water. It would cost a thousand bucks and you almost had it in the bank. Maybe even a wife when you hit forty and you'd got the rank. A couple of boys. Summers at the shore. Sunday baseball games. By that time you could spring box seats with a twist of the wrist. Thum thum thum. It could all be turned off tomorrow. *Jesus*. He got up, poured himself a stiff drink and watched the late late movie. It was vintage Jimmy Cagney. He died in great style, much better than any cop in the picture.

Kurz finally went back to sleep and when he woke up he knew it was late. He was right. It was 10 A.M. His mother puttered in the kitchen. "Why the hell didn't you wake me up?" he snapped.

"How do I know what time you're going anywhere? I don't even know you're *going* until the last minute."

It was perfect revenge. He grabbed his bathing suit and dashed to the Volvo. It took him until 10:30 to find Ann Macy's apartment which was on a dead-end street above the river. The houses nearby were well kept. He was surprised to find that at least half the kids playing in the street were Negro. But they were right on the edge of the Congo. The 13th precinct house was, in fact, only a dozen blocks away.

The apartment was a walk up and Macy was on the top floor. Cursing, he struggled up four perspiring flights. It would take weeks at the gym to get himself back in shape. Three long rings and no answer. Then Ann Macy finally opened the door. She was wearing dark blue Bermuda shorts and a light blue shirt that buttoned down the front. Her feet were bare, a good sign. Kurz had a theory that girls who liked to take off their shoes also liked to take off other things.

"Have mercy on the walking wounded," he said. "I overslept."

"That's all right," she said. "I got some studying done. Come in and sit down. I'll be ready in a second."

She led him down a short hall into a very drab living room. The furnishings must have come from some bankrupt third-rate hotel. There were a couple of fat brown chairs, a sagging grey love seat, a worn blue rug. There were no flowers, no knickknacks or chintz curtains, none of the frilly feminine things Marion Kelsey was always fussing over. But there were a hell of a lot of books, two built-in wooden bookcases from floor to ceiling filled with them.

He glanced idly at some of the titles: *The Condition of Man* by Lewis Mumford, *Psychoanalysis and the Doctrine of Freud* by Dalbiez, *The Art of Living* by Eric Fromm, *Being and Nothingness* by Jean Paul Sartre, *The Victim* by Saul Bellow, *The Plague* by Camus. A few of the names were familiar but he had not read one of them.

"Ready and waiting," Ann Macy said. She stood in the doorway of the bedroom swinging a blue beach bag.

"You're quite a reader," Kurz said.

"I'm trying to make up for a lost education."

"I haven't read a real book in five years."

"You've missed a lot of good ones."

"You'll have to tell me about them."

They rolled north on Michigan Street, which ran through the heart of the Congo. The heat was incredible. The sun beat off the storefront windows and even, it seemed, off the grimy bricks of the flats above them. The sidewalks were jammed with Negroes, lounging in front of stores, strolling aimlessly. The only white faces they saw were some cruising cops in a radio car.

"This isn't a city, it's a furnace," Kurz growled.

"I bet it's cooler up on the hill," Macy said.

"Where the white folks live? Yeah, about five degrees."

At last they were on the thruway and the red needle rocked up the dial to seventy. The wind was still hot but at least it was wind and the farther they got from the city, the cooler it became. Head back on the red cushions, Miss Macy seemed to be enjoying the ride too. Then above the wind he heard her voice: "Have you had any luck with the television set?"

Jesus, she was still back in that stupid hospital. Worse, he had forgotten all about the television set. "I'm having a little trouble," he bellowed, "but I'm working on it."

He turned on the radio and between the music and the wind, there was not much conversation for the next hour. It was one of the things he liked about a sports car. On a long ride there were no worries about listening to an endless monologue from some dizzy dame. But he suddenly discovered he had something else to worry about. "Can I drive?" blithely asked Miss Macy. "I've never driven one of these before."

"That's a good reason right there for saying no."

"I've driven a Jag. This can't be any harder to handle."

He debated. Risk your car and your life, Kurz, or risk the whole purpose of the expedition by hurting her feelings? The first choice was clearly the only sensible one. He pulled into a rest area and changed seats.

"Your license is okay and everything?" he asked as Miss Macy buckled herself behind the wheel.

She laughed. "That's exactly the kind of question I always imagined a policeman would ask in a situation like this."

"Ha. Ha." He explained the overdrive, how to cut it in when the speed passed 50, the importance of cutting it out when she slowed.

She drove with her head up, chin thrust out a little, in the standard feminine style. For the first fifteen minutes, Kurz was too nervous to breathe. But she handled the car very well, shifting like a veteran, flipping the overdrive switch and settling down to a smooth 75. "It's a lot more fun than a Jag," she shouted merrily, above the wind, and he decided to relax. After all, the advertising said a Volvo was practically indestructible. That was one of the reasons he had bought it. The idea of risking his life at high speeds—and simultaneously having a built in safety factor was peculiarly appealing to him, for some reason.

Gradually, he even found himself enjoying the scenery. Mile after mile the turnpike wound through the immense furrowed farmlands of the southern end of the state. Rambling white houses drowsed beneath ancient trees. Beyond a hill a church steeple probed the blue sky. Protestant Hicksville. He preferred the city to that Christmas card tranquility they called the small town.

The scenery was pretty good inside the car too. He studied the curve of Ann Macy's arm, the slim hand on the steering wheel, the line of her leg flowing down to the accelerator. She had really great legs.

By 11:30 she was backing expertly into a parking space only a block from the Paradise Beach boardwalk. She cut the motor and sat there, aglow with almost childish pleasure. "Thanks," she said. "That was fun."

"You're good," he said. "Practically ready for the Grand Prix."

She smiled mockingly. "That sort of flattery could get you somewhere."

Kurz was totally delighted with himself as they strolled up the street to Jorgensen's Pool and Cabana Club. He always took his dates here. It was the poshest part of town, a private deal where you had to be introduced before they let you reach for your wallet. It was expensive, but the pool and beach were seldom crowded. The place was largely patronized by people who rented cabanas or bathhouses by the season.

As they neared the boardwalk, Kurz was puzzled by a mob of people milling at the top of the steps. Their path was suddenly barred by two local cops. "What's up?" Kurz asked, flashing his badge.

"Civil rights demonstration," one cop growled. He was

thirty pounds overweight. His belly bulged at least a foot beyond his belt buckle.

"Some friends from up your way," said the other cop, who was tall with a mean Protestant deacon's face. "The kid gloves you guys use on 'em, they got the idea they can push anybody around."

"They don't push us around," Kurz said. "Nobody pushes us around."

On the boardwalk the mob was in an ugly mood. They were mostly teenagers with a scattering of women. "Bastards," they shouted. "Who do they think they are? I'm not going to swim with any damn Nigger. Kick hell out of them."

Some eighteen demonstrators, three of them white, were sitting six abreast in the entrance to Jorgensen's pool. They were flanked by two others with big signs declaring: INTEGRATION IS THE LAW OF THE LAND. In the wooden passageway behind the seated demonstrators, the manager of the pool was arguing vehemently with another Negro, probably the demonstration leader. Four or five cops walked up and down in front of the entrance keeping the crowd back. Once more Kurz thanked God he had made detective before this civil rights stuff started. Sure as hell he would have belted somebody with a nightstick and been put on the promotion blacklist. It had happened to a half dozen good cops already. For a few months last year they had had half the force going to classes on how to handle these so-called non-violent demonstrations.

Opposite the pool, Jorgensen operated a big two-storied pavilion with a ballroom and restaurant. His office was on the second floor. Suddenly Jorgensen appeared on a little balcony outside his office, with a bullhorn in his hand. He was a round butterball of a man, always red-faced and perspiring. Now his face was magenta. "Ladies and gentlemen," he bellowed through the horn. "I want you to know that Jorgensen's Pool and Cabana Club is not going to be intimidated by leftist demonstrators." The crowd cheered. "We intend to retain the right to select out clientele." The crowd cheered even louder.

"This is the United States of America, not Soviet Russia." Another cheer. "These people are trespassing on private property and the Chief of Police has assured me that they will receive appropriate penalties." Another cheer.

It was well timed. A police siren wailed in the street. A few minutes later the Chief of Police appeared on the balcony beside Jorgensen. A tall, grey-haired man with a big, beaked nose, he took charge of the bullhorn and spoke into it in a calm, matter-of-fact voice. "You people are going to jail. Why don't you be sensible about it and get up and walk?"

They just stared at him.

The demonstration leader appeared out front. He had a barrel chest and a wide thick neck. His nose was wide too, and flat. His black skin glistened in the noon sunshine. "These people will move when Mr. Jorgensen agrees to end his ridiculous pretension that this is a private club." His voice was shrill. "Everyone in this town knows he uses it to discriminate against Negroes and Jews."

Jorgensen tried to grab the bullhorn away from the chief but he wouldn't let it go. The chief stepped in front of him before he could start screaming. "That's something you can take up with Mr. Jorgensen in private," he said. "My job is to preserve law and order. You're trespassing on private property and causing a public disturbance. I'm giving you one more chance to move out quietly."

The leader went back and sat down with the rest of the demonstrators. They all immediately went into their nonviolent crouch, heads down, legs and arms locked together. "Take them away," the Chief said.

Three more cops arrived. The Chief had turned out the whole force. They waded in, grunting and cursing, and tried to separate the demonstrators. It was a job. The demonstrators all began singing "We Shall Overcome." Sometimes it took a couple of raps from a nightstick to extricate an arm or a leg but the cops disentangled them one by one and dragged them down the boardwalk. The crowd yelled insults as they went. "Nigger. Commie. Bastard."

It was not especially inspiring but then neither were the demonstrators. They were scroungy, most of them in sneakers, the whites badly in need of haircuts. Kurz was more interested in the police work. They did their best, but they had no training for this sort of thing and most of them were in terrible physical condition. They got tired and irritable and a little brutal. They dragged the last few demonstrators by the feet, whacking their heads on the boardwalk. That was when the photographers leaped out of the crowd and took their pictures.

In twenty minutes it was all over. The paddy wagon, jammed with singing demonstrators, rolled off to the jail. The crowd melted away. "Well," Kurz said, "let's go swimming."

"Where?"

The way Ann Macy asked the question warned him. But it also made him stubborn. "Right here."

She shook her head. "You won't get me in there."

At least she kept her voice low. On each side people strolled past without even glancing at them. They might have been a couple of lovebirds billing and cooing.

"Look," Kurz said. "I'm not for them and I'm not against them. If they can browbeat old man Jorgensen into letting them in, I'll swim with them. But——"

"No one's neutral," she said. "You give that man money, you're on his side."

"No I'm not," Kurz said. "I'm on my side. I want to go for a swim. I can't go in the ocean. This is the only pool in Paradise Beach and in the last place it's my money, not yours, and it's none of your goddamn business how I want to spend it."

Her eyes filled with tears of rage. He had never seen a woman look so ferocious. "I can't stop you," she said. "But you won't get me in that water."

The pool was visible through a high wire fence—a long gleaming green rectangle. "That's fair enough," Kurtz said, and walked over to the window and bought two tickets.

Undressing in his bathhouse Kurz winced once more at the

ugly scar on his chest and decided to wear his T-shirt right up to the water's edge. He found a chair opposite the ladies' locker entrance and waited for Miss Macy to appear.

It was quite an appearance. She was wearing a red, white and blue two-piece bathing suit which was well on its way to bikiniland. The figure more than fulfilled his fondest expectations. For some reason, he found the long flat midriff especially delectable. It was a lovely contrast to Marion Kelsey's over-thirty-five bulge.

Miss Macy retained a grumpy look on her face. She sat down in a chair beside him without a word. "Still not going in the water?" he said.

She shook her head.

"It's pretty hot."

The two-story bathhouses enclosed the pool and their white walls concentrated the noon sun.

She shook her head again. "I meant what I said."

"Well, I'm going in," he said.

He flipped off his T-shirt and eased himself into the green water feet first. It was marvelously cool. He swam the width in an easy crawl and was pleased to find his chest was not hurting at all. He swam back under water and popped up wet and smiling only a few feet from Ann Macy's lovely legs. "It feels great," he said. "You don't know what you're missing."

She said nothing.

He swam away and it became very clear that this was a test of strength. Let her win this skirmish, Kurz, and you have lost the whole damn war. He swam the length of the pool twice in the same easy crawl, pondering strategy. She was watching him. He could see her when he raised his head to breathe. He knew he looked good in the water. He had won the state free style championship three years in a row. It never hurt to let them see you as a good athlete. No matter how intellectual they were, there was always that primitive desire for brute strength.

Ah, yes, Harry, when you grow old and tired you should

write it all down, a manual for the stickmen of the next generation. And if you believe in your own theories, there is only one solution.

He hauled himself up the brass ladder and padded over to where Ann Macy was sitting. "As an officer and a gentleman," he said, "I can't let anyone who looks so good in a bathing suit sit and swelter." He grabbed her by the wrist and spun her out of the chair into the pool.

She came up spluttering, furiously brushing hair out of her eyes. "You are the most arrogant—of all the—"

He sat down on the side of the pool and grinned cheerfully through her abuse.

"It feels good, though, doesn't it? That's something I've never been able to figure out. The more forbidden a thing is, the better it feels when you do it."

"You know," she said, "I could very easily learn to hate you."

He slipped into the water and swam out to her. "You could learn to like me, too. It's just as easy."

He could see her thinking about it.

"Come on, be reasonable. You can catch a lot more flies with honey. You know, you might even end up with me the hottest picketer in the movement."

That was good for a smile. A little rueful, but lively enough. "Sometimes I think you're just a nut."

"There are things that drive me crazy," he said. "People like you, for instance, who take life too damn seriously."

"But it is serious," she said with a frown.

"Honey, you don't have to tell me that. When I help put a guy away for five or ten years and I see his wife sitting there in the courtroom ruining her handkerchief, I don't make jokes about it. But when I get away from it, I want to be far away."

"Now who's being serious?" she said, and shoved half the pool in his face.

It was over. He was on his way. They swam for a half hour in the pool and had hot dogs and beer for lunch at the pavilion bar and retreated to the beach for the afternoon. Kurtz produced his transistor radio and they lay there side by side on the blanket smoking and listening to some symphonic music. It was a lovely way to live. He could put his head down on the blanket and through his dark glasses follow the curve of Ann Macy's outstretched arm all the way up to the shoulder. He could prop himself on one elbow and study the soft rise of her breasts. The two-piece bathing suit was a great invention.

She had interesting skin, tan and rather glossy with very little hair on either her arms or legs. "You have an Italian mother or something?" he asked.

"Why?" she said.

She lay on her back. The dark glasses made her face a mask.

"Dark skin, dark hair."

"I don't know who my mother was. Or my father. I was one of those abandoned babies you read about. Brought up in a home."

"No kidding. In the city?"

"Holy Family Home for the Homeless. You know it?"

"A big grey barn up in the North End with a spiked iron fence around it?"

"That's right."

"We used to play your basketball team in high school. They were pretty bad."

"Everything about Holy Family was bad."

"For instance."

"When I was eight or nine I got caught taking a shower with a boy. Neither one of us knew what we were doing. They shaved off all my hair for punishment. I looked so awful, the kids started calling me Monster. The nickname stuck, even after my hair grew back."

"Are you sure this wasn't the Home for the Blind?"

"If you menstruated early, they thought this was a bad sign. It meant you had an unnaturally strong sex drive. I menstruated when I was eleven. After that if they caught me even looking at a boy I was dragged into Mother Superior's office and told I was going to hell."

"Nuns are a nutty bunch. I had a few beauts when I went to school. There was one we called Dynamite Aggie. I had her in the seventh grade. She used a yardstick on the back of your legs. She gave me fifty in a row once. It was the only time I cried in school. The old bitch."

"Do you still believe it?"

"Believe what?"

"Catholicism."

"Sure. I'm not the greatest Catholic in the world but I believe it. I mean—it hangs together."

She chewed on the tip of her sunglasses for a moment, eyeing him. "How would you feel about it if you were little Harry?"

"The kid in the hospital?"

"He was abandoned at birth. They put him out for adoption at the age of six months but he developed nephrosis—kidney disease. His would-be parents gave him back and he's spent the rest of his life in that hospital. What would you believe if you were in his place?"

"Not much, I guess."

"But you are in his place," she said fiercely, leaning toward him. "We're all—everyone of us is in the other person's place. That's what being human means. You can put yourself in the other person's place. If you can't or won't do that, you're just an animal."

Fantastic, her intensity. She carried him with her right off this sunlit beach to that weary, stifling ward, the small face, hard eyes, saying: *I don't believe in God.*

Kurz yanked off his glasses and looked across the glaring beach. Other couples on other blankets listened to other radios. A muscleman was balancing a cute giggling blonde on his shoulders. Kids dug holes, trundled pails of water. Matrons sat, magazines in their lap, gassing to other matrons. It was the beach. He looked down at Ann Macy, still leaning toward him. The sun glistened on the tawny skin, the bright bathing suit, the black hair.

"Let's go for another swim," he said.

"In the ocean?"

He studied the breakers. The doctor had said no, but Kurz could not think of any better way to escape this ridiculous conversation. "Sure," he said. "The Führer will never know—unless you squeal."

She followed him down to the water without another word. They swam out to where the big ones were breaking. She was a fair swimmer but he could see she was just a little alarmed by the size of these white monsters, close up. "Dive way under," he called to her, "or the suction can get you."

A really big one came surging toward them, the bending lip white with blowing spray. "Oh," Ann Macy cried, and he put his arms around that soft flat tummy and took her down with him. They repeated the performance for the next three or four waves until they finally came up in a calm sea beyond the surf line.

Casually she unwound herself from his sheltering arm. "I'm not a championship swimmer," she said.

"I'd love to ride one of them," Kurz said.

"No, don't—" she said. "I mean—I'd rather not go back alone."

"Ride one with me," Kurz said. "You just make yourself into a surfboard, chin up, head out, back stiff, arms at your side."

"It sounds like fun," she said.

He could see her vowing not to admit she was scared. They swam back to the surf line and waited for a likely candidate. A ten-footer finally came looming and Miss Macy swam beside him as it slowly seized them in its giant hand. Up, up, it mounted and they stayed with it until that lovely moment when they were poised on the crest, ready for the big slide. "Now. Now. Swim hard," he roared.

Over they went, the wave curling behind them. Miss Macy started fine but she took him too literally. Instead of spreading her arms for balance on the way down, she kept them tucked in too tight and the wave sent her slewing to the right. She flipped over on her face and a mountain of white water fell on her. Kurz dove for the bottom and swam swiftly back to find her.

She was all right, aside from some gasping and coughing. "What did I do wrong?"

He explained and they tried again. They caught another big one and this time they rode it all the way, laughing, shouting, like a couple of adolescents, right onto the beach.

"Oh, that's marvelous fun," Miss Macy said, happily unaware that the top of her bathing suit was showing a lot more than usual.

They rode waves for another hour. Kurz finally had to admit he was pooped. "Remember you've got an ex-patient here," he said as he labored back to the blanket.

The beach was almost deserted now. They sat and watched the lifeguards pull up their boat and tip over their stand and blow their final warning blast to the one or two swimmers still in the water. For another half hour they watched the waves break, while the radio whispered in the background. When it came to establishing romantic moods, you could not beat that old man ocean. It had orchestrated more than one big evening for Harry Kurz, Esq. Miss Macy was loving every minute of it. She sat up, letting the breeze play with her hair, drinking in the scenery as if it was an all-star cast in cinemascope.

When he thought she'd had enough he said, "Hey, I'm hungry. Are you?"

She looked at him, completely relaxed and very friendly. "I could be persuaded."

They dressed, checked out of Jorgensen's and ate in a restaurant farther down the boardwalk, an arty shack on a pier with the surf breaking beneath them.

"Drinks are absolutely necessary," Kurz said.

"Why?"

"We're celebrating your initiation into the Noble Order of the Surf."

"All right," she said, smiling.

They had two martinis on the rocks and she got just a little silly. She told him all about her courses at the state university, especially the one in philosophy. Existentialism was her way of life, apparently. She talked about commitment, reality, creativity. She was very warm for the philosophy professor.

"He makes you feel the search for meaning is . . . really important."

Ordinarily Kurz would have scoffed at such balderdash. But things were humming and he looked very interested and said he had been fascinated by philosophy in his college days and would like to meet the professor some time.

Bulging Bill O'Reilly, the proprietor, appeared and treated Kurz as if he'd just won the Medal of Honor. O'Reilly had been one of several captains who resigned one step ahead of Mayor O'Connor's new broom. He'd bought a house and this restaurant with his loot.

"Jesus, kid, how are you," he said, and clapped Kurz on the back, sending a spasm of pain through his chest.

"I'll be dead if you hit me once more like that."

"Christ, I read it in the paper and I couldn't believe it. I always used to say they never kill the smart ones, it's only the jerks that stop the slugs. But you made me wonder, kid."

"Whether I was smart?"

O'Reilly whooped. "Hell no, I never had to ask that question twice." He gave Macy an approving leer. "Yeah, honey, you got to watch this guy every second. That's how smart he is."

Kurz felt like planting his foot up O'Reilly's big behind but he didn't pursue the joke and Miss Macy seemed to miss it. "He's a retired cop," Kurz explained. "He stole more than any other captain in the history of the police force."

"Really?" Miss Macy said, peering across the room at O'Reilly, who was pounding some other unfortunate on the back. "He looks so—good-natured."

"If I could steal thirty grand a year, I'd be good-natured too."

"But you wouldn't."

"Steal? That's one reason I stayed a bachelor. So I wouldn't be tempted. Guys like O'Reilly with eight kids by thirty-five, they're the ones who start taking it. Not for themselves—for the children."

Miss Macy looked sad. "The world is—awfully complicated."

"Not for a surfer," Kurz said. "Surfing is like drinking martinis, a nice cool simple feeling. I like simple feelings."

"I'll drink to that," Miss Macy said.

They had lobsters for dinner with a good white California wine. They talked mostly about food, here and elsewhere. Miss Macy's restauranting was rather limited—another good omen for the evening.

After dinner they walked out to the end of the pier and watched the ghostly white breakers charge across the dark water toward the pale beach. Beyond, the sea lapped endlessly beneath the stars.

"I love the ocean," Miss Macy sighed. LAKE MICHIGAN

"Me too," Kurz lied.

He had been seasick all the way to Korea. But for his present purposes old ocean's mood music was even better medicine after dark.

Casually he put his arm around her waist. "I kind of like you, too."

She let him kiss her, yielding very little, but definitely not protesting.

She waited, cradled in his arms, looking up at him. "I never met—a girl like you," he said.

"Is that good or bad?"

"Good, I think."

He kissed her again and there was just a little more surrender in it. It was a great opening routine, especially effective with the college girl type. They all thought they were different, uniquely fascinating, because they could talk about the meaning of meaning and the purpose of existence.

"Let's go for a walk," he said.

It was a silent stroll with a cool sea breeze caressing them. The boardwalk was almost deserted except for clumps of teenagers in dungarees, wandering barefoot. She let him hold her hand. Ah, that little gesture carries you back, doesn't it, Harry. All the way to high school days when that was the quiet way to saying, yes, I'll neck. Now it was only a small part of the buildup. Not to be scoffed at, of course. Even the smallest part of the buildup was important. What made it really interesting was the lack of formula. There were certain tried and true signals, but these were like basic skills that any good quarterback possessed—the ability to fake, to think on his feet, to take the options as they came. Basically what made the whole thing interesting was the unpredictability. You never really knew if you were going all the way until you crossed the goal line.

"Oh, I'm glad you asked me to come down here," Miss Macy said. "I didn't realize it, but I think the city was really getting on my nerves."

"It gets on everybody's nerves," Kurz said. "I don't know how you can go to school in the summer in the first place. It's practically against a law of nature."

"School's the only thing that makes life halfway interesting for me. It's hard for someone like you who's been to college to understand how exciting it can be to find new ideas."

New ideas. That was good for a laugh. The only new ideas Kurz could remember finding at St. Ingatius of Loyola were better ways to conceal crib notes. But he assured Miss Macy that he knew exactly what she meant.

They strolled in silence for a while. It was time, Kurz decided, for the next phase and the move was there glowing in his agile brain. You may not know much about existentialism, Harry, but you are good at other things.

"I've got a great idea," he said, stopping their stroll. "Barbarry Park."

"What's there?"

"Whoopee rides. It's a great way to end a day."

"Oh, that sounds like fun."

In a half hour they were on the Barbarry boardwalk. The Steeplechase clattered in the distance, Dodge-ems roared and crashed, the Whip clanked and whirled. Blue, red, green and yellow lights swayed everywhere like candles on a giant birthday cake. Perfect, Harry, perfect. Here is someone who never had even a tiny slice of this marvelous cake in childhood. Remember that little girl manner beneath the professional poise, the intellectual jargon.

"We'll start with the Whip."

Away they went, whirling laughing, his arm around her, each wild curve flinging her against him, the wind blowing her hair in his mouth. And the Steeplechase. On the first drop she flung both arms around him and closed her eyes. "We're still alive," he shouted, and she sat up a little but she did not let go. On the curves they practically blended. "I hope you brought a needle and thread, I think my stitches are going," he howled as they headed for Suicide Slope.

"Let's do it again," she said when they got off.

This time she let him hold her and she did not close her eyes.

The Dodge-ems were equally useful. The car was so small they were practically Siamese twins by the time they had crammed into it. The floor was crowded with teenagers and they had a slam-bang three-ride series. On to the rocket ship, two long tubes on giant metal arms that swung them up thirty or forty feet and left them hanging there at the apex upside down while the mad, mad world blinked and swirled beneath. Crushed in the narrow seat, warm and laughing, was a no longer frightened Miss Macy. Next came the Fun House, crazy mirrors, a walk through the spinning barrel. Kurz fell, taking Miss Macy with him and they rolled the rest of the way in a laughing tangle. And the Magic Carpet. She sat between his legs, his arms around her waist and away they went down the long polished slide, tobogganing around curves with his hands spread wide, wandering just a little, unnoticed in the laughter.

They did everything twice. Kurz was suggesting round three when Miss Macy caught his wrist and looked at his watch. "Is that eleven o'clock?"

"I can't believe it," Kurz said.

They strolled hand in hand to the car. "What did you like best?"

"The Steeplechase. I conquered that."

More laughter. He held the door, she slipped into the front seat. He got behind the wheel, shoved the key in the ignition and then without a word drew her to him for a long, clinging kiss.

"I don't feel like going home. How do you feel?"

She kissed him again. It was yes. He flipped the ignition key and drove with one hand, holding her close to him with his free arm.

The motel was owned by lean, balding Eddie Osgood, another police department fugitive from the city's new morality. "Harry, how's it goin'?"

"It's going very good," Kurz said, "if you keep your trap shut and give me a nice quiet room in the back."

Osgood's small dark eyes glittered enviously. "You son of a bitch, I don't think even a bullet in the brain would stop you."

"That's one experiment I'll skip," Kurz said, signing the register and throwing a ten dollar bill into Osgood's open hand.

Miss Macy was standing beside the car. Kurz put his arm around her and they walked past the silent front rooms and across the courtyard where a few lights were shining from windows. They had Room 13 in the east wing, which was entirely dark.

He dropped his coat on a chair and kissed her. He did not even bother to turn on a light. The courtyard lights came in through the blinds, spilling across a big double bed. Only two or three pieces of clothing now. Another reason why summer was wonderful. In January, it took a half hour to get them undressed. His fingers reached for the buttons on her blouse.

She broke off the kiss and stepped back. "I want to do it myself," she said. "I don't like being undressed."

"Shall we race?" he said.

He was still in his socks when she turned on the light. She turned toward him, smiling. "I'm not ashamed. Are you?"

"No," he said, reaching back and closing the blind.

The rug felt good under his bare feet. And Ann Macy. The waist was flat all the way down, the hair very black, lustrous, thick, the breasts not really as large as he had imagined them but very firm and coned.

She let him come to her, eyes wide and aglow, reaching for his eyes. "Ann," he said.

The last necessary word. She opened her arms to him, clinging, passionate, her tongue finding his tongue, her hands moving on his body. And then suddenly very still, taking the first long sweet thrust with a shudder, a momentary closing of the eyes, a soft opening of the lips.

Jesus, she was good and he was full. After two goddamn weeks in that hospital and a month before trying to swear off Marion Kelsey he was full, rich, foaming. And alive. Every square inch of his flesh alive. All the way down on her now, his hands on those breasts and then fistfuls and mouthfuls of that rich black hair, tasting of delicate perfume. Woman. Jesus, woman, I am alive. That long finger of life leaping in you, that savage arm, that sword, that gun, is going to explode you into Loveland any moment. Woman. Woman alive.

Locked in her arms now, twisting the rough hair of his chest into those soft breasts, hearing her breath wild with words and small cries. *Oh—you—I—Oh—I.* Was she trying to ask him something? Mr. Kurz, do you really love me? Don't you think we should discuss our wedding plans? Too late, sweetheart, too late. The Kurz buildup is about to reach its climax.

He came. He could feel the love juice beating against the condom. She felt it too. She cried out—a strange cry, almost joyful. Most of the others, especially old Marion, gave a little whimper—of relief, as far as he could tell.

They lay side by side on the bed. The light made him feel vaguely uncomfortable. He never really thought about it before, but he preferred the dark. This way there were too many things to notice. His own hairy left thigh, for instance, a veritable jungle growth that descended to the top of his bent knee. Suddenly her hand was in the hair, moving softly up and down.

He dropped his leg and she stopped. Did she want another round? He thought about it and decided it was a long ride home.

Maybe in her apartment. After a nightcap.

No. She might decide you are a pig.

He went into the bathroom, got rid of the rubber and washed himself. While his hands worked up a lather below, he studied himself in the mirror. It was a reasonably handsome face, a heavy jaw, a nose that was a little too thick, eyes set close together. Some girl had told him once the eyes meant he was an egotist. Probably true, and why not? How many other bachelors were capable of such finesse? He paused in his lathering for a moment to compose the opening lines of the story for the listeners in the squad room. *There I was with twenty-five bucks already invested, absolutely nowheresville. Holding hands, for Christ's sake, on the boardwalk and suddenly the idea, another Kurz original.* He could practically see the husbands drooling.

But that was the old squad room. Nobody in the 13th precinct seemed especially interested in his personal life. He dried himself, pulled on his shorts and stepped back into the bedroom. She was still on the bed, staring up at the ceiling, still not wearing a thing. It bothered him. According to the standard routine she should be dressed by now, combing her hair, replacing her lipstick, pretending nothing had happened.

"Hey," he said, "it's a long ride home."

She did not just hear the words. She seemed to absorb them. The softness drained from her face. Her body, which had been lying loose-limbed and inviting, visibly stiffened. She rolled over on her side, away from Kurz and lay there for a brief moment. Then she stood up, took a comb from her purse and walked slowly over to the mirror. She ran the comb through her hair once and flung it at her face in the mirror.

"What the hell's the matter?"

She spoke to herself, the enraged face in the mirror. "It's a long ride home. And now that I've paid for my transportation, not to mention swimming and dinner——"

"What the hell are you talking about?"

"I'm talking about the way you just made me feel, Kurz."

"You don't want to go home?"

"I do now."

"I'll stay for the night," Kurz said. His fingers closed on the soft flesh of her upper arm. "I'll stay for ten nights if you feel like it."

"I don't feel anything now."

He pulled her into his arms for a long rough kiss.

"Does that restore some circulation?"

She just looked at him. He stepped out of his shorts and smiled sardonically at her. "It looks like you need extensive shock treatment, Miss Macy."

It was delicious. He wanted her again in a completely different way. All the original antagonism flickered between them. He toyed with the right nipple. The left. His hand wandered slowly down the soft belly to the luxuriant pussy.

She just stood there, slim and shining in the lamplight. His finger went deep into her soft wet darkness. Her mouth trembled. The answer was still no. An unbelievable excitement swept over him. It could not be true. She was not going to let him do it this way. Any moment she would scream and try to slash his face with those neatly trimmed nails. But he was wrong. Slowly, like figures in a minuet, they returned to the bed.

He took her slowly, with long, deep thrusts. Her response was zero. He began to tease. First a quick flurry, then long and slow again, then nothing. "Come on, Miss Macy," he whispered, "you can't deny the superior quality of the goods, even if you don't especially like the owner."

Still nothing.

Suddenly he was angry. He gouged her body as if his penis was a weapon. Once. Twice. Three times. Four times. Five.

Six. Seven. I will make you beg, Miss Macy. I will make you crawl. I will make you plead. You will come to that trembling brink and I will wait, laughing. Eight. Nine. Ten. Eleven. Twelve.

A small cry strangled in her throat. Her body bent against him, her lips found his mouth with a fantastic, almost insane intensity. Vanished his dream of savage control. She went past him like a wave cresting without warning. But he quickly caught her and from there it was truly wild. Her nails tore at his back. Her teeth found his shoulder. He pinned her arms against the mattress and held her while she writhed and sobbed beneath him. Those gasping sounds are music to my ears, Miss Macy, wordless little pleas that are the prelude to complete surrender. Personally Harry Kurz may be an s.o.b. but right now he is at the center of your little world and you do not want him to go away; no, that is the last thing you want. Instead you want Harry Kurz to happen in you again, oh again again again.

But he wasn't ready yet. Deliberately he changed the tempo. Long slow and easy now. Hesitate a moment long and slow. Hesitate a moment long and slow.

She would not wait. With a cry she bucked against him and flung him off the precarious point of power. Down they went into the roaring hollow of another wave and all he could do was ride, cowboy, ride, taking her tempo, her fury as darkness poured over them and he came in her with a thudding finality that echoed deep in his own body. She took it with a last furious arcing lunge and then dwindled away beneath him to small mournful murmurs.

Silence. He lay on top of her feeling almost dismembered. Never had he had one so wild. Martha Tully in those good old backyard days was frigidity personified, in comparison. He tried to think of one other woman who came close to matching it and drew an absolute blank. Maybe it was taking life seriously which made you take sex seriously which helped you get lots of practice. He rolled off her and lay beside her feeling drained. She had really taken it out of him.

"You're good at that game, Miss Macy," he said. "Almost too good for a guy flying on one wing."

She said nothing. She just lay there staring up at the ceiling. He pushed himself up on one elbow and saw to his amazement she was crying. Small quiet tears trickled down her cheeks.

"Hey, what's the matter?"

"Nothing."

"Did I hurt you?"

"No."

"But you're not exactly happy?"

"Why should I be?"

"I'm happy."

"Three cheers."

He let his hand come gently down on her right breast. "Come on, Miss Macy, where's that girl I saw in the hospital—all fire and ice."

"She stepped outside for a second. But she'll be back."

She rubbed her eyes with her fist. It was a strangely childish gesture. Kurz was surprised how much it touched him.

"I thought you liked it," he said. "You came all the way. You came a lot farther than any woman I've ever known."

"I wasn't there, Kurz. You—drove me out. It's my body, Kurz. You have no right to—do that."

"What the hell are you talking about?"

She had stopped crying now. She looked up at him, much more like the girl in the hospital. "You're a monster, Kurz, and you don't even know it."

"That's a hell of a thing to say when I've just—"

She clapped her hand over his mouth. "I know. You just told me I'm the best piece of ass you've ever had."

He jerked her hand away. "I did like hell."

"Oh, you didn't say it in so many words, but that's exactly what you meant, Kurz, and I'm supposed to be flattered. Well let me return the compliment. I've never been so thoroughly fucked before either."

For a second Kurz almost got mad. She wasn't playing the game according to the rules. Either she should bewail her shame and call him a beast or murmur her love and call him Mr. Wonderful. But he saw just in time that she wanted him to get mad. Then he would automatically admit she had broken the rules.

He waited a moment and finally smiled. "Okay, so we're not romantic. Now what?"

"Now nothing," she said. "That's what we are, where we are. Oh, Kurz, don't you see——"

There were tears in her eyes again. She let her head fall back on the pillow.

"No, you don't."

"Do you want to go home now?"

"I don't care."

"I think it would be better if we stayed for the night and got an early start in the morning."

She nodded, got up, and went into the bathroom. He called his mother and explained he had met a few friends and decide to stay overnight. She guaranteed him that he was going to ruin his health permanently. He thanked her for this reassuring advice and hung up.

Miss Macy came out of the bathroom and got under the covers, still wearing nothing. For some reason it made him feel uneasy. Marion Kelsey was the only other woman with whom he had spent the night in bed and after they did it (in the dark) she was always so giggly about not peeking and eventually showed up wearing an ankle-length nightgown. There was a hint of mockery, even contempt, in Miss Macy's careless nudity.

But you are too tired to think, much less do, anything about it now, Kurz. He washed and staggered back to bed in the same state of nature. Sleep came almost instantaneously.

He awoke and did not know where he was and lay absolutely still in the darkness listening to the hum of the air conditioner. They had left it on full and the room was Arctic temperature. His shoulder and arm were outside the blanket and they felt as if they had spent the night in ice water. He pulled the blanket up over his ears and snuggled down under it, rolling on his side in the close warmth. He was still mostly asleep when his fingers touched her breast. No cold here, warm and yielding. His hand moved slowly down her body and he came awake thinking: *it happened, it all happened.*

She murmured sleepily and suddenly put her arms around him and drew herself close. It was completely different from the first two times. In some ways more exciting, kissing sleepily, everything warm beneath the blanket and the cold on their faces. It was like dreaming except you know you were not going to wake up and find yourself alone in bed with your mother snoring on the other side of the wall. This time there were no sounds. They seemed to be above or beneath them. It was relaxed and deep like music in lower octave, more perfectly physical and rhythmic. *Like two animals, two beautifully functioning animals. What a lovely way to live.*

When it was over she clung to him for a moment, her arms around his neck. "You know," she whispered sleepily, "if we keep this up something terrible could happen."

"What?"

"We might fall in love."

Not a chance were the instinctive words on his lips. But he suddenly remembered the crumpled fist on those streaming eyes and his brain was too sleep-fogged to intervene before he spoke out of a surprising tenderness. "I'm not scared," he said. "Are you?"

"Yes."

"Sissy."

He drifted down into sleep again.

They awoke at 6 A.M. with Kurz's wristwatch alarm tinkling in their ears. Miss Macy gathered up her clothes and retreated to the bathroom and come out looking positively innocent. They stopped for breakfast at a turnpike restaurant about halfway to the city. In a booth Macy cradled her coffee and peered at him over the cup.

"You're a funny detective."

"Why?" Kurz said, briskly peppering and salting his eggs.

"I thought all policemen were squares pretty much. But you seem to enjoy breaking rules."

"Some rules."

"Me too," she said after a moment of silence.

"How old are you?"

"Twenty-four. You?"

"Thirty-six."

She sipped her coffee. "You don't act it."

"I remember reading about some philosopher who said a man didn't hit his stride until he was thirty-five."

"Aristotle. How can you stand being a cop?"

"What's so hard about it?"

"It's such a—repulsive moral position, always being the accuser, the persecutor. You must know that ninety percent of the people you catch are innocent."

"Innocent of what?" Kurz said incredulously.

"Of any real guilt. They're victims. Of our sick society."

He shovelled in a few more mouthfuls of eggs to let things settle a little.

"Like the guy that put a hole in me and killed my partner."

"He was only defending himself."

"A hero, in other words."

"Maybe—in his own twisted way."

"Killing a man from ambush before he has a chance to reach for his gun—that's your idea of heroism?"

"The heroism of the weak," she said triumphantly.

"He didn't look very weak to me," Kurz said, getting madder.

He caught himself just in time. Do not flip your lid, Harry my boy. Miss Macy may not be very good upstairs, but downstairs she is still great and if you want to sample more of that downstairs traffic, let us not worry too much about what goes on upstairs.

"I don't mean I'm glad he shot you, or your partner." Miss Macy was explaining earnestly, "but I am glad he got away."

"Now what the hell do you mean by that?" Kurz snapped, forgetting all the good advice he had just given himself. "A man with a wife and three kids gets killed trying to stop some hood from robbing enough heroin to keep the hopheads in the city on the needle for the next six months—and you're cheering."

"Someone has to speak on behalf of the dispossessed."

That is the silliest thing you've said yet, Miss Macy, but I can easily foresee your reaction if I gave it the name it deserves. So instead I will say, "You know, I never thought of it that way. Where did you get all these ideas?"

"My course in twentieth century philosophy."

"Fascinating," Kurz said.

Maybe your course in scholastic philosophy at old St. Ignatius was duller than dull, but at least you did not wind up with your head screwed on backwards. Common sense was the main conclusion. That was what made the world go round, with God in His heaven and His slightly fouled up creatures down here on earth. Common sense. You preferred it to Miss Macy's brand of logic. But there were other aspects of Miss Macy you preferred a lot more. Let us consider your substantial form, Miss Macy, I think even old Thomas Aquinas would have cast a wondering eye over it in his salad days. As for your prime matter, I am prepared to take just about all of it you can deliver.

They drove back to the city in a relaxed, contented mood. Miss Macy was obviously thrilled at the possibility of converting one of the Neanderthals of law and order to swinging with the twentieth century. He, Kurz, was even more delighted at the prospect of integrating Miss Macy into his schedule. Yes, there are some forms of integration I fervently support, Miss Macy. Male and female, for instance. There is entirely too much segregation practiced in that segment of our society. Thinking of all the unintegrated pubic hair around town is enough to drive a man to the picket line. But we are going to pioneer a change in this unnatural way of life. Olé!

Chapter Four

The city's air was still thick with humidity but the heat of the day had only begun to clog the streets when they rolled swiftly through the almost deserted Congo to Ann Macy's doorstep. Kurz killed the motor and gave her his biggest smile. "What are you doing tonight, tomorrow night, and night after that?"

"Going to school."

"Saturday night?"

"I'm going to a party. Would you like to come?"

"What kind of party?" he said, suspicious at the hint of mockery in her voice.

"Some people from school. Maybe it's not a good idea, I'd never be able to explain—dating you."

"Why the hell not?"

"Policemen—aren't exactly popular with this group. A lot of them are civil rights activists, that sort of thing."

"Why don't you admit the truth?" Kurz said. "You're worried about your popularity, not mine."

She considered this for a moment, then ruefully nodded. "I'm afraid you're right."

You are a strange one, Miss Macy. You not only preach the honesty bit, you practice it.

She was smiling now. "I'm game if you are."

"You can tell them I'm a college graduate. That may raise my stock a little."

"I'm impressed already."

The wind teased her black hair. She brushed it out of her eyes and suddenly Kurz found himself leaning over, kissing her on the mouth.

"I'll see you Saturday."

"Yes."

They were like a couple of school kids working up to the work *neck*. She slammed the car door and vanished into the apartment without looking back. Kurz drove away trying to figure out what had just happened. It wasn't sex. You had more than enough of that last night. You felt—Christ—almost fatherly toward her. She was so goddamn young and innocent and eager and honest. She made you feel like a tired old cynic, even made you feel a little guilty playing a two-faced game with her.

Come on, Harry, come on. You have something very nice going for you there. Let us leave it that way. Nice but on ice.

He went home and slept for five hours. Miss Macy had really done a job on him. He awoke to a ringing telephone. He heard his mother answer it and say, "Well, he's still asleep, Mrs. Moser. He was up late last night and he's still *very* weak."

"I'm awake, Mom," he called, and grabbed the extension beside his bed.

"Mr. Kurz," a soft whispery voice said, "this is Marianne Moser, I hate to bother you. I know you must be feeling pretty awful."

"No, as a matter of fact, I'm feeling—pretty good."

"I'm wondering if you could pay us a visit some evening—or maybe in the afternoon. I'd like you to talk to my boys."

"Sure," Kurz said. "I'll come down tonight."

She gave him the address. It was only a block from Ann Macy's apartment. Another middle class street on the outskirts of the Congo. She thought seven o'clock would be just fine.

Kurz ate a hurried dinner while his mother discoursed on

the latest non-clever remarks from Alice's kids. He drove downtown through the after-five torpor of the city in summer. The dying sun glinted on the windows of the office buildings. People stood languidly on shaded corners. He found a parking place right in front of the house—an old-fashioned two-story affair with a wide belly of front windows on the first floor. The Mosers lived on the second floor and he pushed the bell, the buzzer sounded and he mounted a dark airless stairway. For some stupid reason he had expected an unpleasant odor. The only smell he could detect was Lysol with which the stairs had been recently scrubbed.

At the top of the stairs a door opened and he looked up at a woman with a classic Negro face—full lips, flat nose, rather narrow chin. Her hair was piled on the back of her head in a kind of African topknot. Her body was very long and angular. "Mr. Kurz," she said in that same soft whispery voice.

"That's right."

He was surprised by her appearance. Moser's almost Caucasian features had led him to expect something similar in his wife.

"It was awfully good of you to come," she said, dropping her eyes in a shy hesitant way. "How are you feeling?"

"Pretty good, thanks."

"I'm glad. Won't you come into the living room?"

She led him past some modern Danish dining room furniture through a set of sliding doors into a modern living room—sling chairs, a couch with elliptical cushions. There was a lot of color but it was largely deep blue and purple with just enough red. The net effect was tasteful, even classy.

"The boys are doing their homework," Mrs. Moser said as Kurz sat down on the couch. She hesitated a moment, then sat down at the other end of the couch. "I'd better explain why I asked you to come over. It's about Bill."

For a moment she had to struggle desperately for control.

"He was the best damn detective I ever met in my life." Kurz blurted it out. He had had to say something.

"Thanks," Mrs. Moser said. "I was pretty sure you felt that

way from things Bill said about you." She managed a sad smile. "He used to say you were all business. He liked that in a policeman."

Any place else, that would be good for a laugh, Kurz thought morosely.

"What I wanted you to do is talk to the boys—about a vicious story that's all around town. At least—around the Negro part of town. People are saying that Bill died like a coward. He threw his gun away and begged that man not to shoot him."

"Jesus Christ."

Never in his life had Kurz felt such anger. It catapulted him to his feet.

"Naturally," Marianne Moser said, her eyes down on her dark hands, "the boys have heard about it. It's hurt them a good deal. They were very proud of their daddy. A thing like this could change all their feelings about him."

"Bring them out," Kurz said.

Mrs. Moser came back in a moment followed by three boys. The oldest was about fifteen and he looked like his mother, dark skinned, very African. The next two, about ten and eight, looked more like their father.

"This is Mr. Kurz," Mrs. Moser said. "He was your daddy's partner. I asked him to come down here for just one reason—to tell you what happened that day so you'll know the real truth and not a lot of lies."

The three boyish faces confronted Kurz and suddenly he was tongue-tied. He was back twenty-eight years listening to Uncle Harold tell him how his father had died, tasting again that crazy mixture of hatred and grief that made him loathe Uncle Harold no matter how much he appreciated all his tenderness and kindness because in the brutal logic of childhood he could only ask one question: why not you instead of him? That was what these three pairs of boys' eyes were asking now behind their polite impassive faces.

"I'm not going to give you a speech, fellows," Kurz finally said. "You know the kind of man your father was. My father got killed when I was about your age, so I know how you feel. But I want to tell you this: your father died with his gun in his hand, running towards the guy that was shooting at him. He ran until he couldn't run any more. I only wish—I could have covered him better. But the whole thing was a complete surprise. It's almost unheard of for the kind of criminals we were after to use a gun."

That wasn't very good, Harry. It wasn't very good at all. You can see it on those three faces.

"We were surprised, but that can happen to the best cops in the world. Then we did the best we could. The very best. I was in Korea. I saw a lot of men die. I never saw one die better than your father."

Suddenly the middle boy began to cry. He put his head down and ran out of the room. The other two boys followed him. Marianne Moser watched them go. "Thank you," she said, her eyes still on the boys.

"Who could start such a rotten lousy rumor?" Kurz said. "Do Negroes really hate cops that much?"

"Some do," Mrs. Moser said.

She offered Kurz a cigarette and took one herself. He lit it for her. "I know who started the rumor," she said.

"Who?" Kurz said. "I'll find him tonight and kick his teeth in."

"Dancer."

That same crazy name. "Bill mentioned him—in the ambulance. It was the last thing he said. Who the hell is this guy anyway?"

Mrs. Moser took a deep drag on her cigarette. "He's my brother."

For a moment Kurz recoiled. Something vaguely ominous flickered in his mind, the sort of feeling you might get when suddenly confronted by menacing faces in a foreign country. He was tempted to say: Look, this is not my fight. Thank you very much but this is not my fight. Then he remembered those three boyish faces and he was not sure what he felt.

"To make the understatement of the century, I don't get it."

Mrs. Moser nodded as if to say: of course. "It's not just a family thing," she said staring past him into the rear of the apartment where her three sons studied and Bill Moser had once taken her in his arms but would no more. "It goes beyond family."

She pondered her hands again as if the answer was there in the slim tapered fingers. "We grew up, my brother and I, in a small town in the mountains. We were the only Negroes in the town. There wasn't any prejudice. We were treated exactly like everyone else. Then my father died and my mother had people here and we moved to the city. It changed everything. My brother was older. He was in his teens. It changed him forever."

"Bill said something about it once. About hating."

She nodded. "Bill was born here. He had time to think about it. Dancer didn't think. All he knew was how much he hated it. I know how he felt—at least I used to know. Bill said the only way to fight it was by living day by day—just living it out. Pretty soon Dancer hated Bill more than he hated—white people."

They were quiet for a moment, in the well-furnished living room. Outside there were shouts, steps, pounding, the whop of a stickball home run. Ordinary city sounds. But there is nothing ordinary about what you are hearing in this room, Kurz. You are entering another city inside the one you know, where every street is mysterious, every face a potential enemy. But you could not turn back. Something deep was involved here, more than pride or revenge, something that involved your whole life.

"Do you think Dancer killed your husband?"

"Yes. He arranged it. He didn't fire the gun. He leaves things like that to what he calls the idiot boys."

"What do you want to do about it?"

The angular, rather placid Negro face suddenly became a mask. The eyes were no longer wandering or uneasy. "I want him to die," she said. "I never wanted that before. But now I want him to die."

The ferocity in her voice and manner momentarily stunned him. "Is there anything you can tell me about him—anything that might help——?"

"I'll do more than that. I'll get some people together and you can talk to them. Tell them what you want, what you need to get rid of Dancer, once and for all."

"That sounds great. How soon can you do it?"

"Call me in a few days."

He stood up and she rose with him. Again he was struck by something faintly regal in her grace. "Thank you for coming over."

"Thanks for asking me. I know—I know how the boys feel."

Kurz drove home and called Uncle Harold. "Listen, I feel pretty good. I'd like to go back to work."

Uncle Harold obviously couldn't believe his ears. Kurz could almost hear him wondering if he ought to have him checked out by a psychiatrist first. "That's great, Harry," he mumbled, "but I don't want—you know your mother will worry——"

"I want to get in on this Moser thing."

Uncle Harold sighed wearily. "There's not a hell of a lot happening there. We pulled most of the special assignment crowd off it yesterday. They got absolutely nowhere. The guys in the 13th said they'd never seen anything like it. Not even the stoolies are talking."

"The manhunt bit won't work on this one. I want one really good partner and a full-time assignment. It might take six months—maybe a year."

"You've got it."

Kurz hung up, thinking there was some advantage in having an inside track to the Chief Inspector. He went out in the kitchen and opened a can of beer. Only then did the madness of it all hit him. You have just thrown away two weeks with pay, Harry. Two weeks of luring Ann Macy to the shore for another all-night session at the motel, two weeks of sleeping late and hitting a few night clubs and seeing old friends, maybe even flying down for that mythical orgy in Nassau. All gone now because you ran into three little jigaboos with accusing eyes.

Jesus, you must have your head screwed on backwards.

The next morning he was eating breakfast when he got a call from his fellow bachelor, Eddie Reardon. "How're you feeling, champ?"

"Good."

"Listen. You're off all next week, right? I twisted a few arms around here and got myself four days. I figure we'd head for the shore and a little you-know-what."

"Jesus, Eddie, I'd love it but I'm going back to work."

"For Christ's sake, why? That clout you took is good for at least a month."

There was no denying it. Reardon with his talent as an actor would have made it two months. "Yeah, but—well, I'm feeling pretty good and it's kind of a bore, you know. And—well—I'm kind of bugged on the case, Eddie."

"Sherlock Holmes as I live and breathe. I never thought it could happen to you. Well, live and learn. I'll think of you down there on the beach, kid, up to my ass in bikinis."

"Have a ball. I did pretty good down there myself the other night."

"Can you spare her name, rank and telephone number?"

"Not at the moment."

"Pig. Was it that nurse at the hospital?"

Any other time, for any other girl, Kurz would have said yes. He was tempted to say yes now just to make Eddie Reardon feel it was the same old Harry Kurz, but something stopped him. He didn't know what it was.

"None of your goddamn business."

"Fuck you too," Reardon said cheerfully. "I'll see you."

Uncle Harold followed with a call ordering him down to the Police Department doctor for a complete physical. This was obviously to mollify mother. The doctor was a fussy old bird who refused to let Kurz go anywhere near a precinct house until a board of experts had studied X-rays of his creased lung. Kurz ignored him and drove down to talk his future over with Deputy Chief Inspector Patrick O'Bannon. As commander of the city's south end, O'Bannon did not like cops who went over his head for any reason.

"I don't see the point," he growled, "you spendin' a year chasin' some boogie you didn't even see."

"I'm not chasing a boogie I didn't see," Kurz said, controlling his temper with difficulty. "I'm after the guy who did the thinking."

"Who's he?"

"Strictly from the grapevine, it's this Dancer character."

"Go on, he's just a two-bit bookie. We checked him out seven ways from Sunday. His idea of makin' it big is drivin' up Devaney Street in a cream-colored Jaguar."

"Maybe that's what he wants us to think. And just because it fits into the standard picture doesn't mean——" Kurz stopped, confused by a sudden squeamishness.

"What?" O'Bannon said testily.

"That sports car has a hell of an impact on kids in the Congo."

He knew exactly what was coming and it came. "Now wait a minute," O'Bannon said. "You're a detective, not a social worker. Let them worry about the goddamn social influences. With a cop it's got to be black and white. If a guy commits a crime it's your job to apprehend him. If you got nothin' on him you leave him alone. Just because Moser yells out this guy's name when he's dying doesn't prove a goddamn thing. He's his brother-in-law and he's bugged on him. Dancer's never given us any trouble and I don't see why you got any right to go out and start roughing him up."

You had to be a cop to get all the nuances in those words. Never given us any trouble meant Dancer had paid off regularly. Roughing him up meant scaring off his regular customers. He had heard a lot of stories about O'Bannon's sticky fingers, but he had always liked the guy and more or less ignored them. "I don't give a goddamn how much book he makes," Kurz said. "I think he's got a lot of other things going for him. He's a lot bigger than you think."

O'Bannon curled his thick upper lip contemptuously. But he had done all he could for Dancer. "All right," he said. "Who you want for a partner?"

"I don't know," Kurz said. "I was hoping you'd suggest somebody."

"How about your buddy Reardon?"

Kurz shook his head. "A Negro would be better, I think."

"Now that's out of the question," O'Bannon exploded. "We only got a half dozen Negro detectives and I absolutely cannot spare one of them for this kind of so-called police work."

"Then let's pick a guy from the ranks. Put him in plainclothes."

"Awright," O'Bannon said grumpily. "Go down to the 13th and talk it over with Crotty. Tell him you got my okay."

Kurz drove down to see Captain Timothy Crotty. Long and lean and cautious, he always reminded Kurz of somebody's curate. But he had a brain. He had even read a few book on the Negro problem. Still he was a cop and when Kurz explained what he wanted to do, Crotty looked down his long nose and said nothing for quite a while.

"It's strictly a hunch," Kurz said. "I'll wrap it up in three weeks if it doesn't work out."

"What kind of a guy do you want?"

"Smart and tough—like Moser."

"Powell maybe. Do you know him?"

"No."

"He's just coming off duty."

Crotty called the desk and a minute or two later Patrolman James Powell appeared in the doorway. He wasn't as tall as Moser, but he had the same tan skin, probing eyes, and even-featured impassive face.

"Powell," said Captain Crotty, "how'd you like to do some plainclothes work?"

"Who wouldn't," Powell said.

"Kurz here has got a special assignment from Chief Clark. He's looking for a partner and I suggested you."

"Did you know Bill Moser?" Kurz asked.

Powell nodded.

"You want to find out who killed him?"

Powell's eyes came alive. "I sure would."

"Let's go talk."

They retired to an empty cubicle off the squad room where detectives interviewed people who came in with information or complaints.

"Where do you live?" Kurz asked.

Powell gave him a slightly off-center look which seemed to say: Where the hell do you think I live? "Couple of blocks from here."

"You married?"

Powell shook his head. "Got a flock of kid brothers and sisters."

"What do you hear about Moser?"

Powell shrugged. "Not much. Guys I know, they don't say much to me about that sort of thing any more."

"Did you know Moser?"

"Sure. He's the reason I'm on the force, pretty much. He used to come around and talk to the guys in our gang. After a while he sort of concentrated on me."

"What do you know about a bookie named Dancer?"

Powell shrugged again. "Flashy cat. Throws his money around. I remember one time he took a whole gang—the Raiders—to New York for a weekend. Saw the Yankees play. Had a helluva time."

"I think he killed Moser. I want you to help me prove it."

Powell thought about this for a minute. Kurz tried in vain to penetrate the expressionless face. It was appalling how little he knew about these people. How could you trust any one of them? This guy could be on Dancer's payroll right now.

"If he did it," Powell said finally, "I'd like to help nail him."

There was something about the way he said it that steadied

Kurz's nerves. He held out his hand. "Okay," he said. "Let's go."

Kurz went home and called Marianne Moser. "You got any of those important people together?"

"Some," she said. "How about tomorrow night?"

"Sounds good."

He asked her if she knew Powell. "No," she answered. "Bill worked with a lot of kids that way. He'd get friendly with a gang and try to do something with one or two of them at least. I remember once I told him it would take a hundred years to get anywhere his way. And he shook his head and said, two hundred."

A twinge of pain ran through Kurz's chest. "We'll see you tomorrow night," he said.

He spent most of the next day briefing Powell on everything they had accumulated about the warehouse robberies before the shooting. Powell didn't say much, but he studied every report, pondered every picture as if he had an X-ray machine inside his skull. "And you think Dancer ran this deal?" he said softly.

"Yeah, but he's dropped it," Kurz said. "They haven't made a move since—that day."

He took Powell with him to the meeting at Marianne Moser's house. Kurz could see she was a little startled by his resemblance to her late husband. He wasn't sure this was a plus or a minus as they filed into the living room and confronted a half dozen Negroes in business suits.

A portly, solemn man named Clancey was the pastor of a local Baptist church. A big burly guy named Seward was an official of the local NAACP. A trim slim banker in an expensive pinstriped suit was named Shays. Then came Kline and Willoughby, two well built younger men from the city's youth corps, one of the new mayor's better ideas. Finally there was a short thin ugly man with an ex-fighter's nose and a rasping voice. Kurz had met him once with Moser. His name was Wanamaker and he owned a hotel and a string of bars. Kurz suddenly remembered a remark Moser had made as they left him. "He didn't look clean. But he is."

They sat down. Marianne Moser began talking in that whispery voice. She sounded almost proud as she told them that Detective Kurz had informed her that he was "almost sure" that Dancer Washington had killed her husband. "As you gentlemen surely know, Bill was convinced for a long time that Dancer was a dangerous criminal, dangerous to our whole community. Now that murder's been committed, I hope maybe you'll finally agree it's time we did something about him."

The NAACP man looked uncomfortable. He cleared his throat, and spoke with a voice that rumbled from his big chest. "I never thought Dancer Washington was exactly the pride of the Negro community. But I never thought he was quite as dangerous as your husband said he was, Mrs. Moser."

"I was in the ambulance with Bill," Kurz said. "The last thing he said was Dancer's name. He was a lot closer to the truck than I was. I suspect he saw the man who shot him . . ."

"You suspect. But you don't know."

"We're trying to make gains, to get some respect in this city," Marianne Moser said.

"I believe it," barked restaurant man Wanamaker. "I believe it about this cat. I see him in action. He's real bad medicine."

"What do you want us to do?" asked the minister, with barely concealed impatience.

"You could help us collect information," Kurz said. "The sort of information that can't be collected from outside. A guy like Dancer has got to have some enemies. We want to know who they are. And we want to know his friends, too. We want to hear every rumor, no matter how crazy or unlikely, that you and your friends hear about him. But what we really need from people like you is a moral counterattack against this guy. We want it spread up and down and all around town that the police are on to Dancer. We want everyone to hear that he's in real trouble over Bill Moser's death."

He took a breath and looked around him. What he saw was not reassuring. The expressions on the dark faces ranged from blank to frowning. "The way I see it," he said, "this guy is a challenge to you people. Bill Moser knew it from the start. Bill gave his life trying to prove that a Negro could make it inside the law. Dancer's trying to prove that the only way is outside the law. It's up to us to prove he's wrong."

Kurz could see the word *us* hit them like fingernails on a blackboard. There was a long silence; then the NAACP man, after glancing around at the others, said flatly, "Mr. Kurz, as a lawyer I don't approve of many police methods. As a Negro lawyer, I disapprove strenuously. But this idea combines all the worst aspects of both sides of the question. You want us to organize a persecution of a man who has not even been accused of a crime."

"Bill Moser accused him with his dying words."

"Let's not get dramatic, Mr. Kurz. Bill Moser's death was tragic. God knows I mourn him, as we all do, but a statement made by a dying man is not de facto true. The fact remains that there is absolutely not a shred of evidence to connect Dancer Washington to this crime. I will not be a party to persecuting an innocent man. I especially will not be a party to persecuting a Negro."

Kurz looked slowly around the room. There was not a sign of disagreement with the NAACP lawyer's denunciation. In fact, he thought he saw on the dark impassive faces something very close to active dislike.

"I'm afraid," said the minister, "I must substantially agree with Mr. Seward's remarks."

Why the hell didn't Powell say something? His eyes were riveted to the shiny tips of his brown shoes. Marianne Moser stared straight ahead, her angular face rigid, her big eyes swimming with tears. Why didn't *she* say something? It was a shambles.

"We're not asking you to persecute anybody. I honestly don't think I'm asking you to do anything that Bill Moser wouldn't have asked if he was sitting here instead of me."

The NAACP man smiled sarcastically. "Mr. Kurz. By the time he died, Bill had learned that most Negroes don't accept the policeman's solution to our problems. Locking people up, beating them up, there's no future in that, Mr. Kurz. Give the Negro a chance. Give him genuine freedom, economic and political, and we won't need police methods."

"I'm not so sure," Kurz said. "It seems to me there's always going to be a certain number of people who think they can make out better by stealing things, pushing people around, shooting them."

"That remains to be seen," said Mr. NAACP. "You people want to lock the Negro up before he has a chance to prove you're wrong."

Kurz sighed. He was up against a politician. This guy will sit here all night making speeches if you keep feeding him the lines, Harry.

"Look" he said. "I'm not here to debate you. I made you a straightforward proposition. If you don't like it, say so, and let's forget it."

"We've said so."

"Okay. Good night."

All six arose and trooped out of the house. Never in his life had Kurz felt so baffled. He sat there staring at the wall, wondering if he had gone crazy. Did the conversation really take place or had he said something completely different which caused these people to hate him? No, it was real, it was true.

Marianne Moser walked back into the living room. She stood in the doorway, her long slim hands toying nervously with her skirt. Kurz looked up at her. "Now you know what Bill was up against," she said in that small soft voice.

What does this mean? Only one thing, of course—she knew Harry Kurz was going to fall on his face. Again he had the uneasy feeling of having blundered into a subterranean world, of fumbling through unfamiliar darkness.

"I don't get it," he said. "Are they on Dancer's side?"

"No," Marianne Moser said. "They just don't like to think about Dancer. They'd like to wish him away."

"You can't blame them, really," Powell said. "They got

other things to worry about. If all Negroes did nothin' but worry about guys like Dancer, we'd have a low crime rate—back on the old plantation."

"In other words, if we're going to get Dancer it's got to be as cops, not crusaders."

Powell nodded.

"That suits me," Kurz said. "That suits me fine."

Was that a smile on Marianne Moser's face? It vanished too quickly for Kurz to decide. "I'll get some coffee," she said.

She must have had it ready. She was back almost instantly with three steaming cups. They drank it and Kurz asked Marianne Moser to tell them more about her brother. "What makes him mad and what makes him happy, that sort of thing."

"I haven't seen much of him in the last—four or five years," she said. "He came to dinner around that time and got into a big argument with us and Bill threw him out of the house. He was running numbers then and Bill told him to stop it." She frowned for a moment, trying to put Dancer together in her mind. "He doesn't care anything about money. He gives it away or loans it as fast as he gets it. He's really very generous in a sort of crazy way. He likes to impress people with it. He likes children. Even after he stopped coming here he always sent the kids expensive Christmas presents."

"How about women?"

"He never stays with one girl long. He doesn't like women who look like me. He likes them light, with white features. I don't know why. It doesn't fit in with the rest of his ideas. But then I never could make much sense out of his mind. He used to say marriage was for suckers like me and Bill. The way he sees it, the whole world is an arrangement by white people to make suckers out of Negroes. When you get married you've got to have a job to support your wife and kids. That keeps you quiet." Marianne Moser shook her head sadly. "That's the big thing about him, the hate eating away down deep."

"Does he have white friends?"

"Lots of them. People from the university. He's read a lot. He can talk civil rights as good as anyone. From what I hear

—I don't really know—he donates plenty to CORE and some of the action groups. But any white person who thinks Dancer's his friend——" She shook her head again.

"Does he get mad easy?"

"Very easy. It's his temper that started everything, when I think of it. He got into a fist fight with a policeman when he was about sixteen. The cop beat him up pretty bad and arrested him."

"But people like him?"

"A lot of people. But from what I hear—lately they're more scared of him than anything else. He's gotten pretty powerful and he likes to throw his weight around."

"Where did he get that screwy name—Dancer?"

"It was my mother's maiden name," Marianne Moser said softly.

"Oh, I thought——"

Powell smiled faintly. "It was one of those names you see on the blotter—like Royal King Jones?"

"Yeah," Kurz said, and could only suffer through the painful silence. With one more deep breath, he tried to regain his equilibrium. "All right. What do you think of this approach?"

You are supposed to be running the show, Harry, and here you are asking advice from a guy just off a beat.

"For the next couple of weeks we concentrate on roughing Dancer up, making his customers unhappy, giving everyone the impression that the whole damn police force has turned the heat on, the idea being that he'll get mad and make a wrong move."

Powell scratched behind his ear for a moment. "Well," he said, "it's better than doing nothing."

And it gets you off the beat and into plainclothes. The hell with it, Kurz, you've got to go with it now or walk out of here as Mr. Whitefuzz, the original idiot.

"I think we'll find out it's a lot better than doing nothing," he said.

The rest of the week was spent arranging for Powell's transfer to plainclothes and getting X-rayed and probed by a half dozen doctors at the medical center. Powell's transfer should have been perfectly simple but Deputy Chief Inspector O'Bannon suddenly decided to make it a first class beef. There was, he argued, absolutely no need for any more Negro detectives and when you put a Negro in plainclothes you were just getting him used to the idea of making detective. If you put him back on the street, ten to one he'll scream to one of the civil rights organizations and you'll have a big stink about Negro promotion. The plea was so obviously phony, Kurz couldn't really believe Uncle Harold would take it seriously. But he fussed over it for twenty-four hours and Kurz finally had to break him down by threatening: "Okay, if I can't have Powell, the hell with it. I'm putting in for two months sick leave."

"Now, Harry, that's no attitude to take . . ."

He got Powell.

The Reichdoktor at the hospital was almost as much trouble. "You still feel pain, don't you?" he said, punching him playfully in the chest.

"I don't feel a thing," Kurz said as a dancing arrow ran through his chest and down his arm.

"You sure?" he asked, punching him again.

"Absolutely."

"Your X-rays are okay. The lung has healed nicely, but avoid strenuous exercise."

"Jawohl," Kurz said, and got a very dirty look in farewell.

Back at the precinct house Powell reported a call from Wanamaker, the skinny little restaurant man who had been Kurz's sole supporter in the Moser living room. Kurz called him back and got a very friendly hello. "Listen, Detective," he said, "I couldn't tell you this the other night, but I'm ready to go all out to finish this here crumb Dancer. Now I just happen to own the Carver Hotel where Dancer lives. Does that interest you?"

"A lot. Is anybody in the room next door?"

"I can arrange it so there won't be."

"We'll be up this afternoon to check it out."

There was a closet in the room next to Dancer's that was

made for bugging. In the police laboratory Kurz explained his problem to Lieutenant Daniel Muldoon, an excitable genius with a face that resembled a Hallowe'en pumpkin. "That's easy," he said. "We wire the closet with a couple of these new voice-activating mikes. If you don't want to leave the tape recorder in the room, we can run a wire down to the owner's office."

"Let's do that," Kurz said. "I don't trust the help."

By five o'clock that afternoon Dancer was wired for sound. Everything he said above a whisper would go down five floors onto a 1200 foot reel of tape in Wanamaker's office.

"Ain't progress wonderful," Kurz said as he drove Powell back to the precinct house. "Five years ago we'd have to sit there and bug that goddamn room twenty-four hours a day ourselves. Now we just pick up a tape once every two days. Meanwhile, we got time for some social life."

Powell grinned. "I think I'm gonna like being a detective."

After dinner Kurz was trying to decide between TV and a visit to Donahue's Bar & Grill when the telephone rang. "Where's my television set?" Ann Macy demanded.

"Hell, I forgot it," Kurz said. "I went back to work ahead of schedule and it went right out of my head."

"Has the party tomorrow night gone the same way?"

"Hell no, I'm looking forward to it. Every night before I go to bed I flip through another volume of the *Encyclopedia Britannica*."

"I can hardly wait to see you in action," she said. "Pick me up about eight."

He was on time. He stood, sports coat on his shoulder, and watched her fuss with her hair before the hall mirror. She was wearing a bright blue and white summer dress, one of those things that hung straight up and down but had a neckline that showed plenty of bosom.

The party was down on the river in the oldest section of the city. With the culture boom of the last five years, a number of art galleries had appeared in basement stores and on the first floors of old brownstones. Several waterfront bars, hangouts for the scum of the city, had been dubbed picturesque by the college generation and were jammed on weekends. Long-haired types wandered the streets in sweatshirts and sandals.

"Listen," Kurz said as they got out of the car, "this isn't going to turn into a pot party or anything like that?"

She gave him a superior smile. "That's strictly for children as far as I'm concerned."

"Agreed," Kurz said, "but there's a lot of twenty-five or thirty-year-old children down this way who go for it big."

"Never fear," she said. "You have nothing to lose but your self-image."

They fumbled their way down a pitch-dark side street not more than ten feet wide and into a building that had to be a factory. There were six different companies listed in the directory at the foot of the narrow, almost vertical stairway.

"Who the hell lives here?" Kurz growled.

"A very unconventional man."

She led the way up the stairs. There were a half dozen long flights and Kurz was sure by the time they reached the top they were at ten thousand feet. He was sweating and the pain was back in his chest. But Miss Macy was not interested in his troubles. "Here we go," she said, and led him through the door into a vast room.

It was a loft. There were big movable walls suspended from the ceiling. Very modern paintings, smears and blobs of purple, pink, yellow, dangled from wires. One canvas had nothing but a single black line vaguely resembling a tire tread down the center of it. Off in one corner there were a number of paintings stacked against the wall and people were milling around them. They were also milling around a table at the far end of the room, obviously the bar. Elsewhere there were knots of conversationalists on long low couches, others sat cross-legged on pillows on the floor. Above the conversation a phonograph was playing some weird Oriental music.

Kurz felt wildly overdressed in his new Madras jacket. There were quite a few sweatshirts, more than a few dungarees, and a definite preference for sneakers. Here and there

Kurz glimpsed a number of Negro faces. It was different, all right.

"Oh," Ann Macy was murmuring beside him, "there's Tom Telfare. I wonder if he's finished his novel yet. You've got to meet him."

"Well, look who's here in a Pucci dress."

A tall, loose-limbed character with a receding hairline and thick horn rimmed glasses wrapped his long arm around Ann Macy's waist.

"Oh, it's just an imitation," Miss Macy said, obviously flattered. She introduced him to Donald Slater. "My philosophy professor," she said, smiling.

Professor Slater gave Kurz a satisfactory handshake. "You can see why I love my work," he said, giving Ann Macy an extra squeeze, "when I've got this kind of scenery around the classroom."

Slater was so totally lacking in sex appeal it was easy to take him with a smile. "From what I've heard, the feeling is mutual," Kurz said. "Another weekend or two and she'll have me down catching a few lectures myself."

"Any time," chuckled Professor Slater. "What do you do, Mr. Kurz?"

"I'm a detective."

The professor blinked. "Really," he said. "You work—for the city police?"

"That's right."

"Fascinating!" Professor Slater practically flipped what was left of his wig. "It must be absolutely fascinating to be in constant contact with the criminal level of existence. Have you read Sartre's *St. Genet?* Oh, you must, you should. I'm an existentialist myself, leaning more toward Heidiger than Sartre, but Genet, you know who he is, of course, Sartre's analysis of him has given us a fantastic insight into the concept of criminal existence. To be against. Of course, that's not the only aspect of crime that interests me. I'd be fascinated to know if you have found in your experience anyone who committed a purely gratuitous crime. Gide, you know, ultimately came to believe that this was the only way that a man could create his freedom."

For a moment Kurz felt just a little overwhelmed by this torrent of words. But he managed to get the point, although the spray of names meant nothing to him. "I'm afraid most of the characters I've arrested were just trying to make a fast buck the easy way."

"Oh."

Professor Slater wrinkled his elongated brow. "That's rather dismaying. But, of course, a good deal of such perception depends on one's point of view. What interests me is the moment when a man decides deep inside himself that he is a criminal, that this is his mode of existence."

"Who knows," Kurz said. "My job is catching them, not understanding them."

"Ah, yes. Ah, yes," Professor Slater said, "if you define your existence that way . . ."

"Much too narrow, in my opinion," Miss Macy said. "Mr. Kurz is one of these people you discussed recently—who live with only a third or half their potential awareness."

"Really." Professor Slater gazed at him with new interest but Kurz did not expecially like his expression. "We must have a long talk some time, Mr. Kurz. I'm working on a book about forms of protest. I'm in the middle of the criminality chapter now. Oh, look who's here——"

Standing in the doorway was the best dressed Negro Kurz had ever seen outside the movies. His yellow sports coat gleamed against a rose shirt. His brown slacks were so sharply pressed, the edge looked positively menacing. He had one of those bullet-shaped heads but without the long, low Step'n-Fetchit jaw. His chin was firm and nicely rounded. The expression on his face was an odd mixture of pleasure and disdain. At times his smile was almost a sneer as he studied the chattering company, but it broadened swiftly when he waved to a friend. There was something vaguely familiar about his face and Kurz suddenly knew why.

"Oh, there's Dancer," Ann Macy said in his ear.

"Excuse me," said Professor Slater, and hurried down to the door, threw open his arms in a flamboyant gesture of greeting and began talking animatedly to his black guest.

"Is he the star of the show?" Kurz said.

"Who, Dancer? Slater has gotten a lot of material from him —on the Negro revolt. Oh, listen—they're changing the music. Let's dance."

The clang of what sounded like a hundred electric guitars suddenly filled the room. As if it was a signal, a half dozen couples started gyrating and jerking in the latest version of the monkey or the frug.

'I don't do those nutty dances," Kurz growled. "They're for teenagers."

"They're for swingers. Come on."

"Give me a quick lesson."

She gave him a one-minute course in the frug and before Kurz knew what was happening, he was out on the floor endangering his spine with the rest of them. The dance was so simple an idiot could have learned it in thirty seconds. But the real fun was watching Ann Macy do it. Those luscious breasts kept practically coming out of her smock and the rest of her bounced around inside that dress in absolutely sensational style. Her face was all bright, flashing laughter, the hair swirling across her eyes giving her that innocent teenager look.

Kurz kept going for a half hour—enough to safeguard his standing in the swingers' club, then dragged her off the floor. "Remember I'm still walking wounded," he said.

"That's right, I forgot," she said, and suddenly put her arm around his waist as she smiled up at him.

"I need a drink," he said.

They wandered down to a long wooden table where two students, one black, one white, were pouring beer from foaming pitchers. As he picked up his two glasses, Kurz was a little startled to hear the dark bartender say, "That'll be one dollar."

"I thought this was a friendly party."

"You're drinking for CORE tonight, pal."

He paid and turned to find Ann Macy smiling triumphantly at him. "You're going to rue the day you threw me in that pool."

"It's been worth every cent so far," he said, and touched glasses with her.

They retired to a couch in a nearby corner and watched the dancers for a while. Finally, when he thought the question was completely casual, Kurz asked, "You know this Dancer character?"

"Oh, everybody knows Dancer. He's spoken to a lot of activist groups."

"I mean, do you know him personally?"

"Yes. Why do you ask?"

"No special reason, he just interests me."

"What did last weekend mean to you, Harry?"

The question left him momentarily flabbergasted.

"Was it special, or the sort of thing you've done a hundred times before?"

Careful, Harry, this baby knows how to mix her stuff. Slow curves, then a high, hard fast ball. Whatever you say can lead to trouble. If you cool her off the trouble will start tonight. If you warm her up, the trouble, real trouble may come in six months.

"It was pretty special," he said softly, looking straight ahead. "But—it's a little early to say it, don't you think?"

"I felt the same way," she said. "I couldn't stop thinking about you all week. I'm asking you because—if we both feel that way I can be perfectly honest—about someone like Dancer."

She took a deep slow breath. "I had an affair with him last year. It lasted about six months."

He sat there not thinking, only reacting, with images clogging his nerves like the rash of panicky phone calls they used to get during the first civil defense exercises. "You're not—putting me on?"

"No."

He stared at the dance floor. A tall, lanky girl was frugging so hard her streaming blond hair kept obscuring her face. At times it was like watching a vibrating mop.

"You don't like it, do you?"

"No."

"Why? Because he's a Negro?"

What were those images crawling down your nerves? That smiling black face, the pink and white mouth kissing where you had kissed—Jesus! "I don't care," he said, "whether the guy is black, brown, or purple, but if—there is something special here, what makes you think I enjoy hearing it's strictly leftovers?"

"It isn't! It wasn't—I mean Dancer was almost a kind of sickness with me. I was trying to be—completely against. Completely. He just—took advantage of me. It was nothing all the way. I mean it, Harry. Nothing."

Maybe because he was lying, he got the uneasy feeling she was too. But the hell with romantic worries, you are back at being a cop again, Kurz. This dame must know a lot about Dancer and it is your job to get it out of her.

Suddenly brown slacks cut off the dance floor. Kurz stared up into a yellow sports coat, while above a dark voice chuckled, "Ann baby, what are you hiding back here for?"

Kurz stood up. Dancer was a half head taller, but underneath the padded jacket he was strictly stringbean. You could break him in two anytime.

"Is he really a cop like I hear?" Dancer said to Macy.

"Yes."

"You can explain it to me while we dance, baby," he said, taking her hand. "But it's going to take *some* explainin'."

Kurz sat there watching Macy and Dancer frug. He lived up to his name. He was like an animated vine out there, all cool, live grace. The hell with them. He wandered down the room eyeing the scenery. There was plenty of other twill around town. There was plenty right here in this room. He bought another beer for CORE and found himself eyeball to eyeball with a trim, athletic-looking redhead. Not bad except for a pair of fullback's legs, until she started talking. It all came out of the corner of her mouth and he knew he was in trouble right away.

"So you're Ann's latest?"

"Latest what?"

A smirk. "I won't say it. That poor kid is so mixed up."

"She didn't impress me that way."

"Don't be ridiculous! How could she go out with you, a cop. Someone who's synonymous with everything she despises. Authoritarian stupidity——"

"Maybe I'm not stupid."

Another smirk. "Please, I don't mean it *personally.*"

"Where do you know Ann?"

"We were in a therapy group together. I'm working for my doctorate in poly sci."

"Oh." Kurz let his eyes wander down the room to the dance floor. Macy and her dark loverboy were still out there frugging away. From the look on her face, she was having a good time. Too good. Kurz felt a sullen anger, half disgust, half resentment, rise in his throat. The poly sci queen rattled in his ear about the need for a new police commissioner. The music stopped and Macy worked her way off the dance floor and walked toward him, Dancer by her side.

"She still swings, this chick," Dancer said.

"Would you like a beer?" Kurz asked Macy as if Dancer weren't there.

Macy nodded. When Kurz came back with the beer, Dancer was still there. He suddenly said in a very loud voice, "So you didn't tell whitefuzz here this was a CORE party. "I bet that beer is burning his guts out."

"So far I've spent two bucks," Kurz said, "and it's not bad beer."

"Every little bit helps, whitefuzz."

"My name's Kurz," he said. "Harry Kurz. What's yours?"

"Dancer," he said and his eyes changed expression. He was suddenly wary as well as arrogant.

"Dancer Washington?"

"That's right."

"I used to work with a fellow named Bill Moser. He talked about you sometimes."

"I bet he did," Dancer said.

"I thought a lot of Bill Moser."

"That's no surprise."

"Why?"

"He spent his whole life trying to make it as a white man's nigger."

"He wasn't anybody's nigger. But I'm not so sure about you."

"You wouldn't talk that way to me, whitefuzz, if this wasn't a real respectable party."

"You're damn right I wouldn't," Kurz said. "By now you'd be on the floor with a multiple skull fracture."

Ann Macy stood beside them wide-eyed with dismay. She was about to say something when Dancer spun away and bellowed: "Do you hear that, cousins, do you hear what the cop just said? He wants to bust my skull. Ain't that just like every cop you've ever known? Argue for one minute and he's ready to bust your skull."

The party had thinned out and was obviously getting stale. People swarmed from all corners to form a circle around them. Professor Slater was there and the poly sci queen along with two dozen eager, staring, anonymous faces.

"A cop? Who's a cop? He's a cop. With Ann Macy?" the voices babbled.

"Tell them what you just said about a policeman who died in the line of duty. A policeman who happens to be your brother-in-law."

Dancer looked around him with a supremely confident smile. "I said he was a white man's nigger. I'll say it again. I think the man who shot him ought to get a medal."

A murmur of approval ran through the crowd.

"He had three kids," Kurz said.

"All the more reason to shoot him," Dancer said. "Now the kids have got a chance to grow up black Negroes instead of white half-breeds."

"I think it's important for kids to have a father, whether he's black, white, or grey."

"Spoken like a true square."

That got a good laugh.

"I ask the assembled multitude," Dancer said, "has anyone found a father so vital to his psychological development, expecially a father an honest son would eventually despise?"

"Well, they don't despise him now. I've seen to that," Kurz said. "I've talked to them. I told them how their father died with his hand on his gun and his face toward the cowardly fink who shot him from ambush."

Again there was a subtle change in Dancer's expression. He seemed, for a moment, to taste those words and find them extremely unpleasant. "You call it cowardice," he said. "I say the man who pulled that trigger was no more cowardly than the Vietcong sniper defending his country against the U.S. Marines."

Instinctively Kurz said: "I happen to think the U.S. Marines are defending the freedom of South Vietnam."

Hoots, laughter, catcalls. Kurz stared around him, bewildered by the outburst of derision. Were these people Americans? Ann Macy stood among them, her eyes on the floor.

"Sure," Dancer chortled through the uproar, "just like you cops are defending freedom in the 13th precinct."

Another laugh. Kurz struggled to control his temper. It was clear now he was in a hopeless argument. He decided to go down fighting.

"Dancer," he said, "you might kid these people." He looked around him at the frowning, hostile faces. "They're all idealists, they think anybody with a black skin is automatically a hero, especially when he's got a big mouth. But I happen to know how you make your money, Dancer. Not from the white people but from the black people. Quarters and half dollars from the poorest black people. A cop like Bill Moser may have cuffed around a few hoods in his time, but he never picked the pockets of the poor."

"Whitefuzz," said Dancer, with total contempt, "I don't have to explain myself or defend myself. I'm among friends."

"You tell 'em, Dancer . . . Yeah friends . . . Tell 'm."

"And I got one last suggestion, friends. Let's give this fuzz back his money. He said he spent two dollars here tonight. Let's give it back to him because we don't want his kind of money."

"Yeah, where's the dough? Give it back."

"And I'll replace it," Dancer said, "with two of my own dollars."

Punch him, a burning voice whispered inside Kurz. One punch smack in that narrow gut just above the belt buckle and he will fold up like one of those pleated party streamers hanging from the rafters. But ten years of being a cop stood between him and this exquisite satisfaction. He could hear long, lean Charlie Campbell in the police academy telling them for the twenty-fifth time *a policeman does not lose his head*. The memory undoubled his fists. He looked around him with maximum contempt. Ann Macy was standing directly behind him, her face blank with a kind of shock that might include pain.

Kurz turned his back on Dancer and walked slowly over to her. "Let's go home," he said. "I'm tired of being the life of this party."

She stared at him like a zombie. Dancer's hand fell on his shoulder and jerked him partway around. "Hey, whitefuzz, you forgettin' your money."

The black hand shot out and shoved two dollar bills into Kurz's handkerchief pocket.

Again came the voice, terrible now like a streak of white fire. *Hit him now, the left in the belly, the right in those grinning teeth.* Instead he took the two bills out of his pocket and dropped them at Dancer's feet.

"I don't take money from a two-bit bookie."

"You're the first cop I ever met who didn't."

This was good for another big laugh.

Kurz turned away again and took Ann Macy's hand. This time Dancer grabbed her.

"Wait a minute. You're walkin' off with one of my best girls, whitefuzz, and I don't think she wants to go. Ain't that right, Ann baby?"

The guy was a glutton. He wanted nothing less than total humiliation and he was probably going to get it if that frozen look on Ann Macy's face meant what Kurz suspected.

"You're sick, Dancer." Ann Macy almost whispered the words, but they echoed across the crowd as if other voices had snatched them up and passed them on. "I told you six months ago you were sick and now you're even sicker."

The smile fell off Dancer's face, the shine went out of his eyes. "Baby," he said, "I never thought I'd hear you say that. Baby, Old John Law here's really got you."

She just looked at him. Without taking her eyes off his face she said, "Let's go."

Kurz shoved his way through the crowd and she followed him. As he passed the girl with the streaming blonde hair she spit in his face. He wiped it off with his handkerchief and they walked to the door. Professor Slater hustled after them blinking excitedly behind his horn rimmed glasses. "We all tend to find Dancer rather fascinating, but we don't endorse his extreme feelings, believe me. I thought he went far beyond the bounds——"

"Why didn't you stop it?" Kurz said.

"Well, I didn't feel it was my part to interfere with a spontaneous——"

"And you think you're a leader," Kurz said.

They went down the long flights and along the narrow twisting streets to the car. Not a word was spoken for another ten minutes as they rolled past the neon bars and cluttered sidewalks of the Congo. As he drove, Kurz felt a fantastic anger building up in him. He actually found himself trying to think of six friends who were off duty and would go back with him to tear those beatnik nigger-lovers apart.

"I could see you wanted to hit him," Ann Macy said. "I'm so glad you didn't."

"Do you have any booze in your apartment?"

"A little."

"I need a drink."

Up in the apartment she produced a half bottle of bourbon. "This is all I've got."

"It'll do."

He poured himself a double on the rocks.

"I'll have a little, too."

He tossed it off in two swallows. It didn't do any good. Every time he looked at Macy he saw her surrounded by those sneering faces. He prowled around the room, stared out the window at the river gleaming dully in the dark street lights. "Jesus," he said. "Jesus."

"Is it because he's a Negro?"

"No, goddamn it," he snarled, whirling to face her on the other side of the room. "I don't let anyone treat me that way."

"But if you understood why Dancer acts that way. If you saw him as a victim, you wouldn't be so angry."

"I see him as an arrogant son of a bitch and I'm going to make him eat every one of those things he said to me tonight in triplicate."

She shuddered as if the words were directed at her."Don't talk that way, please."

"How the hell do you expect me to talk? Do you think I should love the bastard?"

"No, just—just understand him and pity him."

She shook her head and Kurz realized she was crying. "Don't tell me you still love him?"

"No," she said, her head bowed.

"Did you?"

"I loved—an idea of him. It lasted for a while, which is more than I can say about you."

"What the hell does that mean?"

She looked up at him, a small, sad smile on her lips "We started out with no ideas, Kurz, no preconceptions. You liked my body, I liked yours."

There was more than sadness on her tear-stained face. Was it a kind of question, a vague patina of hope? It stirred something inside him less cold and bitter than his rage. "There could be—worse ways to start."

She smiled ruefully. "Yes. We're honest, at least."

He sat down beside her on the couch and tried to pull her into his arms. "Let's keep it——"

"No!" She shoved him away and all but fled across the room. "No. I couldn't make love to you tonight. All the hate I saw on your face, in your eyes, it was just like Dancer—maybe worse."

"Like Dancer! Did I start an argument with that son of a bitch?"

"You treated him like he was—invisible."

"Which is exactly what I'd like him to be."

"That's what I mean." The lovely head came up, the green eyes aglow, not with anger but a kind of sullen sadness. "That's what I mean."

She paced the floor like an animal in a cage. "All you can do, Kurz, is meet hate with hate. It's no good."

"You met it with love. How did it work out?"

"No good either," she said with a tired sigh. "What two people do in a bedroom can't change what happens outside. Especially what happens to—a Negro."

"Look, Ann, this bleeding heart——"

"Keep quiet," she said. "Let me tell you. Let me tell you the whole thing." Around and around the room she paced, her arms clutched about herself as tightly as if they were bound by a strait-jacket. "When I met Dancer, I'd just come out of—my childhood." She caught the doubt on his face. "Yes, childhood. When you grow up in a home you can be—a child all your life. Why did I become a nurse, for instance? Because I couldn't dream of being something that didn't involve regimentation, routines. But then I—met some people at the hospital. I started taking some courses at the university. I went from child to adult in—well, much faster than you did. Suddenly I was a person with a life. I thought about it—without any help from nuns or priests. For the first time I thought about it. And I saw, for the first time, how silly it was, what I was doing. I was trying to heal one kind of sickness but the real sickness in our society was—is—spiritual."

She stopped by the window and stared into the darkness. "I really thought I could help him. I thought that if someone really loved him it could heal that hate." She started walking again now, head down, the words pouring out. "I knew the hate was there. He spouts it in your face the first time you meet him. But he does it with that wonderful bitter gaiety. Anyway, I fell in love with him—or with this idea of him. For six months I tried to make it work."

She stopped by the window again. "Impossible. It was so impossible. I couldn't stop the hating. I couldn't even stop it from growing. Sometimes I could feel it when I was in the room with him. I could feel it expanding like one of those huge ballons, crushing us against the walls. I—I finally started to feel like his sewer. That's all I was, a sewer, where he vomited his hate. Sometimes I felt hate coming out of every part of his body." She faced him somberly. "Yes, even that part. The part you don't want to think about. There was always a new story, a cop who had given him a ticket, a woman who had sneered at him in the supermarket, a restaurant that wouldn't serve him, one of his teenage friends beaten up by a detective."

She started walking again. "Was he good in bed? Not nearly as good as you. I guess you need confidence to be good that way, and Dancer doesn't really have any. In fact when he was upset, when some personal insult had come his way, like Professor Slater forgetting to shake hands with him at a party, he couldn't do it at all. Which led him to start making—suggestions. He had all sorts of ideas, recommended by the best pornographers. I actually tried—to cooperate for a little while."

She was back to the window again, facing him. "Am I disgusting you as much as I assume I am?"

He looked at her and for the first time felt some consciousness of himself. She had taken him completely outside. He felt dazed, as if he were coming out of hypnosis or ether. You are sweating. In the air conditioner's chill hum, you are sweating. Why? Was it—the dream? The cage dream. Around and around and suddenly the serpent's head. Ridiculous. Answer her.

"It's pretty hard to disgust me," he said. "But you're coming close."

"Why?" she said bitterly. "Aren't you interested in what you can do with me when I'm in a better mood?"

"You want me to walk out of here? Is that it?"

"No I—I don't know what I want." She brushed briefly at her hair and started walking again. "It didn't last very long after that started. It was a kind of downhill acceleration. Finally one night Dancer came up with a friend, a big heavyset Negro. He was going to perform. Dancer was going to watch. I threw them both out. That was the end of it. I've seen him at parties since then, but very much in the distance."

The air conditioner hummed. Kurz stood up and faced her across the empty room. For a moment they reminded him absurdly of a pair of western gunslingers. "What do you want me to do about it?" he said.

"Just understand," she said.

"That's all," he said. "You're not hoping I'll scream and curse and call you a filthy pig for sleeping with a nigger. You'd like it, wouldn't you? That would prove all the conclusions you've drawn about me."

"I didn't draw them," she said. "I don't want to draw them."

It was the cage dream all right, with a new ending. But what do you do now? You have whipped this strange creature back to obedience momentarily. How do you keep her there? Kurz, the swinging cop, is in charge, but for how long? Remember the sweat running down your arms, greasing the palms of your hands while she coiled that heartbreaking story around you. What now, what now? They stood in a paralysis of imbalance, unpower.

"Could you love me?" she said in a small distant voice, as if she had crept deep down inside herself like a snail and was whispering out her only possible greeting.

"Sure," he said.

It was too glib, too easy. It was Detective Kurz, swordsman extraordinary, speaking and with that fantastic sensitivity of hers, she sensed it, no, she knew it. But she was resourceful.

"Let's wait until next weekend. Come have dinner . . . stay."

"All right," he said glumly.

He clumped down the concrete stairs, his chest aching, his whole body feeling strangely battered. Come next Saturday. He felt below his confusion a sullen anger. Screw next Saturday. Now is when Kurz wants you. He stopped, almost turning around, contemplating what she might do if he just grabbed her when she opened the door. But you saw and heard too much tonight, Kurz, to gamble those tactics. It was not her fault. No, the fault, the reason for your frustration was that elongated jig with the big, flashy mouth and clothes to match, Mr. Dancer. Now you have two reasons to go after him. Or is it three? Count those images that had erupted earlier, those black hands on her white skin, that snakelike dark body writhing in and on her, pink tongue darting, and correct that, Harry—three reasons.

Chapter Five

He woke up the next morning with pain gnawing in his chest, trickling like icy water down his arm. It depressed him. He lay there thinking about last night and he could no longer see Ann Macy. Dancer was all he could see, that long black body, that mocking smile, that vaguely musical high-pitched voice crowing *We don't want your money, whitefuzz.* A dull rage seeped through his body. He began to plan in delicious detail the destruction of Dancer Washington.

His mother rapped on the door. "I'm going to 12 o'clock Mass."

The unspoken question was perfectly clear. "Okay, okay, I'll come with you," Kurz growled.

Twenty minutes later, shaved and showered and with a glass of orange juice under his belt, he strolled with his mother down the dusty, tree-lined street to the long grey fieldstone church at the corner. The bells clanged noisily and people streamed up the steps and vanished into the dark orifice. It was hot and his chest throbbed relentlessly.

You should have stayed in bed, Harry. These new evening Masses were invented for guys like you. In the old days when his mother tried to drag him out for the 10, he would promise to go to the 12:50. This was not the easiest dodge in the world; you had to get your ass out of the house and disappear for an hour at the very time when a good football or baseball game was starting on television, or you were only halfway through the Sunday papers. But Mass at 7:30 P.M. was made to order. He was always on his way some place interesting at 7:30. So what the hell are you doing here sweating up your underwear at 12?

Guilt. Every so often you had to pay an installment on it. Especially when you had been a very bad boy and the old lady was on the verge of growing morose about it. But as they trudged through the heat, Kurz felt a new uneasiness. You have forgotten just how much it bugs you to go to church this way. It brings back too many memories of boyhood days when Mother marched heroically to worship, her meek daughter and well-scrubbed son beside her, while from behind the curtained windows the neighbors' eyes watched with the curiosity people reserve for freaks. It had lasted for over a year after his father was killed—as if his violent death had somehow made them weirdos.

You had hated them for it, Jesus, how you had hated them. You could look back at it objectively now, of course. Ten years on the police force would make anyone wiser about human nature. But it was still there under your skin and walking the same route with Mother brought it all back. Except now you can do something about it, Harry. You are no longer that solemn-faced little kid who stood silently while his mother sighed, "It's God's will." Now you are a man and you can do something about a world that makes widows out of simpletons like Mother and wipes out a kid's father when he needs him most. Now you can even the score.

Up the steps they went, through the pall of the vestibule into the vaulted dampness of the church. Two huge fans whirred feebly on the altar, shoving the stale moist air into the faces of the worshippers. After five Masses, the place was clogged with the odors of a thousand sweaty bodies. They sat on the side in the back at Kurz's insistence. Even in his teenage days he had refused to follow his mother up the middle aisle to the front pews—where she had led them every Sunday during boyhood. There were times when he almost suspected Mother liked being a widow. Maybe she was glad to get that big healthy man out of her bed. That crazy Irish attitude about sex. His sister had it in spades.

Mother began fingering her beads. The priest appeared, followed by two weary-looking altar boys. Kurz knelt with his rear end wedged against the back seat to take the pressure off his knees. In the seventh grade you got twenty-five on the legs with a yardstick if Dynamite Aggie caught you kneeling that way. A familiar voice droned in his ears. It was Jim Fogarty acting as lector. He had been a good friend in eighth grade days, a tough stocky character. Now he was a butterball, the boy's face lost in rolls of fat. Kurz wondered how he supported five kids on what they paid him as assistant manager of the Garden Square Hotel. "The priest asks God to accept in Christ's name the people's prayer for forgiveness." The new liturgy was, if possible, more boring than the old show. There was even more standing up, kneeling down, sitting, with lector Fogarty broadcasting the orders as if they were all in the first grade. You should have stayed in bed, Harry. But what the hell, you are here so let us meditate a little while on how to even the score.

Dancer. That was the big way to even the score. Pin that boogie to the wall, Harry, and you will feel better about a lot of things from Bill Moser to Ann Macy. How to do it, that is the question. You weren't going to get anyone in the Congo to help you, that was obvious. But you had the big item, the one thing that made them move in the Congo—that badge in your wallet. With that and Powell you had enough muscle to turn the juice on Mr. Dancer. You would have him doing a buck and wing before the month was out.

The priest was in the pulpit. It was Monsignor McIntosh, erstwhile police chaplain under the old mayor. The cops had called him Monsignor Brainstorm because he was always sending in ideas on how to improve the efficiency of the department. A fat, puffing little man, he had been swept out with a lot of other trash when the new broom came in two years ago.

McIntosh gasped and gargled through some announcements about novenas and funerals and read the gospel about the young man whose widowed mother persuaded Jesus to resurrect him. Two weeks ago you were pretty close to needing the same sort of resuscitation, Harry. But it was a colored nurse who came to the rescue, not Mother. If there was a moral to that one, you can't find it.

"In the name of the Father and of the Son and of the Holy Spirit," puffed Monsignor McIntosh. "My-a dear people, what-a is our Lord trying to-a-tell us in this gospel? He is-a giving us a warning. He is-a saying that the son-a who turns away from his mother's love risks eternal damnation. So many-a young men today, our young people, think they know more than-a their parents—"

Even the score. With only two of them working, it would have to be a slow, steady thing. But it was nicer in a way, that approach. You would be able to watch the boogie squirm. It would start with a beef or two from O'Bannon and the other payoff cops. But they would get the word fast enough and that would be the last you heard from them. Then the noise would come from Mr. Dancer himself. Squawks, yells, finally screams. Maybe in the end a plea for mercy. That would be really delicious, to hear those watermelon lips babbling *What did I do to you, man, a little gas at a party. Come on, man, tell me, how can I square it.* And you would smile and say in your sweetest, most understanding tone: *Kiss my ass.*

"A lonely widow, trusting, hoping-a in her son, but-a she had faith she-a remained true-a to her faith, even-a though her boy lay dead. And-a Christ rewarded that faith—"

That would even our score and we would be on our way to evening the bigger score. Without his numbers wheel, Mr. Dancer would have trouble maintaining that high, wide and handsome style of life. He would start to worry about the old casheroni. It would never occur to him to get a job. He would go back to stealing and that would be the beginning of the end, as they say in the song. By that time they would have at least a half dozen pigeons watching Dancer day and night. Maybe they would even work a willing pigeon right into his operation. They would know every move Mr. Dancer was making and when Mr. Dancer made the wrong one, Harry Kurz would be there waiting for him.

"We are-a too lenient with-a these juvenile offenders," gargled Monsignor McIntosh. "Mothers-a must recognize that God-a has given them responsibility for not only a son's body but his-a soul."

Delicious, that moment. Maybe it would be at a supermarket or a liquor store. He and Powell and a dozen other cops would be staked out waiting. He would pass the word to Powell and the others, *Dancer is mine.* And there in his black flesh would stand Mr. Dancer. *This is Harry Kurz, Dancer. Put down that gun and you won't get hurt.* If his hand moved even one inch to the left or the right, Mr. Dancer would be on his way. You would shoot for the gut, where the bullets really burned. What exquisite pleasure it would be to look down at Mr. Dancer twisting on the ground with that fatal pain exploding in his belly. *How does it feel, Dancer? Not too good? Bill Moser didn't feel too good either.*

"The sacraments-a, there is-a no substitute for the sacraments. The mother who does not make sure her son receives Communion at least once a week—"

But Mr. Dancer was smart. He probably wouldn't let that gun move, even one-quarter of an inch. That was okay. They would take him in and have another kind of fun. Hour after hour Mr. Dancer would sit there in that empty little room while Harry Kurz asked him why he had killed Bill Moser. Hour after hour until he started crossing and uncrossing his legs and a desperate look replaced that nigger pride on his black face. *I got to go, man.* And Detective Kurz goes on asking. *Please.* And finally it goes running down his leg and trickles through the dust, a greenish brown stream, and Mr. Dancer sits there in his own urine while Detective Kurz looks shocked. *Why didn't you tell me?*

"I-a believe-a in one God—"

Monsignor McIntosh had finally stopped gassing and was reciting the Creed. The congregation recited it with him. It reminded Kurz of school days, reciting the Pledge of Allegiance to the flag. Every afternoon after lunch, all of them out there in the school yard, their voices bouncing off the windows of the old red brick building. How the hell did it go? *I pledge allegiance to the flag and to the republic for which it stands* . . . Once Sister Matilda Mary, the fifth grade nun, made them write it out and everyone was appalled to discover how many kids had the words assbackwards.

"I believe in one holy Catholic and Apostolic church . . ."

Ho-hum. A few more bells, the consecration, standing up, sitting down to Fogarty's dull drone, and Communion. Up the aisle went Mary Gilroy, pregnant as usual. That beautiful Irish face was getting lumpier every year. And there goes Terry Matella, looking more Sicilian every year. A teaser until she met Harry Kurz on the beach and found out how to cure her hot pants the quick, hard, easy way. And blond Helen Scully, still looking pretty damn good, and still teaching the second grade at P.S. 109. There was one you never made, Harry, although you tried. In fact, you tried once too often and that was the end of the romance.

And Betty Case, another near miss. Amazing how much she resembled Ann Macy. Betty had you on the ropes for a good month, Harry. File that for future reference.

A tall cool blonde came drifting by. Not much of a figure, but fantastic legs, wearing one of those straight white summer dresses with modern art in geometric lines on it. There was nothing geometric about the rear view.

Another blonde, neither cool nor devout, with a lovely pair practically popping out of the dress. One of those wide mouths with ventriloquist lines running down. Good-natured, always the easiest kind. And young. As young as Macy. Let's face it, pal, you have to start thinking young.

They stood up one last time at Fogarty's insistence. Kurz realized he was soaking wet. The fans whirred wanly as Fogarty read something about the Communion. Jesus, let's wrap this up before we all dissolve. The dumb blonde, her Communion prayers finished, was looking around. Her eyes wandered in his direction and he gave her an interested look. She stared into her missal. She was going to be a good girl for the time being.

"Go, the Mass is ended," gargled Monsignor McIntosh.

"Thanks be to God," murmured the congregation.

"Amen," muttered Kurz.

Out into the sunlight, nodding to familiar faces.

"Hi, Harry." Big busty Ann Broderick with hair piled on top of her head, and Mrs. Broderick beaming at Mrs. Kurz. Still trying to make a match. No thank you, ladies. It would be like trying to knock down the Chicago Bears' best running guard every night.

"Wasn't that a wonderful sermon?" his mother said as they plodded up the hill.

"Great," Kurz said.

"Sometimes I wonder if I should try to influence you more."

"You do."

"When is the last time you went to Communion?"

"Last week," he lied.

"Oh. Well, it was a wonderful sermon."

"Yeah. Really great."

He spent the afternoon watching the Yankees lose to the Cleveland Indians and went to bed early. He slept beautifully, knocked down two eggs and six slices of bacon for breakfast and drove downtown through the semi-coolness of the early morning. He was feeling good. He parked his car in the shadow of the precinct house and trotted briskly up the steps. The eight to four shift was getting ready for morning inspection and he nodded and waved his way past the bluecoats. It always bothered him a little to see guys like Tommy Altman, pals from police academy days, still pounding a beat. About a third of the shift was Negro. The mayor was really delivering on his promise to give them a better shake on the city payroll.

Upstairs Kurz found Powell waiting for him, looking serious and maybe just a little contented at finding himself in plain clothes while the boys were mustering downstairs.

"We all set to go?" Kurz said crisply.

Powell nodded. "I did a little checking this weekend," he said. "Dancer doesn't own that wheel. The real money comes from outside. Probably syndicate dough."

"Good," Kurz said. "Those guys scare easier. They never want any trouble. I met Mr. Dancer at a party the other night. Now I've got two reasons for hating his guts."

"That's funny," Powell said. "Most people like Dancer."

"Do you?"

"Well—yeah, I do. I mean—I kinda wish I was like him, more free and easy."

"Balls," Kurz said, with an unsettling feeling that the conversation was out of control. "He's a loudmouth crumb."

"Okay," Powell said, his eyes shifting past him. "I'm just tellin' you what I think."

"I know, I know, and I asked you."

They settled down to discussing their plan of attack.

There was nothing especially complicated about it. A few hours later they sat in Kurz's duty car outside the ramshackle tenement where Dancer ran his wheel. It was ferociously hot and Kurz found himself wishing he'd bought an air conditioner for the heap. In the middle of the street a few teenagers flipped a rubber ball up and down the block. But most of them sat on stoops, listless, dulled by the fantastic heat. Above the street, black faces in search of coolness drooped from a hundred windows. They soon found Kurz and Powell. Pretty soon the whole block seemed to be watching them. Kurz could practically see the puzzle turning over in their minds. *If it was something big and they knew who did it, they wouldn't just sit there. If it isn't something big, why are they sitting there?*

Around 4 o'clock the sun got low enough to give the street some shade. As if it was a signal, the action also commenced. In cars, on motorcycles, on foot, the runners started showing up with the day's bets. More than one threw an uneasy look at Kurz and Powell, spotting them for cops on the first blink. Kurz just smiled grimly at them, brought his tiny Minox camera to his eye and, click, there was another picture. Powell kept score on a yellow pad, putting down all the names he knew. Pretty soon it was 6:30 and Kurz's stomach was starting to growl. "Let's grab the next one," he said.

Who should it be but the spherical character Moser had kicked in the crotch. "What's his name?" Kurz asked.

"Porky Brown."

"Hey, Porky."

He stopped just outside the tenement door and revolved, until his big belly was pointing at them like a cannon. "Yeah, man?"

"Get in."

"Me?"

"Get in."

Kurz swung open the back door. Porky shuffled across the street. "What's the name of the game, man? I'm clean. I'm just comin' down here to visit my grandmother at number 22."

"Look him over," Kurz said to Powell.

Powell got out, walked around the car and pushed the big belly up against the fender. He pulled a bundle of numbers slips out of each coat pocket. Kurz opened the back door again and Powell shoved Porky onto the seat.

"Man, you're makin' a big mistake. You got no rap against us. We go right up to the commissioner, man. You gonna be workin' a four o'clock cemetery——"

"Shut up," Kurz said.

They drove down to the station house and escorted Porky up three flights of stairs to the squad room. Down the corridor they walked him to one of the interrogation rooms, prodded him inside and sat him on a chair.

"You want a lawyer?"

"What I want a lawyer for, I ain't done nuthin'."

"We're booking you for those numbers slips, fatso. But that isn't the real rap."

He waited until the fat man stirred uneasily. He tried to read an answer on Powell's face, then muttered, "What is?"

"Murder."

He bounced around the chair as if it was a vibrating machine. "Murder! Look, man, you got the wrong cat. I chisel a little here, a little there, sure, who don't, but murder, not me, pal. I take too good care of this little chile I got here" (patting his belly). "I don't want nuthin' but natural juices runnin' through it."

"If that's the way you really feel, maybe you'll sing us a little song about Dancer."

"Dancer?"

"Dancer—and how he killed Bill Moser."

"Dancer? Oh, come on, man, that cat's no killer. Not that maybe he didn't stand up and cheer when he heard Moser got it. That boy was kickin' Dancer in the balls every chance he got. He never let up. But Dancer wouldn't kill nobody, especially a cop who's his brother-in-law. Dancer's got it up here, man. He plays it cool."

He knocked a stubby finger against his skull.

"That was a very nice performance, wasn't it, Jim?"

"Yeah, sure was," Powell said, crossing his arms and giving Porky Brown a deadeye.

"I bet he rehearsed that every night for a week."

"Wouldn't be surprised."

"Rehearsed—listen, I'm just tellin' you what I know—about Dancer."

"If you don't start telling us what you really know I'm going to leave you here with Detective Powell for twenty minutes. If you thought Bill Moser was tough——"

Porky began to sweat. "Man, I swear——"

"You ever hear Dancer say anything about Moser?"

"Sure, sure, I heard him say lots of things."

"Such as?"

"Such as he was a no-good son of a bitch."

"Did you ever hear him say he'd like to kill him?"

"I heard him say—he wish somebody else kill him."

"Since Moser's been dead what's Dancer been saying?"

"He say—a toast to the next one to die. I mean—let's face

it, he don't like cops, especially cops like Moser."

"What did Moser ever do to him besides trying to get him to play it straight?"

"Moser did a hell of a lot to him, man. He busted up two wheels on him. Dancer, he'd be a real cat down here now instead luckin' along on fifty percent of that pissass wheel he got now. Moser, he wouldn't let that boy live."

"All he had to do was get an honest job."

"Sure, sure."

"You've never heard him say anything about hiring anybody to plug Moser? Or doing it himself?"

"No, sir." The big balloon face swung back and forth emphatically. "No, sir."

"How well do you know Dancer?"

"We drink together."

"He ever tell you his troubles?"

"Sure. Dancer tells everybody his troubles. I keep tellin' him right back, shut your mouth, but he never listen."

"Look, fat man, we can put you away for a whole year under that new habitual gambling statute. That little child of yours will get pretty small down on that work farm. The warden is awful proud of how he never spends more than eleven cents per day per prisoner."

"Christ, man!" Porky sprang to his feet, arms flung wide, the crucifixion bit. "What you reamin' me for? You lookin' for more dough, a side payoff? You can get it. Just go see Dancer. I swear——"

"Sit down."

He sat.

"We're going to let you go, fat man. We're going to let you walk around loose like there's no great big ax up here just waiting to fall on your neck. And if you don't want it to fall you're going to have to be the best pigeon in the history of this precinct. Get it?"

"Yeah, I get it," Porky said, his voice suddenly small and weary. "I get it okay."

"And tell this to your friends. We know Dancer knocked off Moser and we're not going to slow down on him until he's laid out on that slab in the death-house morgue, smelling like a quick-fried pork chop."

Porky Brown's mouth went slack, his eyes revolved in opposite directions. "Man, if I thought he did it I'd—I don't buy killin'—I mean I'm a religious man. I——"

"Just start listening. And tell us what you hear. Maybe you'll change your mind."

Kurz opened the door and Porky went down the hall like he was ejected. Kurz stood in the silent room looking at Powell. "Think it will work?"

Powell shrugged. "It might."

They walked back to the squad room. "Listen," Powell said, "I hope you don't take this the wrong way but I really don't appreciate you giving me out as another Bill Moser."

It stopped Kurz dead. "Why not?"

"I just don't want people to think of me that way. I think Moser—well, he went a little too far. A lot of people started wondering whether he liked beating guys up."

"A lot of people, who?"

"People outside. Negroes."

"Listen, Jim, if you want to be a good detective you've got to understand there are times when a slap in the kisser or a jolt in the belly can work wonders."

"Sure, but I don't believe in workin' a guy over just on the chance he might have something to say. That might have been style ten years ago. It don't go today."

"Well—I'll buy that," Kurz admitted. "But I worked with Moser for three months. I never saw him go out of his way to kick anybody around."

Not exactly true, Kurz thought, remembering how Moser had creamed Porky Brown. And that night when they were looking for a certain larcenous character and ran into one of his pals robbing a liquor store. Moser had kicked him all over the sidewalk. At the time, considering what he'd done to the liquor store proprietor—he died of a fractured skull the next day—Kurz had thought the punishment more or less matched the crime.

"I'll tell you something," Powell continued. "Moser was a hell of a problem down here in the Negro community. Most decorated Negro on the force and all that. But a lot of people didn't buy his methods."

"Yeah, people like Dancer."

"No," Powell said, sounding almost angry. "Other people."

"Well—that still doesn't justify killing him, does it?"

"Christ, no. That's why I'm workin' with you. But I—thought I ought to explain."

"Okay. I got you. I got you loud and clear."

Kurz drove slowly home through the twilight, well satisfied with his day. Powell was probably right about Moser's style. What the hell, time marched on.

Which reminded him for no apparent reason of Ann Macy. Maybe it was just the time of day. Maybe he was ready to let her have another crack at giving him something. Why let her set the schedule? The possibility ping-ponged back and forth in his head as he parked the car and trotted briskly up the steps to dinner.

"That girl called," his mother said, without taking her eyes off the television set where a bunch of idiots were playing a game that involved potato racing.

"What girl?"

"Ann Macy."

"Oh, that one. Did she say what she wanted?"

"Just left her number."

He dialed from his private phone in the bedroom.

"Hello," she said. "Are you still mad?"

"About Saturday night? Don't be silly."

"Good. I'm calling you about that television set."

"Oh, hell, I'm sorry, Ann. I've got so damn many things on my mind——"

"Well, I don't need it now."

"Why not?"

"I'm getting it from someone else."

Don't ask, whispered a little voice behind Kurz's ear, but he asked anyway. "Who?"

"Dancer," she said. "He called me up to apologize for the way he acted the other night. He said he wanted to give me a present. I told him I didn't want any presents from him, but if he was feeling so flush maybe he'd donate a television set to the kids. I—didn't really think he'd say yes."

"Send it back."

"Why?"

"One, because it's probably stolen and, two, because I don't want you taking any presents from that son of a bitch."

"He's not a son of a bitch. He's a very mixed up unhappy person and if you want to know it, I was rather touched by his calling me up."

"I'll get you a television set. I'll get you a color television set."

"Go ahead, we can use two of them."

"Ann, that guy's a punk. A killer. I don't want you to have anything to do with him."

"I don't intend to have anything to do with him. But I'm going to accept the television set."

He slammed down the phone so hard he was sure he shattered the cradle. The stubborn, stubborn, stupid bitch. He was so mad he could barely eat his dinner. He just picked at the big juicy pieces of sirloin and shuffled the home-fried potatoes around the plate.

"Don't you feel good?" his mother asked.

"I feel fine."

Even Mother could tell that one was a lie. His chest twinged unpleasantly. He shoved down the apple pie dessert to keep her quiet and went back in the bedroom to call up Eddie Reardon.

"Well, if it ain't the Congo's leading Boy Scout," Reardon said. "What do you hear from Leopoldville?"

"Nothing but trouble. You feel like moving around?"

"Sure."

"What have you got that's new?"

"I met a couple of waitresses from the North End. Real broads. But they're worth a night."

"Sounds good. Call them."

He picked up Reardon and rolled into the North End. Goddamn Ann Macy and her television set and her bleeding heart. You would forget her for the night. Maybe for good.

"I hear O'Bannon's going around town promising to square your ass."

"Shit on him. It's about time he put in his papers. He must have a half million in the bank under six different names."

"That's no lie but he's a tough son of a bitch. What are you buckin' him for?"

"I'm just trying to do a job."

"Sometimes I can't figure you out."

"Why put up with this racket if you don't do a good job? Christ, be a house painter. You'll double your money."

"Sure, I know. But you got to play inside the rules. Until you get where O'Bannon is and then you can make your own rules. If you want to be a scoutmaster——"

"I don't want to be anything. I'm a pro. I know my job and I just want a chance to do it."

"Good luck."

It wasn't the best way to start the evening. But after Kurz got a look at the girls he decided there wasn't much evening to start anyway. They were obviously hookers with enough paint on their faces to rustproof the *Queen Mary*. Still they were built and not bad looking and it was only a night. Dotty was blonde, Billie, brunette; otherwise they were practically interchangeable. But Reardon always went for blondes and grabbed Dotty like she was the last of the big brass rings.

"Gee, it's hot," Billie said. "Ya car got an air conditiona?"

"When they made this heap, air conditioners weren't invented yet," Kurz said.

They drove to the Club Sahara where the continuous music made conversation impossible. A wink to the head waiter and they got their usual table at ringside. The girls left to powder their noses and Kurz said, "This isn't going to cost us money, is it?"

"Not for the boys in blue," Reardon assured him.

Ordinarily he wouldn't have given it a thought, making out with a hooker, although he preferred other types. But tonight for some reason it bugged him. He kept imagining what Ann Macy would say if she walked in and got a look at the company he was keeping.

Moreover these broads talked stupidity like they invented it.

"Ya know Harry Moreska?" Billie squawked above the music.

"Never heard of him."

"He runs a ba. He's a real good friend of aws. He knows a lotta cops. I just thought ya might know 'im."

"Never heard of him."

That was the way it went. They suffered through one of the Sahara's third-rate comedians and a fifth-rate singer and adjourned to the Shanghai, which had Chinese décor and South American music. By this time Kurz was telling himself he was just tired. Tired? He was exhausted. His whole chest was one goddamn ache and his rear end was another ache from those infinitesimal nightclub chairs. He decided he hated nightclubs and would never go near another one.

"And away we go for a nightcap. What do you say, girls?" Reardon chortled.

Why he was enjoying himself was a mystery to Kurz. He had not heard Dotty say anything smarter than Billie, but then blondes were supposed to be dumb.

"Sure. You got a bottle? We're fresh out."

"Here, there's a guy just closing up," Reardon said.

He had the iron grates on his windows, the whole works. But when he saw their badges, he went back inside and sold them a fifth of Scotch. On they zoomed to what Dotty called "our little love nest," a crummy third floor walk-up where everything smelled of garlic, even the furniture.

They mixed drinks and Billie cuddled up to him on the couch. He just barely managed to put his arm around her. The smell of her Woolworth perfume mingling with the garlic made him almost puke. He watched Reardon necking enthusiastically with Dotty on the other side of the room. Billie blew in his ear and he jumped a foot.

"What's eatin' ya, you're like a zombie or somethin'," Billie said and planted a kiss on his lips.

He gave her a squeeze. "Just a little tired," he said.

Reardon took off his coat and headed for the bedroom, giving Kurz the old wink as he went. They were a well trained team. A long time ago they worked out a routine. While one guy hit the bedroom, the other always stayed outside to watch things like guns and wallets.

Billie poured him some more Scotch, blew in his ear again and nuzzled his neck. He gave her another perfunctory squeeze and looked down at her, trying to muster a smile. It never got there because the dark hair seemed to swallow his eyes and all he could think about was Ann Macy. The contrast was too painful to endure for more than a second. He shoved Billie away and walked over to the window.

"I'm sorry, kid, I'm not in the mood. I got hurt a couple of weeks ago. Maybe you saw it in the paper." One look at her stupid face and he knew she never read the papers. "Never mind, it doesn't matter."

"Well, geez, you don't think much about my feelins. Ya coulda leasta tol me."

"I know. I'm sorry."

Reardon eventually came out of the bedroom with a satisfied smile on his face. Dotty flounced demurely, straightening her dress. Again Kurz felt bewildered. Could his old pal really enjoy it with that pig? Actually, thinking back over past outings, there was plenty of evidence that Reardon preferred hookers. Kurz suddenly remembered a speech he had given him once. ". . . No bull about moon, spoon, June. They know what you want and if it's a deal, it's a deal."

You don't really buy that, do you, Kurz? You never really bought it. You prefer the other route, the pursuit and conquest bit. You like the challenge. At least that was how you explained it. Maybe it was more than that. Maybe it involved a whole way of feeling about life, about people.

"What's this?" Reardon said, seeing Kurz by the window and Billie on the couch. "I thought by this time you two'd be making like a pair of television wrestlers."

"He's tired," Billie sneered.

"I can't believe it," Reardon laughed. "You sure that bullet hit you in the chest?"

"Yeah, I'm sure," Kurz said. "Let's go."

In the car Reardon said nothing for a while. Then he leaned against the door and gave Kurz the fisheye. "I still can't believe it. The champion himself hors de combat."

"Maybe I just don't like your taste in broads."

"They weren't that bad."

"If you don't think so, more power to you."

"For Christ's sake, when I think of some of the dogs you've trotted out."

"Sure, five years ago. Then everything was strictly for laughs."

"It isn't now?"

"I don't know. It doesn't seem that way."

Reardon hesitated. "Old buddy, you act like a guy that's got something really bugging you. I think you ought to hit up Uncle Harold for a fast transfer out of that dingy hole back up to the good old 23rd squad."

"No thanks. To tell you the truth the 23rd gets more boring every time I think about it."

"On the level?" Reardon was getting excited now. "We made some pretty good collars up there, Harry."

"And we played a lot of pinochle, too."

"I don't get it," Reardon sighed. "First I thought that bullet had hit you in the crotch. Now I think it was in the head."

"The bullet's got nothing to do with it."

They sat in muddled silence. Why couldn't you explain it? This guy was an old friend, someone with whom you'd shared a thousand working days and almost as many off-duty days. Girls, laughs, hours of batting the breeze, and you couldn't explain it to him. Maybe because you couldn't explain it to yourself.

"I don't know, Eddie. You see a partner get knocked off that way, it does something to you. I mean—we played it for laughs up in the 23rd. But you can't do it that way downtown. There just isn't that much to laugh about, in the first place."

"Come on, are you kidding?" Reardon said. "What about those stories old Benny Clark used to tell, like catching that one boogie going from the second to the third floor on the outside of the house, balls naked. Those coons are good for a million laughs."

"Maybe they were ten years ago," Kurz said. "But not any more."

"They'll never be good for anything but laughs, if you want my opinion."

It was hard to believe. But he and Reardon were having an argument about race prejudice, as they called it in the training manuals. "Christ, I'm not for them, Eddie. But when you work with them, you've got to think of them as human beings."

"Jesus," said Reardon. "The next thing you'll be donating to CORE."

"Like hell I will."

They sat there in the muggy darkness, silent once more. But now Kurz could feel the difference between them, like a wall. Maybe you really have switcherooed, Kurz. Reardon certainly seems to think so. Maybe Ann Macy has gotten deeper into you than you are into her. But it wasn't Macy, it was Moser whispering *Dancer,* it was those three boys' faces in the Moser living room, it was Marianne Moser's damp eyes.

If you have switched, Harry, that means you started on the other side—Reardon's side. You don't want to admit that. But no less surprising was Reardon's total lack of humor. "You're not exactly laughing yourself to death right now."

"You're goddamn right I'm not," Reardon snapped. "I don't think it's funny. These people want to run the fucking country. They want to run guys like you and me right off the police force."

"You're not making much sense, Eddie."

"It's the truth. Don't you read the papers? All that crap about police brutality those bleeding hearts are always handing out. What the hell is it but a gambit to try and stop cops from doing their jobs."

"There's nothing to it? You rode a car down there in the Congo, you tell me."

"Sure we roughed them up sometimes, the ones who needed it. And that's most of them as far as I could see. Stay down there a couple of years, Harry, and you'll be talking out of the other side of your mouth."

"I'm not talking out of any side of my mouth."

But you know that isn't true, Kurz. Maybe this is one game you can't play down the middle. Maybe because the rest of the players won't cooperate. He could almost feel Reardon's sullen anger pulsing in the darkness. There was obviously no point in debating him. "I'll see you around, Eddie."

"Yeah."

He slammed the door just a little too hard.

Kurz drove home feeling very tired. What the hell was happening? You just lost your best friend with that argument. But you could no more avoid the argument than you could stop breathing. All of a sudden everything seemed to be happening in ways that were impossible to control.

He fell asleep thinking about it and woke up realizing he had to make a decision about Ann Macy and her goddamn television set. It took him about sixty seconds. Precisely at nine o'clock he dialed Uncle Harold. "Where the hell can I get a color TV?"

"What do you want it for?"

"Some kids at the hospital."

He explained rapidly but efficiently how he had taught catechism to these incurable kids and promised them a TV set. Now he wanted to deliver in style.

"I'll make a few calls," Harold said.

In ten minutes he was back on the line. "They picked one up at a dispossess yesterday. There's no sheriff's sale until next month but I twisted a few arms and it's yours. This is on the level now, isn't it?"

"You want to help me lug it into the goddamn ward?"

"No. No. I mean—it just sort of took me by surprise. But—you're not the first guy I've seen change after stopping a bullet."

"Where can I pick it up?"

A half hour later Kurz was in front of the hospital, the TV set in the back of the car and Powell in the front seat to lend a hand. They lugged it down a good half mile of corridors and then Kurz spotted a rolling bed which they commandeered for the rest of the journey. Ann was at first surprised, then ecstatic when she saw them.

"Oh, Harry, it's beautiful," she said, clapping her hands in that little girl way.

In the ward the kids swarmed around it. Even the old men sat up and goggled. Kurz plugged it in down in the back where the kids' beds were.

"I don't know how to say thank you, really," Ann vowed. "And to you too, Mr. Powell."

"I just carried it," Powell said with a grin. "Here's the man that pulled all the wires."

"Oh, I know. He's an operator," Ann said, giving him a mocking smile.

"Where's little Harry?" Kurz asked.

"Oh," Ann said, her eyes darkening. "I'm afraid he's had a rather bad relapse. Would you like to see him?"

"Sure."

"I'm afraid he's not—very pleasant to look at."

She led him down the ward to a bed completely surrounded by curtains. She opened one and Kurz stepped through to look down on a boy's face and head swollen out of all proportion to his body. The same eyes, hard and defiant, peered out at him through puffy slits. The small mouth looked like something smeared on the pulpy flesh with a crayon.

Ann miraculously ignored these grotesque details. "Harry," she said in a soft, warm voice Kurz had never heard. "Look who came back to see you just like he said he would. And he's brought us a color television set."

Only the eyes moved in the swollen face. Then the mouth twisted, mumbled.

"He said thank you," Ann said.

"He's going to be okay, isn't he?"

"We don't know. He might die this time. We don't lie to each other around here, do we, Harry?"

The small eyes looked straight at Kurz. Suddenly they seemed to ask him a question that he did not want to answer.

"You'll be okay—I'll be rooting for you, Harry," he mumbled and backed hastily past the curtains into the aisle.

Ann came out a few moments later and they walked together toward the front of the ward, where Powell was waiting.

"On the level. He might die?"

"Any time—if he gets convulsions. He's been losing ground for over a year."

"Why?"

"No one knows. It's a mysterious disease. About half the children get better and the other half die."

"Are you sure you're helping him with that—you-might-die stuff?"

"I think I am," she said. "Everyone else, the priest, the doctors have lied to him. I told him the truth. For the first time someone cares enough about him to tell him the truth. It's—meant a great deal to both of us."

Standing there in the whitewashed ward beneath the glaring fluorescent lights with the old men's shrunken faces staring from beds on both sides, Kurz felt an extraordinary wave of sympathy for Ann Macy. For the first time he understood why she worked in this ward. This girl has been alone all her life, alone with nothing but her own woman's body to help her fight it. And that is what she is doing here, fighting a more serious, more total kind of loneliness. Maybe she was a kook, you didn't know what she was going to do or say next, but you had to admire her guts.

"Did Mr. Dancer deliver his television set?"

"Not yet. But he will."

"Get me the serial number and I guarantee you I'll prove it was stolen."

"Harry," she said, touching his arm with the tips of her fingers, "it doesn't really mean anything, believe me."

He stood there, helpless, a sullen zombie.

"Come to dinner this Saturday," she said. "Just the two of us?"

"Okay."

Kurz and Powell strode swiftly down the long, empty corridors to the front door.

"That Ann Macy," Powell asked, "she your girl?"

"Sometimes."

"Good looking woman."

"I know."

Why does that harmless remark make you uneasy, Kurz? If it came from Eddie Reardon it would be a compliment. Are you so bugged on the situation you can't treat any Negro as an ordinary human being? You lectured Reardon last night on that point. But the feeling obviously isn't there inside you.

"She's a funny dame," he said, forcing himself to speak casually. "The intellectual type, big on civil rights."

"No kidding. That's kind of unusual for a nurse."

"What? To have a brain or be interested in civil rights?"

"Both, I guess," Powell said, laughing.

"You chasing anything?"

"Me?" Powell looked surprised. "Oh, a little dancing now and then. But I've never been too big with the girls. I do a lot of youth work. Work a couple of nights a week at the Boys' Club."

Powell spent the ride uptown talking about the Boys' Club. It was good, Kurz thought. They were both breaking down that stupid reserve, the kind of no man's land between them that had bollixed up all his time with Bill Moser.

They stopped in the precinct diner for lunch and talked boys' club baseball over corned beef sandwiches.

"You ever play baseball yourself?"

"Hell, yes," Kurz said. "I was All-county three years in a row in high school."

"No kidding. What did you play?"

"Third base."

"Christ, we could use a good infield coach. I'm a basketball type myself. I'm teaching these kids out of a book."

"I've forgotten everything I ever knew," Kurz said.

"Come on down anyway. Maybe you'll start remembering."

Why not? You don't even have a convenient excuse. "When do you work out?"

"Coupla nights a week and Saturday morning."

"Let's try it this Saturday."

"Great."

Kurz, you are practically on your way to becoming a civil rights crusader, he thought wryly as they drove through the blazing streets of the Congo to take up their afternoon vigil outside Dancer's tenement.

"You grabbed the right guy last night," Powell said, as Kurz backed into a tight parking place. "That Porky Brown's got the biggest mouth in town. It's like putting the news about Dancer on the radio."

"Good."

Speak of the devil or something, the basement door swung open and who comes out but Mr. Dancer himself. He wasn't wearing his party clothes. He had on a tight dark blue shantung suit, very Italian style. He stood in the doorway staring at them for a moment, then walked across the street and leaned on the fender of the car.

"What's with you guys?" he said.

"What's with you?" Kurz said.

"Not a thing. I got no beefs, no worries, no complaints."

"You'll have all three by the truckload when we're through with you," Kurz said.

Dancer's smile faded. "What's the deal? You want dough? Come on inside."

"Make sure that goes in the record, Jim. He offered us a bribe."

"I got it," said Powell, scribbling in his notebook.

Dancer walked a little closer. "You're Kurz, right? Maybe you're sore about that act I pulled the other night. It was just booze, man. And I get sort of carried away when I'm with those white lefties. I mean they sort of expect me to perform."

"That's your business, not mine," Kurz said.

"Look, what's the *angle?*" Dancer said. "All day I'm getting phone calls about how I'm suddenly hot."

"Who killed Bill Moser?"

"How the hell should I know?"

"We think you know. We think we know," Kurz said.

Dancer gaped, speechless. "Me? You think I knocked off my own brother-in-law? Hell, man, I hated his guts but his kids are my blood. I'm not going to take bread out of their mouths."

"But you're glad he's dead," Kurz said. "You've been telling everybody in town you're glad he's dead."

"Sure. After the fact, man, after the fact. I hated that son of a bitch. I had good reason to hate him."

"Why don't you come down to the precinct house now and tell us what you know? It will save us both a lot of time and trouble."

"It's a bum rap, man. I didn't have anything to do with it."

"We'll be here every day from two to six. Any time you change your mind and decide to tell the truth, just come out and get in the back seat."

"Look," Dancer said, and it was delicious, he was very close to pleading. "You guys know I can't do any business with you sitting here."

"No kidding," Kurz said. "Did you realize that, Jim? I wonder what kind of business he's in when cops make him nervous."

"Funny business, maybe," Powell said.

"Okay," Dancer said, sticking out his chest. "I'm gonna take this to the top, the very top. You guys are gonna be real sorry you started this bullshit."

"I've got a feeling it's going to be the other way around," Kurz said.

You could see Dancer wilt there in the fierce sunlight. It was so obvious that he did not want trouble. "How much you really want? I can stretch——"

"Go in and rig your wheel, wiseguy, and think about telling us what we want to know."

With a farewell glare Dancer retreated down the basement steps into the dim interior of the building. Kurz spent the rest of the afternoon snapping pictures, but the traffic was noticeably lighter.

The next morning practically on schedule, Kurz got a call from O'Bannon. "I got a report here on my desk that says you guys are sitting outside Dancer's shop twenty-four hours a day."

"That's right."

"What the hell are you trying to do, put him out of business? If you do, I'll kick your ass from here to the river. This guy is strictly small fry but he's locked into something a lot bigger. We've had him under surveillance for months."

"Who's working on it?"

"None of your goddamn business. Just remember I'm giving you the word. If you fuck us up I'll hang you good and if necessary I'll string the Chief Inspector right up next to you."

"You take it up with him, Bill. You know damn well I'm working under direct orders from him."

"I'll take it up with him, don't worry. Meanwhile, remember what I said. I've got a few friends around this town too."

Kurz told Powell about the call. He looked worried. "Forget it," Kurz said. "If anyone starts swinging an ax I'll be the target."

After lunch they drove down to take up sentry duty outside Dancer's headquarters again. Like the rest of the city, the street was a furnace and the heat had melted all signs of activity. The teenagers weren't even sitting on the stoops. Kurz was busy parking when Powell said, "I don't like it."

"What?"

"Where's all the kids? And the window types?"

It was just as hot as yesterday, or hotter. There wasn't a kid on the block, not a face at the windows.

"Close the car windows quick," Powell snapped. One second later the first brick came sailing off the roof to land with a tremendous *thunk* in the middle of the hood.

"Jesus Christ," Kurz snarled and threw open the door to get out. A brick hit the door and another one hit the fender as he sprang into the street, gun in hand. Bricks bounced all around him and Powell yelled: "Get back in the car, man, they'll kill you."

Kurz fired a shot well over the heads of the throwers on the righthand roofs and they vanished. He just pointed his gun at the group on the left and they did likewise.

Now there were faces in windows from one end of the block to the other. "Put away that gun, you white son of a bitch," a fat woman screamed from the second floor just above Kurz's head. Similar advice poured down on him from all directions. In another ten seconds people were cascading out doorways into the street, a black river swarming toward him. Powell piled out of the car and joined Kurz in the street.

"I'm stickin' with you, pal, but I wish you hadn't pulled that trigger," he said.

"You and me both," Kurz said. "Follow me now, nice and slow."

Calmly, deliberately, Kurz put away his gun and he and Powell turned and strode across the street into Dancer's headquarters. It was the only move they had left. To walk down the block through that mob would have been suicide. It also took everybody by surprise. No one tried to touch them although there was plenty of noise.

They kicked open Dancer's sagging front door and shoved their way into a grubby basement apartment redesigned as an office. Weary old filing cabinets lined the walls. In the rear were two desks, a couple of typewriters and two brand new, flashy looking adding machines. There were four Negroes in the room, all very busy, two at the adding machines, one at a typewriter and Dancer himself with his nose in a filing cabinet. Without saying a word to one of them Kurz strode down the room and picked up the telephone. He dialed police headquarters. "Get the flying squad fast," he said. "Barrow Street between Sixth and Seventh."

He hung up and walked over to Dancer, who was leaning against the filing cabinet, watching him now. "You think you're going to get away with this, germ?"

"Get away with what?" Dancer said.

"Out there."

"I didn't see a thing."

Kurz walked over, picked up one of the new adding machines and threw it against the wall. The plastic case broke open and bolts and wires sprayed in all directions. "You see that?"

"I saw it."

He picked up the other adding machine and threw it even harder. It practically exploded.

"You see that?"

"Yeah," Dancer said. He looked very unhappy.

Kurz picked up the two typewriters and smashed them on the floor. He walked over to the filing cabinets, pulled out their drawers and dumped them, then kicked the folders in all directions. Numbers slips flooded up to the ceiling, a paper snowstorm.

"You're out of business, crumb."

"You bastard," Dancer said. "You no good rotten son of a bitch."

Outside in the street a siren wailed, followed by a confusion of shouts, screams and stampeding feet.

"What do you want me to do?" Dancer shrilled.

"You know what we want you to" Kurz said, walking to the window.

The flying squad was pouring out of two riot trucks. They had their white tin hats on and the lieutenant in charge was briskly ordering details left and right to clear the roofs. "Everybody back in the house now," the lieutenant began bellowing through his bullhorn. "Everybody back in the house and nobody will get hurt."

A farewell brick came floating down, thrown by someone who didn't have the nerve to come to the edge of the roof. It hit a middle-aged woman on the shoulder and she crumpled to the sidewalk wailing in agony. Cops rushed to her aid. Kurz walked over to the lieutenant whose name was Bruce. He had been his sergeant when Kurz was a rookie.

"What the hell happened, Harry?"

Squads of cops moved up and down the street, melting the crowd back into the tenements while Kurz gave Bruce a fast explanation. They walked over to examine Kurz's car. There were six or seven major dents in the hood and fenders. Somebody had whacked the rear window with a baseball bat. One tire was flat.

"One of these days we're going to have to come down here and teach these bastards a real lesson," Bruce said.

"Yeah," Kurz said. "Can we get a wrecker?"

"Sure, we'll radio."

An ambulance came clanging down the street to pick up the woman who had been hit with the brick. There was a commotion on the sidewalk a few doors from where it stopped. Two cops had come down from the roof dragging a teenager who was cursing and kicking at them. They heaved him into the back of a van. A half dozen more captives appeared in the next five minutes, most of them sullenly submissive.

"We sent details down both flanks and came up the roofs behind them," Bruce said. "I figured we'd get a few of them."

"Nice," Kurz said.

But it wasn't nice. Standing beside his battered car, staring up at all the dark faces in the open windows, he felt fantastically weary. What a mess, he thought, what a hell of a mess.

Chapter Six

An hour later he was at a typewriter in the squad room banging out a report when the telephone rang. "Harry," said Bill Callahan, the desk sergeant. "We're transferrin' those kids who threw the rocks. You want to talk to them first?"

"You bet I do."

"They're ready and waiting."

Kurz sent Powell down to get the first one. He came back escorting a stocky, barrel-chested kid with small squinty eyes, a flat nose and a wide, sullen mouth. He looked like he could put his head down and run through a brick wall. But when they took him into the interrogation room he fell apart. "Don't you hit me," he said, backing into the farthest corner.

"Nobody's going to hit you."

"You hit me and I'll be back here tonight with the Double A and CORE and the Muslims, man, I got brothers and cousins in all of them. You hit me and you'll be sorry."

"Nobody's going to hit you. Sit down," Powell said.

This time the kid sat down. In a relaxed, quiet voice Powell explained that they wanted to know who had told them to throw the bricks.

The kid shrugged. "Nobody. We jus' sorta got the idea."

"Dancer didn't tell you?" Kurz asked.

"Nope, he didn't even know it was happenin'."

"He didn't pay you to do it?"

"Nope, he didn't know it was happenin'."

"He looked like he didn't know it was happening," Kurz said.

"Listen," Powell said, his calm voice making Kurz slightly ashamed of his fury. "Why did you throw the stuff?"

"We had it in for you guys. You givin' it to Dancer on a bum rap. He didn' kill no cop."

"How do you know?" Kurz said.

"He didn' kill 'im. We know. Dancer always tell us, don' kill nobody, that's when the trouble starts."

"It's started for him all right," Kurz said.

"Listen," Powell said, "that woman who got hit, she could be hurt bad. You guys could be in a lot of trouble. You ready to go to jail for Dancer?"

"They didn' catch the guy threw that brick."

"Who was he?"

"I don' know, some guy we never saw before. He come up after we stopped throwin'."

"You think a judge is going to believe that?" Powell said.

"Look, if Dancer started this he ought to take the rap, not you," Kurz said.

"He didn' start it."

It was the same story with minor variations for the rest of them. Nobody would finger Dancer. Every one of the kids was apparently willing to go to jail first.

"You'd think the son of a bitch was a hero," Kurz said.

"He is to them."

"All by itself that's a reason for hanging his ass."

"Is it?" Powell asked, his face deadpan.

"Hell, no. I don't mean it literally, but when I think of Moser's kids——"

He told Powell about the night Marianne Moser had called him over to her house.

"Yeah," Powell said, pulling his ear, "she's going to have a tough time with those kids. When you got a father like Bill Moser and suddenly he disappears, you got to expect trouble. It's like takin' the lid off San Quentin."

"San Quentin? Was he a warden or a father?"

"A little of both, I think, but I don't really know."

Kurz arrived home to find Uncle Harold sitting in the living room looking worried as usual. His mother had turned off the television in honor of the unscheduled visit.

"I'd like to talk to Harry alone, if you don't mind, Mary. This is kind of departmental business," Harold said.

His mother withdrew to the kitchen after making one last try at keeping Harold for dinner. He took out a cigarette, lit it and puffed it in that short, hasty way that always reminded Kurz of a twelve-year-old on his first butt.

"That was quite a rumpus today."

"Nothing really happened."

"I know, but it shook up a lot of people. With all these goddamn riots in other cities the mayor is going all out to avoid one here."

"Yeah."

"And then there's O'Bannon. The Police Department is a funny thing, you know, like any big organization. A guy sort of gets to regard certain areas of command as his private property."

"Sure."

"He's mad as hell about you breaking up that guy Dancer. Says he had him under surveillance for weeks but he's small fry. When they hit they want to get it all."

"Do you believe that?"

"Of course not. O'Bannon's been taking it under the table for years. But he's got a hell of a record and the bigger fish argument is unbeatable."

"The hell with O'Bannon and his arguments. I told Dancer he was out of business and I'm going to make sure he stays that way."

"He'll stay that way now. The Mayor himself couldn't do anything for him now. But I just want you to understand, Harry, you're making yourself a lot of enemies, big ones."

"I'll worry about them later."

Harold stubbed out his cigarette and stood up. His mouth

moved, rubbery, clownlike. At first Kurz thought he was mad but instead he grabbed his arm and said, "I'm proud of you, kid. I really am."

Kurz sat and listened to a faggot announcer on the six o'clock news describing "the near race riot" on Barrow Street and again he had that sensation of weariness—or was it confusion—he had felt that afternoon, standing beside his car. The whole thing was getting more and more like a trip through a dark house without a floor plan or through a city where all the power has failed and streets run at crazy, incomprehensible angles. Somewhere in the middle you have an uneasy feeling you are going to stop dead like a little lost kid and panic.

His mother spent dinner giving him an inch by inch description of a case of poison ivy which his nephew Jack had contracted on a recent trip to the shore. Kurz retaliated by silently wondering why he could not stand one of his sister's children, not even the girls. They were all such quiet, squashed kids. Their fink of a father pictured himself as a great disciplinarian and was always batting them around. Which in turn made him wonder if his old man would have gotten that way as the years passed. Big Jim probably would have taken a very dim view of little Harry playing games in the backyard with Martha Tully.

It was tough to figure percentages in life. Like having a father—something that seemed absolutely automatically great—could actually be a liability—if your father was a fink, for instance. Of course Jim Kurz was no fink. But why had he married this woman sitting across the table from him babbling about poison ivy?

"How come you married Pop?"

"What?" Mrs. Kurz said in the middle of a disquisition on the poison ivy in Jackie's left ear.

"How come you married Pop?"

"Well," she huffed, "what kind of a question is that?"

"I was just wondering. I mean—you seem like different types. You're kind of quiet. You'd rather stay home. He was just the opposite, wasn't he?"

She gave him as good a deadeye as he'd ever seen. "For

your information I married him because he happened to be the best looking boy in my high school class. We started going together in our last year in high school and we got married the first year he went on the police force. And for your further information, I didn't stay home all the time in those days. I stay home now because I'm an old lady and I don't think old ladies belong in nightclubs."

"You're not old, you're fifty-four."

"Fifty-six."

"That's not old. Why didn't you ever get married again?"

"Because nobody asked me. What in the world are you trying to find out?"

"Nothing special, I just thought it was—more interesting than poison ivy."

"Oh."

His mother picked up their empty plates and put them down in the sink with a special clatter. She brought out apple pie for dessert and hacked him a piece as if it were somebody's throat and bumped it down in front of him. She poured the coffee, sat down and stirred her cup violently. A lot of it splashed onto the saucer.

"If I'm boring you, why don't you say so?"

"I didn't mean it that way."

She poured the coffee from the saucer into the cup. "If you want to know the real reason why I never married again, look in the mirror."

"Me? What the hell have I got to do with it?"

"What have you got to do with it? Why do you think I'm still living on this godforsaken block? If you'd gotten married when you should have—ten or twelve years ago—maybe I could have found another husband."

"What do you mean should have? Since when is there an age when someone should get married?"

"Since when. Since the day you started fooling around with floozies like Martha Tully instead of finding yourself a decent wife and settling down."

He stopped eating his pie. The woman across the table was

no longer Mother with a capital M. For the first time Kurz saw Mary Dugan, a chunky, spunky girl with a good figure and bright, snapping black eyes—the girl in the wedding picture that hung on the wall beside her bed. The ghost of her was still alive inside this grey-haired blob of a woman who fed him, made his bed and ironed his shirts. All these years you had assumed automatically that she loved you. And you loved her.

Yeah, yeah, yeah. Now you've heard the ferocity in her voice, you can see what?—maybe hate—in those glaring eyes. It's appalling—there's no other word for it—the ignorance in which you have been living your life, Kurz.

They finished their dinner in silence and he retreated to the bedroom to fill out an accident report for his insurance company. The garage estimated a hundred and fifty bucks to get rid of the dents and replace the back window in his car. It took the better part of an hour to finish the forms and he was tired and looking forward to an hour with the boob tube and then to bed when the telephone rang. It was Callahan down in the precinct.

"Harry," he said, "I hate to bother you, but I think you ought to know about this. We just pulled in four kids for breaking and entering. One of them is Bill Moser's oldest boy."

"Good Christ. What did they hit?"

"A hardware store. They were stealing knives. Carving knives."

"I'll be right down."

He called a cab and shot down to the precinct. The heat wave was holding. Everywhere people sat on porches, gasped at open windows. In the 13th it looked like all the Negroes in the city were on the streets. He could see why City Hall was worried.

Inside, the yellow lights made the crumbling walls of the old precinct house look prehistoric. Callahan sat at the desk, a stolid slab of a man. You could bring in his own mother chopped into a dozen pieces and he would make out an official report without even breathing hard. He'd been the four-to-twelve-desk sergeant in the 13th for ten years now.

"Where are they?"

"Upstairs in the pen. We booked them. The NAACP is sending down a lawyer."

"Is it a first offense for all of them?"

"All but one."

"I want to talk to the Moser kid."

"Go right ahead."

He trudged up the iron stairs to the third floor where the air was boiler room temperature. In the far corner of the squad room was a big iron cage used for temporary detention. As usual about this time of night it was getting crowded. There were a couple of drunks, a junky prostitute who was well on her way to getting the shakes and the four teenagers, all wearing identical black T-shirts and black chino pants. They were having a ball watching a detective named Carlson take down the sad tale of a visiting fireman who had lost his wallet in the Murphy game. It was one of the oldest dodges in the world—holding a clown's wallet and sending him upstairs to Mr. Murphy's for a nonexistent girl—but it still turned up a half dozen times a month.

"Boy, he got sucked in good," one of them said.

"No more black nookie for you, huh, man."

"You lucky they just took your wallet. Sometimes they perform a little operation, too."

"Yeah."

"Shut up, crumbs," Carlson said, spinning in his chair. "If you want to keep your teeth in your heads, shut up."

"Man, he tough," the tallest one said.

Carlson was about to prove it when Kurz strode over to the cage. "Billy Moser," he said, not sure which one he was.

"Yeah?" one of them said and Kurz saw the long, serious face of the boy who had stood in the living room—his mother's face—Dancer's face.

"You remember me, Harry Kurz. I want to talk to you."

"I got nuthin' to say to you."

He took the key off Carlson's desk and opened the cage door. "Come on."

Down the hall they went to the interrogation room and Kurz thought about the six times he had already gone down this hall with Negro kids today. Into the bare furnitureless room, slam the door, the same defiant sullen expression. Bill Moser's kid, he was just like the rest of them.

"I suppose you know you're in trouble."

"Sure. So what?"

"Why the hell were you stealing knives?"

"That's our business."

"You say that to a judge and he's liable to decide it's his business to give you six months to a year in Bentonville."

"So that's bad? You get a real education down there."

"Who told you that?"

"The cats that count."

"What's your mother going to think about it?"

"She doesn't think. She's just a robot that somebody wound up and she keeps on going day after day."

"What would your father think?"

"Who gives a goddamn what that son of a bitch would think? I wish he was standing here instead of you. I'd say the same thing to him."

"And what would he do?"

"He'd beat the shit out of me and I'd let him. I'd take it and just before I passed out I'd tell him—I still don't give a goddamn."

The confused feeling, the exhausting darkness sensation closed around Kurz again. "Jesus Christ," he said. "You're out of your goddamn mind, you know that? Are you trying to tell me that your father beat you up?"

"I didn't say that." The kid was quieter now as if getting all that rage out of his system had helped. "He didn't have to beat us up, we were too damn scared of him all the time. He just had to lift his hand and we grovelled."

"Billy," Kurz said, uneasy at the desperation in his own voice, "he was only trying to give you the right start in life."

Billy Moser laughed in his face. "Mr. Kurz, you are such a goddamn white square. Do you think any Negro my age is really interested in that career crap—a start in life? You think we're going to wait another hundred years workin' our way up from junior executive to assistant manager? Shit, man, we're not going to wait another year. We're gonna do our own starting. That's why we wanted those knives. And then we're gonna get guns. The next time you come down our streets with those riot wagons and white hats you're gonna get a lot more than bricks from those roofs."

"If I was in one of those wagons you'd shoot me?"

"I'd shoot you right now if I had a chance. I'd shoot any cop and that includes the great Bill Moser—the original Uncle Tom."

"You're sick, Buster. Do you know that? You're really sick."

"And you're not?"

Billy Moser gave him a smile Kurz had never thought he'd see on a fifteen-year-old face. He had to catch himself inside, give himself a shake. *This is just a kid shooting off his mouth.* But bugs still kept crawling up and down his nerves. What the hell could he say? Was there any answer to the fantastic hatred that gushed out of this kid's guts?

Screw it. Kurz decided to say exactly what he felt. "You know what you just did? You turned me completely around. You turned me from a friend into an enemy."

"You were an enemy before we started. You're white and you're a cop."

"No, sonny, that's wrong and you know it's wrong. I dragged my ass out of an air conditioned bedroom to come down here and spend an hour with you in this sweat box. I wish now I hadn't bothered."

He sagged a little. "I didn't ask you to come," he said.

"Let's go," Kurz said, opening the door.

Billy's friends were no longer in the pen. They were downstairs, conferring with their lawyer, who turned out to be Mr. NAACP in person, the big, pompous guy who had talked Kurz into the rug that night in the Moser living room. "Did they ask you to sign anything?" he was inquiring as Kurz restored Billy Moser to the group.

"No."

"Did they threaten you, or beat you up, use force in any way after they arrested you?"

"One of them twisted my arm real bad," said the tallest kid, a big butterball with a round, seemingly good-natured face.

"That made him drop his knife," Bill Callahan explained in a perfectly neutral voice.

"And what were you doing upstairs with this boy, Detective?"

It took Kurz a moment to realize Mr. NAACP was looking at him. "I was talking to him. His father happens to be—or was—a good friend of mine."

"Did he interrogate you? Use force?"

"No," Billy said in a subdued voice.

"I presume you know that the Supreme Court takes a very dim view of questioning a prisoner before he has had a chance to obtain advice from his lawyer."

"I wasn't questioning him. I didn't make the arrest," Kurz snapped.

"All right," said Mr. NAACP to his clients. "They'll take you down to the City Jail now. There'll be a hearing in the morning, and your cases will be referred to juvenile court. Behave yourselves and don't cause any trouble in jail. Unless someone tries to mistreat you."

He turned back to Callahan. "You're sure, Sergeant, that these boys will not be sequestered again with adult offenders?"

"If there's an available cell downtown, they won't," Callahan said.

"I'm going to take this issue directly to the Mayor's Office."

"Great," said Callahan. "Maybe he'll tear down this mausoleum and put up a real building. Now, I want to ask you something. What do you think these kids were planning to do with two hundred carving knives?"

"I haven't the faintest idea. Throw them at telephone poles maybe. What do kids do with knives?"

"I got a feeling they were going to throw them at people," Callahan said. "You know who they are?"

"They're four boys who have committed a minor infraction of the law."

"You don't know why they wear those black T-shirts and black pants?"

"Boys like to travel in packs."

"They belong to a new gang, the VC's. Do you know what that stands for?"

"No, I don't. And frankly, Sergeant, I'm not really interested in this routine. Where is the van you ordered to take these boys downtown? I left an important meeting to come down here."

"VC," Callahan said. "It stands for Viet Cong. These kids think they're guerrillas. Doesn't that worry you?"

"Of course it worries me. We'll report it to the youth board. New gangs keep forming and reforming all the time."

Callahan sighed and went back to shuffling his papers. Billy Moser and his friends watched and listened with snide grins on their faces. They were having a ball, watching their man tell off the fuzz. A young cop with a perspiration-stained shirt came in the door. "Them prisoners for downtown ready?"

"Right there," Callahan said, pointing to the VC's.

"Billy Moser stays here," Kurz said. "I'll take him home with me on a Captain's bond."

"That smacks of police favoritism to me," said Mr. NAACP. "Why should these boys spend a night in jail while he——?"

"They're spending the night in jail because you're a windbag lawyer that couldn't get a favor from a cop even if he was your own brother. When you wise up and realize you've got some responsibility for what's happening down here, maybe you'll really help a few of your clients."

Mr. NAACP took a deep breath and said nothing. The Viet Cong filed out, leaving Billy Moser glaring at Kurz.

"I don't want your goddamn help," he said.

"I don't care whether you want it or not, you're getting it," Kurz said. "Now sit over there and shut up."

Callahan called a local bondsman, and Kurz paid his fee. While the papers were being signed, Kurz phoned Marianne Moser and told her what was happening. She burst into tears. "I knew it, I knew it from the way he's been acting."

"I'll have him home in a half hour," Kurz said. "We can talk about it."

Billy Moser sat on a bench on the other side of the big room, a study in morose defiance. Callahan stared at him, shaking his head. "It sounds crazy but a bunch of kids like that could blow up this goddamn thing. All we need is one attack on a cop. He shoots in self-defense and bingo, we'll be calling out the National Guard."

"You really think it's that bad?"

"I know it's that bad. You should hear what the guys are saying—the guys on the beats. Teddy Franciosa had a brick miss him by six inches last night. You know how they walk down the streets now? Zigzag, to avoid the street lights. Anybody that stands under a street light for more than two seconds is asking for a fractured skull. I'm thinking of asking for helmets, I really am."

Out on the street, Kurz remembered he had no car. And cruising cabs were nonexistent in the Congo. The darkness, the black faces swirling past, the hot dirty air, Billy Moser walking sullenly beside him—it all combined to give Kurz the feeling that he was suddenly in danger of suffocating—or going crazy. He needed help. He stepped into a corner phone booth and dialed Jim Powell. Quickly Kurz told him what had happened.

"It sounds real bad," Powell said. "I'll pick you up in my car in ten minutes."

He was there in five. They rode swiftly down the crowded avenues, past the neon bars and the white windows of the clothing and jewelry stores, all with their wire mesh screens up. Kurz told Powell what he thought of the NAACP lawyer, using all the adjectives.

"Sure, he's a buttonhead. A lot of people know it. The younger crowd down there are tryin' to ease him out gradually. But you got to remember all the years he went into that precinct house and those cops shit all over him, wouldn't even let him see his clients. Now he throws his weight around too much. It's human nature."

Another lecture. You were getting tired of lectures from Powell. Maybe because he was telling the truth. Maybe because you were just tired.

There were no parking places near the Moser house. They had to walk two blocks down the dark street past porches filled with laughter and movement. The sound stirred in Kurz a memory of high school nights when he used to walk through Negro streets on the way home from a party or a dance. Once he had stopped, startled by a burst of mocking laughter from a shadowy porch. His fists had clenched. He was sure they were laughing at him, and were about to come charging out of the darkness to pound him into the gutter. Other nights when he and the gang from the block went out on war parties looking for Negroes to beat up. It was considered a combination sport and vigilante activity. It kept them out of the neighborhood. But that night alone on the Negro street, nothing had happened. Only the laughter, the gust of fear—nothing else. Crazy. Why were you thinking about it now?

They clumped up the Moser porch steps, rang the bell and trudged to the second floor. Marianne Moser waited for them at the doorway of the living room, her face sodden with grief. Billy Moser was sent to his room. Kurz explained Powell. "I thought—maybe he could help——"

Marianne Moser managed to smile.

"I think I went to school with you a long time ago," Powell said. "P. S. 31, the fifth-grade."

"Mrs. Emerson?"

"Real fat. Steel spectacles. A nut on arithmetic."

"That's her," Marianne Moser said. "I'm afraid I don't remember you."

"I was just up from the South," Powell said. "I was afraid to talk to anybody. Especially the prettiest girl in the class. I wound up gettin' left back."

She led them into the living room and they sat down.

"You've got a real mixed up boy there," Kurz said. He gave her a very mild version of his session in the interrogation room.

Marianne Moser broke down completely. All they could do was sit there helplessly watching her weep. "I don't know what to do," she sobbed. "I just don't know. He won't even talk to me."

"Where did he get those ideas about his father?"

"Well," Marianne Moser said a little more calmly, "Bill was pretty strict. He always figured we had to be with three boys. And in this neighborhood."

"Did he ever hit them?"

"Not lately. He didn't have to. When they were little he whipped them a lot. I used to stop him sometimes. I thought he was laying it on too hard. But I appreciated it later when all I had to do was say 'I'll tell your father,' and they'd jump a mile for me. But now—" Her voice trembled toward tears again. "It's this neighborhood. We live on a nice block but what's he find when he walks off it? Delinquents, junkies, Muslims. Even before this happened I was thinking—I've got to get them out of this neighborhood."

"Where you thinking of going?" Powell said in that quiet, almost toneless voice.

"I don't know. Isn't there—someplace? I mean the Urban League's been talking about it for years."

"That's all they been doin'—talkin'," Powell said. "I don't know of a place that isn't lily white."

Silence.

"Goddamn it," Kurz said, "that's unbelievable. Have you got the money to move?"

"Yes. Bill carried a lot of insurance."

"You pick out where you want to move and we'll get you in. I think it would be a good idea, don't you, Jim? It would give the kids something to think about besides making like Viet Cong."

"Could be," Powell said. "But it isn't going to be easy."

Marianne Moser's eyes enveloped them in damp gratitude. "I'll never be able to say thank you."

"We'll get to work on it tomorrow."

"In the meantime," Powell said, "I was wondering if Billy liked baseball. We got a league going down at the Boys' Club. I'm the coach. Do you think he'd like to come down to practice at Roosevelt Park two nights a week—Tuesdays and Thursdays?"

"I'll make sure he's there," Marianne Moser said, giving Powell a smile that Kurz noted with an odd pang. It was more alive than anything he had ever gotten from her.

Out on the street Kurz said, "Okay, now I've shot my mouth off, how do I deliver?"

"That's a good question," Powell said. "I think maybe tomorrow we ought to go see the Urban League people. They got a fair housing program going on paper anyway. Maybe they might figure she'd be a good test case. You know, widow of a hero cop and all that bit."

They got in the car and Powell offered to drive him home. After a minute or two he suddenly said, as if there had been no break in the conversation, "I guess when you live with a guy like Bill Moser, you don't need to be strong. And you wind up kind of weak."

"Yeah," Kurz said.

"It's that way in a lot of Negro families," Powell said. "The guys who make it are so tough they beat down their wives and kids to nothing and the guys who don't make it hit the road, like my old man."

"Yeah," Kurz said.

"Bill Moser really got to me. I thought he was practically God for a while there. I guess it was just—not having a father —you know, you get a real man to pay some attention to you and it's like Christmas every day. But since I come on the cops I've been changin' my mind little by little about him. I think he did it wrong in a lot of ways. I mean, his intentions were good but he did it wrong."

"Christ, nobody's perfect," Kurz said.

"I know. But I think maybe Moser was real wrong in some things."

They were on Western Avenue now, only a block from Kurz's home. Donahue's Bar blinked its neon cocktail shaker at them.

"You in a hurry?" Kurz said.

"Not especially."

"Let's go have a beer."

It was just past eleven and Donahue's was still pretty crowded. Kurz came in first and a dozen heads swung, smiles of greeting spread. "Hey, Harry—Harry." But the smiles did not keep on coming, the voices faded prematurely.

"What do you say, men?" he barked, noting the averted heads, the rolled eyeballs, the frown on Blubber Donahue's forehead, behind the bar.

The whole thing was very small and he was sure Powell noticed nothing. There was room at the far end of the bar, out of television range, but Donahue was so busy washing glasses he could not find time to take their orders. Kurz waited one minute and then snapped, "Hey, Blubber, two beers down here."

Blubber waddled down and planted the steins in front of them with an emphatic thud. Nothing to it, he does that all the time, Kurz told himself. You are seeing, hearing things.

They drank beer for a minute or two. "It's funny what you say about Moser. Sometimes I wonder how I'd get along with my old man today. He was kind of like Moser. Big, rough."

"What happened to him?"

"He got himself shot, the stupid bastard. Went down an alley after a mugger. The guy had a gun."

"Must have been tough to lose a man like that."

"It was."

"I don't even remember my old man. He disappeared when I was about three. My mother got married again, and again, and again."

"And you're a cop. According to the magazine stories you ought to be doing ten to twenty somewhere right now."

"I know it," Powell said.

"What pulled you through?"

"I don't know. You get a little something here, a little something there from different people. A lot of guys Bill Moser talked to are doing ten to twenty right now. I can't figure it out."

"Crazy," Kurz said. "What do you hear about Dancer?"

"I'll tap the fat man on the way home," Powell said, finishing his beer.

Kurz said he'd walk home and Powell drove off with a wave. In the house Kurz got another beer from the ice box and watched twenty minutes of a musical on television. One of the ingénues was a dead ringer for Ann Macy, which made him think with more than a little warmth about Saturday night. He was just getting into bed when the telephone rang.

"Is this Harry Kurz?" a muffled voice said.

"That's right."

'This is one of the regula patrons at Donahue's Bar and Grill. I'm speakin' for every regula patron in the place, and the own, when I say this. If you wanna drink with ya boogie friends, do it down in their neighborhood."

"Come up here and say that to my face, you son of a bitch," Kurz roared.

The line was dead.

For a minute he thought about putting on his clothes again and charging down to Donahue's. He was sure the call had come from there. But what could you do? No one would admit it. He lay there seething for another hour before he fell into a restless sleep. He dreamt he and Ann Macy were alone on a wide tropical beach, a world of white sand, blue sky and blue water. She wore absolutely nothing, he likewise. Lazily she rolled over on top of him and began to nibble the tip of his nose. Her skin was silk, her hair soft as the wind.

Suddenly from the jungle burst a fantastic army of Negro warriors, giants seven feet tall with white death's heads painted on their black shields. Slowly, sullenly, they advanced, their long spears upraised. Macy knelt beside him whispering *They won't hurt us. They won't hurt us.* Suddenly the air was black with spears, like a flock of huge birds flying south.

Jesus.

He was awake. Dawnlight filtered greyly past the window. He went to the bathroom, crawled back in bed and lit a cigarette. It was just a dream. Sure, just a dream. But the day after you nail Mr. Dancer, you are going to transfer the hell out of the 13th precinct.

Chapter Seven

Powell was waiting for him in the squad room when Kurz arrived.

"I called this guy I know at the Urban League," he said. "He thought they could do a lot with the Mosers. He's going to call me back this morning."

"Good," Kurz said. "What's the word on Dancer?"

"The fat man says he's out of business. The guy who was bankrolling the wheel pulled out."

"What was his name?"

"Nobody seems to know. Except he's white and has syndicate connections."

"What's Dancer doing?"

"He spent last night gettin' drunk."

"That's good. He's taking it hard."

Powell answered the phone. He listened, hung up and shook his head wearily. "That was the guy from the Urban League. He says they can't do a thing. They had a real estate man leaning their way out in the Dellwood section. But the guy says he won't touch a single woman. Says everytime a man called on her all the white neighbors would be sure she was——"

"What a cowardly son of a bitch."

They sat there. Images jumped through Kurz's mind—Marianne Moser's sodden face, Billy Moser in his all black

Viet Cong suit. "Negroes are living in the suburbs in other cities. What the hell is wrong with this one?"

"Not much punch to our Negro organizations," Powell said, "and the state's Civil Rights Commission is just window dressing."

The first time he got the idea, Kurz dismissed it. But there was that kid in the Viet Cong outfit, the wavering helpless mother, Bill Moser in the ambulance whispering *Dancer*.

"Listen," he said, "what if we pulled an end run? What if I went out and bought the goddamn house and then sold it to the Mosers. What could they do?"

"Raise hell."

"Sure, but they'd be in, right?"

"I don't know," Powell said cautiously. "The Department might not see it our way."

He was right, of course. "Let's think about it for a day or two. There might be another angle."

They spent the next two days on Dancer. The tapes of the action in his room were disappointing. He was almost never there. The few phone calls he made were so monosyllabic Kurz found himself wishing they had tapped the line. But that required a court order, and he was not sure they could have gotten it. Around town, they used the fat man and a few other pigeons to keep them up to date on Dancer's moves. They did not have much to say, either. Dancer was drinking a lot, and talking big, telling everyone he was on vacation, looking around for a chance to invest some real money.

If the money was real, it wasn't coming from numbers. Everything had vanished from the basement flat on Barrow Street. The gambling squad had vacuumed the place—and no one had so much as peeped at Dancer. The head of the gambling squad, Eddie Garrick, was a good friend of Deputy Chief Inspector O'Bannon. Sometimes Kurz wondered whether one lowly detective, telling everything he knew to the mayor, couldn't clean up the whole city in forty-eight hours. The idea was ridiculous, of course. It went against the Department's unwritten law: you don't fink on your own. Solidarity, that's all they had as cops and they needed every bit of it, Kurz thought moodily as a contingent of teenagers, most of them probably rooftop rock throwers, eyed them angrily.

"I get the feeling we're not too popular on this block."

"That Dancer," Powell said, "he was good at sprayin' his money around. I think we sort of broke their rice bowls."

"Tough."

Back in the squad room there was a call from Marianne Moser. Kurz returned it and found her awash in tears and near hysteria. Billy Moser had not come home last night nor had he appeared in school today.

"Maybe he stayed at a friend's house. He just wants to scare you. You know how kids are."

"No, he's with Dancer. I know he is. Dancer's been after that boy for years."

"Do you want us to send out an alarm for him?"

"No—if you could just—do it quietly?"

"We'll check Dancer out anyway."

Powell sat there smiling as Kurz hung up. "Some more babysitting?"

"In spades. I mean—" Kurz floundered, embarassed by the unintentional pun. But Powell did not seem to notice it. "She thinks he's with Dancer."

"Why don't we grab an earpiece and take a run down to the hotel?"

They drove through the hot twilit streets to the shabby entrance of the Carver Hotel. The desk clerk was a tall, spare man with a beak nose and sharp, prominent cheekbones. He peered noncommittally at them through steel-rimmed glasses when they asked for Dancer. "His key is missing. I believe he's in his room."

"Have you seen a kid with him—about fifteen?"

"Quite a few young boys come in to see him. I really couldn't say."

"Mr. Wanamaker around?"

"In his office."

Wanamaker grabbed Kurz's hand and shook it like a politician on the day before election. He was just a little too eager. "You sure puttin' the heat on him," he haw-hawed. "You sure are. Word's all over town Dancer's hot as a pistol."

"Still got a vacancy next door?"

"Absolutely."

"We're going up for a visit."

"Any time, Detective, any time."

The Hotel Carver had not been redecorated since the Civil War. Twenty-five-watt bulbs glowed in gas lamp fixtures. The pattern in the threadbare red carpet had long since vanished. The air was thick and foul in the hall and not much better in the closet next door to Dancer's room.

"Open the window, for Christ's sake," Kurz whispered as he took the bugging equipment out of the brief case. It vaguely resembled stethoscopes. A pair of ear pieces was connected to metal listening discs which attached to the wall.

The first thing they heard was Dancer's voice, loud and clear. *"Listen, Cap, for the tenth time, you can't stay with me. Your mother ever finds out you been here she'll be on my trail with a carving knife."*

"And I told you I don't want to live another day with that dumb bitch."

"Say, steady, pal, she's my sister you know."

"She's still a dumb bitch."

"Kiddo, don't take it out on her. Your old man was the foul ball. What could she do but go along?"

"She could have walked out on him."

"She loved the guy. She don't know what he did on the job. What everybody thought of him. Hell, compared to most husbands in this town, he gave her a good life."

"What Uncle Tom doesn't?"

Dancer laughed briefly. *"Now you got me, kid. Now I don't know what to say. But we can't team up. It's absolutely no dice. I'm down to loose change, kid. I'll be bumming free meals from Whitey by the end of next week if somethin' don't break."*

"They really wiped you out."

"Yeah, that bastard Kurz. Your father must have fed him that line of his. The guy's really bugging me. He's even grabbed off one of my old girls. Only last week I was thinking——"

"She's white?"

"White. But what a body. Like I told you, it's not the color, it's the shape, the response that counts."

"I don't go for white chicks. I never will."

"You got to be cosmopolitan, man. It's the style. You want to be a nigger all your life?"

"I want to be a man and I want them to know it. I want to rip their goddamn guts out."

"Sure, buddy, sure, when the time comes. I'll be with you, man, on those barricades when the time comes. But right now they got the power. We got to swing with them just far enough to get them off balance."

"I think maybe the Muslims are right. You swing with them and they wind up owning you."

"Like shit. Do they own me? Do they own what's in my head? I bullshit them blind, man. They don't know what's in my head."

"What you gonna do, start another wheel?"

"Can't do that without money. The kingpin says I'm too hot, I got to wait at least six months. The Guinea bastard."

"Come on in with us VC's—you got a score to settle. Come on in with us and we'll do something big."

Dancer laughed again. *"Like what?"*

"Maybe hold up a white bank, publish a speech. You can write it. You got the gift of gab."

"A manifesto! Hey—what would it say?"

"The time has come to redistribute Whitey's money."

"Hey, you'd really shake them up with that, wouldn't you? You'd make every newspaper in the country."

"Damn right. And even if some of us got caught we'd get off light. Them white politician judges would be scared shitless."

"Hey—I bet they would. What happens to the money?"

"We'd give it all away just like we said."

"Bullshit, pal. We keep a little. Enough to set me up on my own. I only need twenty-five, maybe fifty grand. When you hit a bank you can walk off with a half million."

"Sure. You write the stuff. You get some of those white professors on our side. We'll give you fifty grand."

Dancer laughed, longer and louder this time. *"Hey, kid, you know something, you're crazy. But I love you."*

"It's not crazy."

"Sure it is. It's crazy smart. Crazy Negro. It makes Negro sense, kid. You let me know when you're ready to move. I'll be there with you."

"We'll let you know."

"But right now—get your ass home and don't tell your old lady where you've been."

"Don't worry."

The door slammed. There was a creak of springs as Dancer apparently threw himself onto his bed. A radio began playing rock and roll.

Kurz yanked his listening button loose and looked at Powell. He took off his earpiece and left his equipment dangling on the wall.

"He doesn't exactly sound like a criminal mastermind, does he?" Powell said, walking over to the open window.

"Do you think maybe Wanamaker's in with him? That whole spiel was an act?"

"Wanamaker's scared of cops."

"Let's pick up the tapes downstairs and go listen for a while."

They went down in the elevator to Wanamaker's office and found one reel used up. They drove back to the precinct house and put it on the machine there. Once more Dancer's strident, edgy voice filled Kurz's ears.

"Professor Slater? This is Dancer. I'm just fine. You know, Professor, I was wonderin'. You were real pleased with that stuff I got for you on your book and you know, it only sort of skimmed the surface. Now I was wonderin' if you could get

me a grant from one of them foundations, maybe three, four thousand dollars and I could really do a job. I mean I could get you conversations with junkies, pushers, second story men, pickpockets. I mean, I know them all. It would be no sweat at all for me.

"Oh. You need a sheepskin. Well, I mean couldn't you sort of front for me? Couldn't you sort of say that you were workin' with me? That would be the truth, wouldn't it?

"Oh. Well, Prof, I just thought I'd ask. I got some free time, you know? Why not make a little money instead of just burnin' it? That's the way I was thinkin'."

The tape went dead for ten seconds. Then Dancer was on the telephone again. *"Garden Square Journal? Let me speak to Jim Devine. Hello, Jim? This Dancer. Listen, baby, remember that time a couple of months ago we got talkin' about maybe writin' a book on my life? I mean, we could blow the lid off this town. I been makin' notes on it, I got enough stuff here about the Negro from the inside to go a hundred, maybe two hundred pages. It would read like a novel, man, with you doin' the writin'.*

"Yeah. Oh, I know you got this other book. But I figured maybe in your spare time . . .

"Well, don't let it worry you. I'm not goin' nowhere. I just thought you'd like to know what's on my mind. Any time you're ready, baby, any time."

There was a crash of a phone against a receiver and a muttered curse. *"He got to listen to me, the son of a bitch."*

Dancer gave the operator another number. *"Hello, Mr. Santini? I want Mr. Santini. This is Dancer. No, I don't want to talk to Lou. I want to talk to Mr. Santini. I'll wait." Pause. "Mr. Santini? Look, I'm gonna put it to you straight. I'm flat, see. This thing couldn've blown at a worse time. I dropped a bundle in a coupla rough games last week. I need some dough bad. Can't you put me on another wheel? You know how many friends I got. I can bring the people in. I deliver, you know that.*

"Shit, Mr. Santini, you can fix those two dicks. All you got

to do is pick up the phone. You're kidding me. You got the mayor in your pocket. He ain't no more reform—Mr. Santini! How about pushin' five hundred my way. I mean just until this thing cools down. Mr. Santini——"

Again the phone clunking angrily into its cradle. More curses. Then another number. *"Hello, Wanamaker? This is Dancer. Yeah, right upstairs. Listen, pal, I've been pretty tied up with other activities, I guess you know. But there's an idea I got for your place. I mean I think you're missin' a real chance to make a bundle here with a nice quiet game in one of these here top floor rooms. Nuthin' big, you know, just blackjack. All you need's a dealer and me to pull the guys in. A little food and booze. It wouldn't cost more'n a hundred dollars a week and I'd split the house cut with you fifty-fifty, split the payoffs the same way. What do you say, man? What? Why, you dumb bastard, I'm giving you a chance to make five grand a month tax free. I mean there are guys who would pay me twice that dough to organize a game for them.*

"Go to hell yourself, you little prick! If you see me comin' you'd better cross the street."

Thunk went the phone and the tape went dead as if the sound had been a knockout blow. Then Dancer was talking again. *"Hey, baby, I'm real low. Buy a bottle and come on over. I could use a laugh."*

Silence, finally broken by a woman's voice. *"What's the matter with you, man?"*

"You didn't hear? You must be the only one. Some cops busted up my wheel. Put me out of business."

"Jeez-us. Here, have a drink. What'd you do?"

"That's the hell of it, I didn't do nuthin', but this one cop got me down for knockin' off Bill Moser. You got any money, baby?"

"You must be kiddin'. I loan my brother fifty bucks last Saturday and he lose it all on a horse."

"Sometimes I wonder, baby, sometimes I really do. Sometimes I'd like to tear this whole goddamn city up. When I think of you out on the street, baby."

"Ah, don't you worry about me. Doris take care of huhself all right. I don't even think about it. I really don't."

"Even when he's white you don't think about it?"

"Especially when he's white."

"You get a lot of white, don't you?"

"Enough. They pay real money."

"Maybe we could get a Murphy game goin'. I'd love to get an act like that with you, baby."

"Not me, lover boy. That's five to ten if the guy puts up a fight and you got to hit him."

"I'd hit him. Oh, I'd love to hit him. 'Boy,' I'd say, 'here it comes, and I'd give him the blackjack right in the teeth."

"Five to ten, lover. Have another drink."

A long silence. *"What am I gonna do, baby? I'm really down."*

"Hell, I don't know. It'll cool off maybe in a week. Things change, you know. If you got to have a couple bucks to pay the rent, I can find some."

"Why do I fool around with white girls, baby, when I got you?"

"You ain't got me, lover, nobody's got me. But—if anybody did—it'd be you."

A kiss. Murmured words.

"Baby—Oh, do that again." The creak of bed springs. *"Lover . . ."*

Suddenly Kurz found himself wishing their equipment was not quite so good. The goddamn microphone picked up every sound. He flipped off the machine and sat looking at Powell. He felt vaguely embarrassed, as if he had been caught doing something stupid.

"I'm starting to wonder about this boy," Powell said.

"Yeah," Kurz said, "me too."

Neither said what he was wondering but it was easy enough to spell it out. Their tiger was looking more and more like a mouse. That was a nice way to put it. That eliminated the feeling you had while you listened to those tapes, the sad, empty feeling that came with knowing the inside of another human being's life. Suddenly he remembered Ann Macy's face, those fierce words on the beach. *We're all in the other person's place. That's what being human means.*

The hell with that, Kurz. Screw the bleeding heart. Can you really start worrying about what happens to a two-bit gambler with the brains of a sixteen-year-old? Does it really matter?

That made him feel better. He was almost cheerful when he said goodbye to Powell. He drove home through the crowded, sweltering streets, barely seeing the black faces, his eyes full of delicious images of tomorrow night's date with Ann Macy.

She opened the door almost instantly and stood there smiling. She was wearing a light blue sweater and jet black pants that were all but molded to her legs. A gold clasp gleamed in her dark hair. He was severely tempted to kiss her, but he restrained himself and simply said, "Hey, you look great."

"Thanks," she said.

She had both air conditioners going. The apartment was cool. Even the sound they made, the steady, rhythmic hum, was cool.

They had martinis, two of them, ice cold, very dry.

They talked about the heat. They talked about little Harry. He was still very sick.

He asked about school. "A bore," she said.

She put on some music, a piano, a violin, playing clear, bright, intricate melodies. "Beethoven," she said, "early Beethoven."

"I prefer early Dorsey," he said.

She laughed.

She went out to the kitchen. Beethoven filled the room with his own coolness. The air conditioners thummed.

"Dinner," she said.

They sat by the window looking down on the river. It was dark and boats went by, lights aglow, ghostly. The city gleamed dully on the water.

Dinner was good, boned chicken in white wine sauce. He opened a bottle of ice cold rosé and let the taste mingle. For dessert there was Black Forest cake, a dozen kinds of sweetness on the tongue.

"You don't look like a cook," Kurz said.

"I'm not. You scared me with all that gourmet conversation at the shore."

They watched the lights move on the river for a long time. Beethoven stopped playing.

"Waterloo Bridge is on television. I've got to see it."

They sat and laughed at the old sob story. It was fun. Amazing, it was really fun.

More music, drowsy. It sounded like Sammy Kaye.

"Let's dance," she said.

He lost track of time. She drifted with him to the dreamy music, her hair full of faint perfume.

They kissed.

There was music in the bedroom too. It drifted around them as they touched each other, lips to throat, breasts. Hands to thighs.

It was like the dream, Kurz thought, the dream on the beach. Only better. Everything seemed to be in slow motion, even their breathing. You don't want it to stop, he thought. You never felt that way before. You don't want it to end.

But it ended. And again there was only the music.

They lay very still, side by side. "Don't go home," she said. "Stay for the night."

"All right," he said.

Later in the darkness her hand touched his shoulder. "Are you happy?" she said.

"What a question," he said.

"I've been thinking about you all week," she said. "I finally decided you didn't believe in anything, not even happiness, and I thought maybe, if I made you happy for a whole night you might start believing in it."

As if he had suddenly emerged from a thunderclap or a lightning flash, Harry Kurz, connoisseur swordsman and professional cop, returned. His reentry was almost physical.

There was a kind of ripple that ran from the back of his head down his spine. *Now comes the pitch, Harry old kid. The why can't we be happy this way forever bit.*

But Harry old kid was wrong. The voice whispering in the darkness only said: "You probably think that sounds crazy. But I didn't think there was any harm in trying."

"Thanks," he said. "It was the best dinner I've had in years."

"And now you think I'm a kook as well as a cook."

"Right," he said, and kissed her once, hard. "But kooks don't scare me. Go to sleep."

She went instantly. It took him longer. He lay there trying to figure out what the hell had happened. Who was that character who sat there listening to Beethoven, drinking wine, laughing at *Waterloo Bridge?* It wasn't Harry Kurz. Somehow, sometime during the evening he had been faked right out of existence. Amazing.

And his emergency return was pretty superfluous.

Still it was good to have him back.

The phone rang and rang. The room was still totally dark. But Ann found it and Kurz listened while she said: "Yes. Oh, no—I thought he was—I'll be there in fifteen minutes."

"What's up?" Kurz asked.

"Harry is dying. He keeps calling for me."

"I'll drive you over."

"No. I can walk."

"Like hell you can. Not in this neighborhood."

In ten minutes they were in the hospital parking lot. The huge white buildings loomed above them. "Do you want to come in?" Ann said.

"Can I do anything?"

"Probably not. No one can do anything now."

Maybe she wanted him to come. Maybe she even needed him. "I'm with you. Let's go."

They walked swiftly down the dim empty corridors, their footsteps resounding. Once as they passed a ward, a voice cried out in pain. The city peered up at them through the long rectangular windows. It was 3:30 A.M., Kurz noted, looking at his watch for the first time.

They finally turned right and walked through almost total darkness to the patch of light coming from the duty office. There sat a plump nurse with a snub Irish nose and a wide mouth fixed in a grimace that made you think she had just swallowed a lemon. Kurz was introduced to Mrs. Dillon.

"He's—a friend of Harry's," Ann said.

"Maybe he can talk to him," Mrs. Dillon said. "The priest is in with him now."

"Oh, why?" Ann said. "All he does is torment him."

"You know where I think that child is going?" Mrs. Dillon said. Her eyes glittered and the puffy lines of her face suddenly seemed to harden. "I think he's going straight to hell."

"He's in hell right now," Ann said.

"You go in there and look at that child. And ask yourself if you still believe in your damn atheism." Almost pointedly Mrs. Dillon turned to Kurz. "She's such a grand girl, as I'm sure you know. But she doesn't have this much faith."

She held up her hand, the fingers pinched.

What do you do? Smile, shrug, admit it, deny it? Say nothing.

She walked swiftly into the ward. Kurz followed her, wishing he'd stayed in the car. They tiptoed past the rows of old men snoring and snorting and snuffling in the darkness. A glow of light came from the curtains around Harry's bed. The curtains parted and Dr. Weinberg's mournful Jewish face peered out at them. "Hello," he said to Ann. "I just took a chance you might be able to come. I just thought—somebody should be here."

"I'm glad you did," Ann said.

"One more convulsion could do it," Weinberg said. "He's had six since midnight."

Ann nodded and stepped inside the curtains. Kurz hesitated, eyeing Weinberg.

"Go ahead," Weinberg said. "It's—nice of you to come."

He lumbered away in his heavy-footed fashion.

The first thing Kurz saw as he stepped through the curtain was Harry's face. He was propped up on his pillows and his eyes blazed out at Kurz with a fierce, contemptuous anger. The hospital chaplain, the same fumbling old priest Kurz had met, sat at the head of the bed. Ann Macy stood at the foot, her hands gripping the white metal frame. The old priest leaned toward Harry, whispering huskily, "I will give you one more chance, Harry, one more chance to make your Confession so you can receive your first Communion."

Harry spit in his face. At first Kurz could not believe what he had seen. He had to say it to himself: *He spit in his face.*

The old priest recoiled, rubbing away the drool. "Harry," he muttered and lurched to his feet.

"Get rid of him," Macy whispered fiercely to Kurz. "Get rid of him."

Why me, Kurz was about to say, when Harry made a choking, gurgling sound and slid down the pillows, his head jerked back and the person vanished from his face. His body arched to an incredible height under the covers.

Ann Macy brushed past the priest, almost knocking him through the curtains. She leaned over the bed and put her arms around Harry. "I'm here, Harry," she whispered. "I'm here. I won't go away no matter how long it takes."

The priest revolved down the bed and stared dazedly at Kurz.

"Why don't you leave her alone with him for a few minutes, Father?"

"Yes," the old man muttered, "maybe—you're right."

Kurz guided him through the curtains into the darkened ward.

"I never saw—anything like it. A child——"

"He's had a rough life, Father," Kurz whispered, "and some of these old men probably——"

"Yes, yes, but a child his age——"

"Yes."

"Do you know him, can you talk to him? His soul is at

stake. I'm sure of it. He *knows* what he is saying and doing. He is accepting damnation."

A tremor ran down Kurz's nerves. Here in this silent humid ward, thirty years away from the childhood classrooms, the old words still had power.

"Can you talk to him?" the old priest murmured, clutching his arm.

"I'll try, Father, I'll try."

"I'll wait—in the nurse's office."

He plodded into the dimness. Kurz stood there trying to assimilate what was happening. Pain twinged in his chest. Five hours ago you were lying on cool sheets making lovely, naked love to the most remarkable girl you have met. Now you are in a hospital at 3:45 A.M. promising to save a kid's soul. Was there a connection? Was there any way to make sense out of it?

He fumbled his way back through the curtains and again stood at the foot of the bed. Harry's body twitched spasmodically beneath the covers. His head was on Macy's shoulders, eyes closed, face still empty, waxen. Macy was sponging his neck with a damp cloth. Kurz inhaled and caught a very unpleasant odor.

"He's a mess," Macy said. "I'll have to change him."

"I'll get Mrs. Dillon."

"No! I don't want her in here. She's worse than the priest."

"Now wait a minute."

Ann put Harry's head back on the pillow and strode to the foot of the bed. "Whose side are you on?"

"I'm not on anybody's side," Kurz said. "But the priest is flipping his wig. He says the kid's soul is at stake."

"What does he know about souls?" Macy said. "He spends fifty percent of his time up in his suite watching television."

Even in a whisper, her ferocity left him floundering.

"The kid's dying. It can't do any harm——"

"He has the right to die the way he *wants* to die."

"Ann," little Harry called weakly.

He retched and some greenish fluid gurgled from his mouth.

Kurz watched Macy wipe it away. What the hell is happening to you—and to the whole goddamn world—

Macy's eyes reached him across the small body on the bed. "Will you help me change him?"

She did the dirty work, the swabbing and scrubbing. All he did was pull away the foul sheets, help her spread the fresh ones. He watched her slim hands move swiftly and surely over Harry's swollen, skeletonic body as she gave him an alcohol rubdown. A few hours ago those same hands had been caressing you, another Harry.

The priest poked his head through the curtains. The sag of his old face was inexpressibly sad. It hung there, disembodied, staring at Kurz, waiting for him to speak. What could he say? Bless me, Father, but my job is arresting people. Permit me to cop a plea. Get lost, Father, you are strictly superfluous on this scene. Hit the road, Father, you have nothing to say to Harry.

Harry who? Harry Kurz or Harry Blank? You did not even know the kids's last name, but he was a human being. And there was another human being on the opposite side of the bed. This girl who had spent a whole evening trying to make Harry Kurz believe in happiness. A kook, Father, but something about her unsteadies me, even unravels me. She couldn't weigh more than 120, but she hits you off balance, Father. She unsteadies you inside and suddenly you're not sure of anything. Which is interesting. I've been so goddamn sure I had things taped it was getting to be a bore, Father, and you are away out there in the distance, a balloon face drifting in the wind, saying things that bored me from start to finish. Bless me, Father, but I have a funny feeling you and I have had it.

Yes, you could say a lot of things to those bleary old eyes, that drooping face, but why bother? Slowly, solemnly, Kurz just shook his head back and forth. The face sagged a little more and vanished. A few minutes later Dr. Weinberg appeared. He put his stethoscope on Harry's chest, murmured something to Ann about pulse and respiration. As he spoke his eyes drifted across the bed and examined Kurz for a hesitant moment. Ann sat down beside the bed again and whispered, "He doesn't think he'll last another hour."

"Yes, I will," Harry said, his eyes closed. "I'll live another two hours."

The first hour passed in almost total silence. Harry broke it once. He asked for water. His body was as still as his voice, as if he was conserving his last vestige of strength for a struggle he knew was coming. And it came. He fought for life through every minute of that last hour, straining for breath, the throbbing heart shaking his body like a rattle. Watching, Kurz found himself gasping each breath down his own dry throat. Each beat of that heart smashed him like a fist in the chest. *I can't stand it,* he thought, *I really can't stand it. Why the hell doesn't he die?*

To his amazement, it was Ann who broke first. Tears streaming down her face, she flung her arms around Harry. "All right, Harry, you don't have to——"

"I *want* to," he whispered.

Never had Kurz seen such intensity on a face. It was Harry against the whole world—doctors, priests, even Ann Macy. Ann sensed it, of course. She withdrew her arms, wiped her eyes, and sat quietly beside the bed holding Harry's hand for the last half hour of the struggle. Once more Kurz felt himself sucked down into that small body on the bed. He would fight it, pull back, and the momentum would carry him back too far past pity into exasperation. Finally he felt nothing. He was numb, a statue.

Harry's eyes opened. Gone was the fierce brilliance. Child's eyes now, weary with oncoming sleep. "Is it—two hours yet?"

"Yes," Kurz said.

"All right," Harry said. "All right."

He tugged his hand away from Ann and slipped the arm under the covers. The eyes closed. One last shuddering breath, and he was dead.

Dawn had broken as they came down the hospital steps and walked slowly toward the parking lot. A cool, moist wind was blowing and the sky above them seemed carved from the grey hill on which the hospital stood. Below, square miles of tenement roofs crowded shoulder to shoulder like upright coffins to the river's edge. They got in the car and Kurz was reaching for the keys when Macy flung her arms about him.

"Hold me," she whispered. "Please hold me. Put your arms around me."

He could feel her trembling. "It's okay," he said. "It's okay. He's better off."

"I know. But he kept taking me with him. Please hold me closer. I'm not strong like you. He kept taking me with him."

"You're not strong," Kurz said. "You're the strongest girl I ever met in my life. I don't know anyone else who could have sat beside that bed for more than five minutes."

"But he didn't need me at the end. He wanted to prove he didn't need anyone or anything."

"I know."

"Maybe I was wrong to let him go that way. Maybe I'm wrong about everything. I know you think I am."

"I stayed there with you, didn't I? I got rid of the priest."

She stopped trembling, but still she clung to him, her face against his chest, and he could smell, even taste, the perfume in her hair. For at least a half hour they sat there in each other's arms while the sun rose above the city in red and purple splendor.

"Look at that sunrise," Kurz finally said. "Just look at it."

She raised her head. "I haven't seen one in years. Not since I was a student nurse."

"I haven't seen one since I was in Korea."

"What was it like in Korea?"

"Lousy. The good guys kept getting killed."

They sat there until they could feel the first warmth of the day striking their faces. "Can we go home now?" Kurz said.

"Yes."

They drove swiftly through deserted streets. Up the four

flights to her apartment they trudged, hand in hand. Kurz closed the door with a kick and kissed her.

"Let's make love," he said. "Now."

"No," she said, turning her face away. "I couldn't."

"Yes, yes you can."

He led her into the bedroom and undressed her and undressed himself and lay down beside her. She did not move, she just stared up at the ceiling while his hand moved slowly up and down her body. "Yes, you can," he whispered. Suddenly she turned her face to him. They kissed. And then they were together in a new kind of loving, a communion that embraced flesh and emotion. Not once did Kurz find himself thinking *what* or *how*. There were larger words moving in his mind. He was taking her into himself and in that taking was also giving, with each slow thrust giving a part of what he knew in his body and in his mind, knew unknowing without words, a fierce certainty, that only he, death's spectator, knew.

It reached her utterly. Weeping, she opened her body to him, let him carry her recklessly toward that unspoken point of power above, below, beyond them, which only he possessed. First a whisper, then a roaring in his blood and brain. First a hope, then almost an arrogance, a swaggering yet solemn, coming, coming. Moment!

She would not let him go. Eventually they fell asleep in each other's arms and awoke to separate, kissing softly. It was better than the dream again, Kurz thought, as he drifted down into darkness. Better than better.

Chapter Eight

Kurz awoke about noon. The air conditioners hummed their song of things, immobilizing rich, white beams of sunlight. Ann Macy was still asleep beside him, her face buried in the pillow, her hands curled in childish fists beside it. Kurz took a shower, put on his shorts, found eggs and bacon in the refrigerator and made breakfast. You feel peculiar, he thought as he scrambled the eggs. You feel like you've just celebrated two weeks of birthdays or made Chief of Detectives.

Ann appeared in the doorway without a stitch on. "What in the world are you doing?" she said.

"A girl gets the services of a master chef, the guy who has sobered up more wild parties with his bacon and eggs than anyone else in this crummy town and she asks, 'What in the world are you doing?' "

Ann laughed and ran her fingers through her hair. "You're marvelous," she said.

"Careful," he said. "You may end up with that on your tombstone. I can just see it stopping traffic in the cemetery every Sunday. 'HE WAS MARVELOUS.' "

She laughed again and kissed him. "Will the eggs wait until I take a shower?"

"How dare you even ask the master chef such a question?" He whacked her on the rear with the skillet. "Get going."

She came out of the bathroom wearing a knee-length blue

negligee. They ate breakfast looking down at the river and talked about what to do for the rest of the day.

"I know what you'd like to do," she said.

"Is that a challenge, an invitation, or a refusal?"

"All three," she said, laughing.

"We could go for a boat ride," Kurz said. "The dayliner leaves at two for that afternoon into moonlight cruise."

"They keep having riots, don't they?"

"Maybe I can quell one single-handed and get a citation."

"No. I don't believe in mixing business and pleasure."

"How about something dull like a walk in the park?"

"Wonderful," she said. "Down by the sailboat lake. I haven't been there in months."

"Sold," Kurz said.

She jumped up, as delighted as if she had just been invited to a weekend in Bermuda. "I'm going to wear Sunday clothes."

She did too. She emerged from the bedroom wearing a pale blue shantung suit, stockings and high heels. She looked so fantastic, Kurz had to say something. "You should dress up more often."

"Why?"

"Look in the mirror sometime and figure it out for yourself."

Outside the sun still beat down with tropic ferocity. The temperature was at least a hundred. The metal on the Volvo was so hot it was untouchable. Along the route to the park the streets were practically deserted. "Everyone with the price of the gasoline is at the beach," Kurz said. "I wish I was there myself."

"Alone?"

Kurz just looked at her. When they got to the park he was surprised to find it crowded. People streamed along the paths, sprawled on the grass. "I bet they're swimming in the sailboat lake," he said.

They strolled hand in hand. It was like high school days, but more fun. They kept meeting people Kurz knew. Most of them were married, many had their kids along and it was great watching the husbands' eyes revolve as they absorbed Ann Macy.

"You're so popular," she said.

"It's the neighborhood. I live only a couple of blocks away."

Lo and behold, his sister and brother-in-law. He introduced Ann and his sister gave her a stare that on a cooler day would have hung icicles on nearby trees. His brother-in-law also recoiled. What was wrong, did they look immoral or some goddamn thing?

"Well, I've *always* wanted to meet one of Harry's girls," his sister gushed. "But I never expected to be so dazzled."

Ann laughed good-naturedly and pretended to look right and left. "You can't mean me."

His brother-in-law began discussing the hot weather and the pennant races. His sister began telling Ann about the latest siege of disease her offspring had survived. It looked like the end of a beautiful afternoon until two of the kids came screaming up to them to announce that a third was trapped in a tree.

"Thank God," Kurz said, watching the parents slew foot it across the lawn.

"I can't believe she's your sister."

"Why?"

"I don't know. She's so—typical."

"She's just married, that's all."

"What do you mean by *that?*"

He took her hand and they resumed their stroll toward the sailboat lake. "Marriage softens a woman's brain."

"Funny, I've always thought it softened a man's brain."

"Maybe we're both right."

That produced silence. Kurz noticed that the farther they walked, the more integrated the park became. At least fifty percent of the strollers and loungers were Negroes now. The side of the park from which they had entered was in the white section, but the northern boundary toward which they were walking was entirely black.

"Come on, smile," he said. "You should be full of happy, happy talk surrounded by all this integration."

"It is good to see," she said. "Does it bother you?"

"Did I say it did?"

"Speaking of Negroes, I've been meaning to ask you about Dancer. Are you—investigating him?"

"Yeah. We think—or at least we thought—he killed his brother-in-law."

"I know this will make you mad. But I hope you're wrong."

"I think maybe we are," Kurz said, "so don't start picketing me."

She laughed. It was good to hear her laugh about something that might have started a violent argument two weeks ago. He took her hand again and they strolled along in dreamy silence, with him thinking absolutely insane thoughts about marriage. Ahead of them the path curved sharply to the right to avoid a mass of glacial rock. Around the curve, practically colliding with them, came Marianne Moser, her three boys and Jim Powell.

"Hello," Kurz said, and introduced Ann Macy. He gave Powell a quizzical look. "You working Sundays too?"

Powell grinned. "Who's working?"

"Jim just met us a few minutes ago," Marianne Moser said, obviously flustered. "He was walking along with us trying to find out why Billy didn't show up at the Boys' Club."

Billy just glowered into the asphalt between his feet.

"Maybe he's scared," Kurz said. "Is that it? You're scared those guys play a better game of baseball?"

"I got more important things to do," Billy muttered.

"I've heard that song before," Kurz said.

They stood for a moment in a slightly awkward silence.

"I—decided to go house-hunting myself yesterday," Marianne Moser said.

"Oh," Kurz said. "Any luck?"

She shook her head. "Pretty discouraging."

"I'm sorry. Jim and I called the Urban League. He probably told you——"

She nodded again.

"We'll see if we can think of something else."

"I'd appreciate it. I really would."

They strolled once more. Macy looked over her shoulder at the Mosers and Powell. "Who, what, where, when?" she said. "Tell me."

Kurz told her everything from his first visit to his confrontation with Billy Moser in the precinct house to the dead end with the Urban League. "I was so damn mad when I heard about the real estate operator," he said, "I was tempted to go out there and buy a house myself and sell it to the Mosers the next day."

"Harry, let's do it!"

Ann Macy had stopped dead in the middle of the path. Negroes and whites streamed around them. The sun beat off the leafy trees, the green lawns, and Kurz had to squint at her through the dazzle. "You must be kidding."

"I'm not," she said, stamping her foot. "We can do it together. We'll pretend we're getting married. You couldn't do it alone. They'd spot you in a minute."

"Listen——"

"Oh, you want to do it. I can tell."

The last twenty-four hours swirled around him, happiness in the hum of the air conditioners, death in the hospital's dawn, his answer, that enfolding moment of giving and taking, the invisible momentum of that lunge toward yes that carried them to this place in the sun, eyes running from those long, lithe, stockinged legs to that imploring beautiful face saying, "Please, Harry, please. You'll never be sorry. I know you'll never be sorry."

"Okay. When?"

"Now. Sunday's the perfect day. Everyone looks for houses."

"Let's go."

From that moment until they walked into the model home he did not think about it. He was like a man falling from a high building who refused to believe that when he hit the ground he would be dead. Something would happen first. A hand would grab him, a voice would wake him up.

The real estate man's name was Flannigan. Round face, button Irish nose, wide, toothy mouth full of friendly chatter.

"We're getting married next week," Ann Macy was saying. "We were going to live with my parents but——"

"There's nothing like a home of your own," Flannigan said. "A home of your own in a nice neighborhood where you put down roots. A nice friendly neighborhood where ownin' property is better than having money in the bank. I tell you, believe it or not, we estimate the value of Dellwood's houses will increase twenty percent in the next ten years. Isn't that somethin'? You a veteran, Mr. Kurz?"

"Yes. Korea."

"Where do you work?"

"Police force. Detective second grade."

"Oh, hell, you got no problems." Flannigan chuckled, briskly filling out forms. "You could raffle off your mortgage and half the bankers in the city would trample themselves to death trying to pick it up. What do you want to put down?"

Kurz stared numbly. "The minimum," Ann Macy said.

It was not really happening, Kurz vowed once more as Flannigan bundled them into his car and drove them noisily up and down leafy streets lined with ranch houses on tiny plots.

"We want at least three bedrooms," Macy was telling him. "My mother and father may want to move in with us when he retires."

"No problem. No problem," Flannigan said. "When we built these houses we took those kind of eventualities for granted."

The house was not new, but it smelled of fresh paint and the floors gleamed with varnish. "—transfer," Flannigan was explaining. "We reacquired the house on a temporary basis to make it easy for the poor fellow. And, of course, it helps us to keep the neighborhood—the way we want it."

Flannigan's laugh rattled through the empty house.

"It's lovely," Ann Macy said. "We'll take it."

Forms to sign. Fifty dollars cash deposit. A check in the morning mail. No problem. Flannigan pumping his hand, babbling about happiness, roots, shrewd investment. Then they were in the car, driving into the heart of the city again.

"We'd better go tell the Mosers right away."

"I guess we'd better," Kurz said.

They found a parking place in front of the door. Ann practically gamboled up the steps beside him. He had never seen her so happy. What the hell, maybe it was the right thing to do. Maybe you do feel good about it. He rang the bell and briskly ascended the stairs. The door at the top was opened by Jim Powell. "Now tell me you're still working."

Marianne Moser came bustling out of the kitchen. "Oh, I asked Mr. Powell to stay for dinner. Do you want him for——"

"No," Kurz said, "nothing like that. We just did something absolutely nuts and we're here to tell you about it."

They went into the living room and Kurz told them. Marianne Moser's eyes filled with tears. "Oh, Harry," she said. "I can call you Harry, can't I? I think that's the most wonderful news—I've been praying and praying and I really was almost ready——"

"You want to go ahead with it?" Kurz said.

"Of course, I want to go ahead with it."

Was the dismay visible on his face? Powell was frowning at him. "Maybe we ought to think about it," he said. "This could get pretty messy. I mean—I don't know whether this particular family is ready to handle what could develop."

"What family is?" Ann Macy said fiercely. "Of course, they'll need help. But there are hundreds of people in this city who are ready to give it. I can vouch for that. I don't think there are ten people in the university who wouldn't support them."

"But there's some kinds of help——"

"Bill would want me to do it," Marianne Moser said, "I know he would."

That settled it. Powell and Kurz just sat there while Ann Macy and Marianne Moser confirmed and reconfirmed the decision. To celebrate, Marianne Moser insisted they all stay for dinner. She and Ann vanished into the kitchen, obviously well on their way to becoming friends. Kurz and Powell sat there looking at each other for a long time.

"Maybe it will work out," Kurz said.

"I hope so."

"We're going to need all the backing we can find."

"I know," Powell said. "I'll make some calls tomorrow. The Urban League, the NAACP. They'll all line up, don't worry."

"Good," Kurz said.

But it wasn't good and they both knew it.

Supper proved to be something less than a celebration. The Moser kids were far from ecstatic when they heard they were moving and when Billy heard how it was being done, his lips curled with contempt. "Why can't we go out and buy a house like other Americans? Why do we have to sneak around this way?"

"You know why," Powell said quietly.

"Of course you know why," his mother snapped. "There are prejudiced people around, but why not look at it the other way? Why not look at the people who aren't prejudiced like Mr. Kurz and Miss Macy?"

"Maybe they're gettin' something out of it you don't know about. Maybe it's all a stunt bein' engineered in City Hall and he's got a nice big fat promotion waitin' for him at the end of it."

"I wish that was true," Kurz said.

"Oh, Billy," Ann said. "You don't know how wrong you are. You don't know how many white people want to help and just don't know how."

"We don't want your damn help!"

"Billy! Shut your mouth and go to your room."

He went. They ate. It was chicken with home-fried potatoes

and it looked delicious but Kurz had lost his appetite. He nibbled at the food while Ann Macy asked the second Moser kid, Daniel, what he thought about moving.

"Well, I don't know," he said. "I mean it's a white school, isn't it? I know a kid who went to a white school. They used to beat him up every day on the way home."

"Oh, that was probably a couple of years ago," Ann said, "and this is a really nice neighborhood. I'll bet you'll find plenty of boys who want to be friends with you."

Daniel shoveled in some potatoes and obviously didn't believe a word of it.

"I hope we're doing the right thing," Kurz said as they drove back to Ann's apartment through the twilight.

"I know we are."

"That oldest kid. I worry about how he'll react if anybody starts roughing him up."

"All he needs is just one white friend and he'll be all right."

Kurz suddenly had an uneasy feeling that she was reciting from something she had read. "Well," he said, "we can't back out now."

"How could you even think of it?"

Up in the apartment she flipped on the record player and did an impromptu watusi all around him. She looked so good, eyes glowing, those perfect teeth flashing, the black hair flying, he had to laugh out loud. "Cut it out, you kook."

"I'm happy," she said. "I haven't felt so happy in—an era."

"You're still a kook. And I've got to go home."

She stopped dancing. "No," she pouted. "Not until we celebrate too. Our way." She gave him an absurdly coquettish smile. He hesitated and to his amazement found himself wondering if he really wanted to do it. Too much of a good thing? Or are you afraid to let this crazy female take you any farther toward wherever she's hellbent on going? That happiness bit, are you really afraid of it, Kurz? Are you afraid of what might happen if you suddenly woke up one morning happy? No, you were happy enough before you met her, at least before Mr. Dancer or whoever knocked a hole in you. But it wasn't her kind of happiness. It wasn't the dancing, laughing kind.

"I'll lure you," she was saying. "I've always wanted to do the watusi with my clothes off."

He watched while she shed shoes, stockings, dress, and kept on dancing. Next went the slip, the bra. The pants she shimmied off and kicked across the room. Then, with absolutely no warning, she stopped dancing and just stood there, the little girl in search of reassurance. "No?"

"You're liable to get me fired, you know that?" he said as he unknotted his tie, "and I don't even give a damn."

Laughing he kissed her, and laughing, she kissed him back. They laughed and kissed and kissed and laughed until kissing and laughter became inextricable. Everything mingled, eyes, lips, hair, the sleek smooth rump, getting, giving, taking, all the words vanished in a new existence without fears, doubts, past, futures, names, new, NEW! It blazed in Kurz's mind as he came in her and she trembled beneath him, seeming for a moment almost to vanish.

He was barely conscious of driving the car home, he did not hear one-tenth of his mother's lamentations about the sleepless night he had caused her by failing to call. "I was at the beach. There wasn't any telephone," he said mechanically, and went to bed.

He lay there in the darkness trying to assemble enough brain cells to think. What the hell is happening to you, Kurz? What is this girl doing to you? Knocking you dead is not a bad description. A few more nights like this one and you will be head-over-heels in love, as they say in the magazines. If you are not there already.

He fell asleep and did not dream once all night. Morning found Mother morosely sniffling phony tears over her coffee. He apologized with a little more sincerity for forgetting to call her and scrammed for work.

Powell was waiting for him, as usual. "You want me to make those calls?" he said.

"Sure I do," Kurz said. "How the hell can we back out now? That Moser kid would give us the horse laugh forever."

"Worse things could happen," Powell said. He sighed. "Well, you're probably right."

"Let's not call from here," Kurz said. "The walls have ears, you know."

"Yeah," Powell said. "I'll see you in about an hour."

Kurz sat and doodled for a while, staring at the sunlight glaring against the dirty windowpane. He finally noticed his doodles were a series of gigantic A's. Bad sign, Kurz. Very bad. You are really in danger of getting hooked. So what? Maybe it was time. What the hell, you never planned to be a bachelor all your life.

Other detectives came in, began making calls, typing reports. Jackson, the Negro detective who had visited him in the hospital, slapped him on the back and practically shouted in his ear, "Hey, Harry, how's the manhunt going?"

"What manhunt?"

"You know what manhunt," Jackson said with that phony minstrel show grin. "You got it all figured out, ain't you? You just settin' here waitin' for Dancer to come up and sign the confession."

Ed Moriarty, an older detective with a razor mouth and a drooping hawk nose, stared at him from a desk on the other side of the room. Several things clicked in Kurz's mind. Moriarty played cards with O'Bannon sometimes. Maybe they were integrating the game these days, or just promising to integrate it with Mr. Jackson.

"I'm just trying to do the job the way I see it, pal." Kurz said. "I was there, you weren't, remember?"

"Sure. Sure," Jackson said. "And you got the cut to show for it. But hell, man, that doesn't give you the right to kick the shit out of some poor guy like Dancer."

"Poor guy," Kurz said. "Since when does a goddamn crummy numbers man deserve any sympathy in a police station? What the hell kind of a game are we playing here?"

Jackson just looked at him, shrugged and went over and sat down at a typewriter and began pecking away. Moriarty picked up a phone and began dialing.

"I don't have to be here," Kurz said. "I could be lying on a goddamn beach."

They did not even look at him.

Kurz grabbed his hat and strode to the door. "One of you guys ought to open a window. Something stinks in here."

He drove down to the warehouse where it had all begun. He sat there staring at the big black building and the even blacker expanse of asphalt loading yard. O'Bannon and his friends are after your scalp, Harry, which means you had better bring home Mr. Dancer's woolly wig fast. Forget about those tender feelings you contracted from the tape recordings. What the hell did those tapes prove either way? Dancer could still be your boy, just too smart to make even the tiniest move. Sure, he tells his girl it's a bum rap. If he's got a brain, does he tell the real story to a hooker? The time has come for you to do some real detective work on Mr. Dancer.

He looked around him. The heat wave had demolished the stickball players. They sat on the steps, playing cards, reading comic books. Kurz got out of the car and walked over to them. "Hello," he said.

They kept right on reading and dealing.

"Listen," he said. "Remember the day that those two cops got shot?"

The kid who was dealing nodded briefly.

"I was one of them."

Again the dealer looked up and gave him the briefest possible nod.

"You guys were playing stickball in the street when that panel truck came along. Did you recognize either one of the guys that was driving it?"

The dealer shook his head.

"Did you see anybody in the back?"

The dealer looked at him this time. "How much it worth?"

"That depends on what you know."

"If it ain't worth nuthin' we don' know nuthin'."

Kurz took ten dollars out of his pocket. "What did you see?"

The ten dollars disappeared like the sun had disintegrated it. "We saw a guy in the back."

"What did he look like?"

"He was kinda tall and thin, with a big hook to his nose."

"What was he wearing?"

"Couldn't tell, man. We just saw him through the window. It was dark in there."

He took a mug shot of Dancer out of his pocket and showed it to the dealer. "Does this look like him?"

"Uh-uh," said the dealer. "He was white."

"You're putting me on," Kurz said automatically. "Who have you been talking to?"

"Nobody, man."

"No other cops talked this over with you?"

"We don't talk to cops if we can help it."

"Why are you telling me?"

"You put the money in my palm, man. And like I said, he was white."

Kurz drove slowly back to the precinct house through the blazing heat of the morning. Was the kid telling the truth? If he was, Harry Kurz was about to qualify for the dodo of the year award. Back in the precinct house he went upstairs and pulled the file on Dancer. Jackson and Moriarty had done the original investigation. According to three witnesses, Dancer had been having breakfast in the apartment of one Mildred Stratton at the very moment Kurz and Moser were getting shot. Who was Mildred Stratton? Just an associate professor of sociology at the University.

Kurz decided to try the other two names first. The first was Michael Collins, a name that surely qualified him to live in the best part of town. But the address was in the heart of the Congo and in five minutes Kurz found himself climbing to the third floor of one of the city's worst tenements. The stench of rotting wood and garbage mingled with the cooking smells and what his old friend Reardon called nigger stink, that musky animal odor he remembered smelling when he played against Negroes in high school basketball. Half way up the clean air seemed to vanish completely and the temperature must have gone well past a hundred. He paused on a landing and with more sigh than crack the bannister gave way and he almost fell two stories into the basement. He had to light matches to find the name Collins on the third floor.

"We don't want any," a woman's voice replied to his knock.

"Open the door, it's the police."

The door was instantly flung open by one of the biggest women Kurz had ever seen. "What you want?" she yelled. "No criminals here. Respectable people here."

"I'd like to speak to Michael Collins. Is he home?"

"He's a good boy," she said, completely blocking the doorway. "I know, I'm his mother. What you want to see him for?"

"About a murder," Kurz said.

"Murder," she shrieked. She must have weighed three hundred pounds and her voice was at least as large.

The uproar produced a young Negro almost as tall as the earth mother, but thin.

"Are you Michael Collins?"

He nodded.

Kurz identified himself and told him what he wanted. Michael Collins, who had Caucasian features and wore heavy horn-rimmed glasses, twisted his mouth in disgust. "I've already gone through this nonsense once."

"It won't kill you to do it again," Kurz said. "You hang around with people like Dancer and you can expect to talk to a lot of cops."

"Come in," Collins said. "There's no need for us to stand in the hall."

"If he say one word about you doing it," his mother cried, "you just holler. I'll call the Double A and P so fast it make his head swim."

"Don't worry, Mama," Collins said. "They're trying to hang an innocent man but it isn't me."

He led Kurz through a clean but dilapidated living room into a big front bedroom lined with books. *Das Kapital, The*

Decline of the West, Escape from Freedom. Titles bounced off Kurz's eyes as they sat down. The sun beat steadily on the window. The heat in the room was fantastic.

"You're a student at the university?"

"Correct. Political science."

"How do you know Dancer?"

"He put up half the money for my tuition last year."

"And what did you do for him?"

"Nothing."

"Except maybe run an adding machine for him now and then?"

"That's my business."

"Sure. It just so happens that we've got a pretty good line on everybody that works or has worked for Mr. Dancer. If we feel like it, we can cause them a hell of a lot of trouble."

"I guess you could," Collins said. His hands clasped and unclasped nervously. "I'm on a half scholarship. If you arrest me, I'll lose it."

"In other words, it might be a good idea to tell me the truth."

"That's what I intend to do," Collins said.

"Let's hear it."

"I was with Dancer from eight o'clock the previous night until twelve noon when this so-called crime was committed."

"There's nothing so-called about it," Kurz said. "I know, I'm one of the guys that got shot."

This shook the student's superior tone somewhat. "Oh. I meant—as far as Dancer was concerned."

"And you stayed awake all this time—he was never out of your sight?"

"No, of course not. It was a pretty wild party."

"Anybody smoking any pot?"

"Some. But I don't think Dancer did."

"Oh, sure," Kurz said bitterly. "Dancer never does anything. He's so goddamn pure I can't understand why they haven't nominated him for sainthood."

"There are some things about him that I find pretty admirable. I don't agree with all his viewpoints on race, of course. He's too close to the Muslims in my opinion——"

Kurz groaned inwardly. Another goddamn academic sermon. Black as he was, this guy was cut out of the same cloth as Professor Slater. Just as windy and just as bloodless. All the blood was in fat Mama out there muttering in the parlor.

"Thanks," he said, cutting him off in the middle of an involved sentence.

The next address turned out to be a Muslim temple. They had converted what had once been a corner bar into a house of worship by sticking two phony wooden columns in front of the big oak door and painting a half dozen crescent moons on the walls and windows.

The door was opened by another large character, a man this time, wearing the usual fez and beard. "You are forbidden to enter," he intoned.

"I'm looking for George Brown."

"There is no one here by that name."

"How about Achmed Abdullah," Kurz said, reading the Muslim name from the slip of paper.

"I will see if he is available."

He slammed the door in Kurz's face and left him standing on the corner while the life of the ghetto swirled around him. A balding Jewish merchant stood in front of his store wiping his neck. Pushcart peddlers wandered by bawling for business. A couple of junkies sidled along, sized him up as a cop and hastily crossed the street. A bunch of kids cruised past in a beatup ten-year-old red convertible. They slowed down to whistle at a girl who was really wiggling it. Kurz found himself smiling, remembering how he used to do the same thing at that age. A patrol car pulled up behind the kids and gave them the horn.

One of the kids in the back seat turned around and yelled: "Blow it out your ass, man."

That did it. The cops pulled them over and wrote out a ticket.

Kurz sighed. There was the difference. They didn't talk back to cops. There was no state of undeclared war with the police in those days. Crazy how life down here could be so similar and yet so fatally different. Kurz looked down at his white hands, then let his eyes move up and down the street. The cops in the patrol car had gone, leaving their victims cursing over their fifteen dollar ticket. There was not another white person in sight now. For a few seconds the whole situation struck him as ridiculous. Why should there be all this hatred because his hands were white and all these other hands were black? It made absolutely no sense.

The genie with the fez on top opened the door again. "Achmed Abdullah will see you in the office next door."

He led Kurz ten steps to the right and through the doorway of a small store on the first floor of a sagging tenement. Achmed Abdullah was also equipped with a fez and a beard but was built along smaller, though solid, lines. Kurz knew from his record that as George Brown he had spent some ten years in state and local penitentiaries, so he didn't expect to be greeted with a warm smile.

"What do you want, cop?"

"We thought you might be ready to tell us the truth about Dancer knocking off Bill Moser. You're still on parole, you know. The board might take a very dim view of how you spend your time."

"He didn't do it. I swear by Allah himself he didn't do it!"

"How much money you owe him?"

"Not a cent. The children of Allah don't gamble."

Kurz took a deep breath. It was really hopeless. They sat there inside those skins like knights in black armor and you were outside, permanently outside.

"You know what I think?" he said. "You guys have the impression that no one can touch Dancer. What have I got to do to prove you're wrong? I put him out of business, didn't I? I'll put you out of business too. I'm serious about this and I go up a lot higher than Dancer."

"I told you the truth," he said, scaring just a little.

"Okay, let's sidestep a little. Dancer didn't pull the trigger, one of his boys did. Maybe one of your boys."

"The children of Allah kill only in self-defense."

"That leaves out Dancer."

Achmed squirmed a little, fiddled with a pen on the desk. "I don't know, that is Allah's truth. I don't know."

"You heard him say some pretty nasty things about Moser, right?"

"That is also Allah's truth."

"And you'd be prepared to repeat them in a courtroom—to keep the parole board happy?"

"Perhaps. Perhaps."

Out onto the blinding heat-clogged street once more. Gas, the last stuff was pure gas. You could not let a hood see you floundering there with the egg still warm on your face. He stood beside his car, seeing but not seeing the black faces, trying to think of the next move. Who would be willing to blow the whistle on Dancer? A name drifted through his mind, and slowly connected with a face. Santini. Michael Santini. Leader of one of the strongest political clubs in the city, a real power with a brother big on the docks, another brother even bigger in the Teamsters. You only heard Dancer talk to "Mr. Santini." But it did not really matter. It was pretty good confirmation of a rumor around town. Mayor O'Connor had put the old Mafia leader Charlie Anfuso away for ten to fifteen. But one jail sentence did no serious damage to a syndicate operation. The others just moved up one rank in the hierarchy. Yes, a visit to Mr. Santini might be worth the time and trouble.

He called the political Santini at his home, and explained that he was working out of headquarters on a special assignment and had been told he could be "helpful."

"Sure, come on out," said a pale, neutral voice. "I'm home until one."

The house was a huge Victorian pile just off the parkway, long the private preserve of the city's Protestant upper class. The Irish had long since sent most of them fleeing to the suburbs, and now the Italians were sending the Irish down the same route. Kurz tried to think of one married classmate from high school or college who still lived in the city. He could not come up with one who didn't have an Italian name, and they were only a handful.

The behemoth who opened Santini's front door had bodyguard written all over him. You could see the bulge on the hip, where the cannon was stashed. He led him through rooms full of gilded mirrors, gold ceilings and chairs with bright rose and brighter green cushions. Santini was on the phone in a small study that was obviously not yet redecorated according to his tastes. It had plain walnut paneling, a high white ceiling, a beige rug. The telephone on the desk was gold, however. Mr. Santini was young—not much older than Kurz, and well built, trim, with a square, bulldog chin and a flat Sicilian nose. To Kurz he looked odd in his expensive dark blue suit and sober tie, like a laborer masquerading as an executive.

"Listen, pal," Santini was saying. "You tell His Honor that we want three seats on that commission, or he can start worryin' about the way Wards Five, Six and Seven vote next year. Does that sound logical? If it don't you tell him to call me. I'm not callin' him again."

He hung up and grinned at Kurz. "The wops are a minority group, too. We got to fight for our rights. What's on your mind, Detective?"

"A guy named Dancer Washington."

"Never heard of him."

"He's a Negro. Runs a numbers wheel. Or he did."

"So?"

"We've been tapping his room. Last night he made a phone call to a Mr. Santini. It was pretty obvious that he was the guy who put up the dough for the wheel."

Santini sat up straight. His face displayed incredulity, then anger. "What the hell kind of an act is this?"

"No act. I'm making an investigation. We think Dancer killed a cop. We're naturally checking anybody who can——"

The friendliness was gone from Santini's eyes. "Who sent you?"

"Nobody."

"You said headquarters——"

"It's a special investigation."

Santini leaned forward, and his head seemed to come across the desk, as if it was on a snake's body. "You tell whoever sent you that nobody's gonna rough us up. We're not gonna take it lying down like Anfuso. We got votes——"

He was yelling. "For Christ's *sake,*" Kurz said. "I don't give a shit about your goddamn numbers. I want this guy because he killed a cop. My partner. You tell me what you know about him and everything else is forgotten."

"Get out."

"I can take that tape to the mayor. He could get pretty excited."

"Go ahead. Take it. Tell him to shove it up his ass and play it there."

Kurz picked up his hat. "I get the feeling you're not exactly on the side of law and order, Mr. Santini."

"Listen, wiseass, one more word out of you and *I'll* take this someplace. One phone call and I can put you back on a beat."

That was too much. Kurz felt anger loose in his belly. "No, you can't. I'm one cop you can't touch."

Santini pressed a button on the telephone. The behemoth and a friend showed up. The friend was even bigger. "I told you to get out. You gonna go?"

Kurz went. He drove back downtown in a daze of sweltering anger. His face, his body felt almost aflame with humiliation. Cool it, cool it, you shouldn't be surprised, he told himself. You knew it was there. Why be bothered by seeing the real thing? But he was bothered. There was, he grimly realized, too much cop in him not to be bothered.

His stomach said lunch. He bought a corned beef sandwich and coffee in the greasy spoon behind the precinct house and hiked up to the squad room. It was empty except for Powell, who was lunching the same way. Kurz gave him a fast run-down of where he had gone and why. Powell smiled bleakly at the Santini story. "All that big talk," he said. "And Dancer's just another white man's nigger."

"He's small," Kurz admitted glumly. "Not big enough to make Santini even look worried. What gets me is why Moser thought he was so big."

"He looked big to Moser. It all depends on where you're standing. Santini looks big to you. He probably don't look big to the boys in Washington. Or even to the mayor."

Kurz nodded wearily. Another speech from the resident philosopher, Professor Powell. Boring but true, like the others.

"Meanwhile," Powell said, "we got other trouble."

"The house?"

Powell nodded. "I talked it over with the Urban League and the NAACP and some other people. Nobody wants any part of it, legally. They say it sounds too much like block-busting. But if we want to go ahead, they'll back us up with everything they've got."

Kurz chomped on his corned beef. "What the hell does that mean?"

Powell grinned wryly. "Well, one way it means go out and get your heads kicked in, boys, you can depend on us to give you three big cheers. Another way, thank God there are people like you around. We're all so hung up with organizational procedure, we're like a herd of elephants when it comes to a surprise attack."

They both ate their sandwiches for a while. Kurz thought about white hands and black hands, O'Bannon and his crummy friends, kids yelling "Blow it out your ass" to cops. Black hands clapping, black lips cheering two cops bleeding to death on black asphalt beneath a brutal sun, Santini leaning across the desk with his snake's sneer.

"The hell with them all," he said. "Let's do it."

Chapter Nine

Kurz took title to the house the following day. The civil rights groups were so wary they would not even supply a lawyer and Kurz had to hire a run-of-the-mill work horse named Dick Harrity, a small wispy Irish type who made most of his money defending two-bit criminals. At the closing, salesman Flannigan fairly bubbled with visions of marital happiness.

"I've seen some good-looking brides, but yours is a real stopper, Mr. Kurz. A real stopper."

In between his visions of splendor, Flannigan was busy sticking Kurz with back payments on the mortgage and everything else he could sneak past a befuddled Harrity. It was probably the first time Harrity had closed a real estate sale since he left law school. His clients did not buy houses. They stole from them.

Kurz figured this out later when he went over the papers in Ann Macy's apartment. But even nicked for an extra $278, they were in a celebration mood. They warmed up on martinis and continued with a magnificent steak, done the way he had been trying to get his mother to cook meat for the last five years.

"Can't you just see the expression on that little fink's face when he finds out what we're going to do?"

"Yeah," Kurz said. "It's a nice thought."

But he found he did not really share her enthusiasm. It was hard to connect Flannigan with those black faces and hands in the 13th precinct, the Moser kid in his Viet Cong suit. After dinner they drove down to see Marianne Moser. Powell was there looking worried but Marianne was raring to go.

"I want you to keep an exact record of how much this is costing you," she told Kurz. "I want to pay back every cent."

"Forget it," Kurz said grandiosely, hoping meanwhile she would remember every word.

"Oh, I've got so much to do," Marianne said. "I'd like to move as soon as possible. That means school transfers, packing."

"I'd love to help," Ann said. "What can I do?"

"That's the trouble, nobody can help. They're all things I have to do myself."

The plaintive note in Marianne's voice made Kurz uneasy. He tried to adjust his mind to cold realism and size up this woman as if she were a stranger. He did not especially like what he saw. She was not strong. She tended to lean on anyone who got close to her. She tended to get rattled easily. But what woman didn't? Answer: Ann Macy.

Goddamn it, Kurz told himself wearily, let's keep that separate. Ann Macy and moving the Mosers and Dancer—all separate. They had absolutely nothing to do with each other. It didn't work, of course. He knew in the back of his head that it was all one big ball of wax. But when you looked at it that way it was too alarming.

The next day Kurz called up Dick Harrity. "Listen," he said. "That house I bought yesterday, is it mine?"

"Sure, it's yours."

"Good, I want to sell it."

"Fast work. Why?"

"I'm not getting married after all."

"What do you know, I predicted it. I met your old friend Reardon in Shanley's last night and told him about you making the big move. He couldn't believe it either."

"You can't change human nature, I guess. I'm a born bachelor."

"Lucky bastard. How'd you find a buyer so quick?"

"It's my ex-partner's wife, Mrs. Moser."

"Mrs. Moser! You've got to be kidding."

"Why should I be kidding?"

"You know goddamn well why. She's dark."

"And that means she can't live in those crummy split-levels?"

"Harry, are you all right?"

"Of course, I'm all right."

"I never picked you for a crusader."

"I'm not. I'm just doing a widow a favor."

"Very nice. But include me out."

"You won't handle the resale?"

"Listen, pal, I got a reputation to worry about in this town."

"I'd worry about it too, if I were you," Kurz said and slammed down the receiver.

He told Powell, who did not look surprised. "I'll get us a lawyer," he said.

That afternoon they had a cup of coffee with a natty young Negro lawyer named Chapman. He looked like Harry Belafonte, but shorter, as if someone had sawed off Harry's legs at the knees. "I'll handle both sides of the sale for nothing," he said.

Toward the bottom of the cup, who should come waltzing into the diner but Dancer. He wasn't looking too good. There was a smudge on his shirt collar and a lot of dirt under his fingernails. But he still had nerve.

"Well, well, well," he said, strolling over to their booth. "You guys arrested somebody else for a crime they didn't commit?"

"That's not our style," Kurz said.

"Sure, it isn't. Sure, it isn't," Dancer said. "No, you just want to run Dancer out of town, that's all. Well I got news for you, fuzz, Dancer's got ways of stayin' in this town that you never even thought about. He can think, see, and that's what no fuzz in this country can do, think."

Kurz realized Dancer was drunk. "He can talk, that's for sure."

"You want to handle my case, Chapman? Dancer versus the City of. False arrest, defamation of character, persecution."

"No thanks," Chapman said.

"No guts, you mean," Dancer said.

He swaggered over to the counter and ordered a cup of coffee.

"There's one nigger I can do without," Chapman said.

"We're working pretty hard on that end of it," Kurz said.

"Work harder," Chapman said.

They shook hands and made a date to meet at noon tomorrow to arrange the resale.

"Where does he live?" Kurz asked as he and Powell drove back to the precinct house.

"In one of the big apartment houses facing the park," Powell said.

"Why hasn't he tried moving out?"

"Nobody wants to be first."

That afternoon Kurz got a phone call from Chapman. "Listen," he said. "I think you'd better stand by for a little stormy weather. I just took Mrs. Moser over to the bank to transfer the mortgage to her name. They couldn't say a word. What the hell, she's got enough dough in her account to cover the full price, but the way they acted! Man, they could have turned off that air conditioning and the temperature would still have been below zero."

"So the word is out?"

"You can bet on it."

Twenty minutes later Kurz got a call from Flannigan, the friendly real estate man. "You son of a bitch," he screamed. "What are you trying to do?"

"I'm not trying to do anything," Kurz said. "I decided not to get married and I want my money back. So I sold the house to a nice respectable widow with three kids. What have you got to complain about?"

"You know goddamn well what I've got to complain about. And, buster, if you think you can get away with this, you're crazy. You're gonna be sorry you ever pulled a stunt like this on Bernie Flannigan."

"Go to hell, you crumb."

Before he could think about it, the telephone rang again. It was Wanamaker, in a near-frenzy. "Mr. Kurz, you better get down here right away. They're upstairs killin' that boy."

"What boy?"

"Your boy. Dancer. A coupla goons busted down his door and they're workin' him over right now. I can hear the noise down here in my office. They're killin' him for sure."

"We're on our way," Kurz snapped and dove for the stairs. Powell had heard the conversation on his extension and was right behind him. "It's Santini," Kurz said. "Dancer probably called him once too often."

Wanamaker met them in his shabby lobby. He looked very scared, which made him talk even faster than usual. "He's out, that boy, if there's anything left of him, he's out," he said. "I can't have this sort of uproar, I run a respectable place."

Kurz pushed the button and the elevator door shut in Wanamaker's face. There wasn't a sound on the fifth floor. Halfway down the hall a pair of frightened eyes peered at them. The door closed and the the bolt shot home, as they charged past. Dancer's room was at the end of the hall. The door was open. The wood was splintered around the lock.

Dancer lay face down on the floor beside the bed. They turned him over and Kurz winced. Half of Dancer's front teeth were gone, his nose was obviously broken. Blood gushed from it, and ran down his chin onto his silk shirt when they propped him up. There was an ugly cut on his cheek, where one of the goons had obviously connected with brass knuckles.

He sat there, his head lolling against the bed, and his eyes slowly came into focus. "Who did it, Dancer?" Kurz asked.

Dancer shook his head.

"You want us to call an ambulance?" Powell asked.

Dancer shook his head again.

"You're beat up real bad, man. You got to see a doctor," Powell said, in the same quiet, almost gentle voice.

"Get out of here, white nigger," Dancer said. "And take your white boss with you."

They left. Riding back to the precinct house, Kurz summed it up. "If Dancer was involved in killing Moser as part of a bigger operation—and Santini was in on it—he wouldn't just beat him up. Those guys would have used guns, not brass knuckles."

"I'm thinkin' the same thing," Powell said.

"Which means we have to believe that Dancer ran the whole thing by himself. Got inside all those companies, had the forms printed, was organized to unload all the loot——"

"It doesn't add up too good, does it?" Powell said.

"No."

"So what do we do?"

For a moment Kurz pondered the possibility of a frame. It would be easy to drag in Dancer's girl friend, Doris, and scare the hell out of her. A hooker would testify to almost anything to stay out of jail, especially if she was on the needle, as most of them were, these days. Then there was Achmed Abdullah, who would gladly violate a few of Allah's truths to stay ahead of the parole board. The rap wouldn't have to be Moser's murder. Any old charge, like selling narcotics, would be enough to salt Dancer away, and keep O'Bannon quiet.

He stole a look at Powell, beside him in the car. His solemn eyes, his earnest mouth were a silent reproach. Forget it, Harry. The guy was too straight. Or maybe just too smart. And maybe you ought to be smarter than to try putting a Negro away on a bum rap these days. You could end up wrecking yourself and half the Department.

"Let's spend another week on it. Check a few more tapes. Watch Dancer move, now that he's out of the bookie business for good. If nothing solid turns up, that's it. I'll have to eat a little crow, but I'll write a report that'll make O'Bannon eat some too."

"And it's back to the beat for me."

"I'm afraid so."

Powell shrugged. "It would've been too good to be true, anyway."

"I get the feeling that just meeting Marianne Moser might make it all worthwhile for you in the long run."

Powell smiled shyly, and gave a small nod.

Ann Macy called at five o'clock and invited Kurz to dinner again. He called his mother to tell her he wouldn't be home and got a twenty-minute harangue on the dangers of eating in hash houses. He drove quickly down the suffocating streets. It was the worst time of the day. People slumped against buildings, shuffled like victims of Buchenwald. Upstairs Ann had the air conditioners going and gin and tonic already mixed on the cocktail table.

He clinked glasses and filled her in on the progress of the Moser move, giving a pretty good imitation of Flannigan squawking like a plucked chicken. Ann threw back her head and laughed delightedly.

Then she went serious on him. "I'm proud of you, Harry. I really am."

"Don't be," he said. "I'm no liberal. I wouldn't do it for anyone else but the Mosers."

"But you are doing it for them."

"That's right, for them."

Was it really true? Didn't all those black hands and faces, the kids on stoops and in cruising cars have something to do with it? No, Kurz told himself fiercely. If that's true, you are just another bleeding heart. You might as well quit the cops and join CORE.

Ann put down her drink and stretched out on the couch, her head in his lap. She was wearing her shift. Lying down the cloth fell away and he could see the figure beneath it. His eyes roved down the whiteness to those marvelous tan legs.

"I missed you last night," she said.

"How?"

"You know how," she said.

"I'm supposed to say that. I guess I'm still recuperating."

"Why can't I say it?"

She reached for her drink and missed and almost fell off the couch. They laughed.

"I wonder if that's the way it gets when you're married. It becomes a habit and you sort of miss it, not the person."

"I wouldn't know," he said.

"Am I an it to you?"

"No, You're a she."

"Let's never become its," she said. "Let's never let it happen."

"Sure," he said.

"Oh, you're not listening to me." She gave him a fierce squeeze around the waist. "Listen," she said. "It's me talking, not just a kookie girl with a good figure. Me. And I'm falling in love with you."

"You have my deepest sympathy," he said.

"No, I don't," she said. "I don't even have your attention."

He slipped his hand down the front of her dress and cupped it over one of those firm young breasts. "If you don't call that attention, what do you call it?"

She kissed him, long and hard. He kissed her back. Slowly, they walked hand in hand into the bedroom.

They had a late supper and Kurz drove home to find his mother in a state of agitation. "The phone's been ringing all night," she said. "Politicians calling you, Uncle Harold, and a lot of people who wouldn't leave their names. Is anything wrong?"

"Not a thing," he said.

The phone rang as they stood there talking. He picked it up and a voice rasped. "I wanna speak to Harry Kurz."

"You've got him."

"Listen, prick. This is the guy who lives next door to the house you just sold to boogies. I want you to know they're never gonna move in. And I also want you to know that if I ever meet you anywhere, anytime, I'll break you in half."

"Now wait a minute pal," Kurz said. "Cool off."

"Don't call me pal."

"This is a widow and three kids. Three nice kids. The widow of a cop who got killed in the line of duty."

"I don't give a shit if she's the widow of the Angel Gabriel, she's black."

"Listen," Kurz said, feeling desperation and rage gathering in his chest. "She's a hell of a fine person. I've eaten in her house. I guarantee you she'll be a credit to the neighborhood."

"Prick, you can love niggers all you want on your own time. But we don't love them out here. She moves in and you know what happens to my house? The value drops five grand and Bernie Flannigan tells me that's a conservative estimate. What do you want to do this for? We don't want trouble. We're nice quiet people out here. But nobody's gonna push us around. When we get pushed, we push back. You're gonna find that out, prick."

Kurz hung up. With the air conditioner whirring only a few feet away, the phone was clammy in his hand. Pain danced in his chest, clanged against his nerves.

"What is it, Harry? What is it? What's going on?" his mother shrilled.

"Nothing," he said. "A crank."

The phone rang again. A heavy, softer voice asked for Harry Kurz. It was Victor Valente, a Democratic leader in the city's north end. "I don't know you," he said. "I spent the last six hours callin' all over town trying to check you out. I still don't get you. What's your angle? You goin' into politics or somethin'? If you think you can do it this way, brother, you need your brains rewired."

Kurz sighed and gave him the planning to get married and then jilted story.

"Sure," Valente said, "and next Christmas Santa Claus is gonna come and give us all a million dollar's worth of presents. Don't hand me bullshit. You tell me your angle and maybe we can work out a deal. Maybe we can't. There's a lot of pretty excited people up here. You let that family move in and someone could wind up getting killed."

"They're moving in tomorrow," Kurz said.

"You're absolutely out of your mind," Valente bellowed.

"One of us is," Kurz said and hung up.

There were more calls, mostly from charming neighbors who told him in obscene terms what they planned to do to Mrs. Moser and her children. It was a bad night. Kurz did not get to sleep until dawn. He staggered out of bed at nine and drove to the precinct house without breakfast. A jolt of coffee at his desk in the squad room brought him half awake. Powell sat in a chair tipped against the wall and listened impassively while Kurz told him about the calls.

"Marianne got a couple herself," he said. "Somebody at the bank must have leaked her name to that real estate character. She was pretty upset."

"And?"

"She still wants to go ahead with it. So do I, now."

Kurz took a large gulp of scalding coffee. "I think I do, too."

"Listen," Powell said, "you did your bit. I think maybe you ought to lay low and let us handle it now."

"And make it an all-Negro show? Nuts," Kurz said.

Jesus, Ann Macy would have loved to hear you say that, Harry. What the hell *is* happening to you?

The Dellwood section was in the 16th precinct. Kurz checked the roster and found the captain was Paul Whelan, only a name to him. He got in his car and drove out to see him face to face. He did not expect much. Dellwood was a quiet section of town and they did not put the best talent out there. Whelan did not look very impressive. He was short, dumpy, with a balding head and a large, red drinker's nose above a small puckered mouth.

Kurz told him the Moser story.

"I know all about it," Whelan said, shuffling papers around his desk. "I got six phone calls already on it this morning. What's your angle, pal?"

"No angle," Kurz snapped. "I'm trying to help a cop's widow."

"Great. Great," Whelan said. "Getting her killed is helping her? Getting the kids beaten up, her windows broken? You move her in and I guarantee you a first class riot. There's a lot of crazy Italians and Polacks in that development. They got every cent they own in those houses. They're out there summer and winter painting them, landscaping, repairing. Now you come along and blow the whole goddamn thing wide open."

"Wait a minute," Kurz said. "Are you a cop or a real estate dealer?"

"I'm a cop, sonny. And I've been a cop a lot longer than you. I knew your old man. He was another headstrong bastard."

"Oh," Kurz wavered. "Look, Captain, believe me I'm not headstrong, I'm only trying to help a family in trouble." Amazing how the mention of his father dissolved his self-confidence.

Whelan sensed he was shaky. "I told you, you're helping the wrong way."

"Maybe," Kurz said, "but it's too late to back out now. They're going to need protection."

"They'll get it," Whelan said. "You didn't have to come out here to tell me that."

"I'm worried, that's all," Kurz said.

"You ought to be worried."

Kurz stumbled out of the precinct house into the baking sunlight. What a disaster. You fell apart in there, Kurz, something you've never done with brass before. What's wrong? What's happening to you?

It was a waste of time to keep asking that question. You are away inside this thing, Harry, whatever you want to call it, the ball of wax, the red hot affair, the jungle. You are way inside and it is too late to worry about where you are going. You can only hope that eventually you will come out the other side in one piece.

Back in the squad room Powell was looking glummer than ever. "Marianne just phoned. She can't get a mover. Those nice people out there must have called up every mover in the city and told him they'd break up his trucks if he took the job."

"Screw them," Kurz said. "We'll hire a Hertz truck. That means we'll need some extra muscle. You know some guys who will help?"

"Sure," Powell said.

And who do you know, Harry? Your brother-in-law? Reardon? Do you know one friend who'd really want to help? No.

"I'll call Ann Macy," he said. "She'll get a couple of college kids."

Ann said it would be a breeze.

They rented a truck, picked it up at five o'clock and drove it to the Moser house. Three tall husky Negro kids were already sitting on the porch. Powell introduced them. "Some of my baseball players," he said proudly.

About ten minutes later Ann Macy arrived with three white volunteers, two long-haired intellectual types and a lively blonde coed. The heat was ferocious on the Mosers' second floor, but it was the most efficient, good-natured group Kurz had ever seen. He tried lifting some heavy stuff but it hurt his chest so badly he had to let Powell and the younger kids do the real work and content himself with playing administrator of the Coke supply. Marianne had her refrigerator full of bottles. They must have drunk fifty of them by the time they dragged the last trunk down the narrow stairs and slung it onto the packed truck.

"Ready to go," sang out one of the baseball players, cheerfully.

"No, we're not," Kurz said. "First we're going to do a little reconnaissance. You stay here and have another round of Coke."

He gave Powell a quick nod and they strode down the street to Kurz's car. Ann Macy ran after them. "Can't I come?"

"No."

By the time they reached the Dellwood development it was almost dark. The street in front of the Moser house looked deserted, at first glance. But as Kurz pulled into the driveway, his headlights caught a flash of white in the shrubbery that lined the property of the house next door. Kurz jumped out of the car and called: "Come on out of those bushes before you get hurt."

Incredible things began happening. A voice roared over a bullhorn: "THE NIGGER LOVERS ARE HERE." Lights came on in houses up and down the block. Out of the bushes emerged a small army of men carrying golf clubs, baseball bats and other heavy objects that looked in the gloom alarmingly like rifles. A heavy duty flashlight beam hit Kurz in the eyes, momentarily blinding him.

If it hadn't been for Powell, it might have been all over right there. Thinking fast, he slid behind the wheel, backed the car onto the lawn and threw the headlights on bright. The glare brought them to a dead stop. Comedy-like they bumbled into each other, pawed at their eyes.

"What the hell is going on here?" Kurz said.

"Free white Americans protecting their neighborhood," someone yelled.

"Listen to me," Kurz said. "I'm a detective. And there's another detective in that car radioing a report to police headquarters right now. I think you all better go home and think this whole thing over before somebody gets hurt."

"It's liable to be you, you son of a bitch," another voice yelled.

Suddenly there was a violent movement inside the crowd, and squirming through the front rank came Bernie Flannigan himself. He ran into the glare of the headlights until he was only a foot away from Kurz.

"It's him, the nigger-lover in person," he screamed. "He may be a cop, but he ain't here on official business. And look, he's got a nigger in the car."

A burly six-footer, built like a stevedore, leaped from the

crowd, one hand swinging a baseball bat like it was a toothpick. "Kurz," he yelled, "I told you what I'd do when I saw you."

Several things now happened very fast. The stevedore charged, screaming hatred. The others followed him. Powell blew the horn with everything he had, threw open the right hand door and drove the car straight at them. They broke in all directions and Kurz heard Powell yell: "Get in, Harry!"

He pivoted and did a swan dive into the front seat, whacking his head on the dashboard. Simultaneously Powell made a sharp right turn and went roaring off the lawn into the street. Lying face down, Kurz could only hear shouts, screams, curses, a clunk or two as flying objects hit the car. Then they were rolling down a typical city street lined with two-family houses. He sat up and Powell slowed down.

"You want to drive?"

"No."

They rode in silence for a while. Finally Powell said, "Well, we're not moving out there tonight, that's for sure."

"Yeah," Kurz said. "But what do we tell the Mosers? The truth will scare hell out of them."

"Maybe," Powell said, "but I think we'd better tell them something pretty close to it."

In five minutes they were standing in the denuded Moser living room, surrounded by shocked, listening faces as Powell told what they had seen.

"It was a real ugly crowd. Baseball bats, golf clubs, even a few rifles. I don't think it would be smart to go out there without a police escort and even if we could get one on such short notice, I don't think they'd let you go in the dark. It's a lot easier to protect people in daylight."

"But what are we going to do?" Marianne Moser said. "Where are we going to sleep? All our beds, sheets everything is in the truck."

"I can take one of the boys home with me," Powell said.

"You can stay at my place," Ann Macy said to Marianne

Moser. "I've got a great big couch I sleep on all the time when friends stay over."

"I can take the other two boys home to my place," Kurz said.

It was settled and they broke up, agreeing to meet at seven o'clock the following morning. Much to Kurz's relief, Powell took Billy Moser home with him. That left Kurz with the two younger boys, Daniel and Peter. Daniel was almost eleven, Peter eight, they informed him as they drove up the steep hill that ran through the center of the city.

"Are you guys in that gang your brother Billy is mixed up with?"

"Not us," said Daniel emphatically. "Billy's crazy. I keep telling him all the time he's crazy. The trouble is he's dumb. You should see the marks he gets in school."

"How about you?"

"I get good marks. So does Pete. Both of us are going to college."

"What are you going to do after that?"

"I think I'll be a Wall Street man," Daniel said. "I'm real good in arithmetic. They make a lot of money."

"How about you, Pete?"

"I don't know. I might want to be a detective."

"That's not a bad idea," Kurz said. "They're looking for guys with college training. What's your favorite subject in school?"

"History, I think."

"Mine's arithmetic," Daniel said. "The teacher told me I was the best in the class."

"That's great," Kurz said. "I never could do arithmetic."

"It's really easy," Daniel said.

The boyish chatter was like a sedative on Kurz's frazzled nerves. It blurred the memory of those screaming figures swinging baseball bats. He pulled into his driveway and escorted the two boys into the house. His mother was watching television in the darkened living room, as usual. He turned off the sound, flipped on the lights and introduced the Mosers. At first his mother was too flabbergasted to say anything but, "How do you do."

"These boys didn't get too much to eat tonight, Mom, on account of moving. You got anything in the icebox we could rassle up? I could use something myself."

This galvanized her. In ten minutes they were sitting down to cold roast beef sandwiches with a big chocolate cake for dessert.

The boys polished off the sandwiches, plus two pieces of cake each. Mother Kurz fussed over them, pouring extra milk in their glasses, urging them to try a third piece of cake or a second sandwich. "I just wish Harry ate that well at your age," she clucked. "I bet he'd be a lot taller now."

"Since when did you ever have trouble getting me to eat?"

"Oh, for a couple years after your father died you were a terrible problem."

"That's news to me."

"Oh, I'm sure it is. You're perfect now and always have been in your opinion. Would you boys like to look at television for a while or are you ready for bed?"

"I think we'd better make it bed," Kurz said. "We're getting up early tomorrow."

They went without a murmur. Kurz put them in his room and asked his mother to make up a bed on the couch for him.

"Will you kindly tell me what this is all about, Harry?" she asked as she spread the sheets on the couch.

He gave her a neutralized version of what was happening and shooed her out in the kitchen so he could use the telephone to call Whelan. He told the captain what he and Powell had seen on their reconnaissance earlier in the evening. Whelan almost went out of his mind. "You think you can get away with this, you bastard? What *are* you trying to pull? You're not assigned to my precinct. You've got absolutely no right to be out there. I'm going to make a full report of this to the commissioner, so help me Christ."

"Make all the goddamn reports you want," Kurz yelled, his

own temper exploding. "I want a detail out there tomorrow morning when we move that woman in."

"You'll get more than a detail before I'm through with you," Whelan screamed, and slammed down the telephone.

A queasy sensation enveloped Kurz's stomach. His chest jangled with pain. Whelan had friends, like every guy who made captain. Christ knew how many friends. He could blow sky high your little dream of making Chief of Detectives before the age of forty-five, Harry. He could really pour some very hot, even boiling, water on you.

He slept badly. The couch seemed full of lumps. His mother banged around the kitchen for another hour, cleaning up. She went to sleep with her door open and started snoring. Five minutes after his eyes finally closed (so it seemed) a hand was shaking his shoulder.

"Huh, what?" he groaned.

"Mr. Kurz," said Daniel Moser, "I'm afraid Peter's wet the bed again."

"Oh, no."

"He does it every so often. My daddy used to whip him everytime. But my mother lets him get away with it. Maybe you ought to whip him now."

What was there in this matter-of-fact boy's voice that made his flesh crawl? He suddenly heard Powell saying, *Bill Moser was wrong*. "You don't whip people for wetting the bed," Kurz said. "He probably didn't even know he was doing it."

"My daddy said he was just too lazy to get up."

"No," Kurz said, "that isn't it. But let's not argue about it. Let's change the sheets and get some sleep."

"He soaked the mattress too, I bet."

"I bet."

Fumbling in the linen closet for some sheets, he knocked six rolls of toilet paper off the shelf. The thumps awakened his mother. She peered around her door looking wispy and frightened. "What's wrong?" she gasped.

"Danny wet the bed."

"No, Peter. I'm Danny."

"Yeah, Peter wet the bed."

It was sounding like a situation comedy.

In the bedroom they found Peter sitting on the side of the bed crying. To Kurz's surprise, his mother took immediate charge. "Now, now," she said. "There's nothing to cry about. It happens to lots of boys your age. Mr. Kurz used to do it when he was a little boy."

"Really?" said Daniel.

"I don't remember that," Kurz said.

"Of course, you don't," his mother said. "Now stand up and let's get those wet pajamas off. Oh, you're lucky, the top is still dry. Go in and run some water in the bathtub and wash yourself and you can wear a pair of underwear pants to bed."

Peter disappeared.

"I still think you ought to whip him," Daniel said.

"Don't be silly," Mrs. Kurz said. "Come on, both of you, help me change the bed."

By the time Peter was back from the bathroom they had clean sheets on the bed and everyone was ready for sleep again. Seven o'clock arrived almost immediately, from Kurz's viewpoint. He staggered into the kitchen, poured coffee down his gullet while the boys slurped cereal. "You know," he said, "I think maybe the best thing would be for you guys to wait here until we get moved in. You can watch television, okay?"

"Are you afraid there might be trouble?" Daniel asked.

"I hope not," Kurz said.

"Billy says there's going to be trouble. He says they're going to try and kill us."

"There may be a little trouble from some crackpots," Kurz said, "but nothing serious."

He drove downtown through the semi-coolness of the morning to the Moser house. Everyone was on the porch, ready and waiting, even Ann Macy.

"I took the day off," she explained. "I said to myself, which was more important, pushing pills down those old geezers' throats—or this?"

"Let's go," Kurz said. "I'll take the girls in my car. The men go on the truck."

In ten minutes they were rolling down the city's western slope and the open streets of the Dellwood development were in sight. Five more minutes and they were braking to a stop in front of the house. At first glance everything looked serene. White, blue, rose, the other houses sat somnolently on their tiny plots in the early morning light like so many dozing animals. Then came the sensation one might get from seeing the Mona Lisa with a penciled moustache. *What is wrong with this picture?*

As they sat there, around the left corner of the Moser house ambled a tall, thin patrolman. A moment later another pudgier patrolman appeared around the right corner. The one on the right walked over to the picture window, turned and casually stuck his head through it. A sudden explosion of breath. They all knew simultaneously: there was no glass in any of the windows.

The two patrolmen met them on the walk. They were strangers to Kurz. The thin man looked worried. The pudgy one, who had put his head through the picture window, was grinning like an idiot.

"Jeez," said Laughing Boy, "they knocked out every pane of glass in the house."

"Every one," the thin man confirmed.

"Where's the detail we asked for?" Kurz growled.

"You're looking at it."

"Two cops. Whelan calls that a detail?"

"What are you talkin' about?" said Laughing Boy. "We been here a half hour without a sign of trouble."

As if his remark was a signal, a voice from the house next door boomed through a bullhorn: "THE NIGGERS ARE COMING. THE NIGGERS ARE COMING."

"No trouble," Kurz said wryly. "Get over there and take that damn horn away from that guy."

He told Powell, who was still behind the wheel of the truck, to back it into the driveway.

Once more the bullhorn boomed: "THE NIGGERS ARE COMING."

Kurz grabbed the more serious cop. "You better call Whelan and tell him you need another twenty men."

"Right," he said. "Is there a telephone in the house?"

"Yes, it was connected yesterday," Powell said as he joined them.

"Marianne," Kurz called, "you and the other girls go in the house. We'll quiet all this down in a half hour if things go right."

The bullhorn boomed again. Laughing Boy came back through the shrubbery. "He wouldn't give it to me," he said plaintively.

"Why didn't you take it?" Kurz roared. "The bastard is inciting a riot."

"What riot? I don't see nuth—" A stone the size of a baseball whizzed past them to clunk against the house. Two burly teenagers howled a war cry from the lawn across the street.

"Hey, listen, you kids," said Laughing Boy, "cut that out." He advanced down the lawn toward them, shaking his club like a schoolteacher. A rock knocked his hat off. As he stopped to pick it up, another one caught him in the leg. With a howl of rage he charged and the kids ran, disappearing behind the houses across the street.

Singly, in groups of two and three, people were moving toward them from both ends of the block. "THE NIGGERS ARE COMING," boomed the bullhorn.

With an oath, Kurz charged through the shrubbery onto the next lawn. In the doorway of a well-painted, red house stood a big muscular man wearing pajamas. A balding head, a wide flat Slavic nose, a massive jaw, was all Kurz could see as he raised the bullhorn to his lips and bellowed his paean of hate once more.

"Give me that horn, you bastard."

"AND THE NIGGER LOVER. NIGGER LOVER KURZ."

As he finished this sentence, Kurz hit him with everything he had right in the center of his big soft belly. He gave a squawk and crumpled to the ground, accordion style. Kurz picked up the horn and raced back through the bushes to the Moser lawn. There was a crowd of thirty or forty people on the sidewalk and in the street, with more arriving every second. The thin cop and Laughing Boy were down on the front of the lawn looking scared. Powell and the male movers had formed a phalanx around the door of the house.

With Mr. Bullhorn eliminated, the crowd had no leader. They just milled around shouting things like, "No niggers in Dellwood." Some of the women were in housecoats; several men wore pajama tops. Only the teenagers seemed really ready for action and were yelling, "Come on, Let's clean 'em out. Let's clean 'em out." Kurz decided there was a good chance to stall them until more cops arrived. He raised the bullhorn to his lips.

"PEOPLE OF DELLWOOD, I URGE YOU TO RETURN TO YOUR HOMES IMMEDIATELY. YOU HAVE BEEN MISLED BY AGITATORS AND EXTREMISTS. THE FAMILY THAT IS MOVING IN HERE CONSISTS OF A WIDOW AND THREE SONS. HER HUSBAND WAS A POLICE OFFICER, KILLED IN THE LINE OF DUTY. THESE PEOPLE WANT TO BE GOOD NEIGHBORS AND THEY WILL BE GOOD NEIGHBORS IF YOU ONLY GIVE THEM A CHANCE."

For a moment it worked, they were quieter, almost listening. Then through the shrubbery staggered Mr. Bullhorn, clutching his ruined stomach. "Bastard," he screamed, "that's my horn."

He turned to the crowd. "He attacked me. Rupture—I know it——" He fell to his knees and vomited on the Moser lawn.

"That man is under arrest for inciting a riot," Kurz said. "We don't want to arrest anyone else. We won't even press charges against him if you all go home now."

"Nigger lover!" screamed Bullhorn, lumbered to his feet and charged. He outweighed Kurz by at least thirty pounds. Kurz sidestepped, stuck out his foot and Bullhorn went sprawling face down on the grass. Kurz leaped on his back and pinned him. The crowd gave a yell and surged forward. The thin man drew his gun and fired into the air. It stopped them dead.

A teenager threw a rock at Kurz. It missed and hit Bullhorn. He gave a scream of pain and thrashed like a maniac. But he could not break Kurz's grip.

Then came the sweetest siren Kurz had ever heard. It growled again and again over the rooftops and down the streets of Dellwood, freezing everyone into an absurd tableau. Another ten seconds and two squad cars and a van were pulling up on the edge of the crowd and cops were piling out in twos and threes.

Whelan got out of the first squad car and ran up the lawn to Kurz. "What the hell are you doing?" he said.

"Subduing a prisoner," Kurz said. "This man is under arrest for attempting to incite a riot."

"Let him up," Whelan said.

Bullhorn staggered to his feet. "Captain Whelan," he blubbered, "this man assaulted me. Punched me in the stomach. Rupture, I know it. I'm sick."

"Go home, Mr. Muraski," Whelan said. "Go home and mind your own business. I'm in charge here now."

Muraski picked up his bullhorn. Kurz grabbed it away from him. "That's evidence," he said. "This is what he used to wake up the whole damn neighborhood."

"Give it back to him," Whelan said.

Clutching his horn with a triumphant leer, Muraski went home. Cops ringed the lawn, then moved out into the street and firmly and steadily pushed the crowd back on the right and left. Whelan went back to the squad car and lectured them over a loudspeaker attachment.

"AS CAPTAIN OF THIS PRECINCT IT IS MY DUTY TO PRESERVE LAW AND ORDER. THAT IS WHAT WE ARE HERE TO DO. WE WILL NOT TOLERATE ANY VIOLENCE FROM EITHER SIDE. I URGE YOU ALL TO

RETURN TO YOUR HOMES AND RESUME YOUR ORDINARY ACTIVITIES."

The crowd slowly melted away until there were only a few teenagers left. They congregated on the lawn across the street and shouted random insults in which the word "nigger" was basic.

"Can't you get rid of them?" Kurz asked Whelan.

"What can I do? They're on private property. And they got a right to demonstrate, too."

Kurz went into the house and found Marianne Moser and the other girls sweeping what looked like a hundred pounds of broken glass. "We called three Negro glaziers," Ann Macy said. "They're all coming out. We'll have every window in the house back before sundown."

"Great," Kurz said. It was 8:35 A.M. and he felt ready for bed.

Ann Macy squeezed his arm and murmured, "I don't know what we would have done without you, Harry."

She was aglow, practically ecstatic. Hurrah. Hurrah. But Marianne Moser was not quite so chipper. In fact, she looked positively mournful.

He went out to the truck to help Powell and the others with the unloading. "Marianne doesn't look too good," he said.

"Can you blame her?" Powell asked.

"Hell, no. Is there anything we can do?"

"Pray," Powell said, and handed him a hassock.

It took them about two hours to unload the truck. By that time the glaziers were busy putting in windows, and the teenagers had gone off to school. But they were replaced by a group of women who took up positions on the lawn carrying placards which read: NO DOPE IN DELLWOOD—MUGGERS WE DON'T NEED—TO EACH HIS OWN. They were organized, too. They managed to maintain a group of about fifteen throughout the morning. When one woman left, another replaced her. Meanwhile, reporters were everywhere. Toward noon a mobile television team appeared to film the ladies on the lawn and the barricade of cops confronting them.

Kurz refused to answer any questions or pose for television cameras. He advised everyone else in the group to do likewise, except Marianne Moser.

She stood in the doorway of her house, gazing across the street at the women with their signs and talked to the television reporters.

"Did you anticipate any trouble, Mrs. Moser?"

"No," she said, "none at all. After all, I'm an American citizen, I thought I could move anywhere I wanted."

"Isn't it true, though, that you had to buy the house through another person?"

"The other person bought it and decided to sell it to me."

"Why did you want to move out here?"

"Because I wanted to bring my children up in a neighborhood where there was less crime and violence."

Kurz walked away. It was too painful.

He wandered through the house. The girls were busy unpacking. Powell and the boys were moving the heavy stuff around. The glaziers were chipping at their windows.

And you, Kurz? What are you doing?

He caught Powell's eye. "I think we'd better check in downtown."

"Yeah," Powell said.

Marianne Moser looked panicky when they told her they were leaving. They assured her the police detail would stay on duty and they themselves would be back in a few hours. They went out the front door and down the lawn to Kurz's car. The moment they passed through the line of cops at the edge of the lawn, and the women across the street saw them, a storm of screams and shouts erupted.

"There he is, the nigger lover."

"Why don't you arrest him?"

"The nigger lover with his nigger."

They drove downtown. Powell didn't say a word. Kurz began to wonder what he was thinking. Maybe at this point he was incapable of talking to any white man without prefacing his remarks with a curse.

"We're in deep trouble out there," Powell finally said. "Those good neighbors aren't going to quit in one day."

"I know."

"And that guy Whelan, he isn't exactly on our side, is he?'

"You can say that again."

"I'm worried about what he said to those reporters. He talked to them for a long time."

"Yeah."

They grabbed a quick sandwich in the diner behind the precinct house. They were drinking their coffee when a kid came in selling the first edition of the afternoon paper.

RACE RIOT IN DELLWOOD, screamed the headlines.

Kurz bought a copy and spread it out on the counter. The story had knocked Vietnam right off the front page. The news part of it ran down the right hand column. Sprayed all over the rest of the page were interviews with housewives, friendly real estate man Flannigan, Marianne Moser. But the black type that caught their eyes first and held them to the last word was an interview with Captain Whelan.

POLICE CAPTAIN DENOUNCES CITY DETECTIVE

Kurz could almost feel his corned beef sandwich turning rancid in his belly as he read Whelan's words: "I regret to say that the entire blame for this situation rests on the shoulders of a fellow policeman, Detective Harold Kurz. He was the man who bought this house and resold it to Mrs. Moser. I don't know what he thought he was doing or what he hoped to gain from it. But such tactics naturally aroused the fear and suspicion of everyone in this neighborhood. Never have I seen a police officer use such deplorable judgment. Moreover, Detective Kurz attempted to act as a police official in the course of these proceedings, in spite of the fact that he is not assigned to this precinct and has no right whatsoever to exercise any authority, use his badge, gun or fists in any way in this precinct. Although Mr. Kurz has some rather important friends on the police force, I would not be at all surprised if the commissioner is forced to find him guilty of serious misconduct."

There was more about how the captain hoped the episode would not mar the city's "perfect record of racial cooperation." He assured the reporters that he and the rest of the police force were "absolutely neutral" in racial matters and were only interested in "maintaining peace at any price."

Beside him Powell whispered: "Jesus, he really reamed you."

Down the short, ferociously hot block to the precinct house, Kurz felt like he was walking on water. Voices kept whispering inside him. *This couldn't have happened. Not to Harry Kurz, the guy who had all the angles figured. Whelan didn't really say that. Somebody slipped you that paper for a gag. What you know is happening can't be happening.*

In the precinct house, the day desk sergeant, a wide-mouthed slob named Brennan, was reading the paper. A big grin spread across his stupid kisser when he saw them.

"Hey, Harry," he yelled, "what's the angle? You goin' into politics?"

"Drop dead."

"We'll see who drops dead. The old man wants to talk to you."

Kurz found Captain Crotty flipping papers on his desk. He studied Kurz for a moment as if he were measuring a freak for a circus act. "This is the last thing in the world I ever figured you to pull."

"I didn't pull anything. I was just trying to help a widow and three kids."

Even he had to wince at how ridiculous that sounded on his lips. Harry Kurz, the angle player, the coolest cat on the force, risking, no, destroying, his career to help a widow and three kids.

"Technically," Crotty was saying, "you're not under my jurisdiction. But everybody thinks you are and I've been getting phone calls from the commissioner, the mayor, you name it. Now, buster, this is going to go to departmental hearings. I want you to make it clear that I didn't know one thing about what you were doing, you got me?"

"I got you."

Kurz climbed the old iron stairs to the second floor, scarcely noticing the heat. He was relieved to find the squad room empty, until he found out why. "This thing's running through the precinct like wildfire," Powell said. "They're talking about organizing a march to Dellwood, a march to City Hall, you name it."

The phone rang. It was Uncle Harold's secretary. "The Chief Inspector would like to see you right away," she said.

"I'll be right over."

He drove across town through the Congo. On at least five corners orators were screaming to big crowds. First he felt bewildered, then trapped, finally horrified. For a moment he was tempted to keep on driving straight onto the expressway and west as far as his money could take him. But he found himself parking in front of the shabby grey sandstone front of Police Headquarters.

Upstairs in Uncle Harold's office, where he had once received bright greetings from secretaries and clerks, eyes avoided him, faces confronted walls. Harold sat smoking a cigarette with fast, fast, fast puffs, the newspaper spread out on his desk in front of him. Kurz sat down and Harold closed the newspaper slowly, as if it were the doomsday book. His face was waxen. His eyes looked like they had been painted onto his head someplace in Japan.

"How could you do it?" he said in a very small voice, almost a whisper.

It jarred Kurz worse than a shout. "I didn't do anything," he replied automatically and almost added the bit about the widow and the kids. But it was too futile.

"You didn't do anything—" Harold's hand made a feeble flailing gesture at the paper. "You didn't do anything——"

"All right, I blew it. I goofed. I got mixed up in something—I don't know. It just got started and I couldn't stop it."

"You couldn't stop it," Harold said in that same small, almost dead, voice.

"No, I couldn't stop it. All I wanted to do——"

They just sat there. A fan whirred in the corner. A typewriter clicked in the outer office. Down on the street horns blew. There he sits, this little wax dummy in the seat of power. Only one step below the Chief of Police.

Where you were going to sit. Once upon a time. Where you were going to sit in ten or fifteen years. Once upon a time.

"I talked to the commissioner," Harold said. "He said there was nothing he could do. They've got to have a hearing."

"It figures."

"And with O'Bannon on your back." His voice slid off, cracked, squeaked like an old 78 record. He swiveled sideways, and stared out the window. "Just like your old man," he said. "Just like him."

"What the hell do you mean?"

Harold glared at him. "Maybe I should have told you a long time ago. Maybe it would have straightened you out. I loved your old man. But you know what he was? A screw-up. When he wasn't on the sauce he was holed up with some dame. I was always half crazy covering for him. The night he was killed, I was working, he was drinking in that bar downtown as usual. He was too goddamn drunk to use his head or his gun in that alley. I knew for years he was gonna go like that. That's why I've been so tough on you——"

Kurz walked down the stairs. He didn't even want to ride in an elevator. He might meet someone he knew. He was tempted to slink down the block to his car, his coat collar up, buy dark glasses, a moustache for disguise. He drove back through the Congo, past the orators, noting that the crowds were getting bigger. Only when he reached the precinct house and walked toward it through the waves of heat was he hit by the full horror of what he now confronted.

Tonight you have to go back there. Without you they might get killed. You have to go back there.

Upstairs the squad room was crowded with detectives now.

But no one paid any attention to him, except Powell. He might have been the invisible man. Finally, he couldn't stand it and said, "Let's get the hell out of here."

They drove down to Wanamaker's Bar and had a beer. Mr. Proprietor served them himself and refused to take their money. "It's on the house today. We're servin' free drinks to all friends of the Negro people. Yessir!" He turned to the dozen or so other drinkers at the bar. "This here's Detective Kurz, the man who got Mrs. Moser in that lily white neighborhood out there."

Necks craned. A short, fat man sitting next to him said, "I'd like to shake your hand."

Kurz shook and drank his beer.

"What's the good word, if any?" Powell asked.

He was trying to be sympathetic. For a moment Kurz felt like telling him the whole sad story. But why bother? How the hell could Powell understand it? If he makes Detective First Grade before he retires, he'll consider it a miracle. "Not good," he said.

"Maybe you ought to—cool it," Powell said. "I can go out there tonight."

"Nuts," Kurz said. "I promised I'd be there and I'll be there."

Why? So Ann Macy could grab you and murmur *Oh, Harry, you were wonderful?* Or taste a little gratitude in Marianne Moser's eyes? Or was it so bad a little more damage couldn't possibly matter? That was probably it.

They stopped at Kurz's house and picked up the two younger Moser boys. They had been watching television and knew the whole story. His mother was remarkably calm. She assumed it was part of his job. "I just hope there isn't any more rioting," she murmured.

"Boy, were you wrong," Daniel Moser said, "when you predicted just a little trouble."

"Yeah," Kurz said. "Was I ever wrong."

At the house Kurz was shocked to find the police detail reduced to five men. The cheerleaders on the lawn across the street now numbered well over thirty and included a lot of men and teenage boys.

"Hey, there's the nigger lover," someone yelled.

"Yeah, he's bringin' reinforcements."

"They're too small to eat for dinner. We'd eat them for lunch!"

They shepherded the kids up the lawn and into the house. Pete kept turning around. "What are they saying? Why are they calling us niggers?"

"They're screwballs," Powell said. "Don't pay any attention to them."

Inside the house everything looked great. The rugs were down, pictures were on the walls and there was food cooking in the kitchen. Marianne Moser and Ann Macy sat in the living room chattering with two men of the cloth, both white.

They were introduced and Ann Macy explained: "These gentlemen are from the local churches. Father Fitzpatrick is from St. Aloysius and Dr. King is from St. Andrews'."

"We wanted to make it clear to Mrs. Moser," said Dr. King, "that these people do not represent the neighborhood. There are many people who are ready and willing to welcome the Mosers."

"Meanwhile," Kurz said, "can't you do something about those characters across the street?"

"I really don't think an appeal to reason will—do much good at present," said Dr. King.

"Appeal to reason, hell," Kurz said. "Excuse my French, but I want you to go out there and blast them." He turned to Father Fitzpatrick. "I bet ninety percent of them are Catholics. Can't you do anything?"

Father Fitzpatrick was very young and almost too handsome. "My pastor gave me permission to make this call," he said. "But he expressly forbade me to have anything to do with any demonstrations. I'm sorry——"

"Harry—we're grateful to them for coming. Isn't that enough?" Ann Macy said.

Kurz sighed. "I don't know, I guess so. You're the expert."

He walked out on them, through the kitchen into the backyard.

Ann followed him. "Harry, that was awfully rude. They're really trying to help."

"I'm sorry," he said.

"Something else really encouraging happened. A woman walked right past that crowd on the lawn and up to the door to give Marianne a cake she had baked. You should have heard what those people called her."

"Will she come back?" Kurz asked. "When she gets four or five phone calls tonight telling her what they're going to do to her house, her kids, her car, will she come back?"

"Yes, I think she will."

"I don't."

"Harry, what's the matter?" Ann said, touching his arm. "You were so full of fire and hope this morning. Without you we would have all collapsed."

"That might have been the best possible thing that could have happened."

"No! Don't you realize what a tremendous thing we're doing? It's going to work. I know it will."

He didn't know why he said it. It was as if some diabolical spirit had possessed him and the words spoke themselves on his lips. "I'll make you a bet," he said. "I'll make you a bet that by twelve o'clock tonight Marianne Moser will be babbling like an idiot, and begging us to get her out of here."

"Not if you stand by her."

"I'll stand by her but it won't do any good."

The clergy departed. They ate supper in the dining room. Pork chops. Again Kurz had no appetite.

"How are we going to get to school?" Billy Moser said. "Those kids are going to be laying for us."

"There'll be other kids who'll be friends," Ann Macy said.

"Where are they? I sure don't see any on this block."

"I hope the white kids aren't ahead of us in school," Daniel said. "I read a story about Negro kids moving into white schools and even the smart ones found they were way behind."

"You'll catch up," Powell said.

It was twilight and they were having coffee when the bullhorn started. "GO HOME NIGGERS."

"Will they keep the police here as long as we need them?" Marianne Moser asked.

"Sure," Kurz said.

"I wonder how long that will be."

"GO HOME NIGGERS."

"I wouldn't be surprised if they give up pretty quick," Powell said.

I would, Kurz thought to himself but said nothing.

They went into the living room and turned on the television. Who was there but His Honor the Mayor Graham (Everything's Jake) O'Connor. "I want to assure you," he said, jabbing a finger in the Kennedy manner. "I want to assure every citizen of this city that my administration is determined to guarantee complete equality in housing, jobs, education. But these things take time. They cannot be achieved overnight. They cannot be achieved by reckless, intemperate gestures. By techniques that smack of subterfuge and double dealing."

The pork chop congealed beside the rancid corned beef in Kurz's stomach. They tuned out the mayor and sat around telling each other, and especially Marianne Moser, that tomorrow was another day. The boys could start school tomorrow. They'd meet friends. Marianne Moser could look up the woman who brought the cake. Unfortunately she didn't get her name. But she would find her somehow.

"NIGGER GO HOME," croaked the bullhorn.

"Why don't they take that away from him?" Powell said. He went out to tell it to the cops and came back looking glum. "It's too dark to find him. He moves up and down the street behind the houses."

"NIGGER GO HOME," croaked the bullhorn.

The boys spent the evening downstairs in the rumpus room playing with toys and watching their own television set. At nine o'clock Marianne Moser told them to go upstairs and get ready for bed. She had just returned to the living room when there was a crash of glass and a scream of pain. They all but trampled each other getting up the narrow stairs and down the tiny second floor hall. In the back bedroom little Pete Moser lay on the floor in a widening pool of blood.

"Mommy, Mommy," he cried. "My leg. Somebody threw a rock. My leg."

Billy Moser came charging out of the room across the hall with a knife a foot long in his hand. "Kill the white bastards," he screamed. "Kill them." Powell grabbed him and threw him back into the room.

"Harry, your handerchief, quick," Ann Macy called. She was kneeling on the floor beside Peter. He handed it to her and she knotted it into a tourniquet above the boy's knee. The bottom half of his leg was wet with blood. It looked abnormally dark on his black skin. On the floor it was red enough.

"Call an ambulance," she said. "I'm afraid they cut an artery."

In five minutes an ambulance came clanging to the door. They carried Pete Moser out in a stretcher. Kurz and Ann Macy followed them, escorting Marianne Moser. On the lawn across the street a whoop of triumph exploded.

"Hey, we got one."

"Three more to go."

"Who threw that rock? Let's give him a medal."

Ann Macy went with Marianne Moser in the ambulance. Back in the house Kurz did not have much to say and neither did Powell. They turned on the television and absorbed stupidity for an hour and a half while outside the bullhorn croaked: "DEATH TO NIGGERS AND NIGGER LOVERS TOO."

The two women returned about ten o'clock, looking grim. "He had to have a transfusion," Ann Macy said. "They decided to keep him overnight at least."

Marianne Moser sank into a chair as if it were her casket.

"I'll make some coffee," Ann Macy said.

"NIGGER GO HOME," croaked the bullhorn.

"Oh, Jesus," Marianne Moser said.

They did not hear the rifle go off until the bullet came through the picture window and hit the opposite wall. "Down on the floor," Kurz yelled. "Turn out the lights in the kitchen, Ann." As he spoke, he reached up and flipped off the living room lights.

One of the cops shoved open the front door. "Anybody hit?"

"No."

"We called for a squad car. We'll get the bastard."

"Good luck," Kurz said.

They lay on the floor for ten minutes. The rifleman did not fire again. "We'll turn on the lights," Kurz said. "But let's lie low for another ten minutes."

He turned on the lights and they lay there looking at each other, prone on the deep blue rug. Suddenly Marianne Moser began to weep. "Oh, Jesus," she wept. "Oh, Jesus, please help me. I can't do it."

"Yes, you can," Powell said, "Yes, you can."

"I can't. I can't. What kind of life is this, crawling on the floor like animals, my baby's blood upstairs. What kind of life?"

"Lousy," Powell said, "but it will get better."

"Not for me," Marianne Moser sobbed. "Never for me. How can I live with those people out there? They want me dead. They want me and my babies dead."

Kurz sat in the far corner of the living room and watched Marianne Moser go to pieces. Jim Powell and Ann Macy tried to talk to her but she was past them into that never-never land of pure hysteria. "Dead," she screamed. "Dead," and pounded on the rug, then staggered to her feet and ran to the window screaming: "Get it over with now. Kill me now." Powell had to tackle her. Together he and Macy dragged her, sobbing and wailing, across the floor into the dining area.

"NIGGER GO HOME," croaked the bullhorn.

"Get me out of here, please. Get me out of here before I go crazy," Marianne Moser shrieked.

Daniel Moser appeared on the stairs rubbing his eyes. "What's the matter? I heard Mommy crying. Did they hurt her?"

"No," Kurz said.

"Why are you sitting on the floor?"

"Because they're shooting at us."

Daniel merely looked puzzled. Like Powell, he was too intelligent to hate anybody.

"Go upstairs and put on your clothes," Kurz said. "We'll be leaving soon. Tell Billy."

"I'm glad." Daniel said. "I don't like this place at all."

"You and me both, kiddo."

One minute later Powell crawled back into the living room. "She's had it," he said.

"I figured," Kurz said.

"We'll put them in a hotel for tonight and move the stuff out tomorrow."

"Sure," Kurz said.

"She's paid up for a month in the old apartment. She can go back there. I don't think they've rented it yet."

"Good," Kurz said.

Good for Marianne Moser, good for Jim Powell, good for Ann Macy. But not good for Kurz. He was the loser. The simple stupid loser.

The kids got dressed. Ann Macy packed two suitcases. The cops escorted them down to Kurz's car. The crowd on the lawn across the street cheered lustily. They drove away.

Chapter Ten

By midnight it was all over. The Mosers were asleep in their hotel room, Jim Powell had plodded wearily home and Harry Kurz was escorting Ann Macy up the stairs to her apartment. She was disconsolate. She talked about how bad, how sad, she felt.

"It's almost as if some of that hate—has gotten inside me."

Oh, so sad. But no sad thoughts for Harry Kurz, no thoughts at all for the real loser. Only Harry Kurz thinks sad thoughts for his career. No one else gives a damn. In the living room he stood there dumbly remembering how she had danced her clothes off, and danced you, Kurz. Oh, how she danced you. You went dancing to disaster with your eyes open.

She slumped on the couch. "Well," she said, "at least we—did our best."

The Girl Scout bit. She was unbelievable. So what do you do? Walk out quietly, thank you very much, Miss Macy, for some great screwing and incidentally for wrecking my life.

No, that was not your style. No matter what happened, Kurz got a dividend. A laugh, a drink, a lay. And you will draw one last dividend here.

He took off his coat and sat down beside her on the couch. "The best thing we can do is forget it as fast as possible."

"No," she said fiercely. "I never want to forget it. I want to remember every word of it. I especially want you to remember it. But not in a hating way. I mean—if the two of us share it as part of—what we mean to each other, we overcome it, Harry. I know we can."

"Sure," he said. "Sure." While his fingers caressed the back of her neck.

She moved into his arms. "Oh, Harry, I never needed you so much. Even worse than the night little Harry——"

In five minutes he had her undressed and in bed. He touched everything twice, the nipples, the honey soft pussy, those firm full thighs. He gave them all a little extra farewell fingering. And then took her, with maximum intensity, a cold, intellectual ferocity that measured and celebrated every wiggle and squirm, touch of the tongue, crush of the breasts beneath his iron chest. That's what he was, an iron man, or a stone man, or an ice man, in the air conditioner's hum, while outside the city sweltered and dark laughter drifted from menacing porches.

Ohhhhhhhhh, how she clung to him, murmuring, crying out. It was over, the load was well dropped and still she would not let him go. But he finally broke free and went into the bathroom, washed himself, put on his underwear, came out, put on his pants and began buttoning his shirt

"Oh," she said, hugging the pillow, "stay for the night."

"No."

Never had Harry Kurz spoken a more deadly word. It transfixed her there on the bed like an arrow in her back. She turned over and sat up.

"What's the matter?"

"Now you ask," he said, buttoning his shirt. "Now you finally ask."

"What——?" she said, pleading.

"While I was fucking you just now I kept wondering whether it was worth the trouble to tell you anything. I figured it would be easier to just walk out of here and never come back."

She was crying already. Standard procedure. "Please, Harry, don't. Tell me what I've done."

"What you've done? Before I met you I had a nice career

going for me. I was on my way to the top of the Police Department. Now I'm on my way to the bottom. Tomorrow they're going to drag me down to the commissioner's office and bring me up on charges. And they're going to find me guilty of every single one. That means I'm through in the Police Department, thanks to you."

"Harry, it can't be that bad. You can fight it. You did the right thing!"

"The right thing."

He looked at her drooping on the side of the bed. That beautiful confident face was falling apart. Those proud shoulders drooped, the breasts with them. She looked like one of those pictures of the victims in documentaries on the concentration camps.

"It's about time you got it through your button head that your version of the right thing is not my version, and it's not the version of ninety-eight percent of the people in this city. You and your friends are a bunch of idiots trying to live out of books. Do you think I ever gave a goddamn for one of your ideas? From start to finish I kidded you along for one reason and one reason only. You've got something very nice there between your legs, and when you're in the right mood you don't have the slightest interest in protecting it."

He took a deep slow breath. His throat felt like he had swallowed a scouring pad. Pain knifed through his chest. "So there it is."

"Goodbye, Harry."

She said it staring straight ahead, not moving from the slumped, broken posture on the edge of the bed.

"Goodbye," he said.

He slammed the door and clumped down the stairs, through the vestibule into the murderous heat. For a moment it felt like the whole sky had fallen on him. How did people stand it without air conditioners? It was enough to send the entire city into a frenzy of claustrophobia. He walked through the murky darkness to his car and sat there behind the wheel just trying to breathe.

You told her, oh, yes, you told her. You got a double dividend up there, Kurz. You really told her.

He drove aimlessly around the city. People had apparently lost interest in sleeping. The streets were crowded. He stopped in a strange bar up in the north end and had a beer. No one paid the slightest attention to him. He got back in the car and drove some more. Down into the Congo he rolled. There were the orators still blatting on the street corners. He stopped and listened to one.

"There's only one hope for the black man in this city," the speaker shrieked. "He's got to set up a separate government, a city inside a city. We got to have our mayor, our own council. We got to gather our own taxes and spend the money our way. There's no other hope, I tell you, no other way of keeping Whitey's hand out of our pockets."

Idiocy. Idiots to the left of you. Idiots to the right of you. The city is full of them. And you are alone, Kurz. Absolutely alone.

He turned on the radio and what was there but the fat-dripping voice of Mr. NAACP. "Thanks to the courage of a small handful of white and Negro citizens, this city is now face to face with the ugly fact that prejudice exists!"

Off. Off with Mr. NAACP. Off with Ann Macy. Off with Harry Kurz.

What to do? Drive west? Get a job in a warehouse? Join the army?

The idiocy is seeping into your brain, Kurz. And you are alone. Absolutely alone.

Jesus. He pulled over to the curb and sat there behind the wheel staring up at strange housefronts on a street whose name he didn't even know, shaking. His heart pounded so hard he was sure it was coming through his ribs. Sweat ran off his nose, drolled down his neck, burned in his crotch. What was it? What was happening? Oh, you read about it in college, remember? Anxiety. And you had almost laughed wondering how someone could work themselves into such a nervous corner. Now you knew. Now you knew.

It lasted about ten minutes. He drove home, totally exhausted. Up the creaky old porch steps, he dragged himself into the living room. "Harry," his mother said through the television dimness, "the mayor's been calling you. He's been calling you all night."

"Did you get a number?"

"Yes, it's on your night table."

His watch read 1:30. A hell of an hour to call anyone. But there was probably some sort of answering service to guarantee His Honor some sleep. He dialed. Jake O'Connor answered the phone himself. "Harry," he said, "I've been trying to get you all night. I want this thing straightened out before I go to bed. Can you come over and see me?"

The mayor's mansion was on the edge of the park, only five minutes away. His Honor met him at the door, in bathrobe and slippers. He was looking good, considering his earlier career as the hardest drinker and biggest lover in the city's history. His father had been one of the kingpins of the old regime and for a long time Jake had been one of the original Irish playboys. But when his father got knocked off politically, Jake had pulled himself together and appeared on the scene as a reformer, no less.

One thing no one could deny: he had Irish charm. Kurz could feel it engulfing him as they shook hands. "You were Red Burke's partner for a couple of years, weren't you?"

"That's right."

Going down a long hall past a series of Early American paintings, Kurz remembered the way he used to laugh at poor Red. So simple he was, so absolutely honest. He was always arresting the wrong gambler, giving a ticket to the mayor's mistress. And what did he get for it? Four bullets in the back one dark night in an abandoned railroad station. Jake O'Connor knew why. But he never really explained it. He just pointed to Red's corpse as the perfect reason why he should clean up City Hall.

Mayor O'Connor led Kurz into a big, square study lined with books. Air conditioners hummed. It was deliciously cool.

The desk in the corner was piled with papers. Jake was working at this job. He talked about Red while he mixed two scotches and soda. "Red broke you in, didn't he? You drove a patrol car together."

"That's right."

"He should have stayed with the car. Life is a lot simpler on a beat. When you get to be a detective——"

The implication—the connection—was painfully clear. Jesus, to sit hearing yourself compared to Red Burke. Harry Kurz, the man with double vision, the both ends against the middle expert.

Before he could answer, the door swung open and a tall, remarkably forceful looking woman walked into the room. "Do you mind if I join you?" she said.

"No, of course not," the mayor said.

With obvious reluctance, he introduced his wife, Paula. She was old Protestant money and looked it, a narrow, haughty face dominated by wide, striking eyes that enveloped you in cool, unabashed judgment.

"Well," said the mayor with forced humor, "now that we've got a caucus, give it to us straight, Harry. What's your angle?"

They looked at each other, the man at the top and the man at the bottom. Suddenly Kurz was so tired he wanted to tell the whole idiotic, humiliating truth. But it was impossible. How could you take another human being through that jungle of experience? How could you make them understand the connections between black boys' faces in a living room and a white girl whispering in a bed and a small boy dying in a hospital ward and a phone call from your favorite saloon? He found himself mumbling inanely: "I don't know. I got hooked, I guess. You know, my partner's wife and kids."

Mayor O'Connor sighed and took a long swallow of his drink. "You goofed, Harry," he said. "I guess you know that. The Chief wants to hang, draw and quarter you."

"So I hear."

"The commissioner feels pretty much the same way."

Nod. What else can you do?

Paula Stapleton O'Connor stirred restlessly in her chair. "I don't see any reason why——"

"Well, I do," the mayor said. "I've got to live with this Police Department. Live with them *and* educate them. But live with them first. Harry understands it."

Nod. Harry understands everything. He is very smart. Or was. And he wishes Madame O'Connor, who obviously wants to help, would pack herself and her bleeding heart off to bed. Harry has had just about all the help he needs from sentimental females.

Jake O'Connor sat there looking tired but astute. So astute, The man in charge. The way you saw yourself, Harry, in ten years. Sitting behind a desk, deciding who gets what. A lovely feeling. "I don't want any departmental hearings, Harry, any more than you do. So let's make a deal. Put in your papers now and I'll smother the whole thing. You're through in the Department anyhow."

There it goes, ten years. There goes your nicely planned life, Kurz, all your stupid little dreams. "You don't have to worry about a job," the mayor was saying. "There's a couple of openings on the State Civil Rights Commission for trained investigators. If you're really interested in this thing you can do a lot for them."

"Like what?"

"Investigating discrimination complaints against unions, employers. They need somebody who can dig out facts. Nine times out of ten that's what stops them."

"I think we need Mr. Kurz right here. In this city," Mrs. O'Connor said.

There was a moment of very tense silence while the mayor stared down his wife. "I do too," he said, "but not now. Not for six months anyway. These things take time, Harry. You've got to work on people, soften them up. We're going to buy that house, give Mrs. Moser back her money. In six months I guarantee you there'll be a Negro family living there."

They were at the door shaking hands, Mrs. O'Connor

frowning. "Please come see us," she said, "if there's any difficulty——"

Doors slammed. You were on the steps in the hot darkness with the finality of it burning in your guts. Suddenly, there was a voice calling: "Harry."

Jim Powell walked toward him. "I phoned your house. Your mother told me you were down here. What's the story?"

What do you say? *Get lost you black bastard. Get lost with all your coon friends?* Oh, sure. And what would Powell do? What would those sad knowing eyes say? Face it, Kurz. Face it for the first time. You are the spoiled boy. This is the man. He has been through it, and you, tasting the first two or three swallows, are screaming and kicking like a six-year-old on castor oil.

"I'm through. He wants me to hand in my papers. Nice and quiet. No hearings."

"Oh, Christ."

"But you're okay. He didn't say a word about you."

They stood face to face under the street light. "I'm not here for that," Powell said. "I'm worried about you."

"Thanks," Kurz said.

"I knew it was wrong from the start," Powell said. "But I—couldn't think white on it, if you know what I mean."

Kurz forced a grin. "Neither could I. Me of all people. I don't give a shit for the movement and I never did."

"Who gives a shit for it, that way?" Powell said. "Personally I think it hurts as much as it helps. What counts is caring about people. Individual people. That's what you did."

"Did I?"

"You did. Don't talk yourself out of it, Harry. You did."

Confusion, weariness, fogged his brain. He fumbled for the certainty and it slipped through his fingers like a muddy football. Fumble, fall on it, Kurz, smother the goddamn thing. You've got to own it. It's your one chance.

Ann Macy. Can you tell Powell what you did, tell him what you said to her? He slumped against the door of his car, rubbed his sleeve across his streaming face. "I did care about those kids. I remember how I felt when my old man——

"But Christ, Jim, I did the worst thing. I was so full of—I don't know. I told Ann I only did it to keep her putting out. I creamed her. I really did. I hit her with the whole thing."

"Christ," Powell said. He stared at his brown shoes. "It's not my business. That's between you and her. But——"

"I'll call her. Apologize at least."

To his amazement, the promise held all the way home. His mother had gone to bed. He muttered a thanks for small favors and dialed Ann Macy's number. No answer. Again and again the phone rang. He redialed the number. Once more he listened to the long rings vanish into the silence.

It was odd. More than odd. It was alarming. Words suddenly tumbled into his mind, *pulling me down—I need you, Harry. Need your strength—more than ever—.* A possibility caromed through his mind. He dismissed it. Back it caromed like a handball in a four-walled court. He ran out of the living room, down the front steps to his car and roared recklessly down the hot dark streets to Ann Macy's apartment. Up the flights of stairs, breath binding in his weary chest, to pound on her door.

No answer.

He dragged out his collection of skeleton keys. Five minutes of cursing, fumbling in the semi-dark, and one finally caught the lock. On with the lights. The living room was empty. Into the bedroom, more lights. There she was.

Still naked, she lay across the bed, her arms by her side, looking like something out of a department store window. She was that still.

"Ann," he said. "Ann."

He touched her shoulder. He picked up her hand. He touched her cheek. Nothing happened. But in spite of his panic, he finally saw she was still alive, breathing in long, slow, shallow breaths. A glance over his shoulder and he saw on the sink in the bathroom the empty bottle of sleeping pills.

Total panic for a moment. Should he run? How do you

explain to the ambulance driver who has to make out a report exactly what Detective Kurz is doing here at three o'clock in the morning? Furiously he dismissed the cowardice. This is your responsibility, Kurz. This human being dying in front of your eyes is your responsibility. Fink out now and you are through forever.

Weinberg. The brain was still working. He dialed the hospital, asked for Dr. Weinberg and finally got a sleepy hello. Kurz explained the situation in three blunt sentences.

"I'll be there in ten minutes. Meanwhile get her into the bathroom and try to make her vomit."

He picked Ann Macy up. A rag doll she was, arms dangling, head lolling. He put her over his knee, pointed her face into the toilet and stuck his finger down her throat. She gagged, retched and finally threw up some fluid and a few pieces of pork chop. Three, four, five times he did the dirty business until he was sure there was nothing left down there that he could get.

He had just put her back to bed and pulled the covers over her when Weinberg knocked on the door. He strode past Kurz into the bedroom without a word, took her pulse and plunged a needle into her arm.

"Get a pot or a pan," he said. "I'm going to pump her out."

By the time he was finished, Kurz was feeling sick himself. He helped Weinberg put a bathrobe on her and then followed the intern into the living room.

"I think she'll be all right," Weinberg said. "I'll drop back before I go on duty. You're going to stay here, I suppose?"

"Sure," Kurz said.

Weinberg busily repacked his bag. "Maybe I'm nosey, but what happened?"

"We had an argument," Kurz said, "and I was a bastard."

Weinberg gave him a pale smile. "That's not hard to imagine."

Kurz held out his hand. "Thanks anyway."

"You're welcome," Weinberg said, ignoring the hand.

Kurz wandered back into the bedroom and looked down on Ann Macy's face. Never had it looked so childish, or so forlorn. It was as if death had come so close it had drained all the vitality and even some of the beauty out of it. Your fault, Kurz. Jesus, how can you make it up to her?

He went back into the living room and lay down on the couch. Sleep was out of the question but he dozed fitfully until dawn. Then he dragged in a chair from the living room and sat beside Ann Macy's bed. It was nine o'clock, sunlight was streaming through the windows, when she opened her eyes.

"Surprise," Kurz said softly.

"What? What happened?"

"I found you. I came back to apologize and I found you."

"Why didn't you let me die?" she said.

She closed her eyes and did not open them for another hour.

"Ann," Kurz said groggily, as she stared straight ahead, "I said I wanted to apologize."

"How can you apologize?" she whispered. "You didn't insult me. You insulted yourself. You showed me what you really are and it made me want to stop living in the same world with you."

"I was—that bad?"

She closed her eyes again. He sat there for another half hour. "Look," he said. "I'm not going away. I'm going to stay here until you get out of that bed and start living again."

"Why? So you can go home to mother and stop feeling guilty?"

"No! Because I love you, goddamn it. I love you and I want to marry you."

She just looked at him for a long moment with total contempt in her eyes. Then she shook her lovely head back and forth, closed her eyes and went to sleep again.

Chapter Eleven

So it began. He did not dare leave Ann alone for five minutes. She was drunk with death. It was all she talked about in a leaden voice that seemed to come from the grave. "I was in a boat," she said, "a small black boat drifting down a dark river with huge cliffs on either side. The water was running faster and faster and faster and up ahead I could hear a tremendous roar of a waterfall and then you touched me and stopped the boat, stopped it right there in the current. I knew it was you and I hated you. Oh God, I hated you."

"I don't blame you," Kurz said. "But I came back, didn't I?"

She did not even look at him. It was evening and he was trying to make her eat. She disdained the delicatessen food that Powell had brought over. Kurz tried talking to her. He told her that little Pete Moser was out of the hospital, that Marianne was feeling better. Still she did not look at him.

"Sure," he said, when they were well into their second day. "I'm a selfish son of a bitch. I always have been. But maybe I'm going to change. Maybe I'm trying to change. And maybe you did it."

"If that's true," she sneered, "what I've got between my legs isn't just nice, it's miraculous."

"I'm not asking for any more of it," he said. "Doesn't that mean something?"

"You don't have to ask," she raged. "You can have it any time you want it. It doesn't matter, Kurz. You're not going to change my mind no matter what you do."

Weinberg returned, examined her, and said: "I hope you won't do anything so foolish again, Ann."

"No," she said. "The next time I'll make sure no one interferes."

This time Kurz did not try to shake hands with Weinberg on his way out.

She slept half the day. The rest of the time she stared out the window or sat on the couch and stared at the wall. Kurz watched television. He read the paper. Smoothly, swiftly, like a master chef whipping up a first class stew from leftovers, Jake O'Connor transformed the turmoil in Dellwood into a statement of policy. A little something for everybody was thrown into the dish and in the course of the stirring the name of a certain detective named Kurz disappeared entirely from sight. It was a dazzling performance. But Kurz hardly felt it. It might have been happening on a distant planet.

He was inside another world now, a world of a woman who watched him with hate-haunted empty eyes, waiting for him to leave. What is the measure of your devotion, Kurz? How long will you stay? That was her challenge. The weekend ebbed into Monday. She watched curiously from her bed as he scrambled eggs in the kitchen, set them on the table by the window and ordered her to eat.

"Aren't you going to work?" she said as she picked at the eggs.

"I'm staying here until I see some sign of improvement from you."

"Won't they fire you, suspend you or something?"

"They already have."

She obviously thought he was lying. He told her in brief calm sentences what the mayor had decided.

"You," she said, "an investigator for the Civil Rights Commission. That almost makes me laugh."

"It is pretty funny, isn't it?"

For a moment he thought he had her. A flash of sardonic humor brought her face alive but she instantly suppressed it.

"Of course," he said, "I may not get the job. All they have to do is find out I'm spending my time holed up in an apartment with a luscious broad. The mayor would love to hear about it. He'd have a perfect excuse to bury me without a trace."

She glowered at her eggs as if somehow they resembled him.

"You think I won't stay for a month? I'll stay for two months. I'll stay until we're both sitting here without a cent left to our names, starving to death. Is that what you want? Will that make you happy?"

"Ecstatic," she said.

Powell called. "The Chief Inspector wants to see you awful bad."

"I'll call him."

He dialed Harold's number. "Where the hell have you been?" he said. "Your mother's almost crazy."

Across the room he saw Ann Macy eye him. Did he have the nerve to tell the truth? "I'm in an apartment on Norton Avenue," he said. "A girl I was going with tried to kill herself Thursday night. Most of it was my fault. I spent the weekend trying to put her back together."

There was total silence on the other end of the phone for a full minute. "Well," Harold said. "I'll call your mother and tell her you went down to the shore to get away from reporters."

"Thanks," he said.

"What did the mayor say?"

"You know what he said."

"I hear he said a lot of things. I think I'm entitled to hear the truth from you."

"Wrap it up. But there's a nice job waiting for me on the State Civil Rights Commission."

A weary sigh. "He couldn't do anything else. No one could do anything else."

"I know."

After lunch Kurz told Ann to put on some clothes and they went for a walk. She obeyed. From the beginning she did everything he told her. But it was all empty, automatic obedience. Zombie-like she trudged beside him to the river and along the promenade. The grim calm he had maintained for three days in the apartment began to slip. He pondered a half dozen insane possibilities. Take her down to City Hall and get a marriage license? Do you really want to marry this crazy broad? Anyway it wouldn't convince her. Every gesture he made, no matter how grandiose, was compromised before he began. She had put him—or he had put himself—in an impossible corner.

No, his only hope was to let life itself slowly seep back into her body and hope it would reach her mind. But even as he told himself this, he was inventing more arguments. "I'm not worth it," he was telling her. "Nobody's worth it."

"I didn't say you were worth it," she said. "You just happened to be my last stop, Kurz. The last of the non-human beings I met in my travels."

Back to the apartment for another night of television and wall staring. Another night of segregated sleep, Kurz on the living room couch, Ann in the bedroom.

Tuesday morning he woke up wondering how long he could take it. He wasn't feeling quite so guilty now. In fact, four days of penance made him feel almost sanctimonious. He thought about a walking-out ploy. Go ahead, Miss Macy, call the drugstore for a new supply of sleeping pills. I'll be back at noon to collect your corpse. Sure. If it happened exactly that way, then what would you say or do? Maybe the psychiatric ward was a better answer. Obviously it doesn't improve her to look at you when she wakes up in the morning and goes to bed at night.

The phone rang. It was Powell. "Harry," he said, "you've got to come down to the precinct house. I just picked up some more tapes from Dancer's room. There's something real hot here."

"What?"

"He's gonna do that bank job with that Viet Cong gang."

"Tell Crotty about it. And O'Bannon. You'll need help to handle it."

"Aren't you comin'?" Powell said incredulously.

"No," Kurz said.

"Harry, if we score with this guy you're back on the force. The commissioner, even the mayor, won't be able to touch you."

He sat there, savoring those words, waiting to see just how much of the old Harry Kurz was left inside his body. Two weeks ago he would have been running for his car by now. It was the kind of ploy the old angle player Kurz adored. The in curve on the out curve. The double reverse. The cake eaten twice and still there ready for a third round.

He looked across the room at Ann Macy sitting sullenly in her chair. "If I leave this apartment today, I'll find a corpse when I get back."

"Goddamn it," Powell said, "handcuff her to the bed. I need your help, Harry. Without you around we won't even get mentioned."

Okay. He would do it for Powell, for the one friend he had left on the force. "I'll see what I can do," he said. "I'll call you back in ten minutes."

Over breakfast he told Ann exactly where he was going and why. "It's not for my great big wonderful career," he said. "I'm doing it for Powell. And for Bill Moser."

"You're so noble. I only wish I could believe one word of it."

"Do you really mean that? Or is it the other way around? You don't want to believe it."

She hesitated for a moment. It was the first time he had reached her. "I can't believe it."

"Look at me," he snapped. "Promise me you won't try anything."

She wilted just a little. "I promise."

He drove swiftly to the precinct house. The heat wave had weakened slightly. It was only about ninety on the street. Upstairs in the 13th precinct squad room, Powell was sitting in front of a tape recorder with a half dozen other detectives. Kurz noticed with grim satisfaction that Moriarty and Jackson were there looking very glum. Powell practically threw his arms around Kurz. Jim was one hundred percent young cop now, raring to make his first big score. They sat down, spun back the tape and listened to Dancer.

"I always told you kids keep your noses clean. But you changed my mind. You made me realize how old I was. You changed my mind. And Whitey out there in Dellwood, he changed it too. When they shot that gun at my sister, they changed my mind. I always figured I could con them. Now I know we got to kill them."

"The stupid son of a bitch. He's flipped. He's really flipped," Jackson said.

A medley of younger voices began telling Dancer about the Dellwood bank. They had it cased. The time figured, everything but the money, which they guessed would be a couple of million.

Kurz looked around at his fellow detectives. They were all listening greedily now, practically oiling their guns. Only you (alone again, Kurz) realize the massive irony of this situation. Here is your master criminal plotting a brainless robbery with a bunch of sixteen-year-olds—a heist that was their idea, not Dancer's.

"We got to have a statement ready to issue to the papers," Dancer orated. *"I'll take care of it. It'll be a manifesto, a kind of Negro declaration of independence. From now on we don't wait, we take."*

"Yeah, yeah, write it out good," the younger voices chorused.

"Is one of those kids Billy Moser?" Kurz asked.

"No," Powell said. "I talked him into quitting the gang, the night after the Dellwood riot."

"Explain that to me sometime. Right now let's get this stuff down to the Chief Inspector's office."

An hour later Powell and Kurz sat in Uncle Harold's office

while the Chief Inspector and Deputy Chief O'Bannon listened to a replay of the tapes.

"I'll be a son of a bitch," O'Bannon said when it was over. "I guess I got to eat crow. But let me tell you guys something. We got proof, at least as close as you can get to proof, that this clown didn't plug Moser. The F.B.I. traced that gun to a Chicago hood named Boom Boom Biagi. They called him Boom Boom because he was so goddamn trigger happy. I'm pretty sure that drug deal was a syndicate operation and they had Boom Boom riding shotgun in the truck to make sure those two Negroes didn't grab any of the heroin. They never figured on him shooting two cops. Lately no one's seen Boom Boom around. I'll bet you a hundred bucks he's at the bottom of the river."

"That's neither here nor there now," said Uncle Harold briskly. "We've got a bank robbery on our hands, and if Harry didn't smell it coming with this guy Dancer, I don't know who else deserves the credit."

"Who's arguing?" said O'Bannon. "Let's get to work."

Powell was absolutely right. You knew it all along, Kurz, you sneaky bastard. You knew Harold would pull out all the stops on the switchboard to make this your production. He sat there in a daze of uncertain self-contempt while Chief Inspector Clark outlined the operation.

Dancer and company were going to hit the bank at 2:55. It was good timing. Customers would be few and they could lock the doors and loot the place with impunity. Harold got Captain Whelan on the phone and commandeered ten detectives from his precinct to man stations inside the building. Ten more detectives from the 13th precinct would cover all possible exits from the outside. They would be backed up by a hundred cops manning key intersections within a mile radius.

Inside, detectives would replace half the bank personnel. They had to keep a skeleton force on duty to handle stray customers. "One last thing," Harold said, wrapping it up, "if there's any shooting, fire low. We want this guy Dancer alive. Harry here thinks he can tell us a lot about other crimes, and the kids who are with him are all a little too young. We don't want the papers screaming about killing sixteen-year-olds."

Orders went humming out over the wires. There were noon briefing sessions for the two squads of detectives, and the uniformed cops. At 2:15 they moved in. The Dellwood precinct house was only two blocks from the bank. It was easy to straggle detectives in by ones and twos. Kurz and Powell used a back door, in case Dancer and his friends were watching the front of the building. Everyone was in position by 2:30. The three tellers were all detectives. Likewise the guard, who did not wear a uniform, and two of the three assistant managers sitting at desks along the right hand wall. The other detectives were operating adding machines and counting change at strategic points. In the manager's office, Kurz and Powell chatted with a cheerful, surprisingly young vice-president named Goss. "I feel like a virgin," he said. "It's my first robbery."

"If you get screwed, it won't be our fault," Kurz said. "Remember, if there's any shooting, under the desk."

"You don't have to remind me."

Precisely at 2:55 a beatup five-year-old Buick pulled to a stop in front of the bank door. Out piled Dancer and three Negro kids. Behind the wheel of the car was another kid.

Dancer and his assistants paraded through the front door and into the center of the bank. Opening the manager's door just a crack, Kurz and Powell watched them. The kids were obviously scared to death. Dancer was his swaggering, overconfident self.

"Now," he said, and all four pulled guns and moved in different directions. Dancer headed for the tellers. One of the kids headed for the assistant managers, the two others for the vault in the rear.

Kurz threw open the manager's door. "Dancer," he said, "put down those guns. Every man in this place is a cop and there's a hundred more outside waiting for you."

Everything froze. Then a clatter of metal as the kid facing the assistant managers saw two guns pointing at him and dropped his pistol. The boys heading for the vault repeated the performance a second later. Only Dancer stood there, gun still in hand. Suddenly he unleashed a scream of animal rage like no sound Kurz had ever heard before. It bounced off the bank's marble walls like something straight out of the jungle. There was rage, and sadness in it, but above all, hatred. As it died away he sobbed, "Kurz. You, Kurz."

With a curse he he threw his gun at the door of the manager's office and ran for freedom. The gun clunked harmlessly against the wood and Kurz sprang out, knelt by the railing between the bank floor and the executive desk and fired one shot. It sounded as if a cannon had gone off inside the bank.

Dancer gave a sharp cry and spilled head first out the front door and down the steps. Three detectives with drawn guns were waiting for him when he landed.

Five seconds later, so it seemed, there was a shouting, yelling, jostling crowd of two hundred people milling around the entrance. News cameras flashed, reporters shouted questions. Uncle Harold was bawling orders and simultaneously giving six different interviews. Five minutes more and the mobile television cameras arrived, the same guys who had photographed Marianne Moser last week in Dellwood. An ambulance clanged up and the intern cut away Dancer's black chino pants. The bullet had hit him just above the knee and he was in terrific pain. Kurz could almost hear his teeth grinding as the doctor applied a tourniquet. But when a reporter grabbed Kurz, Dancer started yelling.

"I want to make a statement. I want to make a statement to the people of this city. We didn't come out here to rob no bank. We come out here to get some of the mortgage money them white slobs in Dellwood pay to this bank, and give it to the black people downtown. I come out here to show this whole city that the black man has taken his last kick in the face. From now on we hit back."

"Tell it to the judge, crumb," snapped Captain Whelan, and they bounced Dancer onto a stretcher and shoved him into the back of the ambulance, still yelling. They stowed the kids in a paddy wagon and scooted them off to headquarters.

Then Uncle Harold marshalled the television cameras and called Kurz and Powell to his side. "I would like to make a statement here," he said, " a statement of pride and praise on behalf of the fine police work which these two detectives have carried out to trap this dangerous criminal. We have reason to believe that this man Dancer Washington, whom we have just apprehended, is guilty of several other serious crimes and may in fact be a criminal mastermind behind a whole network of organized lawlessness. Detectives Kurz and Powell have done this city a signal service by their untiring vigilance and surveillance of this man over the past weeks. In fact, Detective Kurz, who was wounded in the line of duty not long ago, refused an opportunity for sick leave after he left the hospital in order to continue his pursuit of this criminal."

Uncle Harold then shook hands with Kurz and Powell while the television cameras whirred. It was eyewash, Kurz thought grimly to himself, but it would look great in the papers and on the tube. What the hell, eyewash or gospel truth, Dancer had tried to rob a bank. An intelligent twelve-year-old could have done it better, true, but the guy had proved himself to be either crazy or dangerous. He deserved to get put away.

Driving downtown, Powell sat beside him encased in silence, his face strangely gloomy, brow furrowed.

"What the hell is eating you?" Kurz said.

"Nothing, I guess," Powell said, shaking his head. "I was just—thinking about Dancer—and Marianne. I wonder how she'll feel about it when she knows the real story."

"Don't tell her," he said. "There's no law that says you've got to confess your sins."

"You think—we really screwed him?"

"The guy robbed a bank, didn't he? Were we supposed to say excuse me, I'm sorry we bothered you, and let him do it?"

"No. No, I guess not. It's just that I never figured—on police work being so complicated."

"Me neither," Kurz said.

In the precinct house they questioned the four kids for over an hour. All of them lived on the block where Dancer had his office and were already on the books as rock throwers. They denied ever having committed a crime with Dancer before, and as far as they knew nobody ever had committed one.

"He didn' need a steal till his wheel got busted," one of them said. "Man, he was rollin' in it."

They called for a wagon and sent them off to the city prison.

"You want to type up the report?" Kurz said.

"Why not," Powell said.

He sounded so glum, Kurz found himself lecturing. "Look, the guy was a germ, an absolute zero. We're well rid of him. You heard those last tapes. He was getting sicker by the minute."

"You're right." Powell said without a shred of conviction in his voice. "You're right."

He got in the car and drove away before he knew where he was going. He should go see Uncle Harold and thank him. He should call his mother. He did neither. He drove to Ann Macy's apartment. As he came in she was watching the last of the six o'clock news on television. Uncle Harold was just finishing his speech. Ann looked up at him, loathing on her face. "It wasn't to help your career, was it, Kurz? You weren't interested in getting one little bit of glory."

"None of that television stuff was my idea. I told you the Chief Inspector——"

"I know. An old family friend. And you didn't even suspect he was going to arrange that little scene?"

"No. I didn't think about it. I was concentrating on catching your friend, Dancer."

"Oh, Kurz, give up. Admit you are completely repulsive and go home. Stop trying to save me with lies a child can see through. I really didn't think you were coming back now that you've gotten your career back into high gear. I even ordered another bottle of sleeping pills from the druggist."

He dialed the drugstore. "Do you have an order for some sleeping pills for Ann Macy?"

"Yes," the druggist said. "She told me to deliver them about ten o'clock."

"Cancel it."

She smiled ghoulishly at him. "I tell the truth, Kurz."

"So do I," he said. "I'm telling you the truth. Every goddamn word of it is the truth."

She laughed and laughed.

He died a little inside. Once more he was face to face with Harry Kurz, that endlessly conniving hungering self. Face to face with him and this girl who refused to accept anything less than the total obliteration of that self. Crazily he remembered the dream, the coppery coils winding around and around him, crushing out his breath. Death, that was what she wanted. That hatred he had injected into her veins could only be appeased by death.

He did not say a word to her for the rest of the night. At eleven o'clock she turned on the television and made him listen again to Uncle Harold's testimonial. "How many years will Dancer get?" she asked.

"Twenty-five, maybe fifty."

They went to bed.

Chapter Twelve

It took Kurz hours to get to sleep. He lay there thinking about his whole life. He was in this thing so deep now, he was so far inside whatever it was—the jungle, the city, the experience—that he could only go backward in his mind trying to make the connections, the turn here, the twist there, that had brought him so insanely to where he was now.

Now.

Now he had to make some decisions. He had to make them alone. That had always been okay, somehow, in the past. Because he had not really been alone. All the time that Harry the swinger Kurz had been making it on his own, he had secretly been convinced that his hero father had been watching over him. His hero father, close friend of God. Yes, it was that childish, it was that simple. And simultaneously Kurz hated God, that old simpleton who had taken away his father at a time when every boy wanted and needed a hero. So Harry got even with God. He never trusted him again. In fact he never trusted anyone again. He got even with God and his whole goddamn world.

And now you know the truth about God. And about your hero father. And you have to decide whether you love this girl. You have to decide whether you stay a cop. Or get yourself another job.

No, it was impossible, he couldn't decide anything. What son of a bitch had done this wrecking job on him, stripping away one idea after another, to leave him here in the darkness, no longer in love with himself, no longer even hoping that Harry Kurz had it made? Jesus, Harry Kurz had it unmade, his whole crazy quilt world was unmade, unraveling.

An artist at wrecking lives, Kurz, that is what you are. But when it comes to putting them back together you are a three-year-old Frankenstein. All you can create with your fumbling is a monster, like the one sleeping in the next room, or the other one in the hospital bed down town with a cop at the foot.

Jesus. His chest ached fiercely. His eyes burned in his head, devouring the darkness. As Dr. Frankenstein had discovered, there was really no solution to a created monster, you either killed it or let it kill you.

There it was again, the dying part. There was death all around him in the darkness, a smell or a sound, like an uncanny note from a strange keyboard, a note that shivered the nerves in a new way. Up until now death had been failure, betrayal, subtraction, all the conceivable varieties of nothing. Never, never had it been a solution, a welcome thought.

And it was not welcome now. Harry Kurz, alone here in the dark, with nothing in his guts but his confusion, Harry Kurz, one stupid, selfish son of a bitch, but human, one human being says no to you, death. Instead Harry Kurz will decide. He will make up his two-bit mind now to love this girl all her life. He will marry her, knowing exactly what that word means. He will blend his *man* with her *woman.* And he will do it not out of pity, or guilt, but because he knows here in his loneliness that he needs her as much as she needs him.

And he will stay a cop. Because that is what he knows. Copping. He will stay a cop even if the name Kurz is dead in the Department, even if down there on his record there are words like *unstable* and *erratic* and *bad judgment.* He will stay a cop and try to be all the things that word means, too. Not just an enforcer. But a guardian.

O Christ, Kurz, a guardian. You have gone all the way, you have joined the bleeding hearts. Well some goddamn thing. Something that puts more in a cop's hand than a nightstick. Something every cop knows is there, but so many don't use it.

He slept and dreamed he was in bed with Macy. They were in a hotel in the Bahamas, sunlight streaming past silken curtains. Every time he touched her she laughed joyously. The whole room rang with the peals of her laughter. Soon she had him laughing too. Laughing and loving like a pair of children in the world's first morning.

He awoke. Sunlight was all around him. It was late. His watch confirmed it. Nine-thirty.

Odd. Ann usually woke him up much earlier. She slept so much during the day she seldom made it past eight o'clock in the morning. He stretched, wistfully remembering his dream. He would tell her about it. What the hell, it might help. He padded into the bedroom and stopped, numb. Her bed was empty.

Send out a general alarm? There was really nothing to justify it. Dredge the river? Nothing to justify that either. For all you know she might have gone to work. Or to the corner druggist for a bottle of sleeping pills and then on to a convenient hotel room . . .

The phone began ringing. He picked it up and Powell was on the line yelling: "Harry. Harry. What's happened? Are you all right? Dancer's busted out of the hospital. Somebody smuggled him a gun. He killed the cop who was guarding him——"

He knew. Without looking, he knew. The sick knowing curled up from his belly into his chest and throat. "Hold on," he said. He walked over to the closet and opened it. There was his holster, empty. He walked back to the phone. "It was my gun."

"I thought so," said Powell in a dead voice. "He took Ann with him."

"Get me another gun. I'll see you in fifteen minutes."

Another connection. A very big one. Moving toward something huge and final. Kurz gulped some instant coffee, and drove downtown. The heat still hung on, but not quite so tenaciously. A soft, almost cool breeze caressed the city. He could see it rippling the water on the river as he rode for a few blocks on Dock Street. Then he was in the winding streets of the Congo and there was no river, no breeze. The jungle swallows you, Kurz, one last time. Powell was waiting for him outside the door of the squad room. He handed him another .38.

"I didn't say anything, naturally."

"They'll find out soon enough. Who got killed?"

"A guy named Hennessey. Three kids. Dancer made him kneel down and then shot him in the back of the head."

"Did he get away on foot?"

"No. He stole a taxi. He can't get far. They've cut off every road out of the city."

Kurz nodded. "It won't take long."

"Let's go downstairs and listen to the radio."

"All cars. All cars." intoned the nasal voice of Bartholomew Kelly, the same voice that had tormented his eardrums when he was riding in a radio car himself ten years ago. "All cars. The taxi containing the fugitive Dancer Washington and his captive reported traveling north on Granada Street. Fugitive is armed and dangerous, repeat, armed and dangerous."

"Granada Street," Kurz said, studying a map of the city. "They'll cut him off at the intersection of Granada and Michigan. He'll go left up one of these side streets."

"Right into Dellwood," Powell said.

"Right," Kurz said. "And Dellwood's a deadend. You can drive around it but you can't get out of it except on these two streets. Let's go."

They drove out Granada Street and, sure enough, as they neared the intersection of Granada and Michigan, there were two squad cars blocking the street. They turned right and the winding side street carried them right to the edge of Dellwood. There were the split-levels gleaming brightly in the sun. And there were more squad cars, blocking the two exit streets, a half mile apart. Kurz drove to the nearest car and the two patrolmen told them a half dozen other cars were already inside the development pursuing the fugitive. They listened on the radio and suddenly a somewhat excited voice said: "Car 62 reporting. We've exchanged gunfire with the fugitive and shot out two of his tires. He has abandoned the car and retreated into one of the houses. We could not fire because he used the nurse as a shield. The house number is 24 Greenacres Drive. Repeat, 24 Greenacres Drive. We are standing by."

"Let's go," Kurz said.

Down the leafy streets they roared, a strange setting for death. Or was it so strange? The real dying had begun here with the hatred.

It would have been lovely, poetic justice if the house had turned out to belong to good neighbor Muraski. But it was a stranger's house, two full blocks away from where last week's madness had erupted. It might even be the house of the nameless woman who had brought the cake to Marianne Moser. Kurz hoped not. It should at least belong to one of the characters who had done time waving those placards and shouting those obscene slogans. Because before the police were through with it, there were going to be a lot of holes in it.

By the time they got there, Car 62 had been joined by a half dozen other prowl cars. They parked a half block away and walked the rest of the distance. The house was on a corner. The cars were spread down both streets with Car 62 at the intersection. As they arrived a bullet wanged into the hood of Car 62 and they crouched low to join the two patrolmen. Down the line several cops fired in return but Kurz could see that their bullets only dug up the front lawn.

"He uses the girl as a shield. It's going to be real tough," said the cop who had broadcast from Car 62.

"Anybody else in the house?" Kurz said.

The patrolman shook his head. "They ran out the back door when they saw him coming. A housewife and her two-year-old kid."

Kurz looked over his shoulder. An army of cops was arriving behind them. Through the crowd of men and machines wound a big black limousine with siren growling: Uncle Harold. He drove right up to the intersection and Dancer blasted another bullet in their direction. He was obviously out to bag the big ones.

Harold got out of the limousine and ambled casually to the shelter of Car 62.

"We're going to have to go in and get him," Kurz said.

"He's got the girl in there?"

"Yes. The girl I told you about."

Harold's face fell apart. "Then it was your——"

"Yes. I want to go in alone."

"Like hell you will," Powell said. "I'm your partner. Anywhere you go, I go."

"Okay," Kurz said, "but I'm running it. You do what I tell you."

Powell said nothing. He had made his point.

O'Bannon's limousine came up the other street. He crouched low and walked behind squad cars to join them. "There's a lot of bushes behind the house. We can get in close enough to fire tear gas. Then we can rush him, but it's bound to cost us some men."

"No tear gas," Kurz said. "There's an innocent girl in there. I want to see what I'm shooting."

"Harry's going in to get him," Uncle Harold said in a dry, aching voice. "Harry and Powell here."

O'Bannon grunted. "Well, he's their pigeon."

Dancer kept moving around the house, firing from different windows. Each time he appeared he had Ann clutched securely in front of him. Kurz could see the dark arm across the whiteness of her uniform.

"Let's go in the back door," Kurz said. "He hasn't drawn any fire from that side."

Crouching low, he and Powell moved down the line of squad cars and around the back of the house next door. With them came four patrolmen with shotguns. If they had to fire to cover the rush across the backyard, they would wound, not kill. They crawled through bushes until they were on the edge of the corner house property. The shotgunners deployed. Out front, meanwhile, it sounded like the Battle of the Bulge. Harold had ordered all hands to keep Dancer very busy and everyone was emptying his gun.

"Now," Kurz barked and led the way crouched low, infantry style. Into the kitchen they dove, flat on their bellies on the linoleum. The floor plan of the house favored a two-man operation. Only a serving wall divided the kitchen from the dining area and living room. On the other side, a hall ran down the middle of the house from back to front with a wide doorway opening into the living room.

"You stay here. I'll take the hall," Kurz whispered. "Don't make a sound. Let him figure I'm alone."

The cops outside were still pouring bullets at the place. With most of the windows broken, the racket was tremendous. Kurz knelt close to the wall and peered with one eye into the living room. A bullet instantly showered plaster onto his face but he saw enough to plot the problem. Dancer was barricaded in the far corner behind the couch and two chairs.

"Dancer," he called. "This is Harry Kurz."

A shrill laugh. "Kurz, I knew you'd show up. That's why I took this little piece of nookie with me. I knew you'd want it back."

"Let her go, Dancer, and we'll fight it out man to man."

"Harry, don't. Please, please go away," Ann Macy cried. "Let them kill us both. He killed a policeman, Harry. There wasn't any reason for it, he just killed him."

"He was white, that was the reason," Dancer screamed. "Come on and get her, Kurz, I got the gun right up against her head. You gonna come?"

"You hurt her, Dancer, and I'll make sure you die piece by piece."

"I'm gonna die anyway, pal."

Again Kurz peered and a bullet practically trimmed his eyebrows.

"You ain't very brave, Kurz. I guess I gotta make you come out. Here's the deal, white fuzz. I'm gonna let her go. I'm gonna let her walk right toward that door and just as she gets to it I'm gonna pull the trigger. You want to save her, you're gonna have to stop the bullet."

"Man to man, Dancer," Kurz said. "Don't use a woman."

"I'd use my own sister to get you, Kurz. My own mother."

Again Kurz peered, hoping for a shot. Again a bullet drove him back.

"Get up, bitch," he heard Dancer saying. "Get up. You want to die now here's your chance."

"No," Ann sobbed. "No, I won't do it."

"Yes, you will, Ann," Kurz said. "Yes, you will. Get up. Get on your feet and walk toward me."

"No. Let him kill me, Harry. Please."

"Get on your feet and walk."

There was one chance, one chance in ten thousand. Powell was listening, watching, waiting, thinking. You could depend on Powell to think. But would it be the same thoughts? You could only hope.

Outside the firing slackened. Kurz got down on his hands and knees and moved away from the wall. Now he could see about three or four feet into the living room. "Do you hear me, Ann? Walk."

"Step in front of her, Kurz," Dancer crowed. "Step in front of her when she gets to that door."

Beyond his sight there was movement in the room. Then he saw the white shoes, the moving skirt, the white stockings curving up those marvelous legs. He dove.

He hit Ann Macy precisely at the ankles and sent her careening off to the right while the forward motion of his dive carried him into the living room, rolling with guns crashing all around him. Dancer, of course, and Powell on the other side.

Past the center of the room he bounced and up on his knees, gun ready and there was Dancer looming above the barricade, the front of his shirt with three great red stains and

Powell still firing, hitting him with every shot. Another stain spurted above the heart, but Dancer would not go down and Kurz could hear Powell screaming: "Fire, Harry, fire!"

He was frozen. His eyes were on Dancer's long black face. His arm, the gun in his hand, were as motionless and silent as a carving. It had finally happened, he was there on the other side of the barricade. He was Dancer, those bullets were hitting him. He was that weeping, swaying death agony. And echoing beyond this terrible transference were the other truths of Dancer's death. They were all involved in it, O'Bannon with his greedy grafting hands, Powell with his hunger to make it as a man and cop, Santini with his dirty Mafia money, Bernie Flannigan with his crummy little dreams of real estate glory, Professor Slater and his so-called philosophy, Bill Moser with his dead rage, Ann Macy with her love, Kurz with his selfishness. The whole city of white and black out there in the blazing heat of summer, they were all crowded into this room, all one people, impossibly, hopelessly, crazily entangled in their living and their dying.

But some were more entangled than others.

Slowly Dancer's arm came up. Kurz waited there on his knees, the paralyzed involuntary penitent, hating the moment, hating the sight. Too late he tried to fling himself aside and as he lunged the gun spoke and he was struck by a wall, a shield, a cry of whiteness.

Whiteness O Jesus no.

But he knew even as the thunder died and the first cops burst in the front door that Ann was in his arms and she was dying. Dancer was gone, crumbled forever beyond his barricade and he was alone with Ann, his hand in her dark hair, watching as her eyes widened with pain and she tried to speak.

"Harry, O Harry I—"

Now you knew, now you had come around the last turn, and all the connections, every twist and bend of the trip, were visible, too late. You thought you smelled your death—that old familiar nothingness—and all the time it was this new death, this loss that was an infinitely more painful dying. Whoever is running this show knows what you deserve, Kurz. Accept it, along with everything else.

Gently, wearily, he laid Ann's body on the floor and walked past the bewildered silent cops, past Chief Inspector Harold Clark and Detective James Powell, past the squad cars and the squawking reporters and the gawking civilians. Walking he went past them all into the city.

A Note About the Author

Thomas J. Fleming was born in Jersey City in 1927. He was educated in parochial schools, graduated summa cum laude from St. Peter's Preparatory School and cum laude from Fordham University in New York City. After serving in the Navy, he worked as assistant to the late Fulton Oursler and became the literary executor of his estate. He went from there to *Cosmopolitan,* where he remained as Executive Editor until 1960, when he left to become a full-time writer. He received several awards for magazine writing. Previous books by Mr. Fleming include: *Now We Are Enemies; All Good Men; The God of Love; Beat the Last Drum; One Small Candle* and *King of the Hill.* Mr. Fleming lives with his wife and four children in New York City and Westbrook, Conn.